The Nightingale

The Nightingale

Morgana
Gallaway

KENSINGTON BOOKS
http://www.kensingtonbooks.com

KENSINGTON BOOKS are published by

Kensington Publishing Corp.
850 Third Avenue
New York, NY 10022

Copyright © 2009 by Morgana Gallaway

All Kensington titles, imprints, and distributed lines are available at special quantity discounts for bulk purchases for sales promotion, premiums, fund-raising, educational, or institutional use.

Special book excerpts or customized printings can also be created to fit specific needs. For details, write or phone the office of the Kensington Special Sales Manager: Kensington Publishing Corp., 850 Third Avenue, New York, NY 10022, Attn.: Special Sales Department. Phone: 1-800-221-2647.

Kensington and the K logo Reg. U.S. Pat. & TM Off.

ISBN-13: 978-0-7582-2728-7
ISBN-10: 0-7582-2728-0

First Printing: February 2009
10 9 8 7 6 5 4 3 2 1

For my parents

Acknowledgments

I would never have written this book were it not for my father, James, who was a police advisor in Mosul, Iraq, in 2004. His vast knowledge and expertise have been a tremendous help to me; if there are any errors in accuracy, they are mine and not his. Dad, you were (and are) one of the "good guys." Huge thanks also to my mother, Molly, for your proofreading skills, constant support, and boundless love and encouragement.

Thank you so much to my agent, Dan Lazar, for taking a chance on an unknown kid; your enthusiasm and ideas shaped this story into something very special.

Many thanks to my editor, Danielle Chiotti, for your dedication, hard work, and the way you made this novel feel like itself.

To the families of Wadi Musa, Jordan, for your lovely welcome and my peek behind the closed doors of the Arab woman's life. I did not spend as much time with all of you as I'd have liked. One of you in particular inspired me to undertake a full study of the Arab culture, on the chance that I would join it.

To A.D. the translator, whom I never knew personally, and who would have had a bright future.

Journalist Jon Ronson's *The Men Who Stare at Goats* gave me the first inkling that the war in Iraq is not what it seems, and provided some interesting plot bunnies. Other sources of inspiration came from several Internet blogs, including but not limited to "Xymphora," "Smoking Mirrors," and the Alex Jones

Web site. Also helpful were the Web sites of Amnesty International and Human Rights Watch.

For some nice details on weddings, I consulted the blogs of two Iraqi women, both of whom are incredibly interesting to read, and I thank them for sharing their thoughts with the world: "Rosebaghdad" and "Neurotic Iraqi Wife."

For further atmosphere of Mosul and the American operations there, I found Colby Buzzell's *My War: Killing Time in Iraq* to be a wonderful resource; also Mike Tucker's *Among Warriors in Iraq*, about the U.S. forces in Mosul and Fallujah. On Arab culture, *The Closed Circle: An Interpretation of the Arabs*, by David Pryce-Jones, was invaluable.

Street descriptions in Mosul are courtesy of the ever-helpful Google Earth.

Chapter 1

The road to the market was long and dusty, but at least it was paved. The fresh asphalt was the only extravagance that Leila al-Ghani could find in Mosul in recent days. Her shoes had started to wear out along the length of the road, back and forth on trips from her flat-roofed home in the Wahdah neighborhood. A breeze came skittering down the street, flapping her dress about her legs, and she reached up with a hand to readjust her head scarf. The pins kept it attached to her hair, so her black locks couldn't peek out, but as always, wearing the *hijab* and the long modest dress somehow made Leila more aware of her body, not less.

In a way, Leila was grateful for the walk. In Mosul, vehicles were unsafe—they could trigger the explosives, the IEDs, hidden on the roadside, or provoke a burst of gunfire from some idiot bunch of self-appointed mujahideen. At least the horror of antipersonnel land mines had not made their way to her home city, with their hair triggers that the light weight of a foot would ignite. Regardless, the walk gave her a chance to clear her head.

Leila's father disapproved of these walks—a woman walking alone in Mosul was a transgression of its own. Before the war, she could go wherever she liked and even wear Western-style clothing without fear of reprisal. The family had been secure then, with her father's job as a judge and Baathist party official and their high standing in the community. Leila had been a princess of one of Mosul's finest families.

Now she wondered how they would all get through this year alive.

It was just after ten in the morning, the best time to do the shopping, for all the stalls would be open but the noontime rush had yet to start. It was a chilly day, moving toward the outright cold of the winter months. Mosul was high in elevation, rising on the Levant plains toward the mountains of Kurdistan and Iran. Leila's corner of the world—for this was how she thought of Mosul, her corner—was the first to develop agriculture some ten thousand years ago. Now the world thought them uncivilized, barely capable of ruling themselves.

Of course, Leila thought, *there's reason to think that. Civilized people don't blow themselves up every day.*

The midmorning call to prayer lifted through the air from the loudspeakers atop the minaret tower at the Al-lah Al-Hasib Mosque, a scant thirty meters away to Leila's left. It had yet to be blown up, though Leila was glad she was not a man and not beholden to attend mosque, or to pray at certain times of the day. She could pray whenever she wanted—or not at all—and no one would notice. Truth be told, she had stopped praying six months ago when her cousin Inaya had her arms cut off by mujahideen, all because Inaya's husband had been seen chatting with an American soldier. In an insane world, it seemed impossible to believe in the good presence of Allah.

The call to prayer was loud, wailing, and grated on Leila's ears. Leila once again adjusted her scarf into place and emerged from the long, asphalt-paved street into the main market area of Mosul.

It was a chaotic scene, with motorbikes zipping through with honking horns and goods being off-loaded from trucks and donkeys. Large, colorful billboards advertised soda drinks, mobile phones, and grocery stores; fresh new promise in a world that seemed dusty dark. Most of it was only that: promise. The sim cards for the mobiles were unreliable, and the grocery stores usually had empty shelves with a few mean little bags of rice or crates of onions. The soda drinks were all right; Leila was almost addicted to Diet Coke, thanks to her university years in Egypt, and once a week treated herself to a three-hundred-milliliter bottle of it. Not today, however; today she needed to haul a sack of flour back home, down the sand-edged road.

The way was filled with people: men in white robes with their red- or black-checkered kaffiyeh headdresses, loose about their heads; Iraqi men in Western clothes, jeans and baseball caps; women in groups of two or three, dressed in modest dark colors with scarves pulled tight about their hair, as Leila's was. Leila noticed a Western man with a gray mustache bartering with a shopkeeper. This one was a journalist, as Leila had seen him before with his press pass. They had a certain annoying curiosity, that flat blue-eyed "Hi, how are you? I'm here to write about your misery" look. Leila did not care for journalists. It was the journalists in the West who brayed about Saddam Hussein's evilness; it was the journalists in Iraq who fed the flames of anti-American hatred. Without the constant chatter of the press, Leila thought something might be accomplished.

She did not look twice at the gray-mustached American, or his armed, privately hired bodyguards.

Instead, Leila went to the Afdhel Baqqal, the "Best Grocer" shop. It was owned by her mother's cousin Khaled and thus the flour and rice were always a few dinars cheaper for the al-Ghani family. She stepped across the muddy drainage ditch, taking care of her shoes, and ducked inside the low entrance to the store.

"*Al-salaam alaykum*," Leila said.

Khaled, hunched in a lazy posture behind the counter, returned the greeting and asked after her parents.

"They are well," she replied.

"Good, good," said Khaled. "And Fatima?"

Leila smirked. Khaled was engaged to her older sister, Fatima, and had been for five years while he earned enough money to marry. It was set in stone, yet Khaled insisted on acting as though he courted Fatima. "She is also well," said Leila, occupying herself by inspecting a row of imported goods. "Skippy . . ." she read aloud.

"Ah!" Khaled jumped up. "We get this from America. It is called peanut butter. You should try some, I only charge three thousand dinars for it. The other shops ask much more. Your sister will like it!"

"Maybe next time," said Leila. She read the rest of the peanut butter label in English. She was proud of her English. At the university in Cairo, classes had been conducted in English and Leila discovered a natural affinity for the language. It was not as expressive as Arabic, but had greater clarity, especially in terms of science and government—and those were subjects that interested Leila.

"I hear your cousin on your father's side is coming to town," Khaled said. "The doctor. What is his name?"

"Abdul," said Leila, running her fingers along the clean plastic cases of bottled water. "Or, Abu Mohammed, if you like." Abdul the doctor was older, thirty-five, and had a son named Mohammed, hence his title of Abu. His wife had died three years ago in childbirth, resulting in the stillbirth of their second son. The man was on the prowl for a new wife to take care of five-year-old Mohammed. Leila figured Khaled was worried this other cousin might snatch away his fiancée.

"He is still widowed?" Khaled persisted.

"Yes," she sighed. "Still widowed. Probably he will marry Fatima." A look of alarm crossed Khaled's face, and Leila almost giggled at his expression. "I am not serious!" she said. "Fatima is intended for you, cousin, and everyone knows it. Don't worry."

He scowled. "You go too far with your jokes, cousin Leila," he said.

Leila just smiled. "Can I get three kilograms of flour, please?" she asked.

Khaled nodded, but was slow in measuring the flour. He handed the cloth bag to her with a surly glance, which improved a small measure when Leila unfolded her bills to pay him. She thanked him for the flour and settled the large bag into the crook of her arm for the walk home. By the time she wormed her way out of the market, it was nearly eleven o'clock. It was best to get back; Father would want his meal prepared, and Mother and Fatima would need help chopping tomatoes.

Instead of taking the more direct route, Leila circled the outside of the marketplace once and took a spur road that ran at a diagonal to the shiny black asphalt. It was a peculiarity of hers, never taking the same way coming as going; a friend at the university had called her obsessive-compulsive. It was difficult to argue in the safe, cloistered environment of Cairo University, but in Mosul this habit felt like prudence, not eccentricity.

Her intuition proved itself worthwhile as she came out onto the new paved road. An American convoy roared by just as she stepped out, and Leila waited for them to pass. She held a fascinated dread for the wide-slung American vehicles, with their thick armor and fifty-caliber machine guns swinging about from the top. This group was likely from the American base in Mosul, Forward Operating Base Marez, from which daily patrols originated.

They went fast as they passed by the spur road and Leila averted her eyes from the convoy when it got close. It would not do to be seen gawping at the Americans and making eye contact with strange men. The Quran prohibited gazing between unmarried men and women, and as for gazing between Iraqis and Americans . . . Leila could just imagine the trouble. Best to stare at the space in front of her feet as she walked. The growl of the petroleum-fueled engines faded and Leila coughed. The air was tinged with exhaust.

As she walked the rest of the way home, her mind turned over the presence of the Americans. They drove with their windows down and popular music blaring, cigarettes dangling from fingertips and eyes concealed behind fashionable reflective sunglasses that wrapped around their heads. They wore electronic gear to excess, looking half machine with wires and antennae sticking up from their helmets. They gave out chocolate bars. Flashing toothy smiles and thumbs-up to every kid they passed by, the Americans seemed like creatures from another planet. In the first year after "hostilities" ended (Leila felt like laughing at that particular declaration, in retrospect) the soldiers interacted more with the local people, or so her family had told her, but after the Iraqis' insurgency began, the Americans retreated into their technology. The sooner the Americans left, the better it would be for everyone. Leila did not like trouble.

The al-Ghani family's home was large, with five bedrooms, two sitting rooms, the kitchen, and even a bathroom with a porcelain toilet. Ever since Leila's older brother, Naji, had moved out to his own place with his wife, it left the house with four inhabitants, all with their own bedroom. It was a luxury for which Leila was grateful. The house was surrounded by high walls, with a metal gate that faced the street.

It was this gate Leila slipped through with her package of flour, and she took off her shoes at the front door before going inside. Her flat brown leather slippers joined the pile of tennis shoes and sandals heaped outside the door. Clad now in her stockings, she came into the blue-tiled entrance hall.

"Mother!" she called. "I'm home!"

"In here," came the reply. Leila peeked her head inside the kitchen to find a large pot of water boiling on the gas, and a basketful of tomatoes waiting to be chopped. "Ah, there you are," said Umm Naji. She bustled into the kitchen from the small storage pantry carrying a load of potatoes. "You took a long time."

"No longer than usual," said Leila. "The market was crowded, and Khaled wanted to talk about Fatima."

Umm Naji's face glowed at the mention of the betrothal.

"Yes, yes," she said. "I think maybe this is the year they will marry. If all goes well, *inshallah*."

"If God wills," Leila echoed. "Shall I peel the potatoes?"

"Yes, yes," Umm Naji said. She sat her large frame down on a stool in front of the boiling pot, and brought out a knife with which to peel the potatoes. "You chop the fruits, I will do the rest."

Leila sighed. She preferred peeling potatoes. Tomatoes, especially these soft ones, always got away from her in a big mess of seeds. Mother had her ways, though, and it did no good to try and switch jobs around. "I saw an American convoy on our road," she said. "Going fast."

Umm Naji snorted. "Better not mention it to your father."

"I wouldn't," Leila said. She added quietly, "He might tell his friends."

Umm Naji looked up and glared at Leila. "Don't speak of such things," she said. "What your father does is his business, and we must not hold opinions about it."

"Speak for yourself," Leila mumbled.

Several moments of silence followed as Leila chopped tomatoes with a sharp serrated knife. Her father's political opinion was a sore subject. He clung to the old ways, and spoke more and more longingly of Saddam's regime, when he had been a party official, and a judge on the local circuit. Now that she was grown up, Leila realized that he must have participated in Saddam's brutal brand of justice, but she hoped that Tamir al-Ghani had been fair when he could. Besides, those days were over now. At least, everyone had thought them over, until those horrible, insulting pictures came out of the American prison. It made Leila think there was no such thing as a good government.

After the Abu Ghraib pictures, her father had started staying out late at night and getting mysterious phone calls, sometimes shuffling odd guests through the house. He became angry. His bad temper simmered around the house. He attended mosque more than ever before, and sometimes the imam came for supper. Leila listened in on the men's conversation from a hiding place behind the wall where there was a loose brick. She heard talk of insurgency, of the noble cause of al-Qaeda in Iraq, of something called Ansar al-Sunna, of using cell phones in dangerous ways, of how the Americans might be hurt. She heard her father grumble about the occupation and the lies of the West. The imam always spoke of the Quran, quoting the hadith, the sayings of the Prophet, and advocating a return to strict Muslim law. When they were together, the men's voices grew louder and angrier, and Leila heard more of "the new Crusade" and the "final battle against the Western invaders."

Leila twisted her mouth, focusing on chopping the last of the tomatoes. She did not believe in such anger; all she wanted was to be free, open, fashionable. She hated the way Father had become since the Americans arrived. It was like walking on eggshells with him, and where Leila had once enjoyed talking politics with him, now he was a different man. He was hard and strict and bitter.

"Get the oven going, Leila," her mother said. "I'll make the dough for the bread."

Leila nodded.

"Tomorrow we'll start making the delicacies for Abdul's visit," said Umm Naji with a new lift in her voice. "We're all looking forward to that."

Leila made a noncommittal noise in her throat. She was not looking forward to cousin Abdul's visit. Ever since Fatima had let slip that Leila wanted to go to postgraduate school to study medicine, Abdul spoke to Leila in patronizing tones and kept hinting that he could teach her about being a doctor.

"It's too bad about Abdul," Umm Naji said. Her eyes darted over to Leila. "He still . . . needs a wife."

Leila raised an eyebrow. "Not again, Mama."

"I am just making a suggestion," Umm Naji said. "You are twenty-three, Leila! You must get married sometime. It will be shame for our family if a beautiful girl like you cannot find a husband."

"If I married Abdul," Leila said, "I would never get to be a doctor. I would have to take care of a five-year-old who wasn't even mine, and probably have more babies, besides. It's not modern."

"Modern. Bah," said Umm Naji. "In times like these, we need what works. You are a little girl, Leila. You have no understanding of these things—"

"First I'm an old woman at twenty-three, now I'm a little girl. Make up your mind, Mother," Leila snapped.

"Shhh!" Umm Naji gestured toward the kitchen door.

Leila turned to see her father filling the door frame. She stood straighter. "Baba!" she said.

"When is lunch ready? I have brought guests," Tamir said.

"Soon, sweet," Umm Naji said. "The bread will take only thirty minutes."

He nodded, turning away to go back to the men's sitting room.

"Guests, always guests," said Umm Naji when he was out of earshot. "That man is more popular now than when he was a judge!"

"I think these are a different sort of guests, Mama," said Leila. "Where is Fatima?"

"She had to work this morning," said Umm Naji. Leila's sister Fatima, elder by two years, worked at a local kindergarten as a child-minder. In days past, it would have been unnecessary for an al-Ghani daughter to work, but with Tamir out of a steady job they needed more income to keep up the house. Leila herself was looking for a job in the local hospital in Mosul; one of the nurses said she might be able to start as a medical technician. "Fatima will be home any minute," Umm Naji said.

On cue, Leila heard the front door open and her sister's light footsteps enter the house. "Hello," Fatima said, coming into the kitchen.

"Khaled says hello." Leila grinned at her sister. Fatima blushed.

"Leila is in a mood today," said their mother.

"I am not," Leila said.

Fatima removed her head scarf to reveal dark brown hair with dyed light streaks. She sat down and began slicing the peeled potatoes into thin discs. "How is Khaled?" she asked in soft tones.

"Making money," said Leila. "He is selling Skippy peanut butter now. I think you will be able to marry soon."

Fatima blushed again. "I hope so," she said. "I spoke to Hala Rasul today. You remember how she was engaged to Omar, the youngest son of Mr. Habibi? You remember how he was involved with a group against the Americans and was killed four months ago? His little brother was shot in the leg last night. He's in the hospital."

Umm Naji clucked her tongue and shook her head. "I don't understand these times!"

"I do," Leila said. "Omar was a hothead. Hala told me he was always going to mosque and talking against the West. Fatima, at least Khaled is a sensible man who has his eye on the future! He would never join the mujahideen. He is too busy running his shop."

"You're a lucky girl, Fatima, to have a sensible fiancé," Umm Naji added, shooting Leila a glance of regret. "Or a fiancé at all."

Leila groaned, standing up quickly.

The kitchen was silent for a long moment. Fatima looked between her mother and her sister. She gave Leila a sympathetic look. "The potatoes are ready," she said.

The women occupied themselves with finishing the preparation for the noon meal: boiled potatoes with chicken and onions, fresh-baked flatbread, salad of chopped tomato and cucumber. Umm Naji brought out the large, round metal plate and set it atop the big pot, flipping it upside down to serve the food. The platter would be enough for at least five men, and Fatima and Leila carried it out to the sitting room together. Before leaving the kitchen, Leila made certain her head scarf covered her hair and she smoothed down her dress. Her father's guests were conservative types.

The sitting room was large and elegant, covered in Qom carpets that had been in the al-Ghani family for centuries. The furniture was low to the floor, and five men lounged on the cushioned divans along the walls. Tamir al-Ghani presided from his favorite seat, and with a rapid beckoning motion instructed his daughters to set the platter on the small round table in the middle of the room.

Leila stole a glance at the guests. They were all about her father's age, in their forties or fifties, and had a hard look about them. There was no congenial conversation among them; Leila decided they were strategizing. Leila and Fatima set the tray down and retreated in quiet modesty as Umm Naji brought out the finger bowls of water and the utensils.

"I did not recognize any of them," Leila hissed to Fatima back in the front hallway.

"Neither did I," said Fatima. "But there are many new faces in town."

"That's true," said Leila. After the American offensive against the insurgents in Fallujah to the south, most of the jihadists had fled under civilian cover. For reasons unknown to Leila, they had chosen Mosul as their new center of operation against the American occupation. It must have been sheer bad luck, she decided. It brought further violence to her lovely city—police stations were besieged and bombed; markets were sprayed with gunfire; and it was only a matter of time before the mujahideen took up their primary shelter in the mosques and holy places, forcing the Americans to come after them there. She suspected the men in the sitting room were part of these problems.

As they waited for the men to finish their meal, Leila sat in the kitchen with Fatima and their mother on the blue-painted wooden stools, legs crossed and hands clasped in their laps. Fatima was talking about her morning at the nursery. She laughed about one of the boys in her class, but Leila knew it was a hard job. More of the children at Fatima's school were orphans these days. So many parents were hesitant to send their children out of the house anymore.

When Umm Naji poked her head in with a gesture toward the sitting room, Leila and Fatima stood to retrieve the meal tray. The sisters reentered the room and retreated with the tray, bringing it back to the kitchen. They sat with their spoons and ate the remains of the lunch. Leila had a small portion of yellow potatoes and the few bits of leftover chicken. It had grown cold, but she was hungry now and it did not matter.

"Do you want to read the newspaper?" Fatima asked, procuring the day's print from her handbag. "I picked it up for you."

"Thank you!" said Leila, reaching for it. She didn't believe much of what she read, but sometimes there were good tidbits in the papers. She loved reading the opinion columns if only to disagree with them. She scanned the headlines in Arabic, full of body counts and talk about the new Iraqi constitution. It was a ludicrous tangle.

"Will you do my hair for tonight?" Fatima asked. "Hala and her two sisters have invited us over. They have new magazines from Dubai and I heard that Hala has some chocolates, too."

Leila's eyes widened. "Have you asked Father?"

"He said yes three days ago. . . ." Fatima paused. Their father's moods changed like the wind these days. "And Naji has promised to escort us. He wanted to visit with Hala's father."

"Good," Leila said. If Naji was escorting them, it should be all right. Their older brother owned a furniture shop, the largest in Mosul. He was respected in their community, and more important, Naji was respected by their father. They would be home from Hala Rasul's house before dark, anyway. The Americans had imposed a curfew and only the desperate would defy it. Curfew meant no one was allowed out in the streets during certain hours; if anyone made the mistake of not being home in time, they were liable to be picked up or shot by an American patrol. Even though it was for their own protection, the citizens of Mosul felt like unwanted visitors in their own city.

Their father's guests stayed all afternoon, and it was four o'clock before the group of hard-eyed men departed. Tamir moved to the inner courtyard for the sunshine, where he sipped his ninth cup of tea of the day, and Leila took the opportunity to approach her father.

"Father?" she asked. Leila had shed her head scarf when the guests left, leaving her shining hair loose in the crisp October air. Tamir had always been proud of his daughters' good looks, and Leila wanted to capitalize on that now.

"Yes?" he said.

"How is your day?" She sat next to him on the stone bench.

"All right," Tamir said. He stroked his graying beard with one hand, a familiar habit that reminded Leila of better times when she was young, and he would set her on his lap and read out of books. Tamir glanced at her with olive-brown eyes. "I don't like you going to the market alone."

Leila tried not to frown. If he was feeling overprotective, she could forget about going to Hala's. "Well. Perhaps you could come with me sometime?" she suggested.

"Perhaps," said Tamir.

A moment of silence followed, during which Leila rehearsed the best way to ask her father for permission. A crow settled on the edge of the roof, cawing at the humans below. Leila glared at it. She hated crows; they were bad omens. "I hope Fatima gets married soon," she said. If she approached the subject of a visit to Hala's from an oblique angle, Father might acquiesce against his will.

"Khaled will be good for her," Tamir said. "I wish he might have more political conviction, though."

"Not everyone can be as active in the community as you are, Father." Flattery always worked.

"Hmm. Yes."

"Naji is coming by this evening," said Leila.

"Is he?" Tamir asked, adjusting his thin frame to catch more sunshine. "My bones are cold," he complained.

"Yes, Naji is coming," Leila said. "He is taking Fatima and me to the Rasul house, remember? He wanted to talk to Mr. Rasul about selling carpets in his shop."

"You and Fatima?"

"Hala has invited us to visit, while Naji does business with her father."

"Hmm," said Tamir. "You will be home before dark?"

"Of course."

"Naji is a good businessman," said Tamir. "Expanding into carpets is good."

Leila let out the breath she hadn't realized she was holding. She could go to Hala's after all, and read the glossy magazines from Dubai. A smile threatened to break across her features, but she held it in check until she told Fatima.

Chapter 2

The home of the Rasul family, in the graceful neighborhood just off Sa'd bin Abi Waqqas Street, was as familiar to Leila as her own house. The Rasuls had been friends of the al-Ghanis for decades, and there had been intermarriages between various members of the extended family. Mr. Rasul, a textile merchant, was well established in Mosul and had made his money in the early years by trading with the Baathist party members, the officials, the high commandants. It had kept him out of trouble during Saddam's reign.

The house was three stories high, of ancient pedigree, with carved wooden screens on the exteriors of the windows and a columned front porch. It needed a fresh coat of paint, but it was swept clean and there was no clutter about it. There was a fig tree in their front courtyard and a screen of creeping vines that absorbed the sound from the road. The surrounding neighborhood was made of old families who had lived in the same place for centuries.

When Naji escorted them to the house that evening, he assumed an attitude of humility when he shook hands with Mr. Rasul. Business was to be discussed in a roundabout way; Leila knew it would take at least four cups of tea for Naji to bring up the subject of stocking carpets in his shop. The niceties had to be adhered to first, the civilizing influence of small talk and pleasantry. Naji was good at socializing and Leila was sure that before they left that night, her brother would have a deal.

"Inside, girls," Naji said to Leila and Fatima at the front door. The girls removed their shoes and scurried inside to meet their excitable friend.

"Lovelies!" Hala called from the hallway.

"Chocolates and magazines?" Leila said quietly, hugging her.

"Who told you?"

Fatima raised her hand and smiled.

"She was right," said Hala.

"Hala," Mr. Rasul's voice interrupted. "The tea?" He gave her a pointed look; in her excitement, she'd forgotten to help her mother. Leila knew how Hala felt.

"Of course," Hala said, still laughing.

Naji winked at Leila and Fatima. "Wish me luck," he said.

"We'll release a djinn for you," Leila said.

"Only a good one, little sister, I know how you can be."

Leila smiled as he disappeared into the sitting room behind Mr. Rasul. For as long as she could remember, Naji had been an ambitious boy, always trying to better himself, perhaps trying to live up to his father's stern example. For a moment Leila wished he were the current patriarch of the family rather than Tamir. Naji was too pragmatic to be involved in the insurgency. It was Naji's tales of study groups and debates over coffee at the university in Baghdad that had inspired Leila years ago.

"Oh, I want to study those things, too," Leila had said to Naji. She was twelve years old, and Naji, home on vacation, was recounting his politics class at Baghdad.

"You're too little," said Naji, drinking tea with a raised finger and sunglasses pushed back on his head. "The professors are difficult, always asking questions, you have to be on your toes."

Tamir glanced at his daughter and smiled. "She has a mind of her own, your sister," he said.

"Will we send her to university?" asked Naji. Even as a girl, Leila could tell he assumed he would have an equal say in the direction of the family. Leila caught her breath to see if her father minded.

"It would be a shame not to," said Tamir. "Leila's grades are much better than Fatima's." He patted Fatima's head as she set down a silver tray arranged with pastries.

"I would rather get married than go to university," said Fatima softly.

"Universities are good places to meet husbands, though," said Naji. "The best men go to university."

"You would say that!" Leila said.

"All of our children should be well educated," said Umm Naji, entering the room and settling her bulk onto a cushion. "For the girls, it will have a place in their dowry."

"How mercenary of you, my dear," Tamir chuckled.

Umm Naji shrugged. "I am practical."

Leila did not care about practicality or husbands or dowries; she wanted to be like Naji, drinking tea like an adult, wearing jeans and new sunglasses. She picked at her pastry, then brushed her hands rapidly, tugging at a thread on her dress until it began to unravel.

"For heaven's sake, Leila, stop fidgeting," said Umm Naji. "I will have to send that dress to the tailor if you keep at it."

"We can afford it," said Tamir. "Would you like a new dress, Leila?"

"Mmm." Leila hesitated. What she really wanted was clothing like what Naji wore. "Could I have something else instead?"

Tamir raised his eyebrows. But Leila could tell by the way his mouth twitched that he was indulging her.

"Jeans," Leila said.

Umm Naji made a startled noise, but Naji and her father both smiled. "You should have a pair of jeans like your brother," Tamir said. "We are a modern family, aren't we? Would you like the same, Fatima?"

"A new dress would be nice," said Fatima, blushing, and they all laughed. The family, together.

As she waited in the Rasuls' front hall, Leila glanced down at her own *abaya*, and to her eyes it was drab and old-fashioned. She could hear Naji in the sitting room, his soft voice rolling out the latest news of the al-Ghanis.

"Well," said Hala Rasul, appearing in the hall with her hands on her hips. "That's done. Souad and Razan are upstairs, let's go!"

Hala's younger sisters were ensconced in her room, already flipping through the shiny magazines, and Leila settled on the floor with crossed legs. Hala's walls were covered with film posters, pictures torn out of magazines of Arabic pop stars, a board filled with snapshots of Hala, her sisters, her family, and several of Hala and Leila in their days at the girls' school in Mosul. Leila grinned when she saw a section of American movie stars in beautiful dresses.

Leila picked up one of the Arabic-language magazines and flipped through it. "I like that one," she said, pointing at a blond actress in a low-cut red dress.

"I wish I could wear a dress like that," Hala sighed.

"The stares would not be worth it," said Fatima.

"Not if I lived in the West," said Hala. "I could wear whatever I want."

All the girls fell silent for a moment. Leila thought again about how her father had once encouraged her to dress as a modern girl. It seemed like a different lifetime.

The boxes of chocolates were depleted one piece at a time, and the magazines were discussed from all angles. Leila's watch, a simple leather band strapped on her wrist, ticked away the hours and when she thought to check the time, she gasped. It was past curfew.

Just then a knock sounded on the door. "Sister?" It was Naji. Leila and Fatima glanced at each other and shrugged.

"I'll talk to him," Leila said, standing up and stepping outside the door. "Naji?"

"It's past curfew," he said.

"I know. What do we do?"

"We'll have to stay here for the night," said Naji.

Leila suppressed a smile. What fun. She and Hala and Fatima and the others would get no sleep, laughing and gossiping. It was an adventure to be trapped.

Stay the night, they did, and the girls were deep into a giggling midnight conversation when the Americans came.

Leila had darted out of Hala's room for a glass of water when she heard the rumble of vehicles outside, the shouts of soldiers. She froze. Hovering in the hallway and peeking out a window, she watched as two armored Humvees roared up to the house. The lead vehicle crashed through the metal gate, rending it to the side in a twist of broken metal, and the other idled outside. Waiting.

Leila heard the front door splinter open but stood frozen in the hallway as the shouts of soldiers echoed through her friend's house. "Get down! Get down!" From below there were more voices, the soft protests in Arabic, the terse chatter of Americans, a disagreement. They were looking for something. Leila dashed back to Hala's room. The trilling strains of pop music filled her ears and she closed the door behind her, hand tight on the cold doorknob.

"Sister, what is it?" Fatima asked.

There was no time to explain and so Leila just sank down to the floor, on her knees; a few seconds later the door opened and all five girls screamed. The room became a melee of waving hands, of black weapons pointed in their faces.

"*Al yed! Al yed!* Hands up!" one of the American soldiers shouted at them. "Marid or Mahmoud?"

Leila's heart pounded, and with a few deep breaths she tried to calm herself as the American soldiers pushed farther into the room. She was aware that her hair was uncovered, but she also knew the Americans would not think of it as shamefully as Iraqi men would, if they noticed at all. In America, all the women showed their hair, at least according to the movies she saw on ArabSat television.

Her next thought was that her father was going to kill her. It was bad enough that their visit had accidentally gone past curfew, stranding them. After Naji decided they would stay the night, he had called their father's mobile to explain the situation. Such news sounded better coming from a trusted son. Tamir was upset, but as long as they were home first thing in the morning, the girls might avoid punishment.

It was just Leila's luck that the Americans had burst in with their suspicious guns pointing back and forth. There were only two of them, but it seemed like more.

Leila registered the ridiculous strains of the latest Najwa Karam song out of Lebanon, still warbling along in the background as though nothing was wrong. She made herself look up, keeping the fear out of her eyes, and again her breath was stolen.

The tall American soldier looked straight back at her. He had dark hair, judging by his eyebrows, and sky-blue eyes set in a strong face. The eyes were kind, but somehow cold. He might be fair to her, but no more generous than that. He was handsome, too, and Leila instantly hated herself for the thought. Right now it should be easier to see Americans as brutes, without honor or decency.

"Marid or Mahmoud?" repeated the other soldier, a large pale man with a big nose.

There was nothing then, except for Najwa Karam's singing.

"Someone turn that off!" Hala said from her corner. Fatima, who was closest to the CD player, reached over and pressed the Stop button. The silence was worse, and Leila imagined the whole room must be able to hear the pulse of blood through her veins. What would the Americans do? And what would Father do when he heard?

Leila gulped and decided to speak. "Why are you here?" she asked in her lightly accented English.

The handsome American looked at her again. "Are you a member of the Rasul household?" he asked.

"No," she said. "I'm a visitor. We did not mean to stay past curfew."

The big man said again, "We're looking for the cousins, Marid or Mahmoud Rasul. Are they here?"

The girls were silent.

"Can you translate?" the handsome one asked Leila.

"Yes," said Leila. She switched to Arabic and faced Hala. "They're looking for your cousins Marid and Mahmoud."

Hala shook her head. "I don't know!" she said. "Ask my father, I do not know! I have not seen those cousins since I was seven years old."

Leila looked back at the Americans. "Hala says she does not know, and she hasn't seen those cousins since she was a small girl."

The Americans sighed together. "Are there hiding places in the house?" said the big man.

Leila translated this into Arabic, and Hala shook her head again. "Only the pantry, downstairs next to the kitchen. We do not hide people here. Marid and Mahmoud are not here."

"She says only the pantry," said Leila in English. "They are not the kind of people to hide cousins."

"That's what they all say," said the big pale man. He had a swagger about him, a grumbling arrogance that made Leila fearful. Another unwelcome feeling floated to the surface: Leila was glad the other one, the handsome one, was there. Fastened on the front and center of his grayish brown combat uniform was the double-bar insignia of a captain. An officer.

"Well, they're not in here, Ike," said the blue-eyed captain. He turned to Leila. "We need you all to stay in this room. We're going to be searching the house, and it's safer if you stay put."

Leila nodded.

"*Asaf*, sorry for the intrusion," he added. He paused, as though about to say something more, but then he marched out of the room, followed by his companion.

Leila's shoulders slumped in relief. "Oh!" She hugged Fatima tight, then Hala. "They say to stay here. They say sorry."

"Thank goodness!" said Hala, tying her light brown scarf about her long hair, a few minutes too late.

"Why do they want Mahmoud and Marid?" asked Souad, Hala's younger sister.

"They think they might be insurgents," said Leila.

"I don't know why they targeted us!" Hala said. "We've never done anything wrong!"

"I think there are things that our fathers and brothers do not tell us," Leila said, with a glance exchanged with Fatima. "These are dangerous times."

"You don't need to tell me that," said Hala. Her hands were pressed to her sides, trembling. "My Omar is dead, remember?"

"We're sorry, Hala," Fatima said, patting Hala's hand for the dead fiancé.

Leila was sorry for her friend's loss, but Hala was better off for not marrying Omar Habibi, she thought. If Hala had married him, then she could expect more raids by the Americans, dragging off her new husband in shackles under a dark hood. Omar could not wait for the paradise of martyrdom, and let him have at it, thought Leila.

The five girls, two al-Ghanis and three Rasuls, stayed in the room as instructed by the American soldiers. The night took on the feel of a secret slumber party, with the girls crammed in together and chattering away in the afterglow of excited terror. Each had stories to tell of friends or family and her own encounters with the Americans.

An hour later, someone knocked on the door, and the girls scrambled to put on their head scarves. "One minute!" Hala called. "All right!"

The door opened. It was Mr. Rasul, looking shaken. "The Americans have gone. They found nothing."

Leila wondered if that meant there was nothing to find, or if the cousins were still hidden somewhere in the compound.

"What happened when they came in here?" Mr. Rasul asked.

"There were two soldiers," said Hala. "They just came in and asked if we knew where Mahmoud and Marid might be. We said nothing, that we did not know anything."

"Huh," said Mr. Rasul. "You were without your *hijab*?"

"No, sir." Leila spoke fast. "We've been wearing our scarves all evening. The Americans did not see us out of state."

Hala shot her an astonished glance, but did not say anything.

"Good," said Mr. Rasul, nodding. Leila wasn't sure if he believed her, but for his own peace of mind he would clearly not pursue the point. "Hala, the al-Ghani family are our guests tonight. And keep the music down."

"Yes, Father."

When Mr. Rasul closed the door behind him, Souad breathlessly said, "Leila, I can't believe how well you lie!"

"She does it all the time," said Fatima.

"I learned at university," Leila said. "Whenever I had a late assignment or missed a lecture . . . it pays to come up with little white lies. It's not to hurt anyone."

"Still, you're so calm," said Souad. "I wish I could do that! That way Father would never guess how I glance at Rashid."

"Isn't he Kurdish?" Fatima asked.

"Mm-hmm," Souad sighed. "He has light eyes. So exotic!"

When Leila went to sleep in the ladies' guest bedroom next to Fatima that night she, too, dreamed of light eyes. Blue ones, the color of the deep sky on a summer day. When she awoke the next morning, she remembered her strange thoughts in the night, but chalked them up to the American raid.

She and Fatima were out of the Rasul house at daybreak, munching on figs and leftover flatbread for breakfast as they walked. It behooved them to get home as soon as possible. Naji walked behind them with dark circles under his eyes, as though he had not slept.

"Were the cousins really there, Naji?" Leila asked.

"I don't know," he sighed. "It is impossible these days. No one tells the truth; everyone has secrets. Even kin and tribe."

"What should we tell Father?" Fatima asked.

Naji cleared his throat. "The truth," he said. "Let me do the talking. And Mr. Rasul said you had your veils on when the American soldiers came upon you upstairs?"

"Yes," said Leila. "And they were only there for a few seconds. No threat from women."

"They don't know *you*, Leila," Fatima said, low enough so Naji couldn't hear.

"Father will know of the raid already," said Naji. "Just tell him what you told me. There is nothing to it. It doesn't concern you, anyway."

"Yes," said Leila. She threw out her arms. "*None* of this is to do with us."

"Leila . . ." Naji said.

"Sorry."

At home, Tamir al-Ghani stood in the doorway waiting for them. His whiplike arms crossed over his tall figure and his face was stern. It gave him a look of spiritual emaciation, no room for humor or mercy. Leila had already made up her mind that the best tactic would be to play helpless, and let her father comfort her over those evil Americans. She tried to look as bewildered as possible. Fatima she could count on, since the elder girl was genuinely frightened.

"Father!" Leila exclaimed, running forward.

Tamir broke his crossed arms to embrace Leila, patting her on the back as she put on a good show of shaking. "There, there," he said. Next was Fatima's turn, and she, too, hugged their father. "Naji," said Tamir.

"Father," said Naji, also embracing him with a hug and a double kiss. "I've brought our girls home safe. It was not as bad as it sounded, I think."

"What happened?" Tamir said as they went inside to the sitting room. "Were the cousins found?"

Leila paused, watching Naji.

"The Americans came, and broke the front gate with their vehicle," said Naji. "They searched the house, but nothing was found. They left after about thirty minutes, empty-handed. No other damage was done, no injuries, and the women were even veiled at the time. It could have been much worse."

"We're all just a bit shaken up," added Fatima.

"Nothing permanent," said Leila.

Tamir lounged back in his chair, looking down at the back of his hand. "Yet you would not have been involved at all, had you been home before curfew! Now the name of al-Ghani is associated with insurgency."

Leila refrained from rolling her eyes. If Tamir al-Ghani was not chin deep in the insurgency already, she would eat her head scarf. "I didn't give our name," said Leila. "I just said we were visitors."

Her father ignored her. "They know your name?" he asked Naji.

"They asked me directly. I'm sorry, Father. But I told them I owned the furniture shop."

"He's hoping to get business." Leila smirked.

Her father and brother ignored her. "Was there any recognition of your name?" Tamir asked.

"No," said Naji. "The Americans came and went. They found nothing, they know nothing."

"Hmm," said Tamir.

"Father, may we be excused?" Leila asked, grasping Fatima's hand.

"Yes, yes," he said, not even looking at the girls anymore.

Their mother met up with them in the hallway, embracing both girls and fussing over them. They needed a change of clothes, she said, and a cup of tea. Leila agreed with the cup of tea; she had not slept enough the night before. She would need her energy for tomorrow, for her job interview with the head of pediatrics at the Al-Razi Training Hospital. She'd been looking forward to the interview for weeks.

As they sat on the floor in the large kitchen, taking turns kneading dough and drinking tea, Umm Naji was more interested in the affairs of the Rasul household than of the American search. "How is Hala doing?"

"Fine," said Fatima. "Better, I think. She is a lovely girl. She will find another man to marry her."

"Let us hope not one of the mujahideen," said Leila.

"Hala would do well to get married soon," said Umm Naji. "After all, she's Leila's age. Soon she will be old goods."

Leila sighed. Her mother would never quit. If Leila ever did marry, as soon as she had daughters Umm Naji would next be plotting for *their* betrothal. Leila loved her mother, but ever since she returned from the university a year ago it seemed as though Umm Naji's primary emphasis was on marrying off her daughters, rather than supporting their ambitions as she once had. It was the war. Every tiny step of progress was so easily erased, the ebb tide taking away the castles of dreams that Leila built in her head.

"Mother, I don't think Leila is old goods!" Fatima said. "I'm two years older and I'm not married."

"Yes, but you are engaged! You have prospects, Fatima."

"I have prospects," Leila muttered. "My mind and my goals. I'll be more successful than any old man around here."

Umm Naji sighed as she wrapped her fat fingers around the small glass of minted tea. "Leila, you know I want you to be a doctor, and show the world all your ideas. But I want you to be protected. What if your career does not work out, if the violence gets worse and we are all impoverished? Then where will you be?"

"I'll move somewhere else," said Leila. "I think you've been listening to Father too much."

"Your father does what is best for his family and his country," Umm Naji said, leaning back as though to end the conversation.

Leila slammed her cup of tea on the tile floor. "I'm going upstairs," she said.

* * *

Leila's bedroom was simple. She was by nature a tidy person, and kept the room free of clutter. A low narrow bed covered by a patterned duvet occupied one corner, and a row of heavy curtains covered the two windows set in the wall that overlooked the private inner courtyard. Leila's pride and joy was the bookcase, filled with texts and novels, and her desk with its pleasant tasseled lamp and stacks of medical journals. It was the desk that Leila went toward, and she leaned on it with her hands and took a deep sigh.

She was not discouraged. If anything, the disregard of her father and the disapproval of her mother served to crystallize her ambition. She held a university degree in biomedical science, two years of extracurricular training in a Cairo medical center, and more importantly, she held hope for her future. Leila wanted to become a research doctor. She wanted to use her expertise to aid the refugees, the impoverished, the forgotten. She wanted to invent a new drug, or discover a new cure, and work in a shining laboratory. There was much to do with life, and based on the situation in Iraq, men were not to be trusted with the important things. To marry a typical Iraqi man, who would expect her to cook and clean for him, to stay home and raise his sons, would mean putting her own dreams on the back shelf.

She knew the Quran regarded family life as the highest pursuit for a woman, but Leila's interpretation was more liberal. At the university in Cairo, there were plenty of women who did not marry, or who had husbands and a career alongside. She figured that Allah, *praise be upon Him*, preferred that Leila use her talents to help people, not to clean some man's kitchen.

Leila sank down into the chair in front of her desk and brought out a Robin Cook novel, written in English. It helped her language skills, especially with medical terminology. She put a pair of tiny earphones into her ears and pressed the Play button on her CD player. The album was a pirated copy and not the best quality, but it was good enough. The blast of American rap pounded into her head and Leila found the beat appropriate for her mood. With the earphones, her family never had to know what kind of music she secretly preferred.

She read straight through to the lunch hour, and when Fatima knocked on her door at noon, Leila put aside the book with reluctance.

"We're starting the pastries for cousin Abdul's visit," said Fatima. "Mama wants you to make the rice and mutton for Father's lunch."

"Yes, sir," said Leila.

Fatima just looked at her.

"Sorry," said Leila. "I didn't sleep well."

"Oh, Leila." Fatima stepped inside the room and gave Leila a hug. "You know Mama doesn't mean what she says. You're so beautiful, you could wait until you were fifty years old and men would still want to marry you!"

"Fatima." Leila smiled at her sister. "Sometimes I think you're the only one who loves me anymore."

"They love you," Fatima said, linking arms as they walked down the stairs to the kitchen. "It's just . . . the war . . . ."

"I suppose," said Leila.

The pot with the mutton was already boiling when Leila entered the kitchen, and she set to work making the rice and slicing small bits of onion to put in the stew. On the table, her mother and Fatima made the dough for the baklava treats. The dough was paper-thin and fragile, laid out in great sheets and then rolled up and put in the refrigerator for preservation. Leila hoped there were no power cuts between now and Abdul's arrival the next day. The refrigerator situation was iffy, and Umm Naji kept hinting to Tamir that he might procure a petrol-fueled electric generator for their home.

"You girls will be happy to see little Mohammed," said Umm Naji, referring to cousin Abdul's five-year-old son.

Fatima smiled as she rolled another sheet of dough. "He's such a cute child."

Leila said nothing but nodded in agreement, pretending to love the little fiend. Mohammed was on her bad side ever since his last visit, when he unraveled her favorite scarf with his tiny, monstrous little hands. To be fair, that was three years ago. Leila was not opposed to children, but she never cooed over them the way Fatima did.

They finished with the dough and started dressing the whole lamb for roasting. Tamir had brought it home yesterday from the butcher's shop, a child-sized bundle dripping with blood. The lamb would be spiced with rosemary and sage, rebundled, and left to marinate in its juices.

The rice was measured, the spices inventoried, and the dough for flatbread prepared ahead of time and put in the refrigerator. At seven in the evening, the women took a break to have makeshift chicken *shwarma*, cutlets of leftover chicken wrapped in flatbread with yogurt and cucumber. After that, Leila took her leave from the kitchen and went upstairs to review the material for her interview the next morning.

The head of pediatrics at the Al-Razi Hospital was a woman doctor by the name of Amina Dahbawi. Leila had introduced herself to Dr. Dahbawi upon her return from Cairo University and expressed an interest in gaining work experience. It paid off three weeks ago, when Dr. Dahbawi sent her an e-mail requesting further interviews. If Leila made a favorable impression, she might be hired. Leila wanted more experience in surgery or physical therapy, but Dr. Dahbawi was the highest-ranking female doctor in Mosul. It would be inappropriate for Leila to approach one of the male doctors, so it would be upon Dr. Dahbawi's recommendation that Leila be transferred to one of the other stations.

It was the sole opportunity in Mosul that Leila could think of. With every day bringing new bombings, injuries, and shootings, it would give Leila an experience of practical hands-on healing as well as humanitarian effort.

Butterflies flew into her abdomen as she got into bed that night. Leila did not sleep well for the second night in a row, tossing and turning over the events of the day to come. Cousin Abdul was arriving. She had to bake bread. She had to go to the hospital and talk to the doctors; would they laugh in her face? Had the recent events at the Rasul house been real or imaginary? Had Leila dreamed up the past day? Did she miss her interview? Leila's mind turned in turgid circles of nonsense, creating a half-asleep insomnia that prevented deep dreaming.

Leila got herself out of bed at seven in the morning and dressed in a professional black pantsuit, her only set of business clothes. She chose a contrasting dark taupe color for her head scarf, modest but of good quality. She took a folder with her résumé and university transcripts, and letters of recommendation from the staff at the university medical center in Cairo where she had interned. Leila rifled through the pages, triple-checking the contents; she could not think of anything else she might need.

With care, she packed her large square leather handbag with the folder, some cosmetics, a small bottle of water, and her on-the-go first aid kit. It paid to be prepared on the dangerous streets of Mosul. She would call a taxi to take her to the hospital, although cars were not necessarily safe; with her dressed as a professional woman, there was the chance she might be snatched and held for ransom. The insurgency did not seem to care who they targeted, American or Iraqi or Martian, so long as they wreaked havoc.

She arranged the taxi with a cousin named Sami, who was a driver. His small white car smelled funny but was clean, which was more than could be said about many taxis. She almost made it out the door.

"Leila!" her father's voice echoed through the front hall.

"Father, I have to go!" Leila said, as the taxi horn sounded outside. "Remember? My interview at the hospital?"

"I don't remember," Tamir said, narrowing his eyes.

"I told you, Father, a week ago," said Leila.

"Your cousin Abdul arrives today. Your mother needs your help here. Reschedule the interview."

Leila's eyes widened. This could not be happening. It was her chance, now or never, and her father wanted her to reschedule? "Father, I can't. They'll hire someone else."

"Leila, I don't like the idea of you working at the hospital. All those men, strangers, foreigners . . ."

Leila was frantic, but knew she couldn't let him hear that in her voice. "It's mostly children, Father, who've been burned or shot! Young people! Besides, don't you want your family to be upstanding in the community? If I work at the hospital, it will only add prestige to our name. It's a humanitarian effort."

Tamir was silent. He took in Leila's fine tailored suit and leather handbag.

"Please, Father? There's no guarantee I'll even get the job. It's just an interview. I'll be back well before lunch, and I'm going in Sami's taxi."

"Unescorted?"

"This is Iraq, Father! We are progressive, you've said it many times. We are not Saudis."

"The Saudis," grumbled Tamir. "Nothing but trouble."

"Right. And they don't let their women out of the house. I follow the Iraqi way. Your way, Father."

Tamir paused, and for the second time in two days Leila held her breath for permission. *As Allah is my witness, I want to move away from home*, she thought to herself.

"Fine," said Tamir. "If you are not back before noon—"

"I will be!" Leila said, before her father could set a more concrete threat. "Thank you! Wish me luck!"

She was already out the door before Tamir could say anything further.

Chapter 3

Leila sat on a yellow plastic molded chair in the hallway of Al-Razi Hospital. Overhead, the narrow fluorescent lights flickered on and off, the power supply as unreliable in this neighborhood of the city as everywhere else. The hospital had generators, but they were used for long-term power outages. Leila raised her head and watched the lights, counting the small black specks of dead flies and roaches that rested on their glass undersides. The smell of antiseptic was strong, disguising the underlying stench of sickness, of blood, of urine, and the fetid aftermath of human injury.

The Al-Razi Teaching Hospital in Mosul was one of the city's largest, with over four hundred beds and a good emergency ward. It was formerly called Saddam Hospital, but that went out the window in 2003, gone to dust like all the other relics of the old regime. It changed in name, but not in function, and three years later the hospital retained its status as one of the more prestigious medical centers in the city of almost two million residents.

That did not mean things were easy for the staff of Al-Razi Hospital. Even before the war, the economic sanctions imposed on Iraq guaranteed a shortage of medical supplies, food, even basics such as bedsheets and syringes and aspirin. It was a constant struggle for the doctors and nurses to heal people, often with nothing but their bare hands. With the American invasion, things looked better for a brief time. Pharmaceuticals in neat little plastic packs came from the Americans, and despite some minor structural damage during the bombing campaign, the hospital stayed up and running.

These days, it was a matter of overwhelming casualties and not enough specialists. Supplies ran short again. The sheer number of munitions lying around meant injuries of innocents, often children, playing with explosives or in the wrong place at the wrong time. They came in with missing limbs, fragments of metal studded along their little bodies, eyes and fingers and legs ripped to shreds. The only thing to do was to stop the bleeding, bandage the wounds, give out antibiotics against infection. The children, when they survived, reemerged from Al-Razi Hospital carrying permanent handicaps.

For a generation, Mosul would be a city of beggars.

In the face of such hopelessness, the hospital worked. It took in patients, treated them, and discharged them back to whence they came. The staff noticed that the violence went in cycles; Friday, the holy day of rest, was always the worst. Holidays were always the worst. Any time the passions of religious fervor were aroused, the hospital knew to expect blown-off limbs.

But thinking too excessively about all this would just bring on despair, so Leila focused herself and her nerves on the job she badly wanted.

Dr. Amina Dahbawi was a kind woman, large and matronly with a bustling efficiency of manner. She welcomed Leila with a firm, warm handshake and sat her down in a tiny office. They talked, and Leila told of her educational background and desire to work at the hospital. Dr. Dahbawi seemed impressed.

"Your educational background is more than sufficient," said Dr. Dahbawi. "And I have a good feeling about you, Leila. You'll be a benefit to the hospital."

"I might work here, then?" Leila asked.

"Oh yes," said Dr. Dahbawi. "There is a place in the pharmacy for you, as a technician."

"Ah," said Leila. She tried not to sound disappointed. The pharmacy would be all right, of course, but it was not the hands-on experience she wanted. "Is that the best place for me, do you think?"

"I think so. I would put you in the emergency ward, but it is so brutal, and right now it's short of supplies, not helping hands. I'm afraid you wouldn't do much good there."

"Right," said Leila. Really, any job in the hospital would be all right. Perhaps something else would open up, and she must be grateful for whatever fate sent her way. *Inshallah*, as they say. God's Will. Even if Leila was not sure she believed in God any longer, fate she could handle. "I'd be happy to work wherever you believe is best," she said.

Leila waited in the hallway while Dr. Dahbawi processed her paperwork. Tired with staring at the lights, she focused on the aged but clean linoleum floor. It was dirty white with a spattering of tiny gray-black dots, and Leila could not help but think of disease on a clean body. It was an appropriate invocation for the floor of a hospital. At the sound of footsteps, Leila looked up: it was Dr. Dahbawi.

"We can go to the pharmacy now, and I'll introduce you," she said.

Leila followed the doctor's large but graceful frame down the hall, and after two left turns they came to the hospital pharmacy. It was marked by a sign in the hallway and a door with a narrow window set in it. A square waiting room greeted them, filled with people sitting or standing, waiting to pick up prescriptions. There was a window at the front with an open space below it, through which pills passed to the patients, and money from the patients passed back to the pharmacy. She hoped that would not be her job, to physically dispense prescriptions; that was secretarial, not medical.

Dr. Dahbawi took her through a squeaky door and into the back of the pharmacy. There awaited Dr. Abdul Musrahi; Leila read his name on the plastic tag that adorned the breast of his lab coat.

"Here she is, Abdul," said Dr. Dahbawi. "As I told you, a first degree in biomedical science from Cairo University. Very sharp girl."

"Hello, Miss al-Ghani," said Musrahi, bowing slightly. To Leila's relief, he was about fifty years old and had a clean and unassuming presence, unlike the other Dr. Abdul in her life. He did not offer a handshake and Leila did not expect it.

"I'll leave you here now," said Dr. Dahbawi. "I have a line of patients waiting, and so much paperwork today. Leila, good luck! If you need anything at all, come back to me. And please stop by once in a while for a cup of tea."

"I'll do so," said Leila. "Thank you."

"Anything to help a fellow female in the medical field," she said, sharing an amused look with Dr. Musrahi.

The pharmacy was well kept, but the metal shelves were startling in their emptiness. Only a few boxes of drugs dotted the long rows. Leaning closer, Leila saw that the shelves were labeled with a variety of pharmaceutical names: doxycycline, tinadazole, norfloxacin. But the allocated space above was empty.

"There is a constant shortage," said Dr. Musrahi. "But we do the best we can. Come. I will show you to your workspace."

Leila followed him through the shelves to a small measuring area with a desk heaped with stacks of pharmaceutical reference binders. There were small white paper bags in abundance, waiting to be filled with pills. Leila knew that the typical safe-latch orange plastic bottles were scarce and expensive, and would only be used for certain prescriptions or for patients willing to pay extra.

"You will be issued your coat and identification badge tomorrow," said Dr. Musrahi. "If you go now to the front security office, they'll take your picture so your ID can be made up."

Leila nodded. She paused, not sure whether she was supposed to leave, or if there were further instructions.

"Here is my signature." He paused to scribble it on a piece of paper, as though writing a prescription. "And then come in tomorrow morning at nine. Al-Razi is a teaching hospital, so you are most welcome here."

"Thank you!" Leila said. She bowed to Dr. Musrahi and left through the front entrance of the pharmacy. It was on the second floor of the hospital and the security office was on the first; the signs were easy enough to follow. The security office was straightforward and the pieces fell together yet again for Leila's medical career.

When she walked out the front doors of the hospital and down the worn concrete steps into a clear, sunny day, Leila allowed herself a smile. She had a job. She was on her way. The pharmacy would be a good stepping-stone, at the very least.

Leila called Sami the taximan on her mobile, and he picked her up and drove her home through the crowded streets of the city. They wound around the market area with its heavy pedestrian traffic, and it took thirty minutes for Sami to deposit Leila at her front door. With thanks, she paid him, and Sami gave Mr. al-Ghani his regards. She glanced at her watch. It was twenty past noon. A little later than she intended, but not to be helped. Leila's feet felt leaden as she walked onto her front porch and reached for the door handle. Abdul and his son— Leila prayed they had not arrived. She opened the door and hesitated in the door frame, listening. There were no voices, no exclamations or conversation. Thank goodness. Removing her shoes to take them up to her room, Leila tiptoed toward the stairs and made it halfway up before the voice of her mother caught her short.

"Leila!" From the top of the stairs.

"Hello, Mother."

"I've been waiting an hour for you, we need to start cooking!"

"Oh joy," Leila muttered. "I need to change and put my shoes away," she said, louder.

"Well, hurry! Cousin Abdul will arrive any minute."

Leila waited for her mother to ask how the interview went. Umm Naji said nothing more, however, merely ducking her head and descending the stairs. Leila shrugged. Fatima would be happy for her at least. Once inside her bedroom, Leila closed the door, set down her shoes and handbag, and then did a little shake of a dance, twirling three times and smiling wide. "Dr. Leila al-Ghani," she said to herself.

She took her time putting away her nice black suit, and poked around her wardrobe before deciding on a dark blue dress. She kept her taupe scarf on her head. Leila studied herself in the mirror: she was decent now to meet her widowed cousin. She groaned, holding on to the memory of the morning's success at the hospital. She would not let any old relative spoil it.

There were voices down in the front hall, echoing up the stairwell. Abdul must have arrived. As she had done so often as a girl, Leila crept up to the stairs and paused there, listening.

"How is your dear mother?" Umm Naji asked.

"Very well, thank you," she heard Abdul's scratchy voice, followed by the whining of his son, Mohammed.

"Ouch! Ow, ow, ow!"

"Oh, look, he's skinned his knee!" Umm Naji exclaimed. "Poor little dear, let me find Leila to take care of him."

Leila made the nastiest face she could manage in the precious seconds before Umm Naji found her. Like a beat of doom, her mother's footsteps came up the stairs. . . . "Mother," said Leila.

"About time," said Umm Naji. "Come, greet your cousin Abdul."

"Yes, Mother."

Abdul had not changed from when Leila saw him three years ago. He still had a large nose and wide-set eyes, a neat combed mustache, and a receding hairline. And he still had a son.

Little Mohammed was a small kid with a round belly and short hair. He sat on the tile floor of the front hall, grasping his knee like he was terribly wounded. One glance told Leila the scrape was minor; she doubted it was even bleeding. But after Umm Naji threw her a warning glance, Leila knelt and patted Mohammed on the head. He scowled in return. Leila sighed. She glanced around for her elder sister to take the burden of Mohammed off her hands. Fatima must have been in the kitchen, avoiding the company as Leila had tried.

"Abu Mohammed!" Tamir's thin voice echoed from the courtyard door.

Abdul greeted the head of the al-Ghani house with a "*Salaam*" and a hug and double kiss. The men put their arms around each other's shoulders and retreated into the sitting room, leaving the women with the battered luggage, the cooking, and the child.

"Mama," Leila pleaded, as Mohammed tugged at the bottom of her dress with vicious force, threatening to rip the hem.

"Mohammed, Mohammed," Umm Naji said.

"What?" Mohammed said.

Leila thought he seemed immature for a five-year-old. Perhaps he did not get enough nutrition, although with a doctor for a father that was unlikely.

"Let's go into the kitchen and you can have a honeycomb. Would you like that?" Umm Naji said, grabbing the boy's hand.

"I want a big honeycomb," Mohammed said, "but I don't like the white parts."

"I'll cut off the white parts," Umm Naji said. "Leila, get the luggage and take it to the best guest room."

Leila nodded. There were three suitcases: one large, dusty red cloth rolling one, a smaller hard case, and a duffel bag. She put the hard case on top of the rolling one and slung the duffel bag over her shoulder, grunting with the effort. Leila was five foot five and very slender, taking after her father's side, so she was not built for porter's work. The best guest bedroom was on the ground floor, down the left-hand corridor and overlooking the courtyard. She wheeled the suitcases along and opened the door to the pleasant but strong scent of incense; her mother must have set it burning for the welcome. Leila stacked the bags in a neat pile at the foot of the bed and brushed off her hands.

Next came an afternoon of cooking over the hot gas and serving the men their food. Fatima seemed to enjoy it, but for Leila it was grim work, and only the prospect of her job the next day put a slight smile back onto her face.

As it turned out, the day was not so difficult as Leila had anticipated. She and Fatima chattered over their tasks, and as expected, Fatima enthusiastically congratulated Leila for finding a good job. They made bread. The lamb was set to stew. And blessedly, Fatima took over the responsibility for watching little Mohammed.

Then it was six in the evening and they joined their father and cousin Abdul in the sitting room for a family reunion over minted, sugared *shai*. Leila sat with her legs tucked beneath her and her hands clasped in her lap, keeping out of the conversation. She wanted to avoid Abdul's attention if possible.

"And Leila still wants to be a doctor," Umm Naji said brightly. Leila almost winced.

"Ah!" Abdul said, sipping loudly at his tea. "You have finished the university?" He stared at Leila.

"Yes, I have finished my biomedical science course," said Leila. She made sure to sound demure, but as proud as she still could.

"Biomedicine, yes," said Abdul. "I say that it's good for research. Research doctors are not so well regarded in the community, I think, but they serve their purpose."

"Mmm." Leila bit back a retort. If it were not for research, no drugs would be discovered, no new techniques invented. And biomedical science was a good general degree, for every kind of medicine! The points of retaliation rose in Leila's mind, but she did not want to make a scene. If she said nothing to Abdul, he might say nothing further to her.

"She is not engaged?" Abdul asked Tamir, nodding at Leila.

"No," Tamir sighed. "Not yet."

Umm Naji cleared her throat.

"Suprising," said Abdul, rubbing his chin with short fingers.

"When would you like dinner served?" Umm Naji asked. "There is mutton tonight, Leila's specialty."

Leila snorted and had to cover it up with a dainty cough. She had no hand in the mutton, aside from poking at it and setting out the large cooking pot.

"One hour, I think," said Tamir. "Civilized people eat at seven-thirty. We are still civilized in Iraq."

"Excuse me," said Leila, standing up. She disagreed that civilization had a firm hold over her countrymen, despite what her father liked to believe, but it did no good to show her opinion. "I will begin preparing the trays," she whispered to Umm Naji, who nodded in approval.

Ten minutes later, Fatima entered the kitchen with the silver tray and its load of empty glass teacups. "Abdul keeps looking at you," she said, setting the glasses to be rinsed.

"I know it," said Leila. She had avoided looking at Abdul, feeling his eyes upon her, and she hated the creepy-crawly feeling on the skin beneath her dress. She imagined he would talk to her father about a possible betrothal and Leila dreaded the inevitable clash. Umm Naji would approve, of course; it would be a one-up against her sister-in-law, Abdul's mother, to whom she'd never warmed. "I haven't been looking back at him," Leila said.

"He's not the one for you," said Fatima. "Don't worry. Mother and Father can't force you to marry anyone."

"But they can make my life more difficult."

"You're going to be a doctor, Leila! A great one! I know it. Don't worry about anything else."

For the millionth time, Leila felt gratitude to have her sister's support.

Through the rest of the meal, Leila held true and refused to meet Abdul's gaze. For once she was glad for societal boundaries. The sole indication of Abdul's affection would be a formal proposal of marriage, which could be deferred. Leila hoped it would not come to that; men's egos were so fragile and it might cause a rift in the family. However, her actions always contained the danger of familial tension: walking alone, going to the market, taking the job at the hospital, of which neither parent knew as yet.

After dinner, as she and Umm Naji and Fatima worked on cleaning the dishes from the day, Leila broached the subject of her morning schedule. "I need to be away again tomorrow," she said.

"Why?" Umm Naji asked sharply.

"Well, Mother, I've taken a job at the Al-Razi Hospital," she said. "My interview this morning went well, and they want me to start in the pharmacy at nine tomorrow morning."

Umm Naji stopped the motions of cleaning the large pot, soapy water dripping from her fingers. "But you are needed here! Cousin Abdul! And with Fatima working tomorrow . . ."

"I don't have to go to work tomorrow," Fatima said.

"Still, Leila, nine! Until when?"

"Six."

"Nine until six! That's all day!"

"That's work, Mama! It will help the family, and it is a good job, in one of the best hospitals. I already said yes, and I got my identification card and security pass." Leila was prepared to run up to her room to show off the items.

Umm Naji sighed. "I don't like it, Leila. What if the hospital is dangerous? What if there is a bombing?"

"What isn't dangerous anymore?" Leila asked. "I'll be fine. If I die, then at least I was working while I was blown up." She did not mean to be flippant about violence, but it was hard not to be in the face of her mother's surfeit of worry.

In the end, Leila got her mother to tell her father about the new hospital job. Umm Naji had a way of wording things that made Tamir agree with her, a by-product of thirty years of marriage. When Leila went to bed that night, she slept well for the first time in weeks.

She had an old bicycle that she would use to get to work in the mornings. The hospital was a long walk, but to take a car was impractical, as the al-Ghani family owned one vehicle at present and it would be unfair to commandeer it all day, every day. Pedaling along, Leila took twenty-five minutes to arrive at Al-Razi Hospital and she walked in the double front doors at eight fifty-eight. *Perfect*, she thought to herself.

"Pass, please," said the security guard at the reception. She handed over the pass from the day before. "Go ahead."

Leila had no trouble finding the pharmacy for the second time. Dr. Musrahi was waiting for her there.

"Miss al-Ghani. You are very prompt."

"Yes, Dr. Musrahi."

"Today, you meet Sayyid, your fellow technician. He arrived *early* this morning," said Dr. Musrahi.

"Aha," said Leila. She noticed a fresh-laundered lab coat folded on a shelf. "Is this for me?"

"Yes. Just pin your name tag on the front, and you're set. Sayyid will show you the routine. Today I must go to the Al-Zawahwiri Hospital, as they received the latest donated shipment of drugs and will be distributing them from there. But it is Sunday, so it should not be too busy today."

"Right," said Leila, unsure of what to do next.

"Sayyid?" Dr. Musrahi called.

A young man emerged from behind the metal shelves. He was of medium height and build, with dark eyes and a ready grin. "Doctor, sir?" Then Sayyid noticed Leila, and his eyes flicked across her, his grin broadening.

"This is your new colleague, Leila al-Ghani. It is her first day, so you can teach her the routine while I am at Al-Zawahwiri," said Dr. Musrahi.

"Greetings," said Sayyid. "*Asalaama.*"

"Good day," Leila replied, keeping herself formal.

"I must leave you now," Dr. Musrahi said. "I will be back in late afternoon, if all goes well."

"I'll take care of things here," Sayyid said, hopping from

one foot to another. He gave the impression of tremendous energy, almost uncontainable.

As soon as Dr. Musrahi left, Leila was left standing in the back room of the pharmacy with her new coworker. "So," she said, "what now?"

"Do not worry. I will show you everything," Sayyid said. He was almost purring the words, and Leila paused—had he intended some perverted double meaning or was this his natural manner? "Today we must fill the list of prescriptions," he continued, and Leila decided she had imagined the tone. "Once they are in the bags and labeled, we pass them through the glass to Mrs. Turahi, who is the dispensary."

"I understand," Leila said.

It was not a difficult job, finding the boxes of pills, measuring out the doses with the flat metal bar on the table, and putting them in the small white paper bags. Some of the pills looked like candy, such as the pink-tinted amoxicillin. She and Sayyid worked in silence for the most part, and he spoke only to give directions. She hoped that would be the extent of their working relationship, though she did detect his sidelong glances at her. As with Abdul the night before, the proximity to a strange man's eyes gave Leila unpleasant tingles.

She let out a long breath. Would she always be a woman before she was a doctor?

Chapter 4

It had been one month since Leila began her job at the Al-Razi Hospital pharmacy. One month, and every day was worse than the one before it.

She did not want to seem ungrateful. She knew she was fortunate to have a job at all, and this one paid quite well. Dr. Musrahi was a good boss who explained things in clear terms and was understanding of the issues of supply shortages and power cuts. Leila had no cause to complain, aside from the big, pressing, panting problem: her coworker Sayyid.

On her first day at work, Leila had been relieved to not make small talk with the young man. She was not interested in becoming his friend, she was interested in becoming a doctor. Sayyid, however, had other ideas. The second day had been fine, and so had the third and the fourth. But on the fifth day, Sayyid asked her about her family. How many brothers and sisters, what did her father do, what neighborhood did she live in? Leila politely answered the questions in as vague a manner as she could.

Sayyid was a typical male. The miniscule encouragement, the paper-thin crack in Leila's demeanor, had bounced his expectations sky-high. He grinned at her. He chattered to her. He did chores that belonged to Leila, hoping to win points with her. Worst of all, he insisted on doing the difficult aspects of the pharmacy job, thinking in error that Leila wanted the easy tasks. This annoyed Leila to the point of grinding her teeth: she wanted to prove herself capable of the most complex jobs so that she might earn a promotion. Instead, Sayyid always beat her to it with a toothy, smarmy smile.

So it was that one month into her job, Leila was counting pills on the counter for dispensary, and next to her Sayyid was labeling a new shipment of drugs donated from a company in Switzerland. She thought about saying something to him about letting her do the hard work, but even their small conversations were too much for her. She could go to Dr. Musrahi, but Leila did not want to sound petulant, and most of all she did not want to add proof to the myth that men and women could not work together professionally. She was in a delicate situation.

"Do you like baklava?" Sayyid asked. He inched his steadying left hand along the counter closer to Leila.

She took a tiny step away from him. What a stupid question, "do you like baklava"! Everyone liked baklava. It was like asking if you enjoyed breathing. She did not grace him with an answer and just shrugged.

"Have you ever heard the song 'Hauolou'?" Sayyid tried again.

Leila held back a cough. Again, everyone had heard the popular song. "This one is ready," she said, finishing the count of pills and folding the paper bag once over to staple it closed.

"*Sinnah al-ah nemye-ee . . .*" Sayyid sang softly, tilting his head back and forth, his eyes fixed on Leila.

She stared. This could not be happening. Sayyid gazed at her, singing his heart out in soft, intimate tones. She glanced around, desperate for Dr. Musrahi to come in, but he was making rounds of the wards, taking note of which antibiotics and anesthetics to order. He would be at least another hour.

"*Uymde al-e ha naaa!*" Sayyid stood, and took a step toward Leila. "You don't like this song?"

"No," she said. "I don't like it." She moved away.

Sayyid looked behind him. They were alone. He put down his writing pen and ran his hand through his side-parted, longish oily hair. "Come on, Leila. We are friends. You like me, right?"

She bit her lip, looking anywhere but his fervent eyes. Her space felt invaded with each breath Sayyid expelled. "This is inappropriate behavior, Sayyid," she said. "Dr. Musrahi will not approve."

"The boss doesn't have to know," said Sayyid.

Then he did the unthinkable: he touched her. He put his hand around her waist and yanked her close. It was the ultimate indiscretion, forbidden by Quran and society alike. He had no right, and Leila bit back a scream. "Let go of me, Sayyid," she said, trying to keep the fear out of her voice. "I don't like you. Let go of me, if you want to keep your job!"

"Leila," Sayyid whispered in her ear. He did not smell nice; like onions and hair gel and dirty clothes and body odor. "You are so beautiful," Sayyid said. "I will treat you right."

"You won't treat me at all, you pig!" She wriggled, trying to get away from him, but his grip was iron around her waist and on her arm. Leila's eyes widened as Sayyid readjusted his position against her, and she felt him pressing up harder against her lower abdomen. Leila gagged.

"Come on, *habibti.*"

Leila narrowed her eyes and stopped struggling. Let him think she was considering the proposal. He loosened his grip, and then quick as a cat she ducked away from him.

"You will not touch me again!" she said. "I swear upon Allah, I will tell Dr. Musrahi."

"No, you won't," Sayyid said. He put his hands in his front pockets. Leila avoided looking there. She just focused on his sneer. "Musrahi won't hear of it. The other girl who complained got fired. Whatever you say, honey, I'll deny."

Leila flushed in anger and shame. The worst part was that what Sayyid said was true. In a battle of words, Sayyid would win. If she complained he had accosted her, she would be fired, if only to remove her from the situation. That was the way it worked. A boiling rage simmered around the edges of Leila's vision, and she wished that for ten minutes, she could be a man. That way she might get Sayyid fired and beat him to a pulp as well.

Standing with him in the narrow, grimy space of the pharmacy's back room, Leila glanced at the wall clock. It was three-thirty in the afternoon. Leila did not want to be with Sayyid anymore; what if he tried something else? Dr. Musrahi had not yet returned, and might be delayed. "I'm going home," she said. "I don't feel well."

The smirk on Sayyid's face grew wider. He knew he'd won. "I'll finish your work," he said, and again Leila wanted to slap him. If she went home early, it would make her look lazy, and Sayyid would get the credit for doing the job.

It was a choice between staying the afternoon alone with lust-crazed Sayyid, or feigning illness and getting blamed for avoiding work. Leila hesitated. But one more glance at Sayyid made up her mind: no job was worth this. If she was dishonored, that would be the end of her. "I'm going," she said. She grabbed her handbag and rushed out the door before she could be further insulted.

As she rode her bicycle home that day in the light afternoon traffic, Leila could not stop rehashing what had happened. It was so unfair. It was unprofessional and wrong and Leila had no one to talk to about it. She would not go to Dr. Musrahi; if Sayyid was telling the truth, she would be fired. Her parents were out of the question, and Leila did not want to burden Fatima with the worry that she might be attacked at the hospital.

Leila was alone in the world. She swerved her bicycle out of the way for a large honking truck that lumbered down the narrow side street she'd chosen that day. She still varied her route to and from the hospital. Today she was motivated by the irrational fear that Sayyid might follow her, and she could not help glancing over her shoulder, looking for his gleaming hair gel amongst the street crowd.

The entire family was home when Leila entered her own spacious house in the Wahdah neighborhood. Her parents were in the sitting room with Fatima, Naji, Naji's wife and children, and cousin Abdul, on the last full day of his visit.

"Leila! What are you doing home?" Umm Naji said, necessitating that Leila give her greetings to the rest of the family.

"Hello," Leila said in the general direction of the room, trying in vain to keep a flush from edging across her face. She hesitated. "They let us off early today. Until we get a new shipment of drugs, we can't do anything."

Umm Naji made a noise with her tongue against her teeth. "The hospitals are all understocked. It's worse than during the sanctions!"

Tamir grunted. "Just proves that the Americans are not the answer to our problems. They are the problem."

Leila backed out of the room. Once her father was on the subject of the Americans, she would not be questioned further about her day at the hospital. She went upstairs to change out of her work clothes, and as she unbuttoned her jacket her fingers trembled. She'd had a close call today. Sayyid might have raped her, and then what would be her choice? She could report it and bring tremendous shame upon the family, or she could keep silent and suffer. Leila sank down onto her bed, relieved that she had escaped with only a bruised ego. She sent a little prayer up to Allah, her first genuine prayer in a long time.

Leila did not rejoin her family that night. Instead she pleaded a headache, successfully avoided cousin Abdul, and secluded herself into the safe cocoon of her own room. She had every reason to be grateful.

The next morning, Leila knew what she should do. Dr. Amina Dahbawi might offer her some advice. She did not phone in to the pharmacy that she would be late; instead Leila left an hour earlier than usual to call on Dr. Dahbawi in person. At eight o'clock in the morning, the hospital would not be busy.

"Leila!" said Dr. Dahbawi, opening the door of the little office when Leila knocked. "Come in!"

"Hello, Dr. Dahbawi," said Leila. She clasped her hands and sat on the proffered foldaway metal chair.

"How are you? Your job in the pharmacy is good?" Dr. Dahbawi asked, shuffling through a stack of papers on her scuffed metal desk.

"Well . . ." Leila paused.

"You are lucky to have such work. Out of the line of fire, so to speak," the doctor continued. She squeezed into her desk chair and it creaked in protest. "Just yesterday, I saw two children who'd happened upon some old ordnance. Twin brother and sister. The boy lost both arms, and the girl did not survive." Dr. Dahbawi sighed. "You are glad you don't have to see it."

"That's what I wanted to talk about," said Leila. Leila suddenly felt awkward; her problem seemed so trivial compared to the tragic stories of the pediatric ward.

Dr. Dahbawi raised her eyebrows. "Yes?"

"It's Sayyid," Leila said. "My coworker in the pharmacy, you know."

"Sayyid?" Dr. Dahbawi paused and looked up at the ceiling, as though searching her memory. "Ohhh yes. Sayyid. Young man, a bit flighty."

"That's the one," said Leila. "Anyway, I didn't know who else to talk to about this. Yesterday afternoon, he—he—well, I guess you could say—"

"He's giving you trouble?" Dr. Dahbawi asked, peering at Leila. "Is he tardy? Not doing his job?"

"Not that, exactly," said Leila. She felt as if she were on fire, but she had to just say it, blurt it out, get it over with. "He behaved inappropriately," she said in a rush. "He started out just flirting, you know, but yesterday he grabbed me."

Dr. Dahbawi sat back in her chair, her mouth an O of surprise. "He grabbed you."

"Yes," said Leila. "I told him to let me go, that I was not interested, but he wouldn't listen until I got away from him.

Then I left for the afternoon because I didn't want to be alone with him anymore."

"I see," said Dr. Dahbawi. She pressed her large fingers together on top of her stack of papers. "Have you encouraged him in any way? Responded to his flirtations?"

Leila made an involuntary face. "Of course not!" she said. Could Dr. Dahbawi think her capable of sloppy moral conduct?

"Are you certain of it, Leila? Sometimes what seems innocent can lead to other expectations."

"I'm certain, Dr. Dahbawi," Leila said. She stared down the older woman. "I would never consider it. I never encouraged his attentions."

"I see," Dr. Dahbawi said again. "You were right to come to me. Perhaps we can work something else out."

"I want this to be my career," Leila said. She was desperate. She was serious about being a doctor. "Please, I want experience. I want to go to medical school. And I don't want some man to—"

"Take it easy, child," said Dr. Dahbawi. "I know. And we're not going to fire you." She smiled. "You're not the first woman in the medical field to be harassed. It is a constant struggle. Don't let it get you down."

Leila breathed a sigh of relief. Dr. Dahbawi must have experienced similar incidents in the past and here she was, a full doctor of pediatrics at one of the city's best hospitals. It gave Leila some hope for herself.

"Something came across my desk two days ago," said Dr. Dahbawi, rummaging through a drawer on her right-hand side. "I did not think of you at first, since you were settled in the pharmacy, but this might be the right thing. We must not let you stay in the pharmacy where further incidents might happen."

"I agree," said Leila.

"The best solution would be to get rid of Sayyid, but he is a man, and without cause for dismissal . . . Unless, of course, you want to file a formal complaint against him."

"No," Leila said. "No. I'd rather find a new position."

"Good," said Dr. Dahbawi. "It would tarnish your name, and for such a young career, you must avoid controversy."

Leila nodded.

"Here is the job description," said Dr. Dahbawi, finding the paper. "You'd be working directly with two experienced surgeons as an assistant. It's a very prestigious position, with a great deal of hands-on experience. You would also serve as a translator between patient and surgeon."

Leila listened with growing excitement. It sounded perfect for her, and she wanted nothing more than hands-on experience. But the last sentence confused her. "Translator? What do you mean?"

"Arabic to English," said Dr. Dahbawi. "The surgeons are Americans. This job is based at the 67th Combat Support Hospital, on the military base. Camp Diamondback."

Leila was astonished. She, Leila al-Ghani, work at the American base? Her father would never allow it. Tamir would sooner see her dead than working for the Americans. But it would be such an opportunity to work with American surgeons, the best in the world. . . . Leila's ambition overruled her qualms about her family. "Tell me more," she said.

"The position pays 150,000 dinars a week," said Dr. Dahbawi, and Leila nearly choked. That was close to one hundred U.S. dollars per week. It was a fortune. Dr. Dahbawi continued with the details. "The hours are ten in the morning until six at night, and transportation will be provided. You'll take the bus of workers that goes into and out of the base every day."

"Will they even let me work there?" Leila asked. "I mean, my father was a Baathist. They must investigate those things."

"They are desperate," Dr. Dahbawi said. "No one is willing to work there anymore, not after the bombing of the mess hall two years ago, and the shootings. I can't lie to you, Leila. If you take this position, you are putting yourself at risk. You know this."

"Yes," said Leila. "I know." Her hands grasped her knees.

"But," said Dr. Dahbawi, "you'd be doing a lot of good. They need a competent medical assistant who is fluent in Arabic and English, and especially one who can translate medical terms. Based on your English test scores, you qualify."

Leila smiled. But there was still one giant hurdle, and she was determined not to let it get in her way. "My father," Leila said. "He will not approve. If he knows I am working with the Americans, he'll . . ." She paused. "He might just kick me out of the house. So please, will you object if I tell my family I am still working at the pharmacy?"

Dr. Dahbawi paused. "That is deception. . . ."

"Yes, but it's necessary," Leila said. She leaned forward. "I *can* do a lot of good with this position. I can help. And I'll learn a lot. My father . . ." She hesitated again, searching for the proper words. "He lacks tolerance, and I don't want that to affect me."

Leila held her breath as Dr. Dahbawi nodded. "It will be up to you what you tell your family," she finally said. "It is not the business of the Al-Razi Hospital."

"Yes," said Leila. Then she smiled. "The Hippocratic oath, right? First do no harm."

"That's correct," said Dr. Dahbawi. "I'll pass along the word that you've agreed to work for the Americans. Come back tomorrow at this time, and the bus will take you into the military base. You already have your hospital security clearance, but the Americans will do another background check and issue you their own pass." She paused, twirling the wedding ring on her finger. "Leila, you do know why they're looking for a new translator, right?"

Leila did not think she wanted to hear this. But she shook her head. "No."

"The previous one was kidnapped by the mujahideen. His tongue was cut out. I can't let you take this job without telling you."

Leila gulped. Perhaps as the daughter of a Baathist she

might be protected from the mujahideen. It was a useless comfort, she knew, but Leila let herself believe it. "I still want the
job," she said, sounding more confident than she felt.

"Very well," said Dr. Dahbawi. "I will tell Dr. Musrahi and
your change of position will not be held against you."

"Thank you, Dr. Dahbawi," said Leila. She stood and with
a startled glance at the clock, saw it was nine-thirty already.

"Take the day off, be back tomorrow," Dr. Dahbawi said.
She looked at Leila with concern and a faint tinge of respect.
"You'll do the name of Iraqi women proud, my dear."

As she walked out of Al-Razi Hospital into the morning's
cool sunshine, Leila felt tossed about like a boat in a storm.
She had taken a job with the Americans. It was the most dangerous thing she could do, and Leila was exhilarated and terrified and helpless all at once. It was *inshallah*, the will of God,
the wheel of the Fates, spinning round and round, depositing
her somewhere unexpected.

She recalled one of Fatima's acquaintances, a Christian girl
called Tara. She had worked at the American operations base,
Camp Marez, as a cleaner, since her family needed the extra
income. Tara shared a car pool with several other girls, and
one day as they returned along the airport road from their
work at the base, they were attacked by a group of angry jihadis. All four girls were killed, shot to death in the name of
some murky religious ideal. It made sense to no one. A girl in
her prime, dead, all because of a job. Leila knew it was reck-
less faith to believe herself exempt from the violence sweeping
her city . . . yet what choice did she have? To languish in
poverty, to slide down inch by inch until her education was
forgotten? No, if she wanted to make her way in a dangerous
world, she needed to be *in* the dangerous world. *Inshallah* to
the rest.

She spent the remainder of the day at home. There was no
electricity and Leila was, for once, not disappointed because of
it; she was in the perfect mood to sit in the women's sitting
room with the windows open and the small breeze lifting

through the window to chill her. It was an overstuffed space full of knickknacks, cushions, Western-style furniture from Naji's shop, and a glass cabinet stacked with special teacups. Leila had always thought the color scheme of gold, pink, and green garish next to the deep jewel tones of the main sitting room.

She finished her second Robin Cook novel of the month. Umm Naji sat opposite, doing a pile of mending, and Fatima worked on her embroidery skills, to the occasional exclamation of a needle-pricked finger. Leila let her hair down, playing with the long, wavy strands, enjoying the freedom of it.

Cousin Abdul had left that morning with little Mohammed, and to Leila's great relief there had been no mention of a betrothal. Umm Naji was happy because Abdul raved about the al-Ghani hospitality, and Leila and Fatima were happy to have the houseguest gone.

"I found some material for new scarves," said Fatima.

"Where?" asked Umm Naji.

"It was on sale at the market. See, dark blue, and this patterned tan and pink." Fatima pulled the fabric from her plaid plastic shopping bag and it made a whispering noise as she moved it between her hands. "I thought of the pink for Leila."

"I do like it," Leila admitted. Sometimes the *hijab* was not so bad, especially when Fatima was so thoughtful about choosing what she knew Leila would like.

"How much?" Umm Naji asked.

"For all of it, just a thousand dinars," said Fatima.

"I think some new scarves would be nice," said Umm Naji. Fatima smiled at Leila; this meant their mother approved of the purchase. Umm Naji bent her head to her own embroidery, and she murmured a folk tune that she'd sung to the girls when they were children; the lyrics were of the love of a humble shepherd boy for a beautiful princess. Umm Naji's voice was sturdy and soft, and the quiet mood was so congenial that for a moment Leila wondered why she wanted to risk this home for a hazardous career. What if her father was right?

Perhaps the best thing to do was to marry, move out to a tiny village in the surrounding countryside, and wait out the imminent civil war. Never leave the house, get pregnant, raise babies on small cups of rice and the milk from scrawny goats. It would make her family happy.

Umm Naji looked up from her needlework and saw Leila's daydreaming. "You are not working today, either?" Umm Naji asked.

"No," said Leila. "No supplies yet, like yesterday. They will arrive tomorrow, and then we can get back to work." Today would be a temporary supply glitch, and tomorrow her parents would think her back at work at Al-Razi Hospital. She prayed they never visited the pharmacy to look for her, but— as the Americans would say—she would cross that bridge when she got to it.

For all its danger, this job at the American base sparked the flame of that old hope: medical school in the West.

Tamir returned from his day's activities, which were never discussed with the ladies of the household, and accompanying him were six new strangers, plus the ever-present Abdul-Hakam, the imam at the Al-lah Al-Hasib Mosque where Tamir worshipped. Leila swore there were more strangers in the house in the past year than in all previous years combined. All the men were the same: curt, conservative, demanding food and shelter and no questions asked. As had become the routine, Leila and Fatima prepared a large tray meal for the men, and then Leila listened from her loose-brick listening post.

"The martyr brigades are forming across the country," said the gravelly voice of a stranger. "With the proper discipline, we might accomplish something."

"It is with the grace of Allah we'll do this," said the imam. "The country will be purged of infidels and Shiites—"

"No," Tamir said. "The Americans must go first."

At this, Leila bit her lip. She sent a silent prayer up to Allah, and the angels, or whatever other deity might be listening, that her father would never discover her new job.

"My friends, you know what to do," said Tamir. "You are each in charge of your own cell. Discipline, remember. Never stay in one place."

As he continued, Leila backed away from her eavesdropping spot, blinking her eyes fast. Her head buzzed with disbelief—her father was a mujahideen, how could it be true? Tamir could not be plotting, not for real. It must be some religious metaphor. Among scholars of the Quran, jihad was a term of spiritual struggle . . . but she could not explain away the men's very temporal words. *Cells. Brigades. Martyrs.* The evidence was in the false thunder that assaulted Mosul every day. Leila winced and something cold settled in her stomach. This was the price of her eavesdropping, yet she knew that she would listen again.

As she passed by the door to the courtyard, she remembered a past conversation with him, or perhaps it was an amalgamation of many views formed in subtle ways over the years.

It did not matter which. The point to Leila was that she no longer knew what to think.

Tamir al-Ghani, judge of Saddam's regime, had been forward thinking when it came to politics. He, and his fathers before him, had been part of Mosul's power structure for so many years that he had space to be more liberal in some of his views.

He and Leila sat in the courtyard; Umm Naji had brought them their shai. Leila was in high school and that day she had gotten in a near argument with her tutor about the economic loans given by the West to other countries. Leila followed Tamir's thinking, that modernization was the key to success. The teacher, a nervous woman with beady eyes, always suspicious, had told Leila to defer to the government in such matters.

"But, Baba," Leila said to Tamir, "you are the government, so I told her I would turn to you."

Tamir smiled. "Daughter, governments are made of people, and every person has his own opinion. Sometimes he hides what he thinks because he is afraid."

"So how do I know when I can speak out?"

Tamir pulled on his beard and seemed to consider this. "Well. First, make sure your position is strong. Because you are a woman, you must find a husband who agrees with your politics. This way, you will have support for your thoughts." He smiled. "But not yet."

"Does Mama agree with you in everything?" Leila asked.

This made her father chuckle.

"Everything that matters," said Tamir. He pinched Leila's cheek.

"I would never marry a man unless he thought the way we do, and you approved of him," Leila said.

"I trust your judgment," said Tamir. "We are not like our fundamentalist neighbors. Every person should be given a chance to decide for himself, including marriage." Leila's mother, after all, was a Kurdish woman, so Tamir was indeed a representative of free thinking in his version of Iraq.

"But," he continued, "you understand that things are not black-and-white. All things take time, especially good things and great changes."

Leila held her tongue between her teeth as she remembered the things her father used to say. It was most uncomfortable to be confronted with a new Tamir, a harsher version of the man whom she'd so admired and respected. Leila wished it were not so. If the Americans had let them alone, they might have come to their own way of peace in Iraq, and Tamir would still be wise and kind and would never need to talk of bombs and weapons.

The country was on shifting sands, and there were a million degrees of insurgency, of sympathizers and participants and innocent bystanders. There was no universal formula for determining loyalty to tribe or family or religion. Leila did not even know the heart of her own father. Was he a mere pretender, talking about the fight against an occupying force? Or had he taken it further and orchestrated attacks against the Americans? Leila hoped he had the sense to stay out of the worst of it.

When she went up to bed that night, Leila lay in the dark of her room, her bedcovers pulled up to her chin. In just two days, her life had changed so quickly. The light from the waxing moon filtered through a gap in her curtains, and Leila stared up at the light spot on the opposite wall. She was in a fog and nothing was certain. There was nothing to hold on to anymore.

Just before she drifted into a fitful sleep, Leila heard voices and footsteps in the courtyard. She heard the clink of a chain, and the creaking of a metal door. There was an old well in the courtyard, gone dry years ago and covered over with a dusty metal hatch. Why was it being opened in the middle of the night? She did not have time to contemplate it, for sleep came seconds later.

Chapter 5

Leila looked at her reflection on the wall mirror in her bedroom, trying to shake the last remnants of sleep. It was seven in the morning, several weeks after beginning the job with the Americans, and the cool glare of sunshine poked through her curtains and created a smattering of light dots on the far wall. She liked her east-facing window into the courtyard, for the morning light served to awaken her. It was the innocent part of the day, never punctuated by the brief moments of terror when her father asked her a question, or when she heard the backfire of a car or the clattering of AK-47 rounds fired into the sky at a nearby wedding. Leila always thought the bullets were made for her.

She reached over and chose a tube of mascara, expertly sweeping it over her long eyelashes in a thin layer so that her parents would not notice. She dusted her cheeks with light pink blush. She dabbed on some glossy lipstick, then blotted it with a tissue so that it was not obvious; it gave her the coloring of a desert dusk, pink lips and dark eyes. The ritual reminded her of the freedom of her university days, of wearing makeup and dressing like a Westerner, of having debates in English with the American exchange students in Cairo. It was a sunny, relaxed memory.

The Quran instructed against women adorning themselves for beauty, but her application of makeup was natural and unnoticeable, or so she hoped. Someday, Leila thought, the world of Arab women would catch up with the rest, and they could all wear beautiful fashions and high-heeled shoes. Until then, Leila's tiny rebellion was a dash of color on the face beneath her *hijab*.

She yawned, and stretched, and pulled her long hair into its tight bun to go with the head scarf. It was Thursday, the last day before her weekend. Fridays, Saturdays, and Sundays were off, as Friday was the Muslim holy day and Sunday the Christian. Leila was sorry, for her work at the American base meant life had finally taken an interesting turn.

Her first day at the 67th Combat Support Hospital had been like stepping into a small piece of America, fresh and efficient and clean. People—strange men!—shook her hand: the doctors, the nurses, all big smiles and welcomes. The immersion was complete, for there was not another woman in sight wearing the *hijab*, or a sentence, a word, written in Arabic.

In comparison to most of the hospitals in Mosul, the American facility was large and well equipped, three stories high, with a radiology department, a pharmacy, and an operating room. When she first arrived, Leila had been given the tour by a female army nurse who held the rank of second lieutenant; the woman had been briskly cheerful, full of facts, and with a quick double pat on Leila's arm, had left her to fend for herself. Overwhelmed, Leila had sat down on a square wooden chair with a black leather cushion and tried to take deep breaths when her new boss showed up.

"Miss al-Ghani?"

Looking up, Leila found a short man with a paunchy middle and thin glasses perched on his nose. She stood. "Yes?"

"Dr. Harding Peabody," he said, jutting out a hand and giving a quick, tight smile. "You'll be working with Dr. Whitaker and me in the surgery."

"Hi," said Leila, shaking the offered hand. "*Fursa saeeda*—er, nice to meet you," she said, flustered that she'd spoken in Arabic first. It would take practice to remember to think and speak in English.

Dr. Peabody told her that she would be working primarily

as a medical assistant, but that she would act as a translator whenever there was an Arabic-speaking patient. He explained that it was hospital policy to always keep someone fluent in Arabic on staff. That sounded just fine to Leila; she was glad they needed her particular set of skills.

The rest of the day had been an orientation, but it served more to disorient Leila than anything else. She'd felt on the brink of doing something wrong all day. The soldiers were intimidating; when she and Dr. Peabody visited the main ward, a soldier recovering from a broken ankle had looked Leila up and down, then winked. When he saw the furious blush rise on her face, he'd given her a broad smile. She was not used to innocent flirtation.

However, the staff was understanding (Leila was not, she learned, the first female Iraqi translator to work at the hospital) and the first strange day passed without incident. At the end of it, Leila felt as though a million things had happened, the impressions crowding in around her, so when she arrived home she'd been truly relieved to make the tea, serve the meal, and listen to Fatima chat about the children at the nursery.

Each day at the Combat Support Hospital grew more routine, as Leila's rational mind told her it would. The mysteries of the American hospital were decoded and Leila began to adjust to the foreign behavior, the laughing nurses, the soldiers who tried to flirt with her. Leila found herself enjoying the job more each day. On the cusp of her third weekend, she had grown to like her job so much that she wished she could work every single day. She was addicted to the thrill of her learning curve in the American hospital.

She descended the staircase when her outfit was in place, modest and decent. Her thick fringe of eyelashes felt like a luxury. "Good morning, Mother," Leila said, popping into the kitchen for a bite of bread before she went.

"Good morning," said Umm Naji. "You are up early."

"I want to get to work on time, and I never know about traffic," said Leila.

"Leila, do you think you could stay at home a bit more? It's not safe out there. Surely the pharmacy can spare you. Perhaps work only three days a week."

"I can't, Mama," said Leila.

Umm Naji sighed. "Your father was talking to me again," she said. "You know that more civilians die every day. There is no law. And the Americans pick up people off the streets! They disappear into the prisons!"

Leila had seen this for herself, the "detainees," as they were called. Some were guilty of insurgency. Others suffered from sheer bad luck. But they were taken to the military base, then whisked away in unmarked planes that took off from the airstrip, with five or ten or twenty Iraqi passengers who might never again be seen by their families. She ignored the operations for the most part; her job was surgical assistant and translator. When she kept her sphere of attention limited to her duties at the hospital, she slept better at night.

The kettle of water on the gas threatened to boil over, and Umm Naji grabbed a tattered cloth to touch its handle and move it away. "Tea?" she asked.

Leila nodded, and reached up to the top shelf of the cabinet to grab two small clear glasses. She put them on the metal tray, and dropped sprigs of fresh mint into them. Her mother poured the tea, hot and black and sweet.

"You are looking well, Leila," said Umm Naji, peering at her daughter.

Leila dropped her eyes, praying her mother did not notice the makeup. That would be fatal to her budding career, as Umm Naji would tell Tamir, and then Leila might be banned from leaving the house. "Thank you, Mama," said Leila. "And Fatima looks well, too."

"Yes, Fatima," said Umm Naji. "Today, Khaled's relatives are coming for tea. I believe they will want to talk to Mr. al-Ghani!" Umm Naji tittered with laughter, rocking in her chair.

Leila sighed with relief. It sounded like the *mashaya*, when the men in the families met to finalize the wedding plans. If it was, all attention would be on Fatima, and off her. "How exciting!" Leila said, raising her eyebrows and sipping the tea that cooled in her glass.

"It is," said Umm Naji. She laughed to herself and said, not unkindly, "Maybe someday soon, we will have good news for you, Leila."

Leila glanced at her watch. "Oh! I must go." She leapt up and kissed Umm Naji on the cheek. Umm Naji waved her off, in jolly spirits, and Leila slipped out of the house unnoticed by her father.

The month of December was cold in Mosul. The air would not warm up until midday, and even then it would be tepid sunshine, kept in check by the breeze sweeping down from the mountains. Leila's breath fogged about her as she pedaled her bicycle down the fine paved road. She hoped the road stayed intact and that the mujahideen had the sense not to destroy it with IEDs. It was such a joy to feel the tires of the bicycle clip along the smooth surface.

Once she entered into the rabbit warren of old city streets, Leila had to slow her pace and ring her bell to warn pedestrians of her passage. The gentle ding of her bicycle bell sounded over and over, merging with the goats' bells and the car horns and the clatter of the city morning. A large truck rumbled past, spewing toxic black clouds from its dripping exhaust pipes, and Leila coughed. Mingled with the chemical scents were the earthy odors of trampled, stale animal dung; the succulent roasting of meat, already turning round and round in the *shwarma* stands; and the deep rich wafts of coffee from the roadside, where old men stood next to tall gleaming Turkish coffeepots. She turned down a random street that would take her on a new route to the Al-Razi Hospital.

Every morning she left her bicycle chained up to the metal rack outside the big concrete building. She walked a block, went past a security checkpoint, and waited for the bulky square minibus to take her into Logistics Support Area Diamondback. It left at precisely eight forty-five every morning.

Today she was fifteen minutes early, and she sat on a concrete guard barrier in front of the hospital. She smiled and nodded to three other girls who chattered together in a tight group. They were cleaners at the base, from poor families in the Assyrian sector of Mosul. For them, the risk of attack was worth the steady salary. There were other employees who took the bus as well: civilian translators who worked with the Americans, some kitchen workers who washed dishes in the army mess hall, and the two Iraqi policemen who rode back and forth on the bus as protection.

The police would be useless against the normal mode of terrorist attack, the roadside bombs or the random spray of bullets. But appearances must be maintained, and the police stood in stolid discipline, checking the same identification cards of the same employees day in, day out. The police were both young men, fresh as cream, and they took their job seriously, never showing informality. As she boarded the bus that morning, Leila handed over the plastic laminated card with her picture, and her name and title written in both English and Arabic. As usual, the policeman took it, inspected it, checked her face against her picture, and handed back the card.

Leila sat toward the front of the bus, and she felt the vibration through the scuffed leather seat as the bus's engines started up. The other familiar passengers boarded the bus just as the second hand on Leila's watch marked a quarter to nine and the wheels started rolling. She smiled to herself. She had always heard the Germans were sticklers for punctuality, but the Americans? She supposed militaries everywhere were the same. They loved hours and minutes and numbers. In a war zone it must be a reassuring element of control to mark the time like that.

The journey took about twenty minutes, allowing for traffic and terrorist incidents. Leila stared out the window, past the buildings, at the green-brown emptiness of the hills beyond. She felt far away from the rest of the world. In her head, she replayed the rap music she'd listened to last night: Tupac Shakur, the dead American rapper. Judging by his lyrics, there was lawlessness even in the promised land.

As they drew closer to the base, anticipation grew in the pit of Leila's stomach. It was dangerous business, and she lived with the constant threat of discovery by her father, but Leila loved her job. The American surgeons were professional and helpful in their advice to her, and the practical experience was a thousand times better than pill-counting in the Al-Razi pharmacy. Just last week Leila had assisted Dr. Peabody in a delicate surgical operation to repair an American soldier's left lung that had been lacerated by shrapnel from an explosion. Their field hospital lacked the full facilities of a major trauma center, but they'd done their best to keep the soldier alive until he could be lifted off to Ramstein Air Base in Germany. Leila later heard that he was in recovery, and she felt good about it.

It was beyond her required duties to help in surgery often, but the doctors with whom she worked, Whitaker and Peabody, allowed it whenever her translation skills weren't needed. They were supportive of Leila's medical ambitions.

Diamondback Road, the long straightaway to the airport and base, was bereft of traffic, aside from an outgoing patrol convoy of Humvees. The road was colored in flat tones of brown, the distance measured in bumps and rattles of the vehicle. During the journey Leila felt the weariness and the danger all at once . . . as though the terror were a thread woven into the fabric of time itself, a corrupt thread that was a shade darker than the clear blue sky and the bright sandy ground.

She clasped her hands in her lap as the bus slowed to go through the security checkpoint into the American base. This took almost twenty minutes, and bomb-sniffing dogs went all around the bus. Leila and the others stood and got out, walked through the metal detectors, and then segregated into two lines, men and women. Leila spread her arms wide for the female military police to pat her down. When the check was complete, they got back on the bus and continued through to the base.

Leila heard from one of the other women that security had not always been so tight. When the Americans first arrived, the base had been relatively open, even to the point of Turkish merchants gathering outside the gates, selling trinkets and fine carpets at a discount to the soldiers and contractors. It all changed on the twenty-first of December, two years ago, when a suicide bomber wearing a shrapnel IED exploded himself inside the mess hall at midday. Over twenty people had been killed, both soldiers and civilians. Leila had been in Cairo for her last year at the university at the time, but the other women said that relations with the Americans turned to high distrust after the bombing. Leila could not blame them.

The overall impression of Logistics Support Area Diamondback was that it was flat. There weren't many bi-level structures; the buildings of size were the hangars and the mess hall, which was really a glorified tent shaped like a great sharp-ridged sand dune. The rest of the base hugged the ground like the interloper it was, trying and failing not to cause offense. Across the straight-edged road, Forward Operating Base Marez lurked, filled with soldiers.

After she got off the bus and showed her pass for a third time, Leila walked across the base to the hospital. The loose gravel crunched beneath her feet as she passed a row of white prefab trailers, squat and square. The wind, cool off the water of the adjacent Tigris River, threatened to steal her *hijab*. With one hand she held her scarf in place and kept walking past the residential trailers. Leila imagined they had once looked new and shiny, but now they were coated with an ever-present layer of thin dust. The odd one was pockmarked with tiny rusted brown holes from stray mortars. Between the exterior walls, wires were strung, floating with towels and brown T-shirts and socks that never quite got clean. Leila liked the miscellany because it reminded her of Mosul City itself; it reminded her that human beings occupied the base, not frightening and pristine robot soldiers.

After three weeks at work on the base, she'd learned what she always suspected: that Americans were not devils or supernatural tormentors or evil people. They became sick and injured just like anyone else, and in addition, most of them were nice. Polite. Smiling.

On the way past the Special Forces compound, however, Leila shivered; the concrete building was protected by rows of razor-wire fence and a sign outside that demanded NO PHOTOGRAPHY in stern red letters. A hand-painted skull-and-crossbones symbol also hung on the outermost fence, teeth bared, giving Leila the impression of a deadly clubhouse. She'd helped set a dislocated shoulder of one of the men of the 10th Special Forces the previous week; his name had been Nisson and he was of Asian descent, with cool black eyes and a hard demeanor.

At nine-thirty, Leila finally entered the hospital. She retrieved her lab coat from her own locker; the locker had her name written in black plastic block letters and she closed it with an authoritative clang. For a moment, Leila imagined herself as a doctor in an American hospital, safe and sound. Then she heard the dull thump of a mortar series from outside, and the illusion was shattered.

"Good morning, Leila!" said Dr. Peabody, the surgeon, when she walked into the main ward.

"Good morning, Doctor," she said.

"How are you today?"

The Americans always asked her "how she was." Leila smiled. "I am well," she said.

"Busy day today," said Peabody.

"Is it?" Leila said. There had been rumors about another gun battle in the city.

"Ah yes. There are two Iraqi detainees at the moment, and they've been pretty uncooperative. One has a leg injury, from which he'll recover. The other has some nasty shrapnel embedded in the lungs; he was messing with his own IED when it happened. Both are in the visitors' ward. You can start there today—just follow the smell," Peabody said. And she did.

Hours later, among the trays of medical supplies, the ubiquitous IV drips and wall charts, the shining linoleum floor, Leila stood at the foot of one of the occupied beds in the ward. Two wounded insurgents lay at opposite ends of the room, each looking mutinous and resentful. Leila wrote fast on her clipboard.

From behind her, a man cleared his throat. "Excuse me," he said. His blue eyes were lowered out of courtesy, but as Leila glanced up she still recognized him. It was the soldier from the house raid at the Rasuls' house two months ago, the handsome one.

"Yes?" she said, astonished that her own voice could sound so cool and clear.

"Captain James Cartwright," he said by way of introduction. Up close, she could see on his uniform the insignia of the 10th Special Forces, like the compound she'd walked past on her way to the hospital. "Are you the translator?" he asked.

She nodded. "I am Leila al-Ghani," she said.

The captain studied the floor and let the moment slide a little too long. Leila glanced back down at her clipboard. Clearing his throat again, he spoke. "Yes," he said, "we've met before, haven't we?"

Leila nodded.

Clearly, the soldier remembered the raid. "Sorry about that. Please, call me James."

Leila met his eyes once more. "It was not your fault, I am sure," she said. "You follow your orders."

James nodded. "So you work here now?"

"Yes," she said. "I have been here three weeks."

"Really? I haven't seen you," said James.

With a lift of her eyebrows, Leila's mouth twitched in amusement; it sounded like Captain James was on the lookout for pretty Iraqi girls. The impression was unintentional, she was certain, but she could not help smiling again.

"Sorry—er—I mean, I didn't know we had a new translator."

"I work with the surgeons," she said. "Here in the hospital. I am on loan from the Al-Razi civilian hospital in the city."

"Ah," said James. He glanced over at the wounded prisoner, who stared back and forth between James and Leila. The prisoner's brown face betrayed both curiosity and loathing. "Does he speak any English?" James asked, nodding at the wounded man.

"No," said Leila. "Not that he has revealed, anyway."

"Right," said James. "I'm supposed to question him. But I think I'll need your help, if you're willing."

Leila shrugged. "It is my job," she said, not liking it, but she felt James knew what she meant. It was his job, too. He pulled up two metal folding chairs that rested on the wall for himself and Leila and then turned to the bedridden insurgent. Leila cleared her throat. There was no room for fellow-Iraqi allegiance here; she had a job to do and she would do it well. "What is your name? *Ma ismuka?*"

The man said nothing.

"He is called Hazim," Leila volunteered, glancing at the chart. "He has not given a family name."

"Hazim," James said. "My name is James."

Leila translated this in a staccato burst. Hazim turned his head away.

"We have treated you of your wounds," said James, "and given you medicine. We want you to heal, and go in peace. It is a matter of hospitality."

Hazim mumbled something in return.

"He says he thanks you for the treatment, but he has done nothing to be held here," Leila said.

"Is he part of the insurgency? Is that how he wounded his leg?" James asked.

Leila shook her head. "He says the Strykers shot him for no reason." She sighed. "It is impossible to know the truth."

It went like that for about twenty minutes. James asked a question about Hazim's company or family or activities in Mosul. Leila translated. The answers were vague and contradictory and they had to repeat themselves many times, hoping to catch Hazim with the truth. She wondered if it was Hazim's guilt or a general coyness that molded his answers.

At the end of the session, the only solid information was that Hazim was from Tikrit, he'd been in Mosul for five months, and he was visiting a "cousin."

"It's always a cousin," said James, rubbing his eyes.

"That is the way of this country." said Leila. "I have over eight hundred cousins."

"Eight hundred!"

"More on my father's side," said Leila. "He is Arab. My mother has a smaller family, and they are Kurdish. Only three hundred cousins on that side."

James shook his head in total disbelief. "Are they all first cousins?"

Leila laughed. "No," she said. "Just cousins."

"Your mother is Kurdish?" he asked.

"Yes, from Dohuk," said Leila. "Most of her family is still there."

"Huh," said James, stealing another look at Leila's face, and she noticed the motion of his eyes. "I think that's all he's going to tell us," James said, regarding their wounded terrorist. A pause hung in the air and then James forged ahead. "Do you translate all the medical terms, then?"

"Yes," she said. "I am the translator, and also surgical assistant. My degree is biomedical science."

"Oh!" said James, impressed. "Where did you go to college?"

"The Cairo University," Leila said. "I graduated last year. But because of the war, and my father, I cannot go back for my doctor's degree." She sighed. Pity she did not want, yet her situation was beginning to demand it.

"Your father?" he asked.

Feeling bad for weaseling out of his interest, Leila glanced at him, then looked away again. "It is nothing," she said. "If you are finished here, I must go. The bus takes us back into the city at six o'clock."

James barely had time to say, "It was nice to meet you!" and Leila was out the door.

Chapter 6

Yesterday, she'd met him. She'd learned his name, the owner of the blue eyes that so impressed upon her. James Cartwright. A captain in the U.S. Army. Like all Iraqis, she knew the demarcations of U.S. military ranks by proximity. Leila hoped to see him again today. If part of his job was questioning insurgents, it would mean he might appear in the hospital ward again; she wondered about the unit to which he belonged. She'd been told the Special Forces at LSA Diamondback were on something called the "logistics" team, but no one knew for sure what they did. It was very mysterious. Although she couldn't know for sure, Leila imagined that logistics was a cover-all term, a free license to go into battle, test out new weapons, interrogate prisoners, gather intelligence, walk among the locals . . . they were called special for a reason.

Her musings were lost in the day's routine. They sent in an order for more drugs. Leila was allowed to use the military Internet to check her e-mail. She helped Ann Pavlopolous, one of the nurses, to change the dressing on the "detainee" Hazim's leg. Other than the brief burst in the morning, the insurgent mortar activity was low that day. A wind kicked up and rattled the window frames of the building, making Leila glad she was indoors rather than out in the dust.

Leila took her lunch at two in the afternoon along with

Dr. Whitaker. They ate in the cozy break room; it held a folding table with three chairs, a sink, a mini refrigerator, an electric kettle for making coffee or tea, and some military-issue tin cups. Every day Leila brought her own lunch; today it was flatbread wrapped around some salad with yogurt sauce.

Dr. Adam Whitaker's tall, sturdy-boned frame was folded to fit into the squeaky old chair in the break room. He had a graying mustache and a full head of hair, and loved to show off the pictures of his first grandchild, a little boy named Aaron. When Leila first came to work at the American hospital, the rumpled photograph of Aaron had been the first thing Dr. Whitaker presented to her.

She liked Dr. Whitaker. He was a good man and a good doctor, with a gentle manner and a great deal of knowledge about the medical field. He reminded Leila of every town doctor in every storybook she'd read, the kind who would show up at a house in the middle of the night with a black leather valise full of medicines for the child with a fever. Leila felt comfortable around him. They ate their lunch in genial silence. The strains of Dr. Peabody's favorite jazz CD filtered down the hallway.

"He missed his calling as a musician," said Dr. Whitaker, motioning with his head toward Peabody's office.

"He likes that jazz music," Leila said. "It stays in my head all the time."

"Cross-cultural learning," said Dr. Whitaker.

"I prefer American hip-hop."

Dr. Whitaker smiled. "You and my kids both."

Leila swallowed the last bite of her flatbread sandwich and wiped her mouth with a napkin, disposing of it in the little gray plastic rubbish bin. She glanced up; standing in the doorway was Nurse Pavlopolous.

"Adam," said Pavlopolous, "they've brought in a seriously wounded patient, they need you immediately. You too, Leila." The largish woman nodded her head and disappeared at a fast pace back down the hall.

"Let's go," said Dr. Whitaker.

Leila washed her hands off and grabbed her clipboard and pen. She was required to keep written summaries of her translations so they could go into the official medical reports. She and Dr. Whitaker hurried down the corridor, where a cluster of men in U.S. military uniforms and a few in civilian clothes gathered, their voices urgent.

"Dr. Whitaker!" called one of the men. Leila could see from his uniform that he was a first lieutenant. "He's suffering from a strong electric shock." The group of army men split to allow Leila and the doctor through. When they entered the ward, Leila's eyes widened.

A naked man was stretched upon a clean hospital trolley bed. His tanned Iraqi skin was sallow and had the look of curdled cheese. His eyes were rolled back into his head and his tongue hung out, limp and swollen. Electrodes were attached to his fingers, shoved beneath the fingernails. There were angry bruises across his thighs and shoulders, and on his abdomen was a half-healed gash that looked like a bullet graze. No one needed to tell her that this man had been tortured.

"Move aside!" Dr. Whitaker ordered the three men standing alongside the hospital bed, watching. Two were in civilian clothes, and one was in a uniform.

Leila glanced up at them, and her eyes locked once again with Captain James Cartwright's. She felt a queer tug from the base of her throat, followed by a sinking feeling in the pit of her stomach. Was James involved in this? From the look of knowing dismay in his blue eyes, she decided he knew something about it.

"Ask him his name," Dr. Whitaker snapped, in full emergency mode.

"*Ma ismuka?*" Leila said, gentle but firm. The man's lips moved, but made no sound.

"His number is 1256. He's classified as an enemy combatant," said a brown-haired civilian. He had a bland face and long-fingered hands that were clasped in front of him like the pale legs of a spider.

Dr. Whitaker felt the pulse at the Iraqi man's throat. "Weak," he said. "Ann! Get me a drip!"

Pavlopolous's hefty frame appeared from behind Leila, dragging an IV tower. "Leila, get the EKG."

Leila attached the electrocardiogram to the man's right index finger, grimacing at the sharp electrode beneath his fingernail. His finger oozed blood.

"Pay attention to what he says," said one of the three observers. "These Akhmeds are always pretending, cunning little bastards. Can't trust an Arab." Leila looked up, repressing a flare of anger. It was the brown-haired man again, and he spoke as if the pained human body in front of his eyes were already dead.

"Who are you?" Leila could not resist asking.

"Call me Travis," said the man. "Travis Pratt. And you are?" He raised his eyebrows.

"Call me Miss al-Ghani," she returned. Leila glanced back at James, and noted the way he narrowed his eyes at Travis. No love lost there. "Well, *Travis*," she said, "this man is not capable of saying anything at the moment. He has been tortured."

A silence fell across the hospital bed as Dr. Whitaker stopped working and Pavlopolous let out a little huff. "He's just injured," Dr. Whitaker said.

"With electrodes in his fingernails?" Leila asked, incredulous.

"Drop it," Pavlopolous whispered into her ear.

Leila said nothing else. Pratt stared at her; she could feel his gaze. She busied herself with turning on the EKG and the comforting beep filled the air. The Iraqi man's heartbeat was faint, but present. In contrast, Leila's own pulse thrummed angrily in her ears. The U.S. military was deep in this business and Leila's soft feelings for James Cartwright started to congeal into disgust. Every healing instinct, every impulse of compassion flinched at the sight of this "detainee"; even if he was mujahideen, he did not deserve this.

The prisoner had been subjected to electric shock from the look of the red burns and weals on his skin. His pallid skin was flushed around bunches of nerves on his neck and mouth; Leila thought the current had traveled up his arms, through his nerves, the path of least resistance. If it had reached his brain at a high enough voltage . . .

"We have swelling," said Dr. Whitaker. "Could be impaired circulation or necrosis. I'm gonna need to do an exploration—maybe a fasciotomy—get me a scalpel, Ann, would you? And I want a bicarbonate at two m-eq's. Leila, prepare an IV for when he's stabilized, this man needs fluids . . ."

"She needs to stay here in case the *hajji* says anything," Pratt protested. "I'll remind you that he is a security detainee, and was in custody of the Iraqi police—"

"Too damn bad," said Dr. Whitaker. "Do you want me to fix him or don't you?"

Pratt just scowled.

The doctor sighed. "I'll have to ask you gentlemen to wait outside," Dr. Whitaker said, turning to the three observers. "If the prisoner says anything, we'll let you know."

Pratt looked about to object again, but Captain Cartwright intervened. "Let's go," he said. "Let them work."

The hours ticked by. Leila felt metallic and thin and cold, but she put aside the feelings and focused on the tasks before her. Grab the pliers. Lift the man's head. Put a towel down to absorb the blood from his fingers. Insert the breathing tube. The injured Iraqi was an inanimate object to be fixed, and ceased to be human. In one flash of disconcerting insight, Leila wondered if his tormentors viewed him in the same way: inhuman.

Whitaker and Pavlopolous, too, were silent aside from the terse remarks and instructions that accompanied the medical procedures. After an indeterminate time, the man's condition stabilized into hitching breaths and a faint but steady heartbeat. He remained unconscious.

Leila stepped away from the hospital bed, reaching for her

blank clipboard. What could she say in this report? There seemed to be a protocol involving what one could "say" about cases of torture, but Leila did not know the anesthetized words for it.

She returned to the staff room after washing down and sat there with her pen hovering over the blank page when Dr. Whitaker entered the room. "Miss al-Ghani," he said.

If he called her by her formal name, Leila knew it was serious. She regarded the tall doctor and waited.

"You know what I have to say," he said. "You can't talk about what you see here."

Leila nodded. "I know," she said. "You have my silence." She had signed a nondisclosure form when she first arrived here, and since Leila's job was a secret from her family, she had no one to tell, anyway. Besides, what good would it do to speak of these things? Such news would enrage the mujahideen further and put Leila in danger for having witnessed it.

"You did well today," said Dr. Whitaker. "You have the right manner to be a doctor."

"Thank you," said Leila, smiling until she thought of the Iraqi detainee, about her own age, tortured by their own police. He would never have the opportunity to become a doctor, or to be praised by the Americans.

Dr. Whitaker nodded. "Okay, good. Well—it's past six. You should be getting home."

Leila blinked and glanced out the window. Sure enough, the sunlight was fading fast, and the electric lights blinked on against the backdrop of darkening sky to the east. The hands on her watch pointed at a quarter past six. "Thank you, Dr. Whitaker," she said again, and dashed out the door.

A wave of panic flared through Leila's veins as she scrubbed down quickly, washed her hands clean, and changed out of her lab coat. If it was past six o'clock, then she would already have missed the bus back into the city. Perhaps today was the exception . . . perhaps it had waited for her . . . but she knew it had not. The military had its schedule and the Iraqis had been warned that if they missed the bus, they were on their own. She slammed her locker shut and glanced at her watch again. Six twenty-two. *Damn.*

The difficult day suddenly welled up and Leila felt like crying. What was she to do? There was no way she could walk back. It would take at least an hour and the airport road was the most perilous in the city. She would be stupid to attempt it. Leila contemplated what would happen to her, a single woman walking home alone, in the dark, from the American base. When the mujahideen finished with her, the tortured detainee would be a model of wellness in comparison.

As Leila walked out the doors, the cold air hit her like a slap and a secondary panic arose when she thought about her father. Even if there was a safe way home, Tamir al-Ghani would be suspicious of the late hour. Leila tried to think up a plausible lie. Perhaps she could say the pharmacy had been busy. . . . She stood alone outside the hospital beneath a silver-blue spotlight, thinking, arms crossed against the chill.

"Uh—sorry. Excuse me?" A man's voice interrupted her thoughts.

Leila turned, and under the harsh fluorescent light, James Cartwright looked worried.

"Yes?" she said. She felt a tinge of loathing at herself for ever having thought James good-looking. Clearly, he was worse than a terrorist.

"Leila—I mean, Miss al-Ghani, I wanted to tell you something."

Leila crossed her arms and waited.

James stepped closer. "I don't want you to think I had anything to do with that." He waved toward the hospital ward doors. As if reading Leila's thoughts, he said, "We don't involve ourselves with torture. It's not what you think."

She stared at him, unsure what to say. His oath was sincere, but Leila wondered if he made it for his own sake as much as hers. She glanced around; they were alone. "Then who did it?" she asked.

"Do you want to take a walk?" James asked. "I mean, just here, outside the hospital."

Leila was already too late for the bus, so what was the harm? It was most inappropriate, though. If an Iraqi man had ever suggested a "walk," Leila would take it to mean he wanted to take liberties with her. However, the Americans were open as children. If James said a walk, he probably meant a walk. "All right," she said. "Just out here."

He nodded and kept a respectful distance as they left the glowing circle of light and walked into the darkening twilight. Across the grainy asphalt surface, a huge C-5 Galaxy cargo plane waited with blinking lights at the other end of the air- field, loaded down like a bird that had eaten too many fish. The plane's engines had a low, comforting drone that made the ground beneath Leila's feet vibrate. The American base had its own sense of rhythm and order, a down-and-dirty functional- ity that was almost soothing, especially after such a hard day. She watched the Galaxy taxi slowly along, preparing to take off into the twilight sky.

Next to her, James's face was a stark white contrast against his dark hair, and his desert fatigues blended against the shad- ows so that he looked like a handsome head floating in midair.

"I came in at the very end," he said. "I don't want you to think Americans are like this, that we—you know—torture people. It wasn't us at all. He was already unconscious when we took custody of him, from the Iraqi police, and he'd been with . . . contractors, not us."

"Contractors did this?" Leila asked.

"They didn't stop it," he sighed. "They don't follow any laws, and since the contractors are private, they can't be court- martialed." James turned his face away, as though he'd done his duty for his conscience and could move on to other things.

"I believe you," Leila said.

But James was just silent.

"Do you mind if I smoke?" he finally asked. "Bad habit."

"I don't mind," said Leila. A man asking permission to smoke? She was accustomed to men doing whatever they wanted.

With a sharp flick of a metal lighter, James ignited the end of a cigarette and took a long, calm drag. The burning tip glowed in the purple darkness. "Didn't the civilian bus leave already?" he asked.

"Yes," said Leila.

"How are you gonna get home?"

"I don't know," she said, trying not to sound like a lost child.

"Hmm," said James.

A moment of awkwardness followed. Leila did not know what to say next, and she racked her brain for something, anything.

James spoke first. "Do you live with your parents?"

"Yes," said Leila. "My parents and my older sister."

"You could call them, explain you're stranded at the base," he said.

"No!" Leila said. "I couldn't. I can't. I mean, they don't know I work here," she finished, out of breath.

"What?"

Leila paused, and shrugged her shoulders in the growing darkness. "They think I still work at the pharmacy, at the Al-Razi Hospital," she said. "My father would never approve if he knew I worked with the Americans. I would be banished, or locked up in the house."

"Why?"

"He is—" Leila stopped herself before she said mujahideen. "He is a very traditional man. He did not even want me working to be a doctor. And this job he would consider most improper."

"Ah," said James. "Yet you took the job, anyway."

"It is the best opportunity," Leila said. "I need experience, and the American surgeons here are good."

"I think it's brave of you," said James, exhaling and tossing away his cigarette.

She felt her cheeks grow warm, and was glad for the darkness. "Thank you," she said. "But I think now it probably will end. My father will be suspicious that I am so late."

Another pause, and James spoke again. "Do you prefer to be called Miss al-Ghani? Or Leila?"

"You can call me Leila, if you like," she said, and could have kicked herself for the bold move.

"Well, Leila, I know there's a patrol going out in about fifteen minutes. Maybe they can drop you at your house?"

"Oh!" said Leila. "I don't know, I—" She hesitated. All hell would break loose if she were seen disembarking from an American vehicle. "Could they drop me somewhere quiet? Near my house, but out of view?"

"Oh, right!" James said. "Yes. Of course. I'll go along, make sure everything runs smoothly. I just don't want you walking along that airport road."

"That would be good," Leila admitted. She felt better to know James would come along on the patrol. It was the only solution in sight, so Leila would have to make the best of it and pray no one saw her in the Humvee.

"I'll take you," said James. "Do you have everything you need?"

"Yes," said Leila, double-checking the presence of her handbag, scarf, and the folder of reports she planned to read over the weekend.

"This way," said James, stepping forward. Leila walked alongside him past some barracks, each with unit-specific flags flying outside. The American flag was omnipresent, lit with floodlights, as were the crests and mottos of individual units. They walked into a hangar-type building where three boxy Humvee vehicles were parked in a tight column, surrounded by the raucous clanging and shouting of a patrol unit preparing for departure.

Leila was intimidated. These were warriors, strutting in

their desert combat uniforms, bristling with arms. Several of the men stared at her, and Leila felt very conscious that she was a woman in a dress. This was out of her league, this tight activity of war-making, and Leila wanted to run in the other direction, out of the hangar and back to the safe familiarity of the hospital ward and her colleagues. Here, she was surrounded by foreigners—the enemy, according to her father—and it was an effort to swallow her fright.

"You all right?" James asked. "Don't worry about these guys. They're really harmless."

Leila let out a tiny huff of amusement in spite of herself. "I'm all right," she said.

"Captain Hooker!" James called into the melee. A man in a bulky combat uniform appeared before them.

"Captain Cartwright," the man named Hooker said, grinning with big white teeth in a loose mouth.

"I have a special task for your MPs tonight," said James. "This lady is Leila al-Ghani, one of our translators. She needs a lift home."

"Mighty fine," said Hooker, nodding at Leila. "Pleased to make your acquaintance, madam," he said.

"Anyway, if it's all right with you, I'll be coming along on your patrol," said James.

"Sure thing, friend," said Hooker.

"Thanks, Hook," James said with a grin. He turned to Leila and said in a low voice, "You'll have to direct us to the best place to drop you."

"I live in the Wahdah neighborhood," said Leila, and gave her street address.

"I know where that is," said James. "Good road. It's paved."

"It is, isn't it?" Leila smiled. Nice that someone else appreciated the fineness of the new road.

"They'll be leaving shortly," said James. "Let's find a place to sit out of the way." He took Leila's elbow with gentle fingers, and her mouth dropped a little. In her life in Iraq, it was unheard of for men to touch women, but Leila needed to get used to it if she wanted to go to school in the West. She had mastered the Western handshake and thought nothing of it anymore, but for some reason in the midst of these American soldiers, Leila was hyperaware of her sex and status as an Iraqi woman. Her sense of decorum, against which she normally rebelled, reared its ugly head and Leila heard her mother's voice in her head, admonishing her about following the proper rules.

She allowed James to guide her toward one of the square, tan-painted vehicles. They all had drivers in place and their big engines idled; on the tops of the vehicles the gunners sat in slings behind armor shields, hands at rest but eyes alert. One of them saw Leila, caught her eye, and winked.

James opened the heavy plated door and held his hand out to Leila. "Here," he said. "You get a window seat."

Leila slipped her small hand into James's larger one. She felt his other hand linger on the small of her back as she stepped up into the looming metal vehicle. Sliding into the canvas seat, she waited for him to release her hand, but he didn't. Instead he stood next to her in the space of the open door, looking at her out of the corner of his eye in a way that suggested more than professional concern. Leila felt warm, reassured . . . and a tiny bit thrilled. A few seconds later, the driver of the Humvee poked his head around the front seat.

"You check her out, Captain?" the soldier asked.

"I sure did," said James, a private sort of smile tugging at his lips. "She's cool."

Leila understood: they wanted to make sure she wasn't a human bomb with explosives strapped beneath her dress. As she brought her feet to rest in the cramped space in front of her, she let go of the captain's grip and clasped her hands in her lap, feeling very much—as the Americans would say—out of her league. She overheard the other captain, Hooker, explaining to the group that they were going to drop her off. James, still standing outside, appeared to be waiting for the other soldiers to get in their positions.

"Sergeant, battle-lock her door, would you?" James shouted up to the gunner.

"Yes, sir," said the gunner, and he got down from his sling and reached across Leila to grab the steel handle on the door and slam the bolt forward. "Here's how you open it again," the soldier said, making a motion with his hands. "You speak English, right . . . ?"

"Yes, I understand," said Leila.

"Keep the grenades out for us," he said, grinning at her. The stitching on his uniform read HARTMAN.

"I will do my best," she said, forcing a smile. "Thank you."

"No problem!" said Hartman.

When all the soldiers were inside the vehicles, James climbed in from the other side and sat in the back with Leila. They were separated from the driver and the soldier on shotgun in the front by a bank of radios; James picked up a handset and said, "Moving now."

Leila felt a lurch, and then the vehicle was carrying her forward into Mosul, the city glittering beneath a sky that darkened like a bruise above them.

Chapter 7

Until that night, Leila had never imagined the tension and danger the Americans felt on their patrols in Mosul. Curfew didn't begin until nine, so there were still many civilians going about the last of the day's business. The patrol began in innocent fashion; they idled at an intersection and children began to gather around them, in twos and threes, then in larger clusters. They had smiles that gleamed friendly in the gloom; they outstretched their hands and gibbered in a mix of Arabic and English.

In the seat next to Leila, James smiled as he spoke into his headset. "This is Mike Six. If you have any kiddy ammo left, go ahead and unleash it. Out." A response crackled back, and above Leila's head, Hartman the gunner reached behind him into a satchel slouched in the rear storage area of the Humvee. He brought out a soccer ball and three stuffed teddy bears. Popping back up into the cupola, Hartman tossed the toys to the children, who jumped up and down, clapping their hands in anticipation. From the other two vehicles Leila could see the same thing happening. As a teddy bear flew through the air to land in the arms of a delighted young girl in pigtail braids, Leila laughed, too. She wished her father could see it.

"I've told them to drop you off after we do the first section of the patrol," James said, low into her ear.

She nodded.

"In the meantime, you get a rare treat," he said. "You get to *arrive* in one of our first-class Humvees, rather than be taken away in one."

Leila smiled and let out a small chuckle so that James would know his humor was appreciated. Through the speakers of the sound system, an American record played, heavy metal from the sounds of it. Leila would have preferred something else, but she doubted her opinion would be taken into consideration.

"Can't you guys put on something else?" James said to the driver in the front.

"What would the captain like?" returned the soldier.

"Anything but this sh—stuff."

"I've got some Apocalyptica," said the soldier in the other seat.

"Excellent," said James.

The new music was dark, metallic classical, but Leila sort of liked it. It fit her mind-set of impending doom. It was the type of music that suited the Middle East region in general: something bad was coming around the bend.

"Do you ever listen to American music?" James asked her.

"Yes," said Leila. "I like hip-hop."

"Hey. Me, too," said James. He sounded astonished by her again.

"I have all Tupac Shakur's music," Leila admitted, and she saw James grinning in the green-tinged darkness.

"Tupac was the best," he said. "I can't believe you listen to that! Wow. That must drive your family crazy, blaring that stuff from your room."

"They are not aware of my taste in music," said Leila.

James was silent for a moment, and the pounding violin strains from the stereo filled the space between them. "Well, Leila, you're just the little rebel, aren't you?" he asked with admiration in his voice.

"Not on purpose," she said. "It just happens."

He smiled at her again. "You'd fit right in, in America."

She glanced over at his shadowed figure. "In America? Really?"
"Yep," he said. "We love people who defy expectations."

Leila sat back. So James Cartwright liked her. As a rule
Americans were friendly, but he kept saying the right thing to
her. Just as that first meeting at the Rasul house, Leila felt safe
in his presence.

As the convoy rolled through some of the rougher streets
the sense of hostility toward them grew palpable, oozing out
of dark residential windows, and the few pedestrians shot resentful glances. The men in the Humvee became quiet and
watchful. The driver wove through traffic, slowing down and
speeding up at unpredictable intervals. Someone turned the
music off.

"Leila, for the time being, you're one of us," James said.
"The *muj* don't care who's in this vehicle. They'll kill us all if
they can, so please keep an eye open."

"What do you mean?" she asked, confused.

James gave her a gentle smile. "I mean, if you see anything
suspicious or unusual out your window, tell us right away."

"Oh! Yes, of course," she said. But she rearranged her scarf
so that it covered all but her eyes, and kept her head down.
Even though the windows were tinted dark, someone might
recognize her.

As the group of vehicles passed through yet another intersection, heading east toward the Tigris, James spoke into his
radio. "Bravo Two Four, this is Mike Six." The radio gave a
tinny response. "Mike Six on Toyota, passing Chevy, south,
over."

Leila was bewildered by the code names, but as she paid attention to the chatter she figured out that the Americans had
named the major thoroughfares in Mosul after automobiles.
The rest of it was a mystery, however. She stayed silent in her
seat and her watchful eyes glanced out the inch-thick window
next to her face. As they passed several side streets in quick
succession, she saw James look to the left and right at each
one. His face became hard and his eyes narrowed, focused on

something that he considered of interest. . . . When the patrol stopped at the next major intersection, James's attention was glued on something to the left of them.

"Hartman, to the left, white Passat coming up fast! Fire it up!"

Leila peered to the left and saw a battered white sedan driving toward them from the cross street, picking up speed and bouncing in the potholes. Sparks flew from the underbelly as it scraped along the road. In the orangish glow of the streetlights Leila could see the passengers: a woman, her face pallid and frozen in terror, and clutched in her arms was a toddler. A wild-eyed man was driving, staring straight at them. Leila realized with dawning horror that Sergeant Hartman the gunner was swinging the powerful machine gun to point at the car.

Leila opened her mouth to protest, to tell James there was a woman and a child, but nothing but a helpless squawk escaped her lips. It all happened in slow motion. When the white car was about forty meters away, Hartman opened up, and a burst of copper-clad bullets spat forth out of the machine gun, punching through the grill of the car and destroying the engine. The clattering roar of the gun was so loud that Leila did not hear herself scream. . . . The next burst of fire, a split second later, shattered the windshield and the man driving the car seemed to dance in his seat as the bullets ripped through his head and torso. The third and final burst crawled across the front of the car to hit the passengers, the woman and the child.

A hot brass cartridge landed in Leila's lap, burning her right thigh through her dress. She jumped, thinking for a panicked moment that she had been shot.

The white Passat veered across a concrete divider and slammed into a *shwarma* stand next to the road, scattering people in every direction.

"Goddamn," said the soldier driving their Humvee, knuckles white as he clenched the steering wheel.

She heard James mutter something under his breath; then he picked up the radio and said, "All units, stay froggy, be cool. I want a perimeter around this Passat." He turned to Leila. "Stay here."

She could but nod as he jumped out of the vehicle along with several soldiers from the other Humvee. The other captain, Hooker, was among the men on foot. The driver drummed his hands on the steering wheel as they waited. It took about twenty minutes; outside, James and the others were inspecting the car they'd destroyed, and she could see him giving orders, pointing, and finally nodding in seeming satisfaction. A creeping feeling worked at Leila's throat as though she were about to cry. Every time she blinked she could see the mother and child explode in a spray of blood.

When James got back into the Humvee, he told the driver to carry on. "We've got a team to take care of it. It was loaded with explosives."

"Goddamn," said the driver again.

For a moment Leila could think of nothing to say to James. Their rapport from the beginning of the patrol was shattered. Then she gathered her wits and said, in a low voice, "There was a woman and a child in the car."

James regarded her for a frozen moment, his eyes devoid of caring. "Yeah, there was."

"So, why? Why did you order them shot?"

"Because their vehicle was filled with old howitzer shells, ready to attack us. No choice."

Leila opened her mouth again, but the driver interrupted to ask, "Sir—how the hell did you know?"

"Well," said James, considering. "I spotted them a while back, paralleling us. They were at every intersection to the left as we moved . . . thought it might be coincidence but when they turned toward us, I could see they were heavy."

"Heavy?"

"The suspension was low, bottoming out. The car was full of something heavy."

"Goddamn," said the driver.

The Humvee gunned forward, picking up speed again, and

Leila tried to grapple with what she'd just seen. "But," she said, thinking aloud, "what if they hadn't had explosives? What if the car was heavy with luggage, or food, or bricks, or something? You would have just shot innocent people."

"Well, yeah," said James. He shrugged.

There was nothing left for Leila to say, so she rode the rest of the way to her neighborhood in shocked silence. Her heartbeat was hard and fast in her ears. All she wanted was to be safe, home, away from this patrol and the heavy machine gun that swung back and forth above her head. Her eyes still smarted from the lightning flashes of combat in the dark. Then a jolt of apprehension when she recognized the corner grocer's shop and then the sign declaring her street. "This is my house, coming up," she said to James.

"Is around the corner okay?" James asked.

"Yes," said Leila.

"Sergeant, take a left up here, and slow down to two miles an hour, but don't stop," James ordered. He turned to Leila. "Can you get out while we're moving? Then start walking in the opposite direction?"

"Yes, I think so," said Leila, mentally rehearsing the movements she would need. "Yes," she repeated, to bolster her own confidence.

"Good," said James. "I'm going to lean over you to open the door. Take my other hand, and I'll help you out."

Leila nodded assent, but James was already in motion. The two Humvees turned onto the street, one after the other, and they slowed to a steady crawl. James leaned across Leila and grasped the metal door handle, unlatching it. With his other hand he held hers with a hard and reassuring grip. Leila felt the night air on her face as the metal door swung open.

"Now!" James whispered in her ear, and Leila was in motion, swinging out the door to land on her two feet. She stumbled a bit, but James held her hand fast until she found her footing, and then the Humvee moved on. Leila gained her stride and straightened her shoulders. She did not look back at them, but heard the patrol pick up speed again as they disappeared into the night.

Leila glanced about her to see if anyone had witnessed the handoff. She saw no other pedestrians, and she turned the corner onto her own street in faith that she'd pulled it off. But the eyes of Mosul were ever watchful and Leila swore that sometimes even the birds and insects talked. She glanced at the green glow of her watch: it was almost eight p.m. "*Khara*," she swore to herself. Her pace increased, and a few hundred yards later Leila slipped through the metal gate of the al-Ghani home.

For a moment she stood just inside her front gate, trying to collect herself. She could have collapsed on the front porch, for her knees were weak with the relief of being home. When she bent over to remove her shoes, she noticed that her hands trembled. It was not the first time she'd seen death, but it had never been so close to her, so real. It had never been a helpless woman and child, carried along with the lunacy of a man who was supposed to protect them. And the firepower of a single American vehicle dazed her as well. It was no accident, Leila realized, that Saddam's old regime had fallen so fast. It was amazing that the insurgency could even put up the fight they did . . . and Leila suddenly imagined what would happen if the U.S. Army was given free rein over Iraq. There would be no resistance. Not after what she'd seen tonight.

Taking a few more deep breaths, Leila confronted her new, immediate problem: explaining to her family why she was so late. Pushing aside the mental images of the day (*I'll deal with it later*, Leila thought), she rehearsed her lie—a sudden order of antibiotics that had to be filled at the Al-Razi pharmacy. Leila had worked as hard as she could, along with Dr. Musrahi. It took hours. They were not let out until seven-thirty. . . .

She thought she had her story straight, then she remembered her bicycle. It was still at the hospital, parked there from this morning. Would it still be there after the weekend? And how would she explain why she had "walked" back from the hospital in the dark? "I let a coworker borrow it," she whispered. "That's all." Leila slipped inside the front door into the dark, empty hallway.

She thought she was safe until she heard someone clear their throat in the sitting room doorway.

Leila turned to see her father's frame leaning up against the wall. Tamir's face was eclipsed by the dark, but he reached behind him and flipped the light switch in the sitting room, bathing the room behind him in an electric glow.

"*Baba*!" Leila said.

"Come in and sit down, Leila. We need to speak."

Leila nodded. This would not be good. She felt it in her bones. As she walked into the sitting room, the harsh lights made Leila feel that her father was about to interrogate her. She sat on the divan, relaxing her mouth into an expression of innocence. "How was your day, Father?" she asked.

"My day does not matter right now," said Tamir, sitting opposite her. "It is eight o'clock. You have just arrived home. Why are you late?"

"I'm so sorry about that, Father," said Leila. "We got a late order of antibiotics at the hospital. We worked as fast as we could, but didn't get out until seven-thirty."

"Where is your bicycle?"

"I lent it to a coworker," Leila sighed. "She said she would return it today, but she did not. I think on Sunday it will be returned."

"You lent it out," said Tamir. He sounded suspicious, and Leila floundered for something more to tell him.

"I am sorry, Father," she repeated. "But I am finished with work for the week. I do not go back until Monday! I was thinking, perhaps tomorrow I could fix some *waraq dawaaleeh*. It is one of your favorites," Leila smiled, charming as could be. She hoped the promise of stuffed grape leaves with mutton would placate him.

"Leila," said Tamir. "I worry about you. You're our youngest, and you're nothing like your sister." He sighed. "Fatima is a dedicated daughter. She never lets work take her away from her duties at home."

"But, Father, Fatima works at a nursery," said Leila. "It is not the same. You know about hospitals. They are difficult places, and not as flexible. I enjoy my work. I want to make you proud, Father."

"Huh," said Tamir. A hard frown furrowed his brow. Leila stared down at the carpet, at the interwoven threads creating garlands of flowers and vases and bees on the floor. The rest of the house was silent, and Leila wondered if her mother and sister were asleep, or eavesdropping on their conversation from beyond the door.

Tamir cleared his throat. "Cut your hours at the hospital," he said. "You may work mornings, but you must be home by two in the afternoon."

Leila's jaw dropped. "What? But, Father—"

"This is not a discussion," Tamir said. "Things in Mosul City are precarious. It is no longer proper for an al-Ghani daughter to work all day out of the house."

Leila hung her head so he wouldn't see the tears in her eyes, the dark flash of frustration that threatened to ignite into a raging tantrum. It was so unfair! If she were a man, they would not be having this conversation. "Father, please—"

"That is my final word," said Tamir.

"Baba," she said, letting him see the tears. "Please. The hours at the hospital are set. I cannot cut back."

"Then you must quit," said Tamir.

She thought about her progress at the American base, all the things she was learning from the surgeons, the advice and experience. She thought about Captain James Cartwright, his unusual blue eyes, his strong hands. She thought about the metal locker with her name on it. Medical school in the West. A white laboratory filled with specimens. Spiked black high heels. Eating in a café and sipping her coffee, perusing the latest medical journal.

"I'll ask. I'll try to cut back my hours," she said.

"Home at two o'clock in the afternoons," Tamir said. "Leila, I—it's not that I'm trying to make you unhappy. You don't know the true situation here in Mosul. People get caught in things they don't expect. There are things planned . . . I am trying to keep you safe. You will be home earlier in the afternoon. I know what's best in this matter." His stare was serious, but he reached out and patted her arm.

"I'll do my best, Father," Leila murmured, and her shoulders collapsed.

"Go to bed now," Tamir said. "Your mother and I have something else to discuss with you, but it can wait until the morning." He raised his head and stared toward the window, as though his mind had already pushed Leila aside and moved on to other matters. Leila wondered if he was having more "guests" tonight.

She stole from the room in silence, not bothering to count the steps to her bedroom. She sank down onto her bed, fully dressed, and paused to kick off her shoes before biting down on her pillow and sobbing. She punched it into shape and soaked it with tears, and tried to sleep, but a black gloom invaded every corner of her whirling mind. She recalled her classes at Cairo University, the lecture slides with anatomical diagrams, the textbooks chock-full of formulae and facts and theories. As a sort of rebellion, Leila translated word after word that came into her head.

Appendectomy.

Metastasize.

Pharmaceutical. Carbohydrate. Osmosis.

Leila sat up in her rumpled dress, a scowl upon her face.

She had a bachelor's degree in biomedical science. It couldn't end here. Her knowledge of human anatomy would not be chained down to the endless cycle of sex and childbirth. Her father could go to hell.

"I'm going to be a doctor," she whispered. "I'm going to be a doctor. I am. I'm going to be a doctor." For good measure, she added, "And no one is going to stop me."

Later, just as Leila was drifting off to sleep, a strange clang in the courtyard jolted her awake. The cotton curtains hung straight down from the window and Leila moved the left one aside very slowly so that no one would notice the movement. She put her face up next to the crack and looked down into the family courtyard.

Five men stood together. She recognized her father's tall, gaunt figure among them. Three of the men had rifles slung over their shoulders, the familiar silhouette of the AK-47 so precious to guerilla warriors the world over.

The clanging noise she'd heard must have been the hatch to that old well, which gaped open to reveal a dark, square hole in the ground. Leila did not recognize the armed men, and she narrowed her eyes as one by one they dropped into the hole with steady, practiced descent. When the three were inside, Tamir and the other unknown man pulled the chain taut and dragged the cover closed; then Tamir took a reed brush and swept some dust across the hatch to create an impression of disuse.

Leila drew back from the window before her father saw her peeking. *He is hiding mujahideen in the well*, she thought. It explained her father's odd hours, the constant rotation of guests, the strategy sessions with the imam.

She felt sick. She wanted to be a doctor, to heal the sick and mend the wounded, and her own father was spreading the violence like the disease it was. Did her mother know about this? Umm Naji must; she was far from stupid, and kept a keen eye over her domain. Besides, they must be feeding the men who hid in the well: the men of the Al-Sunna Martyrs Brigade, or the al-Qaeda in Iraq, or one of the other groups of ex-Baathist, neofundamentalist crazies.

It took hours to fall asleep, and when Leila awoke in the morning, the solution to her predicament still eluded her. She kept thinking about the mujahideen lurking in the courtyard, and the ride in the American Humvee, the bomb-laden white car with the family who'd been shot and killed by the Americans, and the detainee at the hospital who'd been tortured. Although those experiences had been harrowing, she'd known her job would bring her closer to such events. It was her father's involvement that hit her deep in the soul, that tangled her up into a knot. If home was no haven from violent men, and her father was one of them, then Leila was in a sandstorm without a rock to lean on.

"I can't handle any more of this," she said to herself.

Pushing away her problems—Leila preferred to start her days afresh—she changed into a housedress. Flinging the curtains aside to let in the light, Leila saw the empty courtyard and the metal cover on the well. If only she could un-know her father's activities. If only she could bury them, hide them, the same way those men hid inside her family's old well.

Chapter 8

The *kanafi* made a fine breakfast, even when it was cold and sticky. Umm Naji had made a large batch of the shredded wheat and goat's cheese baked in thick sweet syrup yesterday, and Leila found a half tray left over in the refrigerator. There must have been something for the family to celebrate yesterday; perhaps cousin Khaled's visit had brought a wedding date for Fatima.

Leila sat alone in the kitchen, staring into the dusty corners and chewing on her forkful of *kanafi* with a morose air. She appreciated its sweet taste, but it did not give her the joy she wanted from it. Her eyes were puffy from her previous night's crying.

"Good morning, Leila!" said Umm Naji, bustling into the kitchen. "Let us go into the sitting room, hmm? I have exciting news for you."

"Fine," said Leila. She got up and plodded after her mother into the women's sitting room. The morning light glinted off the glass of the teacups in the cabinet. She and her mother sat on the camel-backed sofa, and Umm Naji brought her hands together with a loud clap.

"Khaled's father and uncles visited yesterday," Umm Naji said. A broad grin spread across her face. "Ten of them in total. They have held the *mashaya* and the men discussed things, you know how they do—they have asked your father for the wedding! Fatima will marry Khaled next month!"

"Good," said Leila, pouring as much enthusiasm as she could into her reply. "I'm so happy for her!"

"Isn't it wonderful?" said Umm Naji. "We have a great event to plan! A family wedding. They showed that Khaled's finances are good, and your father gave his consent to the date. Your father has high regard for Khaled."

"Mmm," said Leila. Poor Khaled. Tamir would probably try to recruit him to be a jihadi now.

Umm Naji rattled off a list of things to do before the wedding, the people to invite, the food they would make. It was a shame, she said, that they would have to forgo the usual round of parties in favor of the main *Nishan* celebration after the ceremony, because of their delicate financial state. Instead of seven dresses in various colors, Fatima would have just three. Leila was truly happy for her sister, and she was doubly glad, for the wedding would put her parents into a happy mood, too. If the focus was on Fatima's nuptials, Leila might sneak back into her normal daily routine at the "pharmacy."

"And I spoke to your father this morning," Umm Naji said, and Leila's attention snapped back. "He said you did not get home until eight last night!"

"I explained that to him," Leila said. "There was a last-minute order, and we had to work to get it filled at the pharmacy. I didn't get off work until seven-thirty. I got home as soon as I could, and it won't happen again."

"That's right," said Umm Naji. "Your father wants you to cut back your hours, and I agree with him."

"Mama, that's not a good idea," Leila said. Maybe if she got Umm Naji on her side, Tamir might be brought around. "With the wedding, my income can help the family and Fatima's dowry. Besides, it would reflect badly on the family, as though I'm lazy, as though the al-Ghanis don't live up to their responsibilities." Leila wished she'd have thought this up last night.

Umm Naji pursed her lips. "Hmmph," she said. "You don't go back to work until Monday, yes?"

"That's right," said Leila.

"We'll see, then," said Umm Naji. "I'll speak to your father."

Smiling, Leila said, "Thank you, Mama." If anyone could bring her father to reason, it was her mother. She excused herself and went upstairs to Fatima's room. Without knocking, Leila burst in the door and leapt onto Fatima's bed.

"Time to get up!" Leila sang. Fatima made a muffled noise of protest and pulled the covers tight. Leila tickled her. "Get up, Fatima!" she said. "You're getting married!"

There was a giggle from beneath the blankets. "I know!" Fatima said. She whipped the covers off her face. "*Baba* said it will be the tenth of January."

"I'm so glad for you," Leila said, leaning over to embrace her sister. "It's wonderful. And you get to move out of the house."

Fatima laughed. "You would think that's the best part of getting married!"

"Well, not the *best* part," Leila said, and waggled her eyebrows at Fatima, who blushed.

"I don't know what to do," Fatima confessed.

"What do you mean?"

"Well, you know," said Fatima. "About being married."

"You mean sex?" Leila asked.

"Shhh!" Fatima glanced at the half-open door and got up to latch it shut, then crawled back into bed. "Yes."

"Oh," said Leila. She didn't have any personal experience with sex, although her medical training left her well aware of the mechanics. She'd had a boyfriend during her university years, an earnest literature student named Farid, but the most they'd ever done together was take walks, hold hands, and share furtive kisses in the shadows of the public parks. A more recent memory arose—of Captain James Cartwright, and how he always found a way to touch her.

"I suppose Khaled will know what to do," Fatima said.

"Yeah," said Leila. She was not sure Khaled would have a clue, either, but she didn't want to worry her sister. "I think it's supposed to be fun."

"You think?"

"Otherwise, why would people be so obsessed with it?" Leila said. "You should talk to Mama."

"I already have," said Fatima. "But she didn't tell me much, except for the best way to become pregnant as soon as possible."

"Figures," said Leila. "I wish we could get some American women's magazines here. Hala looked at one once and told me they have advice, and even include diagrams."

"No!" Fatima gasped in disbelief. "Do you suppose Hala still has these magazines?"

"Don't know," said Leila. "I don't think it belonged to her, she just saw it."

"Maybe some of the women soldiers at the army base have them," said Fatima.

Leila shrugged and laughed. "I'm sure they do."

"We should ask Hala," Fatima said earnestly. "I wouldn't be brave enough to find an American to ask. And I don't speak English, anyway."

Leila sobered. She looked at Fatima. "Can I tell you a secret?" she asked.

Fatima nodded. "Of course," she said. "Anything."

Leila took a deep breath. "I don't really work at Al-Razi pharmacy," she said in a quiet voice. "I left that job a month ago. I've been working at the American base, with the surgeons, as an assistant."

Fatima's eyes widened with each word until Leila thought her eyes would pop out of her head. "What?" Fatima said.

"I couldn't tell anyone," whispered Leila. "You know how Father would take it. And Mother tells him everything. You have to promise not to say a word! Do you swear it?"

"Of course, yes," said Fatima. "I won't tell anyone, not even Khaled. But, Leila, why? It's dangerous! Don't you know what happens to people who work with the Americans?"

"I know," said Leila. "But it's good, too. I'm learning so much, Fatima! They let me help in the surgery, and my English is improving, with the medical terms and translations."

"So . . ." Fatima paused, looking confused. "You're an assistant in the surgery? But also a translator?"

"Yes," said Leila, "I translate for the Arabic-speaking patients in the military hospital. You know, the prisoners. Jihadis who are wounded." She omitted the mention of torture. "And when there aren't any of those, then I act as a normal assistant to the surgeons, along with the nurses."

"What are the surgeons like? The Americans?"

"They're so kind, Fatima. They are both older men with families at home, and Dr. Whitaker said he's willing to recommend me to the medical schools in America."

Fatima gasped. "Like you've always wanted! Do you think it's possible?"

"I hope so," said Leila. "I hope so." She plucked at the bedspread. "You see, I had to take this job. It's my chance, my opportunity. And the pharmacy was not working out so well."

"Oh? Why not?" Fatima asked.

Leila twisted her mouth in distaste. "I've mentioned the man who works there, the other assistant. Sayyid."

"Yes."

"Anyway, after I'd been there a few weeks, he tried to . . . um . . . he tried to kiss me and grab me." Leila made a spitting noise with her tongue.

"Oh, goodness!"

"Shhh! Do you want Mama to hear?"

"Sorry," said Fatima. "But oh, Leila, I'm sorry to hear that. It's because you are so beautiful. Men lose their heads when you are around."

Leila snorted.

Fatima patted Leila's cheek with a warm hand. "I am more

fortunate in my appearance. I am not a great beauty, though not unattractive, either."

"Fatima!" Leila hugged her sister again. "You're gorgeous. And you have a man who is smitten with you. Khaled will treat you right, I know it. He'll be a good provider."

Fatima smiled. "Khaled will make a good husband," she said. "But what about you? I think perhaps you might fall in love with an American doctor at the base. Not if they are married, hmm?"

"No, no doctors," Leila said. For a moment she contemplated telling Fatima about the dashing army captain who kept helping her out, but decided against it. That would be too many revelations for one day. Besides, she was not sure she liked a man who could be warm and cold by turns. Too close to her father's psychology for her comfort. "I am in love with books, and laboratories!" she said.

"And test tubes?" Fatima asked, turning red.

Leila stared at her sister. She had not thought Fatima capable of double entendre. Then she burst out laughing, so hard her sides ached and tears ran down her face. Umm Naji burst into the room, asking what was the ruckus, and Leila could not speak, she was laughing so hard.

"You girls get dressed," Umm Naji said, smiling at her daughters. "Your father wants *waraq dawaaleeh* for supper, and we must mince the lamb."

"Yes, Mama," they said.

"So, Fatima," said Leila in a whisper when Umm Naji left, "since I work at the American hospital now . . . I'll see about those Western magazines for you?"

"Yes, yes, please!" said Fatima, with a muffled giggle.

The tears of laughter returned to Leila's eyes. She put her hand over her mouth and nodded, trying to compose herself. "Come on," she said after a few seconds. "There's some *kanafi* left from yesterday."

"Mmm, I love cold *kanafi*," said Fatima.

But when they opened the refrigerator, the large sweet tray

was gone, emptied and sitting on the floor to be washed. "That's odd," said Fatima.

"Yes, it is," said Leila, and with a chill, thought of the men hiding in the well. Umm Naji knew about the mujahideen, then, and had fed them the leftovers. "Have you heard any weird noises in the night?" she whispered to Fatima.

Fatima pressed her lips together. "No," she said, "I don't think so." Fatima's bedroom window overlooked the front, so perhaps she hadn't heard the activity in the courtyard.

"Huh," said Leila. "You know the old well in the court-yard? Last night I saw three men go into it. Father was there, too. He's hiding people. They had Kalashnikovs—rifles—and I think he's turned it into some kind of room."

"Leila, are you sure?" Fatima was pale. "I hope you're wrong."

"I'm not, I—" Leila broke off and looked up when their mother came into the kitchen from the pantry.

"I've got the grape leaves!" Umm Naji said. "Leila, put on an apron. That dress isn't right for cooking."

The creation of the *waraq dawaaleeh* required concentration, and with Umm Naji in the kitchen, Leila could not speak any more about insurgents. Umm Naji chattered away with Fatima about the wedding plans, and Leila interjected the occasional witticism about the family, but her mind stayed upon the mysteries of the house. Through the open kitchen window, the odd burst of gunfire punctuated the morning; it was Friday, so it could have been from weddings or celebrations. Or it could have been from gun battles.

When they were almost finished cooking, Umm Naji said to Leila, "Oh, and I spoke to your father. He did not object that—for now—you may keep your hours at the hospital, but only if you are very careful with yourself."

Leila thanked her mother and grinned. She even mustered goodwill for her father; perhaps his reasonable self was not lost after all.

Tamir was at mosque until two in the afternoon when he returned with Abdul-Hakam, the imam. With a disappointed sigh, Leila rolled the rice and lamb stuffing into the grape leaves. To have the imam as a guest meant no family meal, and it would put Tamir into a religious mood. It made him strict, conservative, and Leila hoped he wouldn't change his mind about her working hours.

"Fatima, let's practice your hair braids," said Umm Naji, when the men in the sitting room were served with their lunch. "My friend told me of a new style. I think it would look nice on you for the wedding." Leila thought it was premature to start dressing Fatima's hair, but she bit her tongue. If her mother and sister were upstairs, she might eavesdrop on the sitting room conversation, as had become her habit.

She was left alone in the kitchen to clean the glass cups from the *shai*, and she did her task hastily, rinsing the glasses and tipping them upside down on a towel to dry. Then she ducked through the back corridor toward the downstairs toilet. Her house shoes made a whispering shuffle on the tile, but no other sound. Leila knelt down near the little peephole. She pressed her ear against the wall, and the hollow space amplified the men's voices from within the sitting room.

"The Martyrs Brigade is forming well. I am pleased, Tamir," came Abdul-Hakam's voice.

"I'm happy to organize it," said her father. "It is our noble task. Allah has ordained it, and I follow His will."

"Allah's will requires that you house two more fighters," said the imam. "They are experienced men from Jordan. They've been operating against the Crusaders for many years."

"Whatever you require," said Tamir. "And these other three, I shall send to my cousin's house in Al-Walah. They will join with a fourth, and begin their training. Our strategy of engaging the Americans, then pulling back, is working. Our men survive longer and get to know the Crusader tactics. Then, when we have an army built up, we strike."

"Not just against the Americans," the imam reminded him.

"No," Tamir said through his teeth. Leila could picture his face. "These Shia traitors and the Kurds, too, will find no welcome here."

Leila blinked. Her mother was Kurdish, and Tamir had never shown antipathy toward the northern warrior race, not even during those hard years in the early eighties, when Saddam's experiments with chemical weapons had meant fields of dead under a cloud of toxic gas. Leila had been a tiny girl and did not remember much, but she knew their family had lost several cousins, aunts, and uncles. Tamir's position guaranteed the safety of Umm Naji, and to Leila's knowledge the political situation never insinuated itself into their marriage. The Kurds were Sunni Muslims, as well, which meant the inhabitants of Mosul escaped most of the religious conflict with Shias to the south. Leila was grateful for *that* respite from the looming civil war.

"The Kurds are too friendly with the Americans," said the imam. "I even hear the Americans who go up north are welcomed as liberators!"

"The Americans are not welcome here in my city," said Tamir. "They will run with their tails between their legs."

Abdul-Hakam chuckled. "Allah is on our side."

"Yes," said Tamir. "The Holy Quran is the only thing that makes sense to me anymore. The only true thing. I never understood until now why it was so important to fight. This world has gone mad. . . ." Tamir sighed. "But one thing worries me most. The American raids on civilian houses. They're getting wise, and it's becoming difficult to hide our men and our weapons."

"They have informants," said the imam. "Loose men, willing to sell their souls for a few dinars. They listen to our phone conversations, monitor our Web sites and our e-mails. When the Americans enter our homes, we should fight them—"

"But the women and children!" Tamir said. "It would endanger them. It's not fair to bring families as innocent victims."

Leila bit her lip. Tamir had invited the devil into their

house. She wished she could shake her father by the shoulders. He seemed to have gone off the edge of sanity, and yet she knew there was a part of him that knew it was wrong. Once a judge, always a judge, and for all his seditious activities, she knew her father would never advocate the killing of innocents. But if Tamir was worried about protecting the innocents—his family—why would he hide insurgents in their courtyard? It was a matter of time before the Americans came, and what would happen then? Darkness settled over Leila's heart; was no one immune from this madness?

"The Quran is specific about their place in heaven," said the imam. "Any Muslims killed in the conflict as bystanders will go to Paradise."

"Hmm," said Tamir. "Yes, I suppose. But it's too soon to instigate direct fighting. In a few months, I think, we'll be ready. In the meantime, what of those in our ranks who are taken prisoner by the Americans? They could be talking, giving away secrets."

"Have you done as prescribed?" asked the imam. "Kept identities secret, worked in cells of four, shuffling men around?"

"Oh yes," said Tamir. "There are none who know the full extent of our plans, aside from you and me and the rest of our trusted friends."

"The Iraqi police are more concerned about reining in their Shia militias, the corruption in their own ranks," said Abdul-Hakam. "And if the Americans take prisoners, then let them! The Americans are soft. They don't know how to make them talk. They give them cigarettes and cushy pillows to rest their heads."

Leila knew this was untrue. The images from yesterday were burned in her skull, the man with bugged-out eyes and electrodes shoved up his fingers. Her father and the imam didn't know how capable the Americans were. Insurgency was a game to them, and all too real to her. . . . She wished she could warn her father, but instead she remained crouched in the hallway, trapped and worried.

"Ahhh," the imam sighed. "I wish we had an informant, to find out what our prisoners are telling the Americans."

"It would be best to have a translator," said Tamir, and Leila felt a stirring of panic. "Someone to tell the Americans falsities if they get too close to the truth. Feed them disinformation."

Leila stood up. She did not wish to hear more of this. If her father knew she worked at the American base as a translator, he would either punish her or recruit her, and she could not decide which was worse. But to spy on the Americans was unthinkable; she might be taken as a prisoner herself and end up like the tortured man.

Quiet as a cat, she went back down the hallway, rubbing her hands as though she'd washed them in the bathroom. She went upstairs and settled down at her desk to read over the medical journal articles she'd brought home yesterday, and the in-depth text about herbal treatments for Alzheimer's disease soothed Leila into a white calm.

Chapter 9

A few days later, the antique minibus rumbled forward through the gates of LSA Diamondback and ejected its worker passengers, Leila included. She held her head at a stubborn angle, determined to go forward and not act neurotic around the Americans after the horrific scene she'd witnessed the last time she was with them. From a distance, she heard the soft thump of a small handheld rocket, and listened to the whoosh of the round as it cleared the tall concrete fence surrounding the adjacent Forward Operating Base Marez, which was a prime target for insurgent fire from the neighborhood on the nearby hill. Cocking her head, she waited for the corresponding hit. A thin metal crumple. Something harmless, as there were no screams of pain. They were most active at night, the mortars and the rockets; the jihadis had a hard time waking up in the morning. This one must be an early bird.

As Leila walked toward the hospital, she noticed the figure of a soldier standing at about thirty paces from her, a cigarette in his hand. When she was closer she slowed a bit, nodding in greeting.

"Hi, Leila," said James Cartwright.

"Hello, James," she said. She tilted her head at him in curiosity, waiting to see what he wanted. She wasn't sure what she wanted from him, how to thank him for delivering her home safely, or how to forget the blank, cold part of him that gave orders to fire a machine gun.

"So, did everything work out at home? You're not in trouble?" His tone was concerned, caring, and . . . genuine. Leila wondered if all soldiers were lonely in secret. Maybe if she was his friend, he would be hers.

"Mmm," she said. "Let us walk." She nodded at the hospital, and James fell into step with her. "My father wants me to cut my hours," she said, "but I'm not going to. I think if I do not say anything, he will forget about it."

"And she's brave again," said James.

"No, not brave," said Leila. "Stupid, perhaps." She turned to smile up at James, and they walked up the metal stairs into the hospital together. Once they were inside, one of the nurses walked by, and Leila could not help noticing the woman's free-flowing blond hair, contrasted against her own tight head scarf. Self-conscious of her religion, feeling the outsider, Leila was struck with a notion that appealed to her rebellious mood. Reaching up with quick hands, she took off her head scarf and the pins that held her dark locks fast against her skull. *Liberation*, she thought.

She turned to James, who watched her in surprise. "I'm tired of wearing this thing," she said. "It is not modern. In America, they do not wear *hijab*, correct?"

He stared for a few seconds and Leila felt a hot blush rising on her cheeks. "Uh, right," James said. "No one has to wear head scarves in America. In fact," he said in the manner of trying to put her at ease, "if you wore *hijab* in America, you'd get a lot of stares."

"That is what I thought," said Leila, already feeling better about her decision. She shook out her hair, then glanced at James. "I must go to work now."

"Right," he said. "Well, I hope to see you soon. I wanted to make sure you're here, and safe, and all that."

"Safe is a relative term, but thank you," she said, brightening a bit. "Maybe I will see you again soon." She turned and walked down the hallway. She did not look back, although she could feel his eyes on the back of her head. Her heart skipped with a pleasant giddiness. Never before had she made this tiny, wild gesture: walking away from a single man with her hair tumbling loose.

Leila saw her new friend sooner than she anticipated; she was in the main ward later that day when she heard James's voice, speaking to Dr. Whitaker in the corridor just outside.

"—wondering if I might have a word with your medical translator, Miss al-Ghani, when she's free this afternoon."

Leila's eyebrows came together in puzzlement at the tone of formality. She edged toward the door to hear them better.

"Sure thing," said Dr. Whitaker. "Mind if I ask why?"

"Security matter," came the vague response. "I'd rather talk to her myself than bring in the intelligence geeks."

At the mention of the word *intelligence*, Leila had a blooming intuition about why he wanted to talk to her: somehow he'd found out about her father. Guilt by association? Leila swallowed hard and dashed back toward where she'd been reading a chart, pretending that she was fine. She wondered how and why and whether she would be fired. A few moments later, Dr. Whitaker found her and tapped her on the shoulder. "Leila," he said, "one of the officers wants to talk to you. He's outside." The doctor's eyes were kind, but Leila could tell he was reserving judgment. Perhaps it was normal for translators to be questioned regularly?

Leila opened the door to the hallway, bringing with her a spill of fresh sunlight from the window in the ward. James sat on a bench, looking for all the world like a child awaiting a vaccination, and he brought a hand up to shield his eyes as he stood up. "Leila," he said. "Hello."

"James!" Feigning ignorance, she said, "Are you waiting for me?"

"Sorry," James said. "But I need to speak with you, please."

Leila nodded warily. "All right. . . ."

"Where's the staff room? We can talk there."

"This way," she said, indicating with a flash of her hand. She did not look at James again until they sat in the metal chairs at the small table in the break room.

"I'm not stalking you or anything," said James, smiling.

Leila stayed quiet.

"Anyway," he said, clearing his throat, "I wanted to talk to you about this first, before the intelligence guys piece it together. We got some names of possible insurgents and—well, your family's name came up. Al-Ghani. I wanted to ask you about it. It's probably nothing. But I don't want you to lose your job, not if this has to do with some distant cousin of the hundreds you said you had."

A swooping sensation passed through Leila's abdomen. "Oh," she said. Her eyes darted around the room, noting the half-empty cup of coffee on the countertop and the scuff marks on the metal legs of the chair. Hanging on to the details. "Oh," she repeated.

"Leila," said James, and she looked up at him. Eyes blue, full of worry. "I trust you."

She smiled, but it was gone after a moment. "My cousins," she said. "Yes, I have so many cousins. I cannot keep track of their activities. I'm sorry I cannot help you."

"Are you sure?" James stared hard at her. His face was stern, no room for humor anymore. Something in his gaze demanded the truth and so Leila dropped her eyes away from him, aware that it made her seem dishonest. An admission about her father and his hidden mujahideen in the courtyard well hovered in the back of her throat, but she swallowed the impulse to blurt it out, to tell James everything. It would ruin her, and it would ruin her family. Leila could not help but hope that Tamir would come to his senses yet.

"What if it is a cousin of mine, a relative?" Leila said. "I have nothing to do with their activities."

"I know," said James. "I have to ask, though. Here's an idea; just tell me more about your family. In general. I'm curious, anyway." He grinned. "Besides, this way we can sort out who's uninvolved."

Uninvolved, Leila thought, and bit her tongue for a moment. "Well," she said, "there's my father, Mr. al-Ghani. He was a judge during Saddam's time, and he is . . . very dutiful toward his community. I could say that he wants to improve things, but ever since the invasion has become . . . moody. Like he is a different man. He will get better soon, though." She said it, trying to believe it.

James's eyes narrowed a fraction.

"Then there's my mother, Umm Naji, who is Kurdish. My sister, Fatima, who is engaged to be married next month to my mother's cousin Khaled. Khaled's not mujahideen. He owns a grocery shop. Then I have an older brother, Naji, who owns the furniture store. He has family, too, but just women and children," Leila said with a drop of sarcasm.

"Right," said James. "So . . . your dad. What are his views?"

"On what?" Leila asked. She laughed, trying to distract James. "The invasion? Modern artwork? How he takes his tea?" She smiled. "In my home, we make our tea hot and sweet."

"I'm sure you do," said James.

"Hmm. Perhaps as thanks, I'll make some for you."

"Thanks?"

"Of course. You helped me very much, by getting me home, in your patrol." Leila glanced at his shoes, clean combat boots. "Any man, even a conservative father, would admire you for it."

"Your father . . ." said James again.

"He's just my father. . . ."

"Does he sympathize with the insurgency?"

James was forcing her into a corner. Leila shrugged. "My job is not to make speculation about another person's politics. My father doesn't speak of such things in front of women."

"But he's your father—"

"Yes? I am Leila, the translator, and I passed my security check. That is all I can tell you. Maybe some distant cousin is doing something bad, but I'd be the last to know about it."

"Okay, sorry." James put his hands up. "I didn't mean to push you. Whatever you want to tell me is fine. I'm only asking because my bosses told me to." He gave her a wry smile.

Leila found herself charmed by it. "I understand," she said. "But, James . . . even if my cousins were involved, would you arrest me? And my family?"

"As long as you yourself are innocent, don't worry," said James. "If we arrested everyone with any connections to the insurgency, the whole of Mosul would be in jail. I'll make sure nothing happens to you."

Leila saw the slight twitch of his lips, the pretty lie that she knew he wanted to believe: that he might protect her from the powers that be. It was an impossibility but she was warmed by his sentiment. Tamir al-Ghani was probably a terrorist. He was hiding insurgents in the house. Plotting attacks. The facts could not be changed. But someone would look out for Leila, and it seemed that person would be James, as far as he could.

By the end of the conversation the day had lost its sparkle for Leila and she stared, feeling cold, at the floor. She prayed that would be the last of her relationship with the American intelligence racket. She'd told James that she knew nothing; what else could there be? Her shoulders felt tense and when she got up to leave, James winced, but she pretended not to see it. The burden of trust was his now.

Chapter 10

The bicycle waited in its appointed place, chained and padlocked in front of the Al-Razi Hospital. Leila walked toward it, carrying her handbag and papers, fishing out the little metal key that would unlock the bicycle for her use. The cold dry air of winter caught in her lungs and the city grew dark around her. The electric lights flickered on, and stayed on for the most part, as people made their way home before the nighttime curfew kicked in.

The distress from her conversation with Captain James Cartwright formed a tight knot in her stomach. She'd gone through her day on automatic, helping Drs. Whitaker and Peabody, assisting Nurse Pavlopolous with the setting of a broken arm, eating her lunch and not speaking two sentences outside of her necessary work. Dr. Peabody asked her if she was all right, and she'd nodded, but avoided further conversation. When she rode back on the bus with the other workers, the weight of new developments was heavy upon her shoulders.

Leila's bicycle was old but well oiled. The chains never squeaked, and the bell remained in working order. She reached down to put the key into the lock, twisting it twice.

From several blocks away, she heard a *crump*. A clatter. She glanced over and saw a column of smoke rising into the twilight sky. An attack on the police station, most likely. Leila stood for a few moments with her hands on the bicycle's cold metal handlebars. She heard screams, shouts, a siren. Should she wait for the casualties to stream toward the hospital? Did she have a duty to help the injured?

Leila swung her foot over the bicycle and took off in the direction of home. It was not worth the risk of arriving late again. The violence was an everyday occurrence in Mosul City and there was not a thing Leila could do about it. She might treat a bleeding innocent who would be shot the next day. "*Inshallah*," she mumbled. She picked up speed, pedaling hard and fast to arrive home in time for dinner.

Her circuitous route took her through various streets and alleyways, but a few times she glanced back and noticed a dirty maroon car crawling behind her. Frowning, she took a narrow footpath through some bushes and reemerged onto a main road. The maroon car was still there, creeping along. Spooked, Leila took another turn and backtracked. The car did not follow her. Laughing at her own paranoia, she sped away home.

It was a reasonable six-thirty when Leila wheeled her bicycle through the metal gate. A quick prayer escaped her lips that her father would not speak to her about work again. . . . She wondered if the Americans would come, with their guns and radios and black cloth hoods, and drag off her father into the night. She wondered if the whole family might be arrested. Then she got a mental image of James Cartwright carrying her off into the desert over his shoulder, and a pleasant shiver wriggled through her, which she repressed with a pinch of the skin on her wrist.

No, it was no good to think about that sort of thing.

"Mother?" Leila called into the hall. "Father? I'm home."

"In here," called Umm Naji from the big sitting room.

Leila entered and sat. "Do you need help with dinner?" she asked.

"Of course I do," said Umm Naji from her seat next to a silent Tamir. "Fatima's already in the kitchen." She pressed her lips together to emphasize that the good daughter did her duty.

"I'll go change," said Leila, standing up. She was relieved

that neither of her parents said anything about the hour. Silence meant permission in Leila's eyes.

"Leila," said Tamir. She forced herself to make eye contact with her father, positive he could read her mind and see where she'd been spending her days.

"Yes?" Leila said, twisting her hands out of sight behind her back.

"A letter came for you today," Tamir said, pulling an envelope from his pocket. "I believe it is from your cousin."

"Which one?" Leila said with a laugh in her voice, thinking of James's reaction to her eight hundred cousins.

"Abdul, of course," said Tamir. "The one who visited here for a month, or have you forgotten?"

"Oh, that one," said Leila. "Thank you, Father." She took the envelope, glad for the further excuse to leave her parents and their deep stares. Leila tucked the letter away on a shelf with a mind to read it later, perhaps next year.

After a change of clothes into an old black housedress, Leila joined Fatima in the kitchen, where she was in the final stages of boiling rice and chicken stew. Leila plopped down on the stool and unfolded her legs. "How was the nursery today?" she asked.

"Fine," said Fatima, stirring the large pot with a wooden spoon. Her eyebrows darted up. "And how was your day, sister?"

"Fine," said Leila. "Maybe tonight I can tell you about it."

"All right," said Fatima.

"Have you talked to Khaled today?"

"He called on the telephone," said Fatima, smiling. "Everything is good."

"Yes," said Leila, despite her growing sense of doom. "Yes, everything is good." She dreaded the morning for some nebulous reason, as though a great black cloud of dust brewed on her horizon and would soon plunge her into grainy darkness. She could envision that a chain of events might be set into motion, and the great Iraqi war would sweep through the al-Ghani household.

It's not my fault, Leila told herself as she busied her hands with the cutlery for dinner. *It's Father's fault. He's the one who brought danger into this house. He's the one plotting violence, adding to the madness. Not me. Not me.* She walked back into the sitting room, placing the forks and spoons out on the low round table. Fatima followed with the pot of stew and a ladling spoon, and the family gathered round to eat their evening meal.

"We'll have some leftovers," Leila could not resist saying, eyeing the quantity of stew.

"Maybe so," said Umm Naji. "If we do, I'll take it to the neighbors."

I'm sure you will, thought Leila. Her mother was culpable in this, too, although in the face of Tamir's stubborn fanaticism there was nothing a woman could do but go along. She took a bite of stew and the rice tasted like soggy dust in her mouth. With effort, she swallowed. She looked at her father's thin face and graying beard, his hazel eyes bright as though with fever. Umm Naji, next to him, blinked with long lashes in the fat folds of her face, with only the strong straight nose to speak of the warrior Kurd in her. Leila's parents were strangers to her in that moment, people with unknown motives and priorities who brought uncertainty like a cancer.

A daughter should trust her parents. A daughter should rely on her parents as the stalwart guardians against the whirling sands of change, a protection from the harsh reality of a war-torn world. But Leila's faith in her family eroded with each passing day. Year after year, she saw her parents more as they were: clueless people trying to make their way in life, basing their decisions on training and society and instinct.

As the family took their meal in a silent house, with dangerous men lurking in the courtyard awaiting their chance at jihad, and Tamir looking upon the women of his family with pride and suspicion, Leila felt the facade of their old life crumble. She was not like her parents and could not follow their decisions. She was an alien in her own house. Why bother to pretend? Maybe she would move out and seek refuge with a female friend's more moderate family. Maybe she would go to her Kurdish cousins in Dohuk. Whatever she decided, Leila knew that she could not stay with her parents much longer.

After dinner Fatima pulled Leila aside and whispered in her ear, "Let's go up to your room and talk," she said.

"*Na'am*," Leila agreed.

Once they were cloistered in the safety of Leila's bedroom, the girls sat on the narrow bed and Fatima grasped Leila's hand. "How was work today, really?" she asked.

"Oh, Fatima," Leila said. "I don't know what to do." She sighed. "I am lucky, because I have a friend on the base. This—person told me something this morning. Our name, al-Ghani, has come up on a list of insurgents."

"No!" Fatima breathed. "It must be a mistake."

"It's not a mistake," said Leila. "You already know Father's hiding mujahideen in the old well in the courtyard. It's for sure," she said, noting Fatima's look of baffled disbelief. "Oh, come, Fatima! It makes sense!"

Fatima was shaking her head. "I didn't think he would bring them into the house."

"He's a man," Leila said. "Men never think about anything but themselves. All this violence is because of stupid men."

"Careful, you sound bitter," said Fatima.

"What?" Leila said. She could not believe what she was hearing. "I'm hardly bitter, Fatima. That's just how men are. Accepting it doesn't mean I'm bitter, I'm just trying to . . . figure it out. Anyway, I think Mother has affected your mind with all this wedding talk. Even if you are married, you are still Fatima!"

"You're in a terrible mood today," said Fatima.

Leila was about to snap a response; then she stopped herself. This was Fatima's way of deflecting the unpalatable situation of terrorists in the house. "Never mind that," Leila said. "You didn't know about the mujahideen until I mentioned it, did you? I just hate all these secrets in the house."

Fatima's shoulders slumped. "No, of course not, and I don't want to believe what you said before," she said. "Are you sure about this, Leila?"

"One hundred percent positive," said Leila. "If you don't believe *me*, you can run out to the courtyard, open up that well, and see for yourself."

"I believe you now," said Fatima. "I'm sorry. You're right about the wedding, I have been thinking of it too much."

Leila sat back, glad she'd gotten her point across. "The question is, what do we do now? The Americans will come for Father eventually. They'll ask where the mujahideen are hiding. So what do we tell them?"

"I hope they wait until after I am living in Khaled's house," Fatima said. "Then we can rely on you to lie to the Americans."

She had already lied to James by omission, but could she continue lying? She'd changed her mind about who was right and who was wrong. Leila hugged her sister good night, exhausted by the complexities of her life, and she got ready for sleep in a semidaze. She never bothered to open the letter from cousin Abdul; it was already forgotten. In a life where every minute held new import, Leila did not have time for trivial letters from cousins and their bratty five-year-olds.

When she arrived for work the next day, Leila's imagination worked itself into a frenzy that every American looked at her with suspicion; did they all think she was a terrorist in disguise? A spy for the enemy? A woman with dangerous cousins? She looked forward to seeing James, the one steady reassurance in the past days. She didn't have to wait long to see him, for James waited in the hallway of the medical ward as he had the previous morning.

But this time he was not alone. Another man stood next to James, and Leila recognized Travis Pratt, the long-fingered CIA agent involved with covering up the torture of the Iraqi man, dressed in neat civilian khaki trousers and shirt. A slithery feeling worked on her skin.

"Miss al-Ghani," Pratt said. "Good morning."

"Good morning," she replied coolly. She wished he would go away, for his presence brought bad things.

"Hi, Leila," said James, sounding apologetic.

She nodded and locked on to James's blue eyes. If Travis had not been there, the sigh might have escaped her lips. As it was, she bit her tongue and glanced down at her feet.

"Pratt here wants to talk to you," James said.

"I must get to work," she said.

Pratt smiled at her. "You see, Leila—can I call you that?"

"You may call me Miss al-Ghani."

Pratt blinked but kept talking. "I have this little report, you see. It mentions your family's last name—a cousin, was it? Captain Cartwright tells me you might know something about some of this insurgent activity."

"Don't we all know something about insurgent activity?" Leila said. She walked down the hall toward the small closet with her locker. She would not let this business get in the way of her medical duties, and she hoped the American doctors would shoo off the buzzing CIA agent. "We all see children with their limbs blown off, and bodies bleeding in the street. Oh yes, Mr. Pratt, I know something about the insurgency," she said over her shoulder.

Pratt trotted to catch up with her. James followed at a steady distance.

It took a few seconds for Leila to open the door of her locker, put away her handbag, and retrieve her crisp white lab coat. She put it on, ignoring Pratt. It might be a mistake to be rude to the man, but Leila could not help herself. Her small admissions about her family to James yesterday seemed stupid in retrospect, and Leila wished that she could take the words and stuff them back into her mouth. She'd known that James wasn't asking for his own curiosity—that it was on behalf of others. She did not want to walk into the position of lying outright.

Pratt leaned back with a studied air, still smiling at Leila. Calculation spun through his eyes; his forgettable face was blank. He glanced over at James, and back at Leila. "I'm sorry to have disturbed you," he said. "I'll leave you in peace now.

I've heard you're one of the best translators on the base, and I'm sure you have work to do. Have a great day, Miss al-Ghani." Pratt finished off his sentence with a bow and a smile. Then he turned and walked down the hall, nodding at James to come with him.

James threw a sympathetic look over his shoulder at Leila, but said nothing as he walked away with Pratt.

It was a puzzling encounter, and Leila tried to put it out of her mind as she fastened the plastic buttons of her lab coat over her dark blue *abaya*. Dr. Whitaker greeted her in the ward and announced that they would be releasing Hazim, the detainee with the wounded leg, later that day.

"I need you to explain to him about when to take the antibiotic pills," said Dr. Whitaker. "Otherwise you know what will happen."

Leila did know. If the antibiotics course was not followed properly, the bacteria in the wound would not be killed and blood poisoning would set in. Hazim the detainee would either have to go to the civilian hospital for further treatment, or he would die and his family would blame the Americans. Following Dr. Whitaker's instructions, she wrote out a prescription in Arabic and explained to Hazim the importance of taking the pills until they were gone.

"And don't go selling these pills, or giving them to someone else," she said to Hazim in her sternest voice. "Understand?"

He scowled. "Yes, ma'am," he said.

When she walked away, she thought she heard him hiss "American whore" at her. The blood rose in her face and she hoped she'd misheard it.

"Leila, I've been thinking," said Dr. Whitaker, rubbing his mustache. They sat in the break room, along with a pair of nurses who were deep in their own gossip. "Based on your interests, you should consider Imperial College, in London. I know it's not America, but it's one of the best research universities in the world, and they give medical degrees as well." He poked at his bowl of rice, brought over from the mess hall. "You'd like London. It has tons of museums and you can get out to the countryside easily. . . . My sister Anne lives there with her family. I've visited a couple of times."

"London," said Leila, rolling the word over in her mind. It sounded faraway and foreign, a city of white lights and fast-walking people and glittering clean buildings. "You think I would like it?" She tried to keep the desperate hope out of her voice.

"I think so," said Dr. Whitaker, standing up to toss away the paper bowl from his lunch. "Think it over. Like I've said, I'll recommend you to wherever you want to go."

"Thanks," said Leila, staring down at the scuffed plastic surface of the table. Dr. Whitaker made it sound so easy. All she had to do was get to the West, and everything would be all right. The remoteness of the prospect created uncomfortable tears in Leila's eyes. Once she might have allowed the dream to take root, but in recent days Leila felt certain she, too, would be a casualty of the insanity that gripped her nation. Another bloody corpse with a dark blue sheet over it, riddled with bullets and wet with tears.

To her relief, there were no encounters with James or his friend Pratt that day, and when Leila arrived back outside the Al-Razi Hospital at twenty minutes past six that evening, she decided to take a detour. With quick fingers she unlocked her bicycle and sped off in the direction of her neighborhood. At the same time, she brought out her mobile phone from her handbag that rested in the wire basket on the front of the bike.

The phone was old but of good quality, a Nokia with a silver plastic cover. Much of the silver sheen had flaked away to reveal the dull white plastic beneath, but the keypad still worked. It glowed green when Leila touched it, and she scrolled through the on-screen phone book to her home number. She pressed the worn-away Send key. The ringing sound was muffled against her head scarf, but she could still hear. Tamir answered on the fourth ring.

"Hello?" came his gruff voice.

"Hello, *Baba*," Leila chirped. "How are you?" she asked, mimicking the American way before she could stop herself.

"I am fine," said Tamir.

"I'm on my way home from work," she said. "But I wanted to check with you first. Can I go to the Jedd cybercafe? You know, the one owned by Mr. Kateb?"

"Huh," said Tamir. "You're on your way home from work? Where are you?"

"I'm almost to the cybercafe," said Leila. "Thank goodness for this bicycle! I'm riding past all the pedestrians."

"Don't stay at the Internet for longer than one hour," said Tamir.

"I won't," said Leila. An hour would be enough time, she hoped.

She hung up with her father's permission. It made him feel in charge, Leila knew, and she did not want to anger him again. This way, Tamir would think he had tabs on his daughter.

The cybercafe was a tiny room perched on the corner of two streets. One of the streets was a main thoroughfare, but the other was a mere alley, wide enough for two donkeys to stand side by side. It was this alley where Leila parked her bicycle, leaning up against a narrow glass window. Leila chained the bicycle to a set of metal bars protecting the window and accidentally scraped her finger on the raw metal. "Ouch," she said, nursing a shallow graze.

There were six computers in the Jedd Cybercafe. These were hunched together along one wall with dirty plastic chairs in front of them. A narrow, scuffed wooden counter held a big pile of papers and a telephone, connected for international calls. A single fluorescent light flickered on the ceiling, casting the room in a wash of bluish light. It was crowded at six-thirty, and there was just one computer available at the very end of the row.

Leila was glad for the position of the vacant computer. She did not like strange men peering over her shoulder while she was on the Internet. The boy working at the counter had earphones stretched over his head; she could hear the pounding beat of Arabic pop music even from several feet away. His dark eyes slid across her as she nodded to him; he scribbled down her time of arrival in a curling paper notebook. The plastic chair made a scraping noise on the unfinished concrete floor as she pulled it out and sat down, her handbag held secure between her feet.

The connection was agonizingly slow in comparison to the Internet on the American base. The military net was beamed by satellite, but this Iraqi cybercafe had to rely on a dial-up connection over unreliable, worn-down phone lines. Half the time it did not even work. Today Leila was fortunate, and she wiggled the sticky mouse with her hand and typed the address she wanted.

It was an Internet search engine, and Leila glanced over her shoulder to make sure no one observed her. This was the one thing she could not do at work. In the little white text box, she typed the words in English, *torture detainees Iraq*. She clicked on the Search button. She waited as the screen went blank and the computer made a noise as though it were thinking. Then her search results scrolled down the screen.

Leila first clicked on the most reliable-looking link, to an Amnesty International report on torture and human rights violations by the Coalition forces in Iraq. It was a huge file, and Leila could see she would not have time to read it. She took note of the address and moved on. She was looking for first-hand accounts, something to make sense of who was conducting the torture and where the prisoners went afterward. After ten more minutes of searching, Leila found a blog written in Arabic by someone using a server based in Egypt.

She scanned the entries with increasing interest. This person went by the screen name of Sammurabi and claimed to have been a detainee for two years. He said he was taken prisoner in Baghdad and held in Iraq without trial or charges for over a year. Then he was put on a plane and flown overseas to a country with a cold climate. He did not know the location, but the guards in the holding facility spoke a foreign language that sounded Slavic. The Americans ran the facility, Sammurabi wrote, and conducted strange experiments there.

The prisoners were kept in isolation from one another, allowed the clothes on their backs and a copy of the Quran. Sometimes they would be left alone for weeks, the only human contact being the twice-daily mealtimes. The cells were spartan but clean, with a hole for waste and a hard plank board to sleep on. Sammurabi's impression was that the prison was new, for there were no rodents and the concrete-block walls had fresh grout.

Sammurabi wrote that when he first arrived, he was left for five weeks without any kind of interaction with human beings. He counted the days by making notches on the plank board with his fingernails. Then, he said, everything changed. Two American civilians appeared one day and dragged him into a room. They beat him with a shiny black lacquered baton. One of the Americans spoke Arabic, and threatened to have one of the big "native" guards come into the room and rape him. After this threat, the Americans gave him a chocolate bar and a cup of tea.

The next day things got weirder. Sammurabi wrote that the Americans set up a tape player outside his cell, and they put on a CD. It was the sound track from *The Wizard of Oz*. The songs were played on a loop for five days. Even though Sammurabi did not speak English, by the third day he could sing every song. The songs stopped abruptly on the fifth day, right in the middle of "The Yellow Brick Road." After that came two days of full isolation and no food.

As Leila read the account, she grew more puzzled with each word. It was too bizarre to be made up.

In the week after the *Wizard of Oz* incident, Sammurabi was dragged from his cell once again and taken to a room where electrodes were attached to his head. He was afraid of being tortured, he wrote. But that did not happen. Instead, a man who looked like a doctor came in, along with a translator. They asked him a bunch of questions, mundane things like where he was born and what was his name and did he love his mother? But interspersed with these questions were strange things, such as "Have you ever had contact with Abu Musab al-Zarqawi?" which was ridiculous because Leila knew, like everyone else, that al-Zarqawi had been dead for fifteen years, and "How often do you read the Quran?"

Then they asked him if he liked *The Wizard of Oz*.

Leila took out a pen and some paper and jotted down some of the main points of the blog. She wanted to ask someone about them; James, perhaps. The rest of Sammurabi's account was of random acts of abuse, such as the Americans sneering at the Quran, dumping a bucket of urine over his head, and being made to drink pig's blood. At this last, Leila felt affronted for this poor man. However, it added to the veracity of his story: no Muslim would ever claim the shame of drinking pig's blood unless it was true.

At the very last blog entry, Sammurabi wrote that he was released and dumped into a back alley of Baghdad, not a block away from where he'd first been taken two years before. He wrote that he had fled Iraq and was living with cousins in a different country (Egypt, Leila assumed from the Web address). Sammurabi's last entry was that he did not want publicity, and did not want his identity known, but that this was his experience on the American "detainee" circuit. This final entry was dated three months ago, and the site had not been updated since.

"Strange," whispered Leila beneath her breath. She noted the date of Sammurabi's final entry, the URL address, and the word *true* with a question mark after it. With a glance at the clock on the computer screen, Leila saw she had an additional ten minutes before her hour was up. Then she needed to leave, as she'd promised her father.

Her e-mails and other business could be taken care of at

work when she used Dr. Whitaker's military computer. So Leila did something else that was impossible at Camp Diamondback. She went back to the main search engine page, and typed in the name James Cartwright.

A fierce blush worked up her face as she looked over the results of the search. Leila could not believe she was doing this, but her curiosity overwhelmed her. *I'm just checking to make sure he's not wanted for murder or something*, she told herself, though it was silly to think James would be a military officer if he was a criminal back home. After scrolling through some unrelated sites, some genealogical Web sites, and clicking the Next link several times, Leila found something good. It was a news story, entitled LOCAL BOY WINS WRITING CONTEST. The name James Cartwright was tagged to the story, from a newspaper called the *News-Gazette*.

She clicked on the link, and when the page loaded she stifled a giggle. It was an article with a picture of James, holding up a small certificate with a big smile on his face. He was fourteen in the picture. Leila read the accompanying story to learn that James had submitted a fiction story entitled "The House Key" to a national contest and won a college scholarship of five thousand dollars. It was a sizeable sum, even in 1994. According to the story, James lived in the town of Lexington, Virginia; his parents were named Sam and Jenny, and he had a younger sister named Marybelle who was an accomplished dancer. He would be attending the Rockbridge County High School in the fall. He wanted to be a writer when he grew up.

Leila sighed and sat back in the plastic chair. Then she clicked the X at the top of the screen to close it before any of the men in the cybercafe could see her gazing at a picture of some teenage American boy. It was time to leave, anyway. She gathered her handbag, stood up, and paid the boy at the counter for her hour of Internet use. The night was heavy and damp when she unlocked her bicycle from the alleyway and sped down the street toward her house. On the five-minute ride, her mind swam with the knowledge she'd gained: the odd and disturbing account of Sammurabi's experience in the American detention center, the massive Amnesty International report on human rights violations in Iraq, and the innocent normality of an old newspaper article about a boy named James who wanted to be a writer.

When she arrived home that evening, Leila decided that she had to be organized about the things she witnessed. The violence, the conversations, and the strange behavior toward detainees were too much to remember on her own. Therefore she would chronicle the experience: she would keep a journal. Into words would go the interactions with the American intelligence officers; the treatment (both good and bad) of detainees she witnessed at the base; the plans of her father, overheard and illicitly known. Bringing out an old ballpoint pen and a lined school notebook, Leila transcribed her notes from the Internet café. She wrote down her memories of the terrorists she'd treated and what their injuries had been, and how they'd received them. It damned her fellow Iraqis most of all.

The therapy of writing eased her nerves, and by the time she had finished, she felt better. Cleansed. She gathered her notebook papers and opened her wardrobe. In the very bottom drawer, shoved in the back, was a Persian puzzle box, of the kind sold in tourist shops. An old birthday gift from her father. It was tarnished silver and had its own hidden combination lock, set by Leila herself, part of the filigreed design in the form of a flower lined up with a bird. She twirled the flower round and round, the box clicked open, and she folded the papers and shoved them inside.

The journal could get her into major trouble, but her conscience demanded it: keeping her own copies of the worst she witnessed from both the Americans and the mujahideen. It was the thing that made it all manageable. Her journal papers would go in the puzzle box, and there they would stay, occult, waiting. With a deep breath she snapped the box closed.

There was much to do at work.

Chapter 11

The next day at Diamondback, the hospital was inundated, by its standards: a gun battle to the north of the city resulted in five wounded jihadis brought to the field hospital. They were all in bad shape. Two had multiple gunshot wounds to the chest and another suffered from a bullet lodged in the brain. Leila suspected this latter would be permanently damaged. The other two insurgents had shrapnel wounds from a shell explosion, which were a mess to deal with: thousands of tiny pieces of metal, embedded in the skin and bleeding, cutting, sinking their way inside.

Leila asked after the patients' welfare and translated their pain into English for the doctors. As always, she was impressed by the professionalism of Whitaker and Peabody. They took their doctor's oaths seriously and did not distinguish between American and Iraqi, friend and enemy, in their medical treatment. They worked with dedication to heal the wounded, and Leila decided it was the model by which she would live. She again had the impression that the medical patients were not individual humans but entities to be "fixed." This was no longer a negative thing, for it meant that labels such as terrorist or soldier or combatant did not apply. All human beings were made equal by suffering.

In the cool sterility of the ward, Leila and one of the American nurses worked to hook up the brain-damaged man to monitoring equipment. Nurse Jessica Quinn was young, about Leila's age, and a favorite of the men who visited the hospital, for she had gleaming chestnut hair and a heart-shaped face that was both kind and alluring. Leila did not know her well, but she was pleased to discover that Jessica Quinn was efficient and calm in her work. The women did not speak as they added an anesthetic drip to the man's IV, just in case he was in pain, and marked his injuries in preparation to bring him into surgery.

"His name is Ibrahim," said Leila.

"Oh?" said Quinn.

"That's according to his friend with the shrapnel," said Leila. She'd held her requisite questioning of the mujahideen to find out basic information like names and ages. The two with shrapnel were conscious; the other three were not. Before the two descended into drug-induced unconsciousness, Leila wrested the names of them all. Ibrahim, Mohammed, Ravi. She was not sure who was who, except that Ibrahim was the one with the head wound.

"He needs a full hospital," said Quinn. "And a good neurosurgeon."

"Even then," said Leila, "I'm not sure he would pull through. From here, it looks like the bullet has passed through the right temporal lobe. He will be a—what do you say in America—a vegetable?"

Quinn laughed, high and light. "Yep, a vegetable," she said. Then she looked at Leila with curiosity. "I don't know your name," she said.

"Leila. And you are Nurse Quinn, yes?"

"Yeah," said Quinn. "Call me Jessica, if you want."

"Jessica," said Leila. "It is nice to meet you."

"So you're the translator? But are you a nurse, too?" Quinn asked as they wrapped up Ibrahim's head and noted the work on the chart that hung on the bedside.

"I'm not a nurse," said Leila. Then she sighed. "I have a degree in biomedical science, and some work experience. I want to go to medical school, so this job is good for me."

"Oh," said Quinn. "I hope you do. You have the right manner."

"Thanks!" said Leila, happy for the encouragement. "That's what Dr. Whitaker said, too. I hope you are both right."

"Your English is really good," said Quinn.

"Thanks," Leila repeated.

"Do you smoke?" Quinn asked. "I need a break."

"I do not smoke," Leila said. She was still shocked that some American women smoked cigarettes, just like men. "But I will keep your company on your break, if you like."

"Mm-kay," said Quinn. They walked outside the hospital and stood together as Quinn lit up her slender white cigarette. The sky held a heavy haze, though not the sort of clouds that brought rain. It made Leila feel oppressed.

"I saw you talking with Captain Cartwright the other day," said Quinn. The comment made Leila think that Quinn had been paying attention to her, despite not knowing her name.

"James? Yes," said Leila, marking her territory by her familiar use of James's given name.

"He's a handsome devil, isn't he?" Quinn said.

"I had not noticed," Leila lied.

"Really?" Quinn took a drag on her cigarette and flicked the ashes with a dainty move of her wrist. "Every other woman on base has noticed."

"Perhaps the other women should pay attention to their work, not the men," Leila said. She had a horrible suspicion that Quinn was about to confess feelings for James or perhaps tell of a tryst with him. Leila did not know how American women did things, but based on the Hollywood movies she'd seen, they were aggressive and open about romance. They slept with men before they were married and did not hesitate to pursue "handsome devils" like James. It intimidated Leila, as though she were a rabbit standing next to a tiger.

However, Quinn's next words put her mind at ease. "It's no use with that one," she said. "Cartwright has never shown an interest in anyone on base. He's too proper. Closed off, you know. A lot of those Special Forces guys are."

"Huh," said Leila. She hid her relief, and then berated herself for feeling it in the first place. She ought to follow her own advice and concentrate on work, not men.

Quinn chuckled and tossed her cigarette onto the ground. "Let's go back inside. The restless natives need to be worked on. Oh, sorry," she said, noting the look on Leila's face. "I didn't mean it like that. You know what I mean."

Leila did not know what Quinn meant, but she was unsurprised by the veiled slur. She should count herself fortunate that she'd not been called nasty names, words directed at jihadis or sometimes innocent bystanders on the street, when the Stryker patrols whizzed by in their roaring vehicles. She could not help wondering what words played through the heads of the Americans when they saw her, Leila al-Ghani, working at the hospital. Did they condescend to her, too? Did they hide it behind polite concern and big smiles? Perhaps Americans were more complex than she gave them credit for.

"I believe Dr. Whitaker will want us in surgery," Leila said, knowing that the doctor had requested her help. "We should go now to put on our scrubs."

"Coolio," said Quinn. Leila did not know the word, but it must mean assent because Quinn followed her into the ladies' scrub room.

It was a treat for Leila to help the doctors in surgery. These were matters of life and death, and she was in on them. It was a privilege, a frightening responsibility, and the combination was enough to set Leila's pulse on hard beating edge. She loved it. In contrast to her inner excitement, her hands moved in calm coordination and the surgery was conducted with rehearsed expertise. One by one the bullets came out of the man's torso. They were dropped onto a metal tray, making a dull clinking noise. Leila counted eight rounds of 5.56 caliber bullets, and then Dr. Whitaker brushed his bloodied latex-gloved hands together.

"That's that," he said, and Leila, Quinn, and the other assisting nurse, a man named Terletsky, bandaged the wounds and cleaned up the operating room.

Leila's mind was so occupied with the details of surgical procedure that on the way home, she failed to notice the dark maroon car that trailed her bicycle.

As she wheeled in past the front gate, Leila heard the chatter of voices, men all, coming from inside the house. The front door opened and a group filed out. A few of the men were dressed in traditional djellaba and headdress, the rest in Western-style garb. She recognized Abdul-Hakam among them and Leila had an impulse to make a face at him; instead she turned away, trying to remain unnoticed among the crowd of strangers.

Leaning her bicycle against the inner wall, Leila picked out another man who seemed familiar, wearing jeans, an old button-down shirt, and a kaffiyeh tied around his head. He met her eye and with a gasp of horror, she placed him: Hazim, the detainee she'd treated at the American field hospital. He had been released, and he'd gone straight back to her father. Leila closed her mouth and tried to gauge if he recognized her.

A self-satisfied smile spread across Hazim's face. As he and his fellows made their way across the courtyard toward the gate, each to disappear into the chilled golden twilight, Hazim leaned her way and in an exaggerated whisper said, "*Salaam alaykum,* Leila al-Ghani."

Chapter 12

Dry mouthed, with fists clenched tight at her sides, Leila watched Hazim leave, noting the strong set of his shoulders. He was proud of something, and it was far too much to hope he hadn't told her father.

In the frame of the open front door, Tamir stood with his arms crossed, and Leila stopped short at the look on his face. The overhead lightbulb on the porch cast Tamir's face into orange hollows as he stood in silence, watching Leila. Dread settled in her stomach like a peach pit dropped into water. She knew it was her imagination, but the night seemed to grow darker and colder.

"Hello, *Baba*," she said.

"Leila, come inside at once."

She scurried in, not daring to say a word in protest. Her mind reeled with what her father's mood might be. She prayed that tonight love might overrule hate, but the rational part of her mind said that was unlikely.

"Sit down, please," instructed Tamir, following Leila into the main sitting room. It was dark aside from a single electric light that burned from inside a wooden-screen lamp shade. The shade filtered the rays into little flower designs that hung on the walls. When Leila sat down, she stared at her hands, and noted how they, too, had little dots of light on them.

Tamir did not waste his words. "You are working for the Americans," he said.

Leila's breath was strangled. "I'm sorry, Father," she said. "I could not say anything. I am not working for the army, I'm working at the hospital." Of course, the 67th Combat Support Hospital was part of the army, but the other way sounded better. Less traitorous.

"You little deceiver," Tamir hissed leaning toward her, his face hard. Leila cringed. "How dare you? You've betrayed us all! Your family, your country! Death is too good for you, for what you have done."

A wild terror knocked at her insides as she wondered if her father would kill her. Ten years ago, when she was the darling youngest daughter of the happy, secure al-Ghani family, the idea of familial homicide would have been ridiculous. But Leila no longer knew her own father. She would not put it past him to kill her by his own hand. A bullet wound? A knife? Would she be another body dumped on the road, left to the flies and forgotten in the face of nationwide carnage? This war did strange things to people. Her father was the sort of man to retreat into medieval notions of honor when threatened. What was once unthinkable was now quite possible for families across Iraq. The despair of it burrowed deep into Leila's heart.

"I am ashamed of you, Leila," Tamir said. "While your family and countrymen are dying to protect this land, you are helping the Crusaders. You work for them, aiding their cause and fraternizing with them. Because of you, they are stronger."

"But they're not!" Leila cried. "I am not there to help the Americans. I help the wounded det—" She stopped herself before saying "detainees." "I help the wounded mujahideen. When the Americans capture them and bring them into the hospital, my job is to translate and help to heal their wounds. I am training to be a doctor, Father!" As she spoke, her conviction reasserted itself. "I do not distinguish between sides. A human in need is a human in need! Iraqi, American, Brazilian,

African, whatever! The Holy Quran tells us to be kind, and compassionate. I am doing nothing wrong!"

Tamir fell silent for a loaded moment. Leila's mind swung crazily between shame for working with the Americans, and certainty that she had done no wrong.

"You said you work as a translator?" Tamir asked, and his tone was somehow different. Softer, less angry.

"Yes," said Leila.

"You translate what the prisoners say, and tell the Americans?"

"Yes . . ." Leila said again. "*Baba* . . . please."

"Hush," Tamir said. He stroked his thin beard with a wiry hand, and was silent for several minutes. Finally Tamir cleared his throat. He furrowed his brow. Then he met Leila's gaze, and she saw clarity in his hazel eyes. She swallowed the lump in her throat and waited.

"Tonight I learned, without doubt, of the nature of your *hospital* job," Tamir said. "One of my friends, a man who had been held prisoner and treated for injuries by the Americans, informed me for certain that you spent your days there. When you came home late that night last week, I knew you were lying, Leila. You are not so good a liar as you think."

This was bad news. God knew he had enough contacts across the city of Mosul to have someone spy on her and follow her movements. As it played across her mind's eye, Leila could just imagine a jihadi watching her board the bus for Camp Diamondback, coming back to the hospital at six in the evening, pretending a different life. And the Iraqis she treated at the hospital; of course some might be released, some who were genuine terrorists with tales to tell. Like Hazim. What a fool she had been. She tucked her legs beneath her.

"When I learned of your lies, I decided that you must not disgrace the family name any longer. It would be better, I thought, to have you dead. But what you have just told me," Tamir said, "about being a translator . . . This I did not know. You've made me reconsider."

Leila caught her breath, recalling the conversation she'd over-heard several weeks ago.

"You have a chance to redeem yourself," Tamir said, lean-ing back and looking satisfied. "I think you should continue to work for the Americans."

Leila stared at her father. She had a nagging feeling that her life was about to get a great deal more complicated.

Tamir explained his plans, which left Leila feeling like the rope in a game of tug-of-war. She would be recruited as a spy against the Americans. When wounded mujahideen were taken prisoner, Leila's task was to make sure they revealed nothing vital to the Americans. She was to translate disinformation and file false reports. She was to pay attention to the workings of Camp Diamondback, take note of any weaknesses in security, and pass that knowledge to her father. The patrols, the sup-plies, the numbers of men: all must fall under Leila's attention.

Refusal was not an option; it was the only way Leila could keep her job. She felt sick to her stomach. No matter which way she turned now, she would betray someone.

For his part, Tamir crossed his legs and arms, staring at Leila. His eyes shone with the look of bloodlust. Leila was frozen by it, both horrified and fascinated by the face of this new, scheming side of her father . . . she'd never been con-fronted with it like this.

Tamir al-Ghani had once been a good provider for Leila and her family, a man with regular hours, a high-paying job, and a calm demeanor. His position as a judge meant that the al-Ghanis never fell victim to disappearance, death, torture, or economic sanctions that plagued so many of their neighbors under Sad-dam's regime. Tamir was able to secure food, clothing, supplies, and even the occasional luxury item, all because of his high of-fice. The first American invasion of the early 1990s had been a mere hiccup to the al-Ghani family. The occasional violence in Kurdistan did not touch them. Umm Naji was safe from the po-litical dangers that plagued her family in Dohuk because she'd married a Sunni Arab. In those days, he was *Baba*. Perfect and powerful. Kind and giving. The unshakeable family patriarch. The gentle reader of children's books.

Now, as Leila met her father's eyes in the semidark sitting room, she saw an emaciated, bitter man who had been part of a vicious government that repressed its own people. The peaceful, nurturing man of her childhood was now a man with a deadly mission. She felt as though she were in a car hurtling toward a great precipice and Tamir was in the driver's seat, directing the entire family toward explosive ruin.

"This is a new chance for you, Leila, to make up for your lies," Tamir said. "This will be a noble task, one that will bring great honor to your family."

"I see," she said, biting her lower lip. "Yes, *Baba*, I am happy to help you. I would have told you much sooner if I knew you had a job for me."

This was the right thing to say. Tamir's smile grew thin. "You will be aiding the great cause," he said. "Allah will look upon us all with grace. Leila, you were always interested in politics. Now you have a chance to participate."

"Many thanks, Father," she said, lowering her gaze down to the carpet.

"Now. Get some sleep. You will have many things on your mind in the morning."

"Yes, Father." Leila gave her father a quick kiss on the cheek and hastened out of the room. She waited until she reached her bedroom to let out a silent gasp, in lieu of a scream.

Chapter 13

Christmas Day, and Mosul was full of good cheer. A wind had descended off the hills and it howled through the streets of Mosul and whipped dust across the rolling plains, kicking up clouds of particles that laced the breath of all, Iraqi and American. The Christian communities in Mosul, of which there were a significant number, prepared for their day's services. If anyone listened hard enough, they might be able to hear hymns being sung. These were beneath the racket of the city, for no one wished to draw attention to their faith. Faith was an excuse for murder.

The winter wind blew hardest across the American base, or so it seemed to Leila. The airfield at LSA Diamondback was stretched across a flat bank of the Tigris River and so bore the brunt of the weather.

That morning, a celebratory barrage of mortars pock-marked their way across the base, not killing anyone but provoking a clattering firefight from the guards posted along the Texas towers around the perimeter. Then came a white car packed with four mujahideen and some RPGs, and they busted a smoking hole in the fence before being felled by a well-aimed TOW missile. Leila, who was working that day, ended up being late because of the fuss . . . and it took even longer to go through security because she had brought several small boxes with homemade pastries in them, as gifts to her hospital coworkers. She had even brought one for James, just in case.

In the field hospital, a festive plastic wreath hung on the wall and a blinking string of Christmas lights was strung aross the door to the reception office. From somewhere in the building a jazzy strain of Nat King Cole floated through the air, at odds with the strong antiseptic smell and functional atmosphere of the hospital. In the main ward, Leila stood, writing on a clipboard, a frown on her face, her mood anything but festive. Her long dark tresses were looped into a messy bun on the back of her head, and although the lack of *hijab* made her feel modern, she could not shake away the troubled feeling that had set in shortly after her talk with Tamir. With a yank, she switched out an IV bag, wrote it down on the chart, and turned to the door.

James lounged in the doorway, and Leila's instinct told her he'd been there for quite some time, watching her.

"Hey, Leila," said James in a soft voice, mindful of the sleeping patients.

"James." She nodded. "Let us step outside."

"Okay," he said, following her into the corridor.

She crossed her arms, looking down at her feet. "I have not seen you in some time," she said.

"Sorry," he said. "Things have been busy around here. Everyone's pretending to celebrate."

"Ah yes, it is Christmas today," Leila said. "I wish you a happy holiday."

"Thanks," said James. "You, too. I mean, I realize you don't celebrate Christmas, but . . . anyway."

"Thank you," said Leila. "You know, in Islam, Jesus is considered a prophet, too. He is much revered. So I can take your Merry Christmas," she said. She flashed him a smile. It was the truth; there was no dogmatic reason why an Iraqi Muslim could not wish a Christian a good holiday, and receive it in kind. And so Leila and James had one more thing in common: Jesus the second prophet. Jesus and rap music. It was a start.

"That's right," James said. He grinned back at her.

"Oh!" Leila said, startled. "I have something for you. Wait here." She whirled and walked down the hall at a rapid pace, leaving James puzzled. It took her just an instant at her locker to retrieve his gift, which she presented to him with a bright smile. "I hoped I might see you today," she said, "because I brought you something. For Christmas. Here." She thrust the package out and he took it.

The small paper box was striped in red and white. He flipped open the lid and stared down at the beautiful little honeyed square pastry, with a lacework design of frosting on the top. "I, uh—thank you!" said James.

"It is a *zalabiyyeh*," she said. "It is one of the few things I like to cook."

"You don't cook?" James teased.

"To the chagrin of my mother, no," said Leila. "But I make dessert quite well. This is a sweet pastry dipped in rosewater to give it flavor, with my little design on the top. And"—she smiled again—"it's safe to eat. Not poisoned."

James laughed. "Thank you, Leila," he said again. "Really. This is—" He stopped and cleared his throat. "I didn't expect such a nice Christmas gift."

"It's nothing," Leila said, blushing. "Just a little . . . something."

"How's work?" he asked.

"Oh, fine. Busy. And in a hospital, busy is not a good thing."

"That's for sure," said James. "I hope they're not working you too hard."

"I bring it on myself," she laughed. "I want to work as much as possible. That means more experience."

"Do you want to sit down somewhere?" James asked. It was a good idea; Leila did not enjoy standing in the middle of a hallway with soldiers and nurses walking to and fro, giving them speculative looks. "We can walk over to the MWR. They serve good coffee there. Or tea, if you prefer."

"Well—" Leila hesitated, biting her lip. She glanced about.

Having never been to the Morale, Welfare, and Recreation Center, she found the prospect made her nervous, as though she would be judged there.

"That's fine," interjected Dr. Whitaker, who popped out of his office. "Sorry. I couldn't help but overhear." The doctor grinned at James and Leila. "Leila, it's okay if you want a break until, say, fifteen-thirty."

"All right, then," she said, now that she had express permission from her boss. "Let me get my jacket," she said to James, who nodded.

It was 1430, two-thirty civilian time, so Leila looked forward to the hour ahead. After retrieving her jacket, she reappeared and James made a gallant gesture with his hand toward the doors. "After you," he said.

James kept a comfortable distance and set his pace alongside Leila as they headed toward the MWR Center. Most of the soldiers would be at the holiday party in the main dining facility, Leila recalled, watching their president's address, the same one being broadcast on the Al-Hurrah television station, on the big screen. Across the sky, thick heavy clouds roiled like an upset stomach, and Leila smiled a little at the thought of the American president being cut off by bad weather. She had no use for political leaders anymore.

"Have you ever been to the MWR?" James asked.

"No," she said. "I have not been outside of the hospital."

"Well, you're in for a treat," James said. "Not only is there good coffee, but there are actual cushions on the chairs. Plus a billiards table."

"Ah," said Leila. "Impressive."

"It is," said James with a laugh in his voice. "Here we go." He nodded toward the door of the hall. Outside, the American flag fluttered in the wind, and someone had put up plastic Christmas decorations across the door.

"Do you like coffee?" James asked Leila as they sat opposite each other at an enamel-topped table.

"I do," she said. "How unfeminine of me!"

"Is it?" James asked. "I always thought of women as drinking coffee."

"Perhaps in America," said Leila. "In the Arab culture, only men drink coffee. But I am more modern than that. Besides," she laughed, "I do not trust you Americans to make tea the correct way."

"Can't blame you there!" James said. He pulled rank and told a corporal to get them some coffee. "Two coffees, if you would, soldier. Milk? Sugar?" he asked Leila.

"Both," she said.

"With both," James said to the soldier. "Thanks."

"Yes, sir," said the private.

Leila felt sure the corporal pulled a face when he turned to get them coffee. She liked the way James took charge. It made her feel more comfortable.

"So," James said, "you're a modern coffee-drinking sort of girl, are you?"

"Oh yes."

"Do you still want to be a doctor after working here?"

"Yes," she said. "Yes. More than ever." Another instant blush rose in her cheeks and she was annoyed with her tendency to color when feeling emotional; it could not be helped.

"Where do you want to go to medical school?" James asked. He leaned forward on his elbows and his gaze was unwavering upon her. Leila wondered if he could discern her rebelliousness, her ambition; he was a soldier and trained to observe. It made things somehow easier to think that he understood.

"In the West," she sighed. "But I think that is not possible. Even if I were accepted to a school, I doubt I would get a visa. You know, we are all terrorists over here."

James shrugged. America was no longer the land of the free, and its once-open doors were closing fast. Leila knew that many of the Iraqi translators who worked with the Americans tried in vain to get entry visas; one translator at the detainment center had attempted six times to get a visa, denied every time.

"It is hard to get a visa," James agreed. "I don't know what's wrong with our customs people. They're paranoid."

Leila wrinkled her nose. "They have to be, I suppose."

"Naw," said James. "They'd be crazy to say no to your visa. I mean, look at you!"

"Sorry?" Leila laughed aloud. "So you are saying they accept visas based on photographs alone?"

"I mean, uh—" James smiled, caught off guard. "I mean your qualifications," he said. "And you look nice. Not at all like a terrorist."

"I see," Leila said as her father's face floated in her mind's eye. Would the Americans spot him as a terrorist? She shook the thought away and smiled back at James.

The lower-ranking soldier reappeared with two cups of coffee in white ceramic cups on matching saucers. The plain, sturdy dishes were reminiscent of the kind that might be found in some little roadside diner in middle America . . . something out of a Hollywood movie. "Here ya go, sir," he said.

"Thank you," said James, and Leila nodded her thanks as well.

"This is good coffee," said Leila after inhaling the aroma and taking a tiny sip. Steam from the cup floated up in front of her face.

"Yep," said James.

Leila's spirits lifted with the caffeine. With a bit of hard imagination, they might be in a coffeehouse in America, one of those places like she'd seen on TV, with cushy sofas and dark décor and designer coffees written in an artsy font on the menu, without a war zone a scant few meters out the door.

"I hope you're not getting a hard time at home, for working here," said James.

"Oh," Leila said, pretending that her pause was due to the hot coffee. "No, it's all right. Tamir, my father, he knows and has gotten better. There is nothing wrong with working in any hospital, I have convinced them."

"Tamir al-Ghani? That's your father?" James asked. There

was a shard of awareness in his voice; Leila immediately wished she hadn't said his name. She wondered how much James knew and how much more he wanted out of her.

"Yes, he is my father . . ." she said.

"Huh. For some reason he sounds familiar, maybe from your background check or something."

"He was a Baathist, before the war," said Leila, hoping that would explain it.

"Yeah," said James. "Keep an eye on him for us, would you?"

And just like that, Leila agreed she would. She couldn't say no; it would make her look more suspicious to James. Besides, if her father wanted her to spy on the Americans, why could she not return the favor? Now she had the upper hand. Inside this rapport with James, this friendly agreement, there was a piece of her that Tamir could not control.

"You'll really let us know if you see anything suspicious?" James asked. "Not officially, of course, but you can tell me if you see anything."

"I will," said Leila. And she would, to an extent. Something inside her squirmed, knowing it might be easier promised than done, but it was too late to back out, and she felt as though she were walking a quivering line above an endless chasm. Blinking once, she raised her eyebrows at James. If she focused on him as a goal, her fixed point of reference, perhaps she could navigate the betrayal . . . and extend the connection.

"And you're still enjoying your job," James said, easing the conversation away from Tamir al-Ghani.

"So much," said Leila.

"Our misbehaved soldiers haven't put you off healing people?"

Leila smiled and took another sip of coffee. "Oh no. I am thinking of medical school in London. Dr. Whitaker recommended it."

"Oh!" said James. "Do you have a list of schools you would attend?"

"Imperial College. Also I have thought about the Johns

Hopkins, in America. If neither of those work out, then there are other places in London I would consider. If I can get out of this country, I would have options."

"I'll say," said James. "I overheard one of the nurses talking, and she said that you were the most skilled assistant in the hospital."

"Really?" The comment lit up her mind like a bright beam. "Who is saying such nice things about me?"

"I didn't know her," said James. "She has a nickname, though: Baby Doll. Some of the other guys call her that because she's kinda . . . sweet. Pretty, you know. She was the one who said it."

Without a doubt, it had been Jessica Quinn. All the soldiers seemed to like her and Leila could imagine her with such a nickname. . . . For a moment she wondered if James liked her as well. "Hmm. And what does Captain James Cartwright think?"

"About you, Leila?"

"Yes. About me."

James grinned. "From where I'm sitting, you're perfect."

She raised her delicate eyebrows in feigned surprise. "Perfect? Surely no one is perfect." James's eyes glinted with fun and Leila felt like dancing because of it.

"You're perfect to me," said James.

"You are not so bad yourself, James," said Leila, and it came out in such a breathless way that if the table had not been between them, she might have leaned in closer.

They noticed the singing first, coming from outside. It was the rude version of "We Three Kings." Then the door slammed open and a boisterous group of army officers came in, howling away the lyrics.

"Oh God," James said.

"That is your Captain Hook," said Leila, nodding at the group. The ringleader, the officer in the Military Police whose name was Hooker, put Leila in mind of the phrase "bull in a china shop."

"Yeah," said James. "Listen, can I walk you back to the hospital? These guys are trying to sing away their Christmas blues. It might get messy." He stood, clutching his Christmas pastry box.

"Sure," said Leila, standing up.

The movement drew Hooker's attention. "Whoa-oh!" he shouted.

James took the initiative and grabbed Leila's elbow, ushering her out the door as fast as he could. When she was outside, they turned back to see Hooker making a rude gesture and laughing. James drew his hand across the throat, and mouthed the words, "Cut it!" The vehemence of it broke through Hooker's jolly mood and he put his hand up to his mouth with a snicker.

"Sorry about that," said James. "These guys have no manners."

"I did not notice," said Leila. She cast her eyes down demurely, then lifted them again to meet James's eye. After a few congenial minutes of walking along the road, the dust gritty and soft beneath their feet, they stopped at the field hospital.

"Thank you for the coffee," said Leila. "My father would be furious." And she laughed.

"Glad I could aid your rebellion," said James with a small bow.

"I will see you soon," said Leila; then she turned and disappered into the hospital.

Chapter 14

The city of Mosul exploded that night of December 25 with three suicide bombings. The violence tended to go in cycles; there would be some weeks of relative peace with the usual shoot-outs and minor bombings. Then something else would set off the mujahideen. In this case, it was the Christian holiday that sparked the carnage; at least, most people agreed it was Christmas. Others said it was the recent appointment of a Shia as minister of oil in Baghdad that enraged the mostly Sunni insurgency. Like most things in Iraq, the reasons for murder were never straighforward.

One bombing was at the police station in the Al-Nahrwan neighborhood; another was on one of the market streets. These attacks killed innocent Iraqis, not "Crusaders," but no one noticed. There were just bleeding bodies, crying children, more funerals in the city of Mosul. A third bombing targeted the Americans at Camp Marez, but did not get past the outer gate before being disabled by military police firing from the towers. The flattened tires left the big old truck sitting like a lump outside, a model of unrealized potential.

Leila was almost home from her day at work when she heard the shock waves from the bombings roll across the city like thunder. She pedaled her bicycle faster. In the distance, there were sirens. A smattering of gunfire. Someone's mobile phone ringing from inside a house. "*Inshallah*," said a man on the street with a shrug.

Leila left her bicycle in a heap in the front courtyard in her haste to get inside. It was time to hunker down and wait for the violence to pass, like having bad menstrual cramps. "Mama!" she shouted as she burst through the front door.

"There you are," said Umm Naji, bustling toward Leila from the direction of the kitchen. "Have you seen your father in the city?"

"No," said Leila. "There have been bombings. I heard them."

"Is that what it was?" Umm Naji said, shivering and crossing her arms across her ample bosom. "I thought thunder."

"The weather is clear outside," Leila said curtly. "Where's Fatima?"

"Upstairs," said Umm Naji. "She's choosing from material samples. For her wedding dresses, you know."

"Eh?" asked Leila. It boggled the mind to think of someone getting married at a time like this. At the rate bad things were happening, the city of Mosul would obliterate itself into dust by next month. Did life go on? *Not for some people tonight*, Leila thought.

Then the night fell into waiting—for the violence to end, and for Tamir to come home. Leila snuck a glance into the inner courtyard; the hatch to the old well was wide open and empty.

Leila sat down in the women's sitting room and switched on the pretty lamp with the green silk shade. She had changed out of her work clothes into comfortable track pants and a T-shirt. She crossed her legs beneath her and listened to the sounds of the night. Despite Umm Naji's glares at the open window, Leila left it open. She wanted fresh cold air. She wanted to hear what was going on. There was not much to be gleaned from the dark crack that allowed the night inside: no cars passed on the road, because of the curfew, and the neighbors' houses sat in breathless wait. Leila's mobile phone rested on the carved wooden coffee table, silent.

"Some tea?" Fatima asked, peering into the room. Leila jumped at the sound of her sister's voice.

"Yes, please," Leila said.

"Please, dear," said Umm Naji. She picked up a pile of mending and, wielding a needle and thread, made use of the waiting time.

When Fatima reentered the room with a tray of *shai*, she and Umm Naji discussed the material to be used for the wedding dresses, with Fatima insisting on the least expensive option and Umm Naji wanting the imported satin.

Leila stared into the black sweet swirl of her teacup. Toward the bottom of the glass, the grounds floated as tiny dark specks in the rich liquid. She drained the tea down her throat and then looked down to see what shape the leaves formed. All her mind saw in the tasseomancy was death.

Sirens still wailed in the distance. They would be looking for survivors now; the body counts would come later. Her mother and sister chattered on about the wedding against the distant rattle of gunfire. Somewhere in Mosul, people were fighting and bleeding and dying.

Leila's father was off in the night; he was likely at the mosque, although that could mean anything these days. But overriding her concern for Tamir was the knowledge that James might be out in the city.

For a brief, horrible moment, she pictured him broken and bleeding. She imagined him as yet another Internet-broadcast victim, bound with cords, and then a hooded mujahideen steps behind him with a long sharp knife and—Leila choked, and disguised it with a cough. Umm Naji gave her a searching look, then went back to the conversation with Fatima. Whatever was going on in Mosul City tonight, Leila knew that her friend James was a part of it. There was too much gunfire to believe otherwise.

"Mama," said Fatima, "can we talk about this some other time? I can't concentrate on my wedding."

"What do you mean?" Umm Naji said.

"She means there are people dying out the door," said Leila. "Stop pretending you can't hear it."

Umm Naji wilted in defeat against the back of the chair. "I don't know what's gotten into your father," she admitted in a small voice. "He never used to be like this. Not in the days when Saddam Hussein was in power. He was a practical man, never running off to start a fight."

"We know," said Fatima. "The war has made everyone crazy."

Umm Naji shook her head. "I would not have married a crazy man," she said. "Fatima, it is good that your Khaled is not a jihadi."

"So we're admitting that Father is a jihadi now?" Leila said.

Discomfort passed over Umm Naji's face. "Leila, daughter, I wish you wouldn't say things in such bad ways."

"The truth isn't always pleasant," said Leila.

"Girls . . ." Umm Naji set down the shirt on which she was working. "I don't want you to think badly of your father for what he does. When we first married, he was kindness itself, that is his character. This is a deviation, his—involvement—in the insurgency. The situation is extreme."

"Mama, he's perfectly aware of what he's doing," Leila said. As much as she loved her father, she worried that his cruel streak had existed long before the war. Yet Leila could see the soft glow in Umm Naji's eyes as she thought of Tamir, and in her mind's eye Leila imagined her parents as newlyweds, perhaps shy like Fatima and Khaled. Loving each other.

Fatima said, "What was it like when you first married, Mama?"

Umm Naji smiled. "Those days were good for me," she said. "I was young and I was even slim." A chuckle escaped her lips. "Your father and I had a happy life. He was a lawyer in those days, you know. Before he became a judge. We were safe and we lived here in this house with his parents before they died. Do you know the pomegranate tree in the garden was planted as a wedding gift for us? It's always given such good fruit."

Leila did not mention that the pomegranate tree was looking withered and dry these days. The upkeep of the garden was second fiddle to the men hiding in the well beneath it.

The same thought must have occurred to Umm Naji, because she muttered, "I must water that tree tomorrow," and then lowered her head to resume her silent mending.

Like the al-Ghanis, the rest of the neighborhood went dead quiet, drew their shutters, and prayed against the battle. They hoped there would not be an urgent pounding on the door, and a scared or wounded cousin bearing an AK-47 and demanding shelter. They hoped that this night, like the others before it, would end in survival.

The women did not sleep. It was a silent pact, a truce against argument, and the girls waited all night for their father to come home. Umm Naji mended shirts. Leila leafed through a book. Fatima wrote letters to their female cousins in Dohuk. Each was too preoccupied with her thoughts to speak more than a few words. In houses across town, women were doing the very same thing. They awaited their men, and prayed that they came home in one piece, whether they were fighters or innocents or just in the wrong place at the wrong time.

The front door unlatched at two fifty-eight in the morning. Three heads snapped up at the sound, and Umm Naji rose from her seated position, clutching the shirt she'd been working on.

Tamir al-Ghani walked in the door. There was blood on his starched collar. "Go to bed now," he said, his face expressionless. He might have been coming home from an average day at work. His utter calm terrified Leila more than anything.

The night was never spoken of again.

For days, no one left their houses. Mosul was on lockdown, a twenty-four-hour curfew. American military police patrols zoomed around, and some Strykers, too. The police manned every corner, and the Iraqi army was brought in. Aside from their dark faces, they could have been Americans, for they carried the same equipment and rode in the same vehicles. The civilian population kept their heads low and knew better than to speak to their neighbors across fences, even if just to exchange news. The mujahideen, having made their statement, went back underground into cellars and rooms and the sewers below the mosques.

When Leila woke up the morning of December 27, she found Umm Naji in the kitchen cooking up a pot of rice that was much too large for their family of four.

"Mother, why do you need all that rice?" Leila asked, although she already knew the answer.

Umm Naji pressed her generous lips into a thin line. "Your father asked me to make it. It is not my place to question him."

Leila raised her eyebrows but said nothing more. Umm Naji had gotten the message across: the mujahideen were back, hiding in the old well in the courtyard.

On the third straight day of military curfew, a cold day with the wind blowing and the shutters of the house locked tight, Leila sat down next to Tamir in the big sitting room. He gazed at her with pride now. "How is my best daughter?" he asked, patting her knee with a too-thin hand.

"I'm fine, *Baba*," she said.

"We got them," Tamir said. He clasped his hands; his eyes were alight. "The Americans are swarming around like ants disturbed from their hill. We got them."

"Were many killed?" Leila asked, concentrating on keeping the hitch out of her voice.

Tamir smiled. "Allah is on our side, Leila," he said. "His justice is wrought. The Crusaders are learning of our dedication now."

"You sound like an imam," said Leila. Even though part of her dreaded knowing the truth of what had happened, she was disappointed with her father's lack of detail. No one else knew what was going on. Even the televisions were unreliable; power cuts rolled through the city, a deliberate attempt to stave off the spread of bad news. The few clips of the Arabic news from Al-Jazeera Network that Leila watched spoke of the bombings in Mosul, violence, and the rest, but no specifics. No body counts, no names or faces.

"Father, what happened that first night? I was on my way home from work, from—er, my job of spying on the Americans— and I heard the bombings. The gunfire. What was it, Father?"

"You do not want to know, little nightingale," said Tamir, and Leila got an unexpected prickling of tears at the back of her eyes. "Nightingale" was her father's nickname for her as a child. She had not heard him use it in years.

"The Americans are terrible," she said, hoping that he might tell her something useful. "I have been learning much about them. They are arrogant. They walk around as if they own the world."

"Oh, my poor ambitious girl," Tamir snapped. "Now you know the truth about the Crusaders who you wanted to emulate."

Leila blinked. She hated how her father's mood swung back and forth like a drunken pendulum. "I'm glad I'm able to help you, Father. Allah must have . . . some sort of purpose for me . . . in all of this."

"Yes, Allah must . . . Just as you are helping me." His voice softened. "When you return to work, I expect details on their casualty numbers. More Iraqis will be taken into custody after this. With you there, Leila, you can prevent damage to the cause."

"Yes," she said.

He laughed then, a harsh grating sound without humor. "I was at the mosque three nights ago. Then I did my part. I saw a Humvee blown up with an RPG. It was like cracking open a dragon's egg, all fire and shell. The Americans bleed hot." He chuckled again. "Then some other Crusaders were wounded. Shot. Shelled. I would say they were a bit stunned by the whole thing."

Leila listened in horror. Her doctor's sensibilities were disturbed, of course, but above all she worried about James. What if he had been in the blown-up Humvee? And Tamir spoke in tones of fondness toward it all. It disgusted her. As much as she wanted to piece together the details, she couldn't bear to hear it.

"I'm going to go finish my correspondence now," said Leila, rising.

"Good," said Tamir. "Have you written back to your cousin Abdul?"

"Abdul?" Leila drew a blank, then remembered the letter she had stowed on her shelf. "Oh, Abdul," she said. "Yes. I should write back. Good afternoon, Father." She planted a kiss on Tamir's papery cheek and hastened herself upstairs.

She stood in the middle of her bedroom, looking around at her things, pretending she was a stranger seeing it for the first time. Pretending she was James. If she knew nothing about herself, what would her bedroom tell her? A woman, a girl. Interested in medicine and politics. No photographs of a fiancé or boyfriend. Fashionable shoes and unfashionable clothes. A girl with secrets.

She reached up and felt along the top shelf of her light-bluepainted bookcase. There was the letter, dusty and still unopened. With a frown, Leila tore open the envelope and opened the two pieces of folded paper inside. *Dear Cousin Leila*, the letter began. Leila read on, her dread growing with each word.

Abdul wanted to marry her. It was a proposal, complete with a list of reasons why Leila ought to consider it. He said that little Mohammed needed a new mother, and said that there would be more "precious" children to come. He hinted at his virility, which made Leila wish she could share the funny contents with her friend Hala Rasul. Then, as though making an inventory, Abdul described his house and its furniture, amenities, and location.

He had worked hard on the letter. The penmanship was better than the scribbled address on the envelope, and it looked as though Abdul had put a lined paper behind the white stationery to keep his handwriting in straight lines. The paper was of good quality, as was the ink. No ballpoint pen for this kind of letter.

With a stifled laugh, Leila thought that Abdul must be hopping back and forth in Al-Hadr, waiting for her reply. And here she had not even opened the letter for weeks!

The idea was preposterous, of course. Not for a moment did Leila entertain the thought of accepting Abdul. She would sooner throw herself into the Tigris River than vow a life with her pompous cousin. His visit to the al-Ghani home must have impressed him more than Leila knew and put crazy notions into his head. It was all Umm Naji's doing, Leila was sure; the special food, the little hints about Leila's domestic qualities, the kindness above and beyond familial hospitality.

She wondered if her parents were aware of the proposal. They must have a clue, for in the Arab culture the first cousins always had the priority for a girl's hand in marriage. It was not an Islamic practice, but rather a tradition for fathers like Tamir to keep the family fortune in the family. Leila wanted no part of such tribal nonsense.

As the sound of another distant explosion rolled across the rooftops of Mosul, Leila sighed and sat down on her bed. She crumpled Abdul's letter in her hand, then smoothed it again. She saw her parents' plan for her clearly: Tamir wanted her to keep working at the field hospital as long as she was useful to him; then Umm Naji would get her way, and Leila would be married off to Abdul and sent away to live in Al-Hadr and raise babies.

"Goddamn it," she said aloud, mimicking the curse she'd heard on the American base. She never gave Adbul an ounce of romantic encouragement during his monthlong visit in Mosul. The problem was that men made assumptions. They thought that just because *their* feelings were ardent, the woman must return them by default.

Abdul's letter demanded a response, though Leila could not think of what to say in a polite manner. She grabbed a blank sheet of paper and a pen from her desk. Out of morbid curiosity, she wrote her own name, followed by Abdul's name. "Ugh," she said. Then her pen hovered above the paper, as though in contemplation. She pressed it down and wrote out *Leila Cartwright*. It looked foreign, two cultures mashed together to create a name. She was not sure what to think of it.

Mrs. James Cartwright, she wrote next. As a hasty postscript she wrote, *May Allah bless you*. Feeling guilty, she tore up the paper into tiny pieces, so small that not even the arc of a character could be discerned from the pile of waste. Leila would not put it past her mother to search her rubbish bin.

On the fifth day after the Christian holiday, the announcement came: the twenty-four-hour curfew was lifted. New restrictions included no vehicle traffic in the markets at any time; no vehicle traffic from nine in the evening until five in the morning; no pedestrians out after ten o'clock. It was almost the same as before the triple bombings, and it meant that the city of Mosul might go back to normal, at least for a while. As usual, the curfew was enforced by MPs, Iraqi police, and the unpredictable Stryker patrols that hammered through the city, teeth bared for destruction.

For understandable reasons, people were afraid to go back to work. The curfew was lifted on Saturday, and Leila stayed home on Sunday, for it was her normal day off and the bus to the American base would not be operating, anyway. But on Monday, Leila awoke and put on a pair of black trousers and a modest, loose-fitting blouse. She wore black polished shoes on her feet.

Now that her job at Camp Diamondback was in the open, Leila reasoned with Tamir that if she dressed like a Westerner, it would help her gain the trust of the Americans. They might tell her things. During breakfast, Tamir's eyes fluttered disapprovingly over Leila's trousers, but he nodded in silence.

The city was quiet as Leila pedaled her bicycle to the Al-Razi Hospital. The Western clothes made riding her bicycle much easier. Her *hijab* fluttered loose about her head, ready to be taken off at the hospital. She had stopped wearing the head scarf some weeks ago, ever since that day when she wore her hair loose in front of James. The Americans treated her as more of an equal when she showed her hair, and she stopped getting those annoying looks of sympathy from her female colleagues, as though the *hijab* made Leila oppressed . . . which, she admitted, it sometimes did.

Without vehicle traffic on the roads, her commute was more peaceful, though it did not speak well for Mosul's prosperity. It was a wonder to Leila that all the shops did not just close up and dry out. But the shopkeepers kept opening their doors, and Leila suspected they would until they were dead, or received direct orders to stop. Khaled at the Afdhel Baqqal did his share of business; in times of war people still needed to buy rice and flour and cooking oil.

The bus to Diamondback was the same old bus, but security had been augmented around it. The waiting point was now surrounded with razor wire and big concrete blocks to prevent car bombers. It was conspicuous, and Leila could feel the stares of curious passersby as she stood in the line to board the vehicle. She dipped her head away; even if Tamir knew of her job, it didn't mean his mujahideen friends did, and she didn't want to take any chances. Leila had a feeling that the insurgency was not as organized as it appeared from a distance; just like the Americans and their intelligence, the mujahideen operated with each other on a need-to-know basis.

"Leila! There you are. Thank goodness," Dr. Whitaker said when Leila came into the field hospital that morning. "We wondered if you were okay."

"Yes, I am all right. Thank you." Leila smiled at Dr. Whitaker's concern.

"And your family?"

"Just fine," she said, looking away. "Fine."

"We've been busy," said Dr. Whitaker, nodding for her to follow him into the ward. "We've got several muj—sorry, security detainees, and they're not talking. Treated 'em the best we could, but can't explain what we're doing. So," he said, pushing open the door to the main ward, "good to have you back."

The hospital was more crowded than Leila had ever seen it. Almost every bed was filled, rows of the wounded, and a good fraction of these were ragged-looking jihadis. They could be identified not just by the miscellany of their clothing but by the plastic shackles that kept them confined to their beds.

"Goodness," she said.

"You've got your work cut out for you," said Dr. Whitaker. "I believe that one of the intelligence people is coming by to work with you on questioning them. Unfortunately that means you won't be helping us in the surgery today, but there's plenty of time for that later, huh?"

"Yes," said Leila, resigned to a long day of translating. She didn't want the jihadis to tell her anything of substance; the less she knew, the better. She was growing to dislike the feeling of being tugged at for information.

"Okay, kiddo. I'll be around." Dr. Whitaker clapped her on the shoulder, then removed his hand so that it hovered about six inches away. He lowered his awkward arm. "Sorry."

"Do not worry," said Leila, smiling at him so he knew she didn't take offense. And truly, she did not mind. Dr. Whitaker was just being a friend in his American way, and Americans were so touchy-feely. Leila had seen total strangers hug each other. It was bizarre to her, but sort of nice, too. Their mental hang-ups were not in the realm of male-female relations.

At least six nurses worked among the wounded, brisk and efficient in the face of pain. Several of the men had serious injuries, Leila saw. With cool eyes she moved her gaze over a soldier with extensive burns. His entire head was wrapped in gauze, with holes for the eyes and mouth. It made him look like a mummy. He was unmoving, under sedation, though he could not move while wrapped up like that even if he'd been able. The gauze turned yellow in places from the drainage of pus and burn treatment salve. He would be airlifted out soon.

She noticed that the nurses tended to the American side of things with greater attention, and in comparison the insurgents looked abandoned and resentful. Leila wandered along the ward, peeking behind the hanging privacy curtains and gazing into the faces of the wounded Iraqis to see if there was anyone she knew. She wondered if any of these men had done time living in her family's old well. None of the faces looked familiar, however, and she turned around to head back down the ward.

Leila stopped. Her shoes made a skidding noise on the linoleum floor. Sitting upright in the hospital bed opposite was James Cartwright. His eyes were closed, and his face turned to the right. Unexpected emotion threatened to overwhelm her. Forcing the worry down her throat, Leila assessed his condition in as professional a manner as she could. James had his left arm in a sling; from the dressing, Leila could tell it was a shoulder wound. Otherwise he seemed all right. She darted forward and grabbed his chart from its hanging place on the bed, reading it, parched for information.

Yes, there it was. Gunshot wound to the shoulder, clean, and slight bumps and bruises. On full course of antibiotics against infection. The wound took twenty stitches on both sides. Healing on schedule.

She exhaled a long, steady breath, and James's eyelids fluttered open.

"Hey," he said.

"Hi," she replied.

There was a moment of silence, in which Leila heard her father's voice:

The Americans bleed hot.

Her rage at her father rose to the surface once again, and she fought to compose herself in front of James. She sat down on the bed, and reached out to adjust the dressing on his shoulder. "You are wounded," she said, redundantly.

"Yeah," he said. "It's not a big deal, really. I'm just here to get the stitches checked."

"Shoulder wound," Leila said.

"The bullet passed in and out," said James. "It's just a scratch." He grinned at his own bravado.

"Silly," said Leila. She found that she did not want to take her hands away from his shoulder, away from him, but settled for resting them on the clean white cotton of the bedsheet. "What happened?"

"After the bombings—you know about them, right?"

"I heard them when I was coming home that day."

"Right. Well, anyway, we had to scramble out, of course. I was in one of the MP vehicles, and we got out on foot to flush some *muj* from an alley. They were up on the roofs across the street, too, and shooting down on us like fish in a barrel. They were bound to hit something, and my shoulder got it." He tried to shrug, then winced.

"Oh!" said Leila, reaching out again.

"It's all right," said James, and he took her hands from their position in midair. He held them longer than was necessary. "Hey, I want to say thank you again for the pastry. It was really good."

"You are most welcome," said Leila. She met his blue eyes, and decided they looked even more vivid in the combination of daylight and fluorescence in the hospital ward. "I think pastry is a better Iraqi Christmas gift than a bullet through the shoulder."

James laughed, causing a few of the nurses to glance over at them. "That's the gift I'll remember, then," he said.

For a moment Leila was tempted by honesty. She wanted to tell James about the new developments at home: her father's request, and her agreement to spy for the mujahideen. But something stilled her tongue as she sat there looking down at him. She wanted to keep the moment—and their relationship—innocent. Instead of hiding secrets, she imagined she had nothing to hide. Instead of a hospital ward, she imagined they were in a restaurant. Instead of a war wound, she imagined James had been injured by a kicking donkey. It was a flight of fancy, but it made it easier to laugh with him.

"So," said Leila, smoothing out a wrinkle in the sheet. "Have you written any stories about Iraq yet?" She smiled as she watched the surprise float across his face.

"How'd you know I write—who have you been talking to, Leila?" James smiled up at her.

"Fourteen years old, winning essay contests, according to the *News-Gazette* newspaper." She raised her eyebrows waiting for his response, letting it sink in.

"You Googled me!" James accused. "You did! Don't try to deny it, Leila al-Ghani."

"I can work in intelligence, too," she said, then wished she'd said something different, something further from the truth. "Actually, no. I was looking at old Virginia news for fun. It was pure, um—coincidence that I found your name."

"Likely story," James said. He sat up a little straighter on the hospital bed. His olive drab T-shirt stretched across his broad chest and arm muscles, and Leila tried not to look. It was difficult. The Special Forces had leeway as far as personal appearance was concerned; they could grow mustaches, have longer hair, and wear civilian clothes at will, in an effort to blend in with the population. James had taken advantage of the opportunity, and a lock of his dark brown hair curled over his forehead; she longed to brush it out of the way.

"So, did you go to university?" she asked.

"Yep. University of Virginia. I studied English literature. Far cry from what I'm doing now," he said.

"Literature. So you will be a writer?"

"I'd like to be, someday," said James. "Better than this war business. I've thought about writing mystery novels."

"Mysteries!" Leila exclaimed. "I read Robin Cook."

"Yeah?" James beamed at her. "His stuff is pretty good."

"It helps with my vocabulary."

"Your plan worked," said James. "Your English is fantastic."

"It is, isn't it?" Leila giggled at herself.

"And so humble about it you are," said James.

They gazed at each other for a good moment. All Quranic prohibitions against unmarried "gazing" fled from Leila's mind.

"Leila! I mean, Miss al-Ghani!" said a cheerful, ringing voice from behind her. She turned. There stood Travis Pratt, arms crossed and looking so smug that Leila wanted to run away. If this was who she was supposed to work with today . . .

"Yes," she said, sullen.

"You could be an American, girl! Keeping up the morale of the troops like this," said Pratt, rocking on his heels with amusement. Every one of his mannerisms seemed an affectation, like something he'd seen in a film and decided to imitate. It irritated Leila, and must have irritated James, too, for he swung his legs off the other side of the bed and stood up.

"Pratt. Nice to see you." James's tone made it clear it was anything but nice.

"Since you're incapacitated, Captain, my job today is to interrogate some of the *muj*. I was hoping Leila here might help me out."

"I'm not at all incapacitated," said James. "I was just having my stitches checked, and dressing changed. In fact, I know that Dr. Whitaker has Leila working on it. So if you don't mind . . ." James made a shooing motion.

A shadow of annoyance passed over Pratt's unremarkable face. "Really, Captain. One of the other nurses can do that. I need a translator. I have orders, just like you do, and just like Leila does. You wanna catch these guys, right? What if one of them"—he jerked his head toward the collection of wounded terrorists—"is the one that shot you?"

"I doubt that," said James. "Anyway, Jesus tells us to forgive." He smirked as though at a private joke.

"You Southerners," said Pratt, laughing. "Always proselytizing. Tell me, Leila, do you Muslims ever try to convert other people, you know, ask 'em if they've found Mohammed?"

"No," said Leila. "We always just converted people by pointing a sword at their throat. Would you like a demonstration?" She gave Pratt her most pleasant smile, and James stifled a laugh.

Pratt looked back and forth between the two, and his arrogant smile faded. "I need Miss al-Ghani to help translate. That's the way it is, James, old buddy. Find yourself another pretty nurse to flirt with. How about Quinn? She's always willing, as I think you know."

Leila narrowed her eyes at Pratt, a pinch of unexpected jealousy rising at Jessica Quinn's name. She followed Pratt away, tossing a regretful look back at James, who gave her a little wave with his fingers.

Chapter 15

The al-Ghani household was in an uproar. The day before a family wedding was always a nightmarish sequence of flowers, dresses, people, food, and things gone wrong. The normal custom for weddings in Mosul was a several-week affair of parties, showers, gift giving, and officiated ceremonies. Thirty years ago, the family might have come from all over the country for a wedding, creating a party of a thousand people, especially for a family as prominent as the al-Ghanis. But times had changed, and wedding parties were big targets for bombings and raids, so people were afraid to congregate, and travel was hazardous.

For Fatima's wedding, the flowers were picked off the trees of neighbors' gardens, and the dress was an embroidered, modified *abaya* of simple white muslin—the famed fabric named after the city of Mosul itself—that could be dyed to some dark, modest color after the wedding. The food was simple and the people were limited to close friends and relatives.

Umm Naji planned for about seventy people at the *Nishan*, the main reception after the ceremony. She kept a stiff upper lip for Fatima's sake, but everyone in the family knew she wished for a big, grand event, such as Naji's wedding had been. Everything would be restricted to family except her *Nishan* after the marriage; the *Arb't Ayam,* the four-days-after party, would be forgone altogether.

For her part, Leila was told to keep out of the way and bake some pastries. That she did with zeal, for she enjoyed baking, and she threw supportive glances and smiles at Fatima whenever she could. *Nishan* would be held on a Saturday so Leila would not have to work. With a tiny feeling of triumph, she noted that her own salary from the Americans helped pay for the party, for the food, for the dresses.

Though Leila was happy for her sister, she was also jealous of the fact that Fatima would be moving away from home. With Fatima moving out, Leila expected the full attention and overprotection of both Tamir and Umm Naji, and she dreaded it. It almost made her want to get married, since there appeared no other way to get out from under her father's thumb. Then Leila thought of spending life with Adbul, and she quickly banished the thought.

In the days before the wedding, time seemed to slow down, each moment packed with a million tasks. The sun moved across the sky, but no one noticed the long shadows. Fatima's face was a constant blush as her friends came for *shai* and went again, teasing Fatima about the imminent wedding night and making ribald remarks about Khaled. The day before the wedding was a Friday, which meant that the men were at mosque and the women left free to hold the *Laylit al-Henna*, the bridal shower.

Hala Rasul came bearing a lovely embroidered cushion for Fatima, courtesy of the women of the Rasul household, and pulled Leila aside for a moment. "I'm engaged again," she hissed in the corridor behind the crowded women's sitting room.

"What?" Leila asked, her eyes wide with gossip.

"Yes, to Rami Hamdoun. I didn't want to say anything to take away from Fatima's day, but it's being announced next week."

"Congratulations, Hala!" said Leila, squeezing her friend's hand.

"And my sister's about to ensnare that Kurdish boy, Rashid

Mehran," said Hala, her dark eyes glinting with fun. "Mother will have a conniption, but I don't care. I told her to be more open-minded, because then Souad can go north to Rashid's family, away from the violence here."

"Interesting," said Leila.

"Maybe tomorrow *you* will meet someone interesting, mmm, Leila?" Hala nudged her in the ribs and grinned. Leila remembered Naji telling stories of when he studied business at the university in Baghdad, and where men and women mixed as equals, and women did not even have to wear *hijab*. But that was all before the war. Now weddings were one of the few occasions where men and women could socialize together without censure.

"Meet someone, Hala? I think my parents would die of joy," said Leila. "They're already threatening to marry me off to my cousin Abdul." She dropped her voice to a whisper, for fear of Umm Naji overhearing her.

"Abdul? Is he the one that visited?"

"Yes," said Leila. "Short fingers."

"Small hands are never a good sign," said Hala.

Leila thought of James Cartwright and his solid, well-formed hands. She nearly said something to Hala about him and held her tongue before she blurted it out. It was hard not to speak of her crush to her friends and analyze every movement, every word, every glance. On the subject of James, Leila could have spoken for hours. But to tell anyone would complicate matters even more.

"Who are you thinking about?" Hala asked, interrupting Leila's thoughts. "It cannot be Abdul."

"I'm not thinking about anyone, Hala!"

"You might lie to your parents and my parents, but you can't lie to me, Leila al-Ghani! I think you're in love."

"Don't be absurd," Leila said, feeling the heat rise in her cheeks. "Come on, let us go back inside before anyone misses us." She pulled Hala by the arm back into the ladies' sitting room. A woman had been hired to paint Fatima's hands with henna designs; with her needle-thin brush and pots of henna paste, she made delicate lacelike designs on Fatima's pale skin. Fatima was basking in the attention of the other women who gathered around her, exclaiming over the beauty of the design. Fatima's nails were already painted with red nail varnish and they gleamed like rubies. Leila, glancing down at her own bitten nails, wrinkled her nose at the sight of an orangish antiseptic stain on her palm that refused to go away.

"Look," she said to Hala, showing her hand, "we get designs at the hospital, too."

"Not the same," said Hala. "We should have our fingers painted while we can. A simple design will take just an hour or two."

"All right," said Leila, plopping down next to Fatima with a grin. She'd had her hands hennaed once before, as a treat when she was a child at Naji's bride's *Laylit* party. Because Leila's skin was darker than her sister's, it did not show up as well, but the effect was still pretty.

Several hours of chat later, and when Hala and Leila had the fingers and palms of each hand covered in flowerlike designs of henna paint, the other women left the al-Ghani house in plenty of time to be locked safe away before sunset. The last to leave was elderly Umm Mohammed, who lived next door. Once the house was empty of guests, Leila, Fatima, and their mother swept around the room, stacking used teacups and tossing pillows back to their preordained places on the sofas.

"I have a present for you," Leila whispered to Fatima. "Let's help clean and then go upstairs."

Fatima nodded agreement and filled her arms with the last of the teacups. Umm Naji chattered away with the gossip she'd learned that afternoon, oblivious of Leila's smirks and rolling eyes. When the kitchen sparkled and the food for the next day was set in the refrigerator, prepped and ready to cook, Leila and Fatima dressed in their nightgowns and settled into Fatima's room for a talk. A sort of finality loomed in Leila's mind; this might be the last heart-to-heart she would have with her sister for a very long time. Marriage stole sisters away. Leila tried to keep her heart light and happy for Fatima's sake.

In her arms she carried a bundle wrapped in newspaper. "These are for you," she told Fatima. "I thought you might use them." She could hardly contain her giggles as she settled down next to her sister on the narrow single bed.

"What's this?" Fatima asked, unwrapping the package. A stack of glossy magazines spilled out of her hands. She gasped. "*Cosmopolitan!*" Fatima said, running her fingers over the cover. Her eyes shone with mischief and gratitude, an odd combination in her plain, balanced features.

"I got them for you from the Americans at the base," said Leila. "As a little wedding gift."

It had taken some doing to procure the five issues of *Cosmopolitan* women's magazine. First Leila had fished around the stack of magazines in the tiny reception area of the field hospital, finding only military-life magazines and some old issues of *National Geographic*. Then she'd kept an eye out in the staff room and elsewhere, thinking the nurses might leave something around. In the end, Leila had approached the ever-intimidating Nurse Jessica Quinn.

"I was wondering," Leila had said, standing with Quinn during one of the pretty nurse's frequent smoking breaks, "about American magazines."

"What about 'em?" Quinn had asked.

"My sister is getting married," said Leila. Because it was for Fatima's sake, she was bolder than she might have been otherwise. "We have heard about American magazines for women. Fatima is a virgin. But she wants to teach her new husband about sex."

Quinn had laughed loudly at that. "And you think I'm the kind of girl who would have issues of *Cosmo* lying around here?"

"Er . . . yes?" Leila said.

"You're right. I am." Quinn took a last quick drag on her

cigarette and ground it into the dust with her heel. "They're the best. Advice on sex, on makeup and fashion and everything a girl needs. You should take a look through them, too, Leila."

"Thanks," said Leila, repressing annoyance at the implication that she needed fashion advice. "Do you have some old copies that you do not use anymore? That I might give to my sister?"

"Sure," said Quinn. The next day, the nurse brought in five issues of the magazine, from May through September of the previous year, and handed them to Leila with a grin. "Don't get too carried away with the 'Cosmo Sutra' sections," she'd said. Leila did not know what Quinn meant until she thumbed through the magazines herself when she got home that night.

On the eve of the wedding, Leila pointed out the contents of the magazines to Fatima, whose eyes widened in guilty curiosity. "You do not think Khaled will find me . . . forward, do you? For knowing these things?"

"You know men," said Leila. "They never pay attention to anything. If he notices your expertise, just say you learned it from Mama. Or better yet, from Scheherazade."

With a snort of laughter, Fatima muffled her voice with a pillow. "From Mama. Who told me to lie flat on my back and think about becoming pregnant."

Leila laughed so hard the tears rolled down her cheeks, and Fatima laughed with her. Leila grabbed one of the magazines, a well-thumbed copy from August featuring a popular American actress with a sultry smile on the cover. She rolled it up and let it flop out again. "You're going to love these," she said to Fatima. "It's not just love advice . . . it's all about how to be modern."

Leila found the fashion pages most interesting. The artful poses of the models and their strange, wonderful, expensive clothing caught her eye and she could not help seeing herself in a tight cashmere sweater or diaphanous short skirt. She placed her hand, adorned with henna designs, against the foreign gleam of the page, wishing she could be that contemporary woman who never worried about mortars or arranged marriage. She closed her eyes for a moment and she saw herself sitting at an outdoor café in some vague Western city, drinking coffee in broad daylight and wearing high heels.

"Now, Fatima," Leila said, turning serious. "I want to hear the details. Not right away, I will give you time to adjust, but I want to know about married life! I could never ask Mama."

"Of course!" said Fatima. "I will tell you how it is. And thank you for these magazines. They'll help me. And," she giggled, "they will help Khaled, too. He just doesn't know it yet."

The gravity of the next day settled upon Leila again. Fatima was getting married, leaving their home forever, assuming a new name and a new identity as the "wife of Khaled." Leila swallowed. She wanted to confess her secrets to Fatima while they were still loyal as deepest sisters, before Fatima entered into the drudgery of keeping her own home. She tugged at her lower lip and gazed down at the floor from her cross-legged position on the bed. "Fatima," she said, "do you remember back in October? When we were stuck at the Rasuls' house after curfew, and there was an American raid, and they searched the house?"

"Of course," said Fatima.

"Do you remember the American soldiers? There was a big bulky one, and then there was a tall man with very blue eyes. Do you remember him?"

"Yes . . ." said Fatima, looking confused.

"His name is James Cartwright," whispered Leila.

Fatima raised her eyebrows in surprise. "Leila—"

"He is a captain in the American army. He is my friend."

"Does Father know?"

"No!" Leila exclaimed; then she lowered her voice. "No. He's allowing me to continue work at the hospital, but I must keep the personal details away from him—that I've made friends. If he knew I was speaking with the Americans, talking with men, then it would be too much for him. You must swear to secrecy, Fatima!"

"You have many secrets for a person so young," Fatima said. "You're always telling me these things, and then asking me to keep quiet!"

"I had to tell someone," Leila said miserably. "And besides, you don't need to keep it a secret that I work at Diamondback." After Tamir's discovery of Leila's true job, it was open in the family, although Leila had to keep quiet about her espionage on the Americans. Fatima and Umm Naji knew nothing about that, and thought Tamir had mellowed in his attitude toward Leila. Family conversation was a tangled knot of covert sentences.

"What's he like?" Fatima asked. "I shouldn't be curious about the Americans but I am."

"They're not devils the way *Baba* talks about them," said Leila. "James—er—Captain Cartwright is such a good man. He's very kind, you see. He watches out for my welfare."

"Is he married like the surgeons?"

"Oh!" Leila said.

"You have not discovered if he is married?" Fatima asked. "Leila, really! He might have a wife and children in America!"

"He does not wear a wedding ring," Leila said, but it sounded plaintive to her ears. Many of the married soldiers did not wear wedding rings because they were in a war zone, and during hand-to-hand combat a ring on the finger could break the knuckles.

"That is the first thing you should discover," said Fatima, shaking her finger at Leila. "If you are going to like this man, do so within the bounds of propriety."

"You sound like Mother," Leila said. She made a face. She had hoped for more support from Fatima. She wanted someone, anyone, to tell her it was all right to have feelings for an American man.

But Leila knew that the feelings of warmth that sprang up whenever James was around would bring nothing but ruin. The Quran was clear about the rules of marriage for a *Mus-*

limiyah, a woman follower of Islam. She had to marry another Muslim, and that was that. The reason was simple: a woman subordinated herself to her husband, and it was forbidden to subordinate to a non-Muslim. To do so would make Leila an apostate, the worst sort of person, and apostasy was a crime punishable by death.

There had been cases of it before, of *Muslimiyahs* marrying Western men, Christians, and fleeing their countries in fear of death. She remembered one instance of a Saudi princess, beheaded in public for the crime. Leila had no doubts about her own family: given his new political leanings, Tamir al-Ghani would kill her himself if she went off with an American.

The solution to the problem would be for the man to convert to Islam. But Leila doubted there was much incentive in that. Most of the time, she did not even like her own religion, and to sell it to someone else would be difficult. And to sell it to an American soldier, who had been shot through the shoulder by Muslim extremists . . . the idea was laughable.

Besides, Leila was not sure about James's feelings in the first place. Theirs was a tentative friendship, and just because she baked Christmas pastries for the man did not mean he was her future husband. She decided to banish the thought from her mind; too much fixation on marriage made Leila feel like her mother. She would enjoy the time she spent with James, and that was all. That was how they did it in the West, right? Had coffee, talked as equals, gave thoughtful holiday gifts. Leila could be modern, too, and modernity started with attitude.

The girls read through the magazines together for another hour or so, but Leila was restless. No matter how much she wanted to pretend this was just another normal night with Fatima, the air between them was heavy with Leila's revealed secret, and Fatima's imminent change in marital status.

"Well, I guess you'd better get some sleep," Leila said. "Big day tomorrow."

"Yes," said Fatima. "Big day."

They looked at each other but said nothing. What more could be said in this awkward space of farewell? Leila hugged her sister good night and closed the door softly behind her.

The next day, Saturday, dawned sunny for Fatima's wedding. The ceremony itself, the *Mahar,* would take place in the al-Ghani sitting room, and the papers would be signed there and the vows taken in front of the imam. Then the *Nishan* would be held at the Mosul Officers' Club, the organization for city officials to which Tamir al-Ghani belonged. The club had a function room that could hold about one hundred people, and it was decorated at the expense of the al-Ghani family. Once again, Leila felt grateful for her hospital job. Even her parents had to admit it was nice to have Leila's income. Fervent politics did not buy food.

Leila wore her best *abaya* for the wedding, a dark silk-cashmere blend dress that had little flowers embroidered in matching black and gold along the edges. At the center of some of the flowers were tiny white pearl beads. She wore a thin head scarf with an elegant drape about her face; it looked almost like black hair. She'd fixed her battered nails herself that morning in a French style, tiny white crescents at the ends of thin fingers, and Leila took a moment to gaze down in admiration. Her steady hands in the laboratory and the surgery meant that painting her nails was never a challenge. The lacy dark henna added a pleasant effect and made her hands appear even thinner and more feminine than they were. Finally, Leila put in some solid gold hoop earrings, which had been a gift for her sixteenth birthday, and wore a set of matching gold bangle bracelets. The effect was almost fashionable.

Only the bride and groom's families would be witnesses to the *Mahar* ceremony itself. The other guests would arrive at the Officers' Club on their own, for no one wanted to take responsibility for transportation in these treacherous times. Leila went into Fatima's room to help her dress, and both girls were uncharacteristically quiet. Fatima bit her lip and twisted her hands together and could not stop playing with the strands of hair that fell to her ears as she gazed into the face mirror mounted on her wall.

"Stop that fidgeting, Fatima," said Umm Naji, taking up a large volume of space and wielding a small needle to cinch in the dress at the proper places. "And you've stopped eating this week. Look how thin you are, skin and bones! Best not let Khaled see you before he makes the vows."

"Thin is popular now, Mama," said Leila just to be contrary.

Umm Naji clucked disapproval. "In the West, maybe. In Iraq, a girl should have some meat on her bones. Otherwise she looks no better than a starving person."

"I think she looks beautiful," said Leila.

Fatima stayed quiet, the shy bride.

When Fatima left her bedroom a few minutes later, trailed by their mother, Leila stood in the middle of the room gazing at the door, still as a statue. She caught a glimpse of herself in the mirror, a woman with forlorn eyes and a sad mouth. Fatima was Leila's last ally and confidante at home and now she was leaving. Of course, Leila would visit Fatima at the home of Khaled, but it would not be the same. Leila sighed and followed the sound of the footsteps down the hall.

Khaled was downstairs in the sitting room, drinking tea with Tamir and Naji and a few other assorted cousins and uncles. They were all men aside from Umm Naji and Leila; Tamir, in a sudden burst of forward thinking, had insisted that they be allowed to watch the proceedings, too. Cousin Abdul, praise Allah, was not in attendance. The imam sat on a chair with a Quran open in his lap, slumped over a little bit and with his belly protruding over the edge of the book.

Leila took the chance to study the imam in detail. She had only ever seen him while serving tea or food, or heard his voice through the crack in the sitting room wall. Nothing about

Abdul-Hakam was impressive. His eyes were rheumy and brown, his posture was loose, and his mouth was a thin line that looked forever turned-down. He frowned upon the wedding party with a sort of distaste. Leila imagined that a jihadist would find weddings annoying; too much happiness in the world led to complacency. The imam cultivated rage as other men might cultivate olive trees.

Khaled and Fatima stood together in the sitting room, each afraid to look the other in the eye, as the imam began reciting the verses that would make their marriage official. Tamir, still the judge, had a stack of legal documents that bound the two together in matrimony. The imam asked Fatima if she accepted the terms of the marriage.

"Do you, Fatima *bint* Tamir al-Ghani, agree to marry Khaled *bin* Abdullah al-Ramzi?"

Fatima was silent.

The imam asked again.

Smiles began to break out among the men; the more times the imam asked and the more times she did not answer, the more it meant the al-Ghani family wanted to keep their daughter. Tamir would have told the imam ahead of the ceremony how many times to ask Fatima. Leila smiled, too, although she felt that if she'd been in Fatima's place she might be asked just once by the imam.

As the imam asked and asked, and the smiles turned to outright laughter, after nine times the red-faced Fatima said, "Yes."

"Finally!" Khaled said.

The dowry was settled, the vows taken, and Fatima became the property of her husband. The dowry was substantial by standards of the day in Mosul, and Leila did not know of any other recently married woman who brought so much to the marriage. It included a piece of land just outside town that edged the Tigris River, a modest sum of dinars, some furniture, pillows, and linens, clothing, three baby fig trees, and a herd of goats in a village to the north that were tended by Umm Naji's relatives. Khaled was coming away with a steal, and from his satisfied expression upon reading the terms of the marriage, he knew it.

Then Khaled and Fatima smiled at each other in relief, Fatima blushed on cue, and Tamir embraced his new son-in-law. Over Khaled's shoulder, Tamir met Leila's eye. Something behind his pale umber gaze told Leila that he had plans for her. Tamir glanced at the imam, and Abdul-Hakam turned his watery eyes onto Leila. She met his cold stare for a few seconds before looking down at her feet. The approval in the imam's face disturbed her. He knew of her work for the Americans, she was certain.

The strange moment was forgotten in the hubbub that came after the vows. Leila's cousin, Sami the taxi driver, showed up to help ferry people to the Officers' Club, and Tamir himself drove the women of the family in the al-Ghani car. The car was about five years old, a Toyota sedan painted brown, and the inside smelled of herbs. Umm Naji liked to hang dried mint from the dashboard to disperse the dusty air. Since no one had driven the car in some weeks, the mint was very dry indeed, and the smell was stale but strong.

Leila stared out the window on the short drive to the party, seeing the reflection of her face on the glass against Mosul City. There were few vehicles on the road, but plenty of pedestrians and goats. There were no cars parked in front of buildings anymore, because if a large vehicle stopped for any length of time, someone would ask the driver to move. Too many large vehicles turned out to be bombs.

Leila sent a quick prayer to Allah and the angels that her sister's wedding be exempt from violence this day.

The Officers' Club of Mosul was on a spacious stretch of road near their home neighborhood. Tamir dropped the women off at the door and Leila clasped Fatima's hand as they went inside. From the corner of her eye, she saw Tamir drive off to park the car on the shoulder of the road, away from any buildings. Then she turned from the glare of the winter sunshine into the darkness of the hall.

The music was already going, high trilling notes of Arabic pop music, tinny over the aging speakers. It was exciting music, designed to arouse the senses and create celebration. Leila felt her hips wanting to move in time with the dance. She released Fatima's hand with a smile and spotted Hala and Souad Rasul, giggling together across the room. She gave a wave and walked toward them.

Hala did a little shake of her hips, a move that would have been forbidden anywhere in mixed company except a wedding. Leila suspected that the world over, wedding parties were an excuse to get other young, eligible people to meet each other, the friends of the bride and groom. Leila laughed at Hala and embraced her.

"Trying to entice your man Hamdoun?" Leila teased.

"He has already fallen for me," said Hala. "He is going to speak to Father this week."

"Oooh!" Leila said.

"And Rashid!" Souad piped up from next to Hala. "I will become Kurdish. Our babies will have blue eyes."

"Congratulations, Souad!" Leila said to the younger girl. "But you know, brown-eyed genes are dominant. So your babies will have your brown eyes."

Souad shrugged with teenage indignation. "There's an exception to every rule, Leila."

Leila gave an indulgent smile to the girl. Souad and Rashid's babies would have brown eyes, but a wedding party was not the place to explain the principles of genetics. She wished she could shake the feeling of being older, wiser, and very much single in comparison to Souad Rasul. Instead she grabbed Hala's hand.

"Let's dance," she said.

"You're my girl!" said Hala.

They danced together for a while, conscious of the looks of

the men around the room. Some perverse instinct in Leila wondered what they would do if she showed up wearing a tight-fitting sweater and a short chiffon skirt, like in the American magazine, and she entertained herself for a moment with the thought of the look on Umm Naji's face. *Someday*, she thought, *when I'm somewhere else, I'm going to wear that outfit and take a picture and send it to Mama and* Baba. She smiled at the room around her.

Fatima and Khaled danced together, not really touching, and Leila cringed. A man and his new wife should want to touch each other, not suffer from anxiety. Leila willed Khaled to just hold Fatima's hand, for heaven's sake, and quit shuffling his feet. Fatima looked lovely in her white dress; it made her skin glow dark against it, and because she was a bride her hair was left uncovered and fixed in an elegant coif. It shone under the lights of the hall because of the large amount of hair spray Umm Naji had insisted upon.

There was no violence at Fatima's *Nishan* party and for that, at least, Leila was grateful. When she returned home that evening, muscles sore from dancing, it was to a desolate house. Leila felt her parents' eyes on the back of her head after she bade them good night and retreated up the stairs . . . perhaps they were wondering when it would be her turn for marriage. The party had been fun, and Leila enjoyed seeing Hala, but she was filled with a sense of loss at Fatima's empty bedroom across the hall from her own. When she switched off her lamp before sleep, she could not help releasing a despondent sigh.

Chapter 16

Home was quiet in the aftermath of Fatima's wedding. For several days the refrigerator was full of leftover food from the party, but it disappeared with suspicious rapidity. Leila kept a nighttime vigil over the well in the courtyard, and there were always noises, which meant the mujahideen benefited from Fatima's wedding, too, in the form of pastries.

As anticipated, Tamir got worse with Fatima gone. Leila felt his eyes watching her all the time, keeping tabs, plotting. It gave her the feeling of a pawn on a chessboard. And Umm Naji did not help, for she did nothing but talk about Fatima's imminent pregnancy now that she was married. Leila thought that if her mother wanted Fatima to be pregnant so soon, she ought to have sent Fatima off into the desert with Khaled even prior to the wedding, but when Leila said as much at dinner one night, she earned herself a sharp word from Umm Naji and disapproving looks from both parents.

Leila's days at the hospital were the best part of her life: translating for the surgeons, assisting in surgery, helping the nurses, and Whitaker and Peabody often gave her independent tasks because she could be trusted with them. Once in a while one of the military intelligence officers would come to the hospital to question the mujahideen, and it was Leila's job to translate for them, too; her father's orders were to disguise any real information the wounded mujahideen might betray. In reality, Leila rarely had to do this, for many of the insurgents did not know anything useful to begin with. The military interrogators were always frustrated. Leila did not help them out very much, but she did not purposefully obfuscate their questioning, either. Then she returned home to tell her father about how nothing had been said. She walked a fine line every day.

She saw James sometimes, but not as often as she'd have liked. He seemed busy and distracted whenever she spoke to him, and often he was with someone else like that obnoxious Pratt person from civilian intelligence. Leila avoided James on those occasions.

The weather stayed cold in January and Leila wore her warm wool *abayas* to work, every day more conscious of the difference between her clothing and that of the other nurses. It was not just the occasional dissimilarity of attire, for sometimes Leila wore trousers; it was the way the American nurses walked and talked with confidence. They held their heads high and their shoulders straight and weren't afraid to roll their hips a little when they walked.

Leila began contemplating the purchase of some tight Western-style jeans. Her parents never said anything about her garb, ever since her rational argument with Tamir that to dress like the Americans meant trust from the Americans. She worked on her posture, keeping her shoulders stiff and proud, remembering some of the women at Cairo University who had careers and beautiful clothing. Every day at the field hospital she felt more like a potential doctor and a woman of the world, a feeling divorced from the hunkered-down existence she had at home. As the days went on, Leila al-Ghani became two people. It was more and more difficult to shed her "work" self when she bicycled home in the evening.

One night a few weeks after Fatima's wedding Leila returned from work and found the al-Ghani home in the dark. The power was out again, and the house looked aloof in the twilight. She could hear her parents' voices drifting outside from the sitting room. The front porch was dusty and little drifts of sandy dirt had built up around the columns, probably from the foot traffic of mujahideen coming through the house. Leila retrieved the reed broom from the kitchen pantry and went to sweep the porch herself.

She whisked the broom back and forth, sending gravel and dirt skittering off the cement and into the front drive. Leila remembered the days when they had hired help. When her father was a judge and a party official, in good with the local power thugs, and had an income enviable for the rest of sanctions-crippled Iraq.

It was fully dark when Leila finished sweeping and entered the house.

"Leila." It was her father, standing in the arched doorway of the sitting room. His tone was that of his nightly summons.

Just as arriving at the field hospital in the mornings was the best part of Leila's day, arriving home was the worst. It meant the "debriefing," as Leila thought of it, by her father about the operations of the Americans. Months ago she might have welcomed the dedicated conversations with her unstable father, but now they filled her with guilt. With every word she spoke to Tamir about the Americans, she wondered if it would get someone killed, someone she knew. Every day it was something sensitive . . . which gate the patrols used to get in and out of Camp Marez, the operations base. The security procedures with the bus she took. A lie about how she didn't know the names of her fellow Iraqi workers.

Umm Naji hustled out of the sitting room with raised eyebrows at Leila. Leila wondered if her mother knew about the listening post by the hole in the wall; she must, for Umm Naji was a relentless gossip.

Leila sat on the floor next to the table with her legs tucked beneath her. The carpet was soft and clean even after centuries of use by the al-Ghani family. Her mother had left a pot of hot *shai* on its engraved metal serving tray and Leila poured herself a cup, wrapping her hand around the small glass to relish the warmth of it. The sugary tea took the edge off debriefing.

Tamir sat down and Leila could hear the creak of his bones.

She glanced up at him. There were new wrinkles around his eyes and new gray hairs in his beard. His hands, which he now clasped and unclasped like a nervous habit, were cracked with dry skin and the nails looked jaundiced. Insurgency was hard work. *It will get him killed*, Leila thought, and was taken aback by her lack of reaction to the idea.

"Tell me what happened at the base today," Tamir said.

Those words were how he always started their evening talks. "There were three mujahideen in the hospital," Leila said. "They say their names are Hamid, Da'ud, and Omran. No surnames that they have told the Americans. One has a wounded leg, a bullet wound. That's Omran. And Hamid is unconscious with burns from an explosion; he has not been able to say anything at all. Da'ud is ill-tempered with his hand blown off."

"What do the Americans think of them?"

Leila tried not to roll her eyes. "They give them biscuits and Coca-Cola, Father. What do you think?"

"I mean, dear *daughter*, what do the Americans know about their positions within the mujahideen?" Tamir snarled.

Leila looked straight at him, unfazed by his tone. His only power over her would be to ban her from working at Diamondback, and she knew there was no way he would do that now. Not while she was valuable. "The Americans are clueless," she said, telling the truth. "They're still trying to figure Sunni from Shia. Father, I've never even had to mistranslate yet, for the mujahideen are well trained not to speak."

A ghost of a smile crossed Tamir's face. "I see," he said. "There's something else you must do, Leila. This is all fine, the way you watch and listen. But I want more specific information. If we pursue the Americans individually, it will scare them out of Mosul, because they have courage only in numbers. I want names."

"Oh," Leila said in a small voice. She'd hoped to avoid anything like this. There was too much responsibility in naming names. It was easy to tell her father how many mujahideen were in the hospital and what kind of wounds they had. That was harmless, almost public information. But Leila knew what would happen if she gave out specific names of specific Americans.

Just as the Americans had their "deck of cards" with prominent Saddam loyalists and various terrorists assigned as the Ace of Spades, or the King of Diamonds, the mujahideen had their lists, too. There were lists of American workers and soldiers and intelligence officers working in the holy territory of Islam, along with listed bounties for whoever killed them. To Leila's slight amusement, the bounties were always stated in U.S. dollars.

But there was nothing amusing about the Americans on the "kill" list. The names would go on pro-jihadist Web sites that sprang up like mushrooms; most insurgents communicated via the Internet. They had to get their information from somewhere . . . and it was from informants like Leila.

"Names, Leila!" Tamir repeated.

"Oh," she said again. "Yes, well, Father, these are doctors that I work with. They never leave the field hospital and even if they did, they would help us and not hurt us!"

"Not the doctors, you silly girl. The intelligence officers. I know they leave the base. What about the Special Forces? They're always causing us troubles. The Stryker Brigade is easy enough to handle; they cower in their vehicles and never come out. Pathetic. But it's the military police, the Special Forces, the civilian contractors that we want. They venture into our streets and into our homes. You have been in homes during raids and searches, Leila, you know how brutal they are!"

She nodded weakly. She had never seen brutality for herself; the only raid she'd ever experienced had been at the Rasuls' house when she first saw James. But there were other stories of people she knew, people who were shot during house raids for no reason, or beaten or kicked or dragged away in a hood without charge or warrant. "I can give you a name," she said, hating herself for it.

"Well?" Tamir said.

"He is an officer with the CIA. The American civilian agency. His name is Travis Pratt."

"Travis Pratt," Tamir repeated, struggling with the English syllables.

Leila felt a little sick to her stomach. She did not know what would come of it; probably nothing. She'd given Pratt's name because he did not seem the type to ever go wandering outside the logistics base into dangerous territory where he might be kidnapped or murdered. She did not like him as a person. But even with this revelation, she felt herself dig a little deeper into the muddy, bloody pit of her father's politics.

Tamir reached out with one of his delicate aged hands and cupped Leila's cheek. In a rapid turnaround from his sour mood, his face softened. "You will have great rewards for this, my little nightingale," he said. "Great rewards."

"Thank you, *Baba*," said Leila. She was unable to look at his face for a moment longer and dropped her eyes to the familiar carpet.

Leila spent a sleepless night tossing and turning, filled with guilt. The next morning dawned fresh and new with no violence in Mosul. Leila dressed in black trousers and shiny black shoes and a cream-colored cashmere sweater, Western-style.

February would begin the next day and Leila wanted January to end on a good note, so she remembered to pray to Allah during her morning bicycle ride. Leila had no idea if her prayers would be answered (they most often were not), but it didn't hurt to have the right mind-set and expect a good day. She also prayed not to run into Travis Pratt; she didn't think she could look him in the eye. Without even thinking she swerved out of the way to avoid a herd of goats, her mind catapulting forward to her day at work. She was a girl who lived in the future most of the time. The present was unbearable.

The other women who worked at the American base gave Leila looks of either respect or disapproval as she boarded the bus, because of the way she was dressed; ten years ago it would have been unremarkable. After the war Iraqi women had begun to retreat into the strict wardrobe mandates of the hadith. It was safer that way with all the men going crazy. It made Leila angry, just as it made many Iraqi women angry, but what could they do? In Mosul, the American bases were the few areas where Western dress for women was accepted and expected.

When she arrived at the hospital, Dr. Whitaker put her to work in the supply room filling IV bags with morphine, a delicate process, for the dosage had to be just right. The army did not want any morphine addicts on their hands. It was such a joy to work in a place where the supplies were abundant and there was no shortage of the basics, such as aspirin and antibiotics and needles. After the bare-bones pharmacy of the Al-Razi Hospital, the difference was like night and day. Leila thought that if the Americans wanted to make a good impression on the local population, they would share their medical supplies freely and publicly. It might stem the tide of hostile feeling and alienation among the ordinary citizens of Mosul.

Helicopter blades hummed overhead, and she hummed along with them as she worked, turning the sound into a replay of the Arabic dance music that had played at Fatima's wedding. The noise of military hardware was so common that she almost did not notice it anymore. Even the bombardment of mortars was a faint worry at the back of her mind. The field hospital was strong enough to withstand them, unlike some of the residential hooches, which were flimsy white prefab things.

"Hey, Leila," said one of the nurses, jumping into the supply room for a pack of saline drip.

Leila turned and saw one of the younger nurses, a curvy woman with blond hair and a quick smile. She racked her brain for the name—all these Americans looked alike to her—and remembered: Bonnie Klein. "Hello, Bonnie," Leila said aloud to help her recall the name in the future.

"What's that you're singing?" Bonnie asked.

"An Arabic song," said Leila, topping off the liquid plastic bag full of painkiller. "It is by Hossam Ramzy. Very popular."

"Oh," said Bonnie.

Leila smiled down at the counter. The nurses were funny.

Sometime they acted as if they were at summer camp, a very perilous one, and did not make much of an effort to understand the Iraqi culture. For all the mortar rounds and occasional explosions, they might as well have been in America. She had yet to meet a single nurse who spoke a word of Arabic, or knew any Arabic singers or film stars, or even had an inkling about the foundations of the Muslim religion. The doctors were a bit more educated; Dr. Whitaker often liked to make comparisons between Islam and Christianity and how they were similar in many ways. He was too busy to have long conversations with, however; Leila took every word with him as a blessing.

She turned and started humming to herself again, thinking she was alone, and at the right place in the song did a little roll of her hips. She murmured the words and artfully dipped the bottle of morphine to and fro in time to the music in her head.

"Do you know how to belly dance?" asked an astonished-sounding Nurse Bonnie from the doorway.

Leila turned, startled, and looked into Bonnie's wide blue eyes. "Oh! I did not know you were still here."

"Can you belly dance?" Bonnie asked again. "I mean, if you can, then . . . wow."

"Every Arab girl knows how to belly dance," said Leila. It came out more condescending than she meant. "The basics, at least. Some are better than others." She shrugged.

"Jessica!" Bonnie called to Nurse Quinn, who was walking past the supply room. Quinn poked her head in. "Leila knows how to belly dance."

"No way!" Quinn said.

"Way," Leila responded with the Western phrase she'd heard the nurses use so many times.

"Dude, can you teach us?" Quinn asked.

"Yeah!" Bonnie said.

"Oh, I, um—" Leila blinked back and forth between the two women, each of whom had an eager and hopeful expression on her pale face. She did not want to disappoint them. And if she were truthful with herself, Leila wanted to be popular among the

American women. She'd always been a popular girl in school and it was a nice feeling. "I can teach you some moves, I think."

"Yesss!" Quinn pumped her fist. "Thanks, Leila! You're awesome."

"Hey, she can teach a class," said Bonnie, speaking to Quinn. "Like with all of us. We can have it in the gym."

"Oh, good idea," said Quinn. "We can use that exercise room. The empty one. I've heard belly dancing is a really good workout."

"*I've* heard it helps in other areas," Bonnie said, nudging Quinn with an elbow. "It's the same movement, you know. Drives guys wild. You can use it, *Baby Doll.*" The two nurses laughed together.

Teaching Bonnie and Quinn to dance was one thing, but the idea of an entire class made Leila nervous . . . yet she didn't want to back out. So she stood like an outsider on a private joke between American girls, hands resting on the counter in front of her and her head turned, waiting.

Quinn turned to Leila, her eyes gleaming. "We would love if you'd teach us, Leila," she said, looking Leila direct in the face. "Please?"

"All right," said Leila.

The word spread fast among the female nurses and by the end of the day Leila had twenty women asking to learn belly dancing. She could not say no. After she'd secured permission from Dr. Peabody, who chuckled a bit, it was decided that Leila would teach an hour-long class the next afternoon at 1500 in the gymnasium at the Morale, Welfare, and Recreation Center on base. Although Leila had no idea what she was doing—her belly dancing was reserved for silly moments with Fatima and Hala—it filled her with smiles to be sought after by the American women. The invisible culture barrier might be broken; Leila might become real friends with them.

When she got home that night and told her father about the ongoing medical status of the mujahideen in the field hospital, Leila left out the part about giving dance lessons.

Chapter 17

The gymnasium at Diamondback was nice, outfitted to the max with weight machines, cardio machines, a basketball court, and heaps of sporting equipment glinting beneath fluorescent lights. There were several exercise rooms and even a nice room with windows and a wall of mirrors, like a dance studio. It was this mirrored space that the women of the 67th CSH commandeered for Leila's dance classes.

She walked between Quinn and Bonnie from the field hospital to the large gym at 1445. It was amazing to Leila how natural she felt among them. Perhaps that culture barrier was a wispy thing, thin and easily broken. The trio was trailed by eight other nurses; not all of the staff at the hospital could take the afternoon to learn sultry dance moves. Leila would teach the rest of them the next day. The gym was filled with soldiers lifting weights and running on the cardio machines. They were almost all men, but there were a few women in track pants and the standard-issue khaki T-shirts. The parade of nurses got quite a few stares and one or two ripe comments from the male soldiers sweating it out on the main floor of the gym. Leila's cheeks burned from the comments, but the other women just laughed and smiled and waved.

Once in the mirrored room, Leila swallowed her intimidation. This was not hard, they were all women, and she knew she was good at dancing. She and Hala had practiced belly dancing together since they were little girls watching it on television. Still, to stand up in front of ten American women . . . Leila did not know what they were expecting. But she would try her best in the spirit of fun.

She handed a CD to Quinn, who'd brought a portable stereo player for the music. Leila had chosen a copy of a popular series of dance songs. She cleared her throat.

"All right," she said, and the women stopped their giggling and talking to listen.

"Everyone quiet!" said Quinn. In her sweet voice, even a command sounded like a suggestion.

"Thank you," said Leila. "I will teach you the basic moves of belly dancing. First I must tell you—these moves are not meant to seduce men. They are usually performed in gatherings of women, with mothers and sisters and friends, and this dance celebrates friendship." Leila's throat was dry as ten pairs of American eyes trained on her, listening. A sudden, wild doubt in her English-speaking abilities came and went, and Leila plunged ahead. *Just keep talking.* "I will start by telling you the fundamental movements, and showing you; then we practice together. So . . . um . . . sit down, please."

The women sat in a loose semicircle around Leila. With a flourish, Leila pulled her dancing scarf, a pretty dark purple sash with jangling metal beads and coins sewn onto it, out of her handbag. The women gasped and grinned on cue. "This," said Leila, "is the traditional belly scarf to be worn. It is very sensitive to motion, see?" She shook the scarf a little, and the movement rippled through the fabric, sending the metal pieces clinking and dancing against one another. "And without the scarf, the belly dance is just shaking your hips a bit."

Laughter.

Leila kicked off her shoes and tied the scarf around her hips over the top of her black trousers. "Now I am a belly dancer. I will give demonstration. Please, Jessica, could you start the music?"

Quinn reached over and pressed the Play button on the little stereo. The strains of the music began, echoes of home in this foreigners' gymnasium, and Leila got ready to dance. She went up on tiptoe and spread her arms up over her head. Then, just when the drums began and the lute went into high notes, she rolled her hips in a full figure-eight rotation. The dancing scarf sent sweet metal jingling sounds into the air around her. She moved along with the familiar music, doing the dance that she'd done since she was a child, and her hips swayed and jerked in expert timing along the way. At the same time, her arms and hands went in slower circles and elegant, held positions. Her waist and breasts did not move at all. As she moved she grew in confidence, feeling the smooth flow of energy down to her fingertips. This was the stuff her girlhood friendships were made of; this was the feminine warmth and celebration that made her toes turn and her hips move. She felt all eyes on her and she smiled, wanting to share with these American women that liberation could be found in many places.

When the short song finished, the room was hung with silence for a moment as the nurses stared at Leila. The applause started with Bonnie, who broke into a grin and clapped; then they all clapped for Leila amid exclamations.

"Wow! I can't believe that! It looks so hard!"

"I want to do that," Quinn sighed.

"All right," said Leila, smiling and holding her hands out. "Now I will tell you about the moves I did. It is less difficult than it looks, if you believe, and the most important thing about the belly dance is muscle control." She placed a hand on her own flat stomach. "It is the abdominal muscle groups that are strengthened by the dance. That is why it is a good workout for the woman."

Bonnie nodded enthusiastically, along with several of the other women who sat up straighter in interest.

"The most important thing to know is the *tamsiq*," said Leila. "It is the rolling of the hips, and keeping the hips separate from the rest of the body. You are like two pieces, bottom and top, and you move . . . um—independent of yourself."

She did the move to demonstrate again. The nurses watched with avid eyes.

After explaining the names of each of the dance moves, Leila had the women stand up and try for themselves. She set the music going again, and there was a great deal of laughter, false starts, and giggles as the Americans attempted it. Leila was unsurprised to see that Nurse Quinn was doing well for her first try.

"Watch Jessica, everyone," Leila said.

"Oh, Leila!" Quinn said, and laughed. The pretty American nurse walked over and put her arm through Leila's. "Here," Quinn said, trying a Western-style dance move, shaking her hips and shoulders, dragging Leila with her. It would have turned into an all-out dance party, had Leila not regained control of the group by clapping her hands together.

"Now we will learn, move by move, a basic belly dance," she said. "You see the moves, now we put them together."

At the end of the hour the Americans were dancing with varying skill and Leila moved around the room, readjusting positions and making suggestions. For an hour, the war was forgotten, and the loud Arabic music drowned out the sound of any fighter jets or rockets that might have been flying overhead. It was a relief to narrow reality into this small exercise room and the sound of the music and the laughter of fellow women. Leila was sorry when Nurse Bonnie's watch beeped, signaling the end of the lesson.

They all walked back to the hospital together. Leila was surrounded by nurses, some whose names she didn't know, all asking her questions. She wasn't a stranger anymore—she was a person of interest—perhaps even a friend.

"So, are you married, Leila?" asked one woman, older, in her forties, but clean-cut with healthy dark brown hair.

"No, I'm not, um—"

"Sal," the woman volunteered.

"No, Sal, I am not married," said Leila. "Although my mother would like me to be."

"Isn't getting married, like, really important in your culture?" Bonnie asked.

"Very important," said Leila. "Every girl's biggest dream should be to have a family."

"Weird," said Quinn as she puffed on a cigarette.

"Jessica, you shouldn't smoke!" one of the other women admonished.

"Eh, we're all gonna die, anyway," said Quinn, undeterred.

"So, Leila," said another woman. She had black skin and hair in long, tiny braids that were tied up in a bun. "My name's Michelle, by the way. Do you have a big family? Someone said that Iraqis have big families."

"My immediate family is five," said Leila. "But I have a sister-in-law, brother-in-law, and eight hundred cousins." She knew it would get the same reaction as from James: shock and awe.

"Eight hundred!" Michelle said. "I have forty cousins and I thought that was a lot."

"Michelle's from Atlanta," Bonnie said. "Deep South girl."

"Oh," said Leila, picturing Georgia on a map. In school, her geography marks were always high, perhaps because she was so desperate to travel outside Iraq. By staring at a map, sometimes Leila waited for the "right" place to jump out at her or start flashing red. It never happened, but Leila's desire to see the world went unquenched. "What is Atlanta like?"

"It's wild," said Michelle. "It has everything in the world."

"Even mortars?" Leila said.

The nurses laughed. "Sometimes," said Michelle. "Depends on what neighborhood." But she was joking and she winked at Leila.

When Quinn was finished with her cigarette she tossed it on the ground and pushed through the group as they reached the doors of the field hospital. "Don't crowd her, now," Quinn said. The nurse took Leila by the hand. "Thanks so much for the lessons, Leila!"

"Yeah," the others echoed.

"You are most welcome," said Leila, smiling and shy again under the attention.

"So," said Quinn in a confidential tone. "How's your sister with the magazines?"

Leila grinned as she and Quinn walked into the hospital together. "Fatima is very well. Every time I see her she looks flushed."

Quinn giggled. "That's what I like to hear! *Cosmo* magazine, spreading the love."

"I think it has spread the love to my sister's marriage bed," said Leila archly.

"Come on, let's go change the bedpans," said Quinn. They walked together to put on their medical coats. Leila wasn't sure where this new level of connection with popular Jessica Quinn would take them, but it felt nice to have another friend at the base, so she did not analyze it too much.

Changing bedpans was not part of Leila's duties as a medical translator, but Whitaker and Peabody were busy and she did not want to interrupt Quinn's goodwill toward her. So she breathed through her mouth and went along the ward, lifting unconscious feet and legs as Quinn did the pan-changing. It was distasteful work but Quinn seemed not to notice as she moved with practiced, quick efficiency. Leila tried to follow her example and acted as though she were not at all bothered by the excretions of the ill and wounded.

"So," said Quinn, raising her eyebrows at Leila over a sleeping soldier who had shrapnel wounds. "Your sister's married. But what about you? Any prospects?"

"Mmm . . ." Leila said. She looked up at the ceiling as though thinking about it. "Not really."

"Oh!" said Quinn. "You mean your marriages are arranged or something?"

"No," said Leila, and it was sharper than she intended. "Not arranged. But the parents should approve." She sighed. "I have told my parents I want no wedding until I am educated as a doctor. I refuse it."

"Good for you," said Quinn.

"Are you married, Jessica?" Leila asked. She already knew the answer.

"Heck no! I'm too young to settle down. I want to marry a soldier, though, if I ever *do* decide to get hitched."

"And in the meantime?"

Quinn gave Leila a smirk. "In the meantime, I have my fun. I guess Arab girls don't do that. But American girls can do whatever they want."

Leila shrugged. "There are always ways to get what you want," she said with broad meaning. "All it takes is determination."

"Like with Captain Cartwright?" Quinn asked.

Leila's head snapped up at the name and she kicked herself mentally for giving herself away. "What about Captain Cartwright?"

"Oh, come on. Everyone sees the way the two of you talk. He stares at you and shuffles his feet. And the Special Forces *never* shuffle their feet." Quinn gave a rueful little laugh. "We've all tried to get that one. He's the bachelor of the month around here. If you can do it—" She shrugged.

"I'm not trying to do anything," said Leila. She had to conceal a smile at the word *bachelor*, though; it meant that James was not, in fact, married back in America.

"Riii-ight," said Quinn. "I'm just teasing, girl." She gave Leila her famous sugar and spice smile.

"Just be glad I don't tease you, Jessica," Leila said. She reciprocated Quinn's smile. "I have plenty of material."

"Hey!" said Quinn, threatening to throw the bedpan she was holding at Leila, who ducked and giggled. The soldier lying on the bed between them looked alarmed. Quinn teased him by poking him in the shoulder, and Leila told her to get serious and put the pan away before someone got hurt.

"Leila?" said a deep male voice from behind her.

"Hi, Captain," said Quinn, flashing a brilliant smile.

Leila turned around to see James and she, too, smiled. "Hi," she said.

"Hey," said James. He glanced up at Quinn. "Hi there, um—"

Leila took vicious satisfaction that James did not know Quinn's name.

"Jessica," said Quinn.

"Right, sorry," said James. "I know you by your nickname. Baby Doll. It's a good thing, trust me."

"Baby Doll!" Leila echoed. "Even I know of your nickname."

"Not a word out of you, belly dancer!" Quinn shook a playful finger at Leila. "I'll leave you two alone now." She walked off still carrying the used bedpan.

Leila snapped her surgical gloves off, tossing them into a nearby bin and brushing the latex residue from her fingers, then looked up at James. "How are you doing?" she asked.

"Great, great," he said with a nod. "Belly dancer?"

"I was teaching some of the other nurses how to dance. Giving a little lesson."

James laughed. "Can I watch?"

"Absolutely not," Leila said primly.

James shuffled his feet, which Leila now noticed for the first time, and his handsome face grew sober. "Can I talk to you alone?" he asked. "It's kind of important."

"Sure . . ." said Leila.

As they walked out of the ward, James thrust his hands into the pockets of his combat fatigues and frowned. Leila gave him a sidelong glance, not understanding why he was so reluctant to speak to her. He was not nervous, she did not think, but rather seemed upset about something. "Are you all right?" she asked when they reached the empty staff room.

"Yeah, I'm all right," he said. "I just don't like my job sometimes. And today is one of those days."

"I see," said Leila. She paused, wondering if there had been another incident. . . . "A bad time at the interrogation center?"

James looked up at her words and their implication. "It hasn't been like that first time," he said in a quiet voice. "With the guy that got electrocuted, I mean. We don't do that here. If the API guys do something when I'm not present, though . . . not my jurisdiction, see."

"API?" Leila asked.

"Asset Protection International. They're the private contractors that help with the interrogations. Sometimes they go out on home searches, too."

"Oh," said Leila, very much aware that James was giving her valuable intelligence to take back to her father. She had to mull over whether to share the information or not.

"Anyway, that's not the reason why I hate my job today," said James. He sighed and rubbed his temples with the fingers and thumb of his right hand. Then he stopped the motion and let his hand drop. "Leila."

"What?"

"I have to ask you something. I've been putting it off because I didn't want to bring you into this—this mess, but my superior officers are on my back and I have to ask, because I said I would."

"James, whatever you want to say, please do not hold back," said Leila. She wanted to ease his torment, whatever the reason. "I will not judge you."

He met her gaze with his electric-blue eyes, blinking fast as though looking at her through a fog. "Okay, I'll just say it," he said. "Your father's full name has come up on our lists of mujahideen. We know about him, Leila. He's more than a sympathizer, he's an active terrorist. I've let it go for a while, but now . . . I have to speak with you about it."

Leila plucked at a loose strand of hair that hung near her face. *Caught at last.* Leila was dead certain she was about to be dismissed from her job. She would be lucky to not be interrogated and imprisoned herself, all because of her father. Helplessness made her knees go weak. She'd known this day would come . . . she just hadn't planned for her racing, terrified heart. "I hate this," she said. "I want to get out of this city."

"Leila, I have to know," James said. "Please. I wanted to

give you the chance to do the right thing. We want you to keep an eye on things for us. Add to your duties and your paycheck, too. They—I mean we—think you're ideally placed as a daughter in the home of a mujahideen. It would mean daily reports from you on the activities you witness, and maybe you could try to talk to your father and get some specific details—" James broke off at the expression on Leila's face.

She stared in shock and dismay at the man she thought of as a friend. He was using her. He was just like her father. She had not thought the Americans capable of such deep deception, but all of James's friendly overtures in the past weeks must have held a purpose. He'd suspected all along that Tamir al-Ghani was a terrorist. Without realizing it, Leila reneged on her own words of a few seconds earlier and *did* judge James Cartwright, harshly and with the turmoil of hurt feelings. How could he? She trusted him. She thought he liked her. In all her admiration of his manners, his looks, his big blue eyes, Leila had forgotten that he was a Special Forces officer and a soldier for his country. His loyalty was not to her. To James, Leila was a means to an end. Pinned under the weight of these men's games, whom could she trust?

"Oh, Jesus, I'm sorry," James said. "I know how it sounds. Bad, right? Listen, they don't want to make you into a traitor. They just want to help end this insurgency and save some lives. You'd get extra pay for it, like hazard pay, and no one would be the wiser."

Leila searched for the right English words, but her thoughts buzzed and screeched in her native Arabic, with a few Kurdish swear words worked in there, too. She stared at the linoleum floor, unable to look James in the eye, afraid that his earnest gaze would disarm her from her righteous anger. The most insulting thing of all was that he offered her money for her information, like some common tattletale. For a moment Leila understood why informants, when discovered, got their tongues cut out.

Sal, the nurse with brown hair, came into the break room to

get a cup of coffee. She glanced between James and Leila, awareness dawning that she'd interrupted something. "'Scuse me," she said, pouring her coffee into a paper cup and hastening back out the door.

"Listen, Leila," James tried again when they were alone. "I'm sorry I brought this up. I want to emphasize that it's your decision. You don't have to do this if you don't want to. It's just part of my duty to ask, you understand that, right? If you choose not to be an informant, then your job here at the field hospital won't be affected. You're already doing enough for us, anyway, I—Leila, please say something."

"What can I say?" she said. "You want me to spy on my own father."

"I don't want you to!" James said, so loud that Leila wondered if one of the doctors would come running. "I don't want you to," he said again, quietly. "Listen, you know Pratt. He's been on my case for weeks about you. Now I've asked, and now I can tell him to shut up about it. I'll tell him no. It's fine."

Leila bit the inside of her cheek, hard, tasting the metallic tang of her own blood. It was the flavor of her anger. "I trusted you, James," she said. "I thought you were my friend. And now I think you were trying to get me to like you so I would agree to be a spy for you."

"I am your friend, Leila," James said. "I am. And I'll tell you something else: I don't want you to become an informant, now or ever. I'm not naïve. I know what the mujahideen do. And, Leila, I *don't* want you in that position. Stay safe. Stay low. And stay alive." His hands were clasped in a position of prayer and his eyes trained on hers.

Leila saw his sincerity, but she did not want to believe it. She wanted to be mad at James; it was easier that way. The truth of her own duplicity tugged at her insides, but she shoved it away. She had no choice in that matter; it was spy for her father, or lose her job. Besides, she was doing her best to be vague in her reports to Tamir, so as not to get anyone killed. James's proposal was something else altogether.

"I cannot believe you think I would be a regular spy on my own people," she spat. "You must think very low of me."

"No!" James said. "It wasn't my idea, Leila. I've been trying to protect you from this mess. I didn't want to ask this of you to begin with, I've just told you that. Don't you believe me?"

"Do I believe an American officer? A man who works with the intelligence? No." Leila blinked away the furious tears that clouded her eyes and turned her head away from James, her hands clenched into stubborn fists at her sides.

"Fine," said James, standing. "Fine. It's up to you, Leila. You have my word and that's all I can give you. I'll tell Pratt and the intel guys that you're not to be disturbed or recruited. I'm sorry I even brought this up. But . . ." He paused, half turning from the door. "You know, you might show a little gratitude. You're not a . . . a pristine island of medical holiness in this war, you're involved, too! When your father hides the *muj*, they go out and *kill* people. Did you stop to think about that? He's not just putting your family in danger, he's putting every citizen in Mosul in danger. And you can't sit here in the hospital, translating for us and treating our soldiers, and expect us not to ask you, Leila! Of course we had to ask if you might keep an *eye* on your *father*, the *terrorist*." James hit the white wall with the palm of his hand. In his eyes, his blue eyes, a glint of exasperation lurked: once again Leila was reminded of Tamir. Then James turned on his heel and left the room without saying good-bye.

Leila stared at the door where he disappeared. Reeling from James's words, her emotions swung between trust and distrust, love and hate. Leila remembered what James had said about the mujahideen and what they did to informants, and how he wanted to protect her. "I don't want you to be an informant," he had said.

How could he put her in this position of choosing between her career, her life, her new American friends, and her own father? There was a cold calculation to it that she didn't like, a realm of "all's fair in war" to which she remained subservient.

She scowled down at the scuffed break room table, sniffed away her remaining tears, and glanced at her watch. It was almost five o'clock. She needed to see Dr. Whitaker, pick up some medical journals for her perusal, and get back to the main gate to catch the bus into Mosul City.

As she rested her head on the glass window of the minibus on the way back toward Al-Razi Hospital that night, Leila's only thought was that it was impossible to do the right thing in Iraq. No matter where she turned, someone was betrayed.

Chapter 18

For several days Leila tried to forget about the unpleasantness with James and his proposals of espionage. She went to work as usual, did her job, and talked with Nurse Quinn, who after the belly dancing lessons was more and more like Leila's friend. Leila was fascinated with the cute American nurse because of her brazen ways. One moment Quinn would be sitting innocent with criss-crossed legs on the floor, working her hair into braids like a small girl and chattering away . . . and in the next turn would exchange racy flirtations with the soldiers. It was the most foreign thing about working on the American base.

The other nurses, too, greeted Leila and talked to her more after the dance lessons. Leila agreed to think about making it a weekly thing. It made her feel more normal. It also anchored her warm feelings about her job with her new friends, rather than with James Cartwright. She didn't want to see him, and yet she yearned to see him.

On a Thursday evening, feeling no better about her situation and uncertain of what to do next, Leila did something she had not done in a long time: she went up to her own bedroom, closed the door, and got on her knees to pray to Allah. A vague sense of guilt descended at first, because it had been years since she'd engaged in devout prayer. She felt that the admonitions in the Quran about women's greater capacity for sin were jus-

tified, judging by her own behavior. Allah would not even recognize her voice, so long it had been since she sent up more
than a quick, fearful demand or vague wish.

Then a knock on her door sounded. Her father's voice came
through, asking her to come out and speak to him.

"I'm praying!" she called as his footsteps retreated. Then
she had to ask forgiveness for using prayer as an excuse to
avoid her father.

Leila sighed and closed her eyes again, put her hands together, and readjusted the position of her knees on the carpet.
She did a quick direction check to make sure she faced Mecca.
"I pray to Allah for my family, for Fatima in her new marriage,
for our happiness. I pray you keep us alive and well. And I
pray that my path clears.

"I want to be a doctor! I must leave Iraq to do it, and I must
stay alive. I hate the way this life is going. I'm being made into
a terrorist by my father and something more useless by my
mother. Please take me away from them. Please let this clear
up, let me feel better about my days at the hospital. I don't
want to come home and feel like a bad person when I sit in
front of my father and talk about the Americans. I don't want
any more violence, or harm to come to anyone!" Leila was
aware that she was babbling in her mind, talking to Allah as
though in a conversation, not in a respectful and pious prayer-
ful request. She wondered if God minded it.

"And please, this prayer goes to Allah and the angels, please
keep James Cartwright safe, even though I'm very angry with
him, and let him be my friend again. Please." Leila stood and
rubbed her knees. "Oh, and *aameen*."

Perhaps it was her imagination, but Leila felt a little cool
trickle of white calm as though poured on top of her head. She
took a deep breath and opened her creaky bedroom door and
went downstairs to "debrief" with her father.

There was not much new to report; Leila had vowed not to
tell Tamir about how the Americans wanted her to be an informant. Tamir would either become enraged by it and forbid

Leila to work at the hospital any longer, or he would come up with a crafty, complicated way to feed the Americans disinformation. Leila wanted no part of either. So she just mentioned the presence of private contractors from Asset Protection International (which many people in Mosul could know about) and omitted identifying details, saying she did not know their names or what they looked like.

The API contractors with whom James worked were not seen in the field hospital often; the Australian one called Reaper, a man in his mid-forties with a bristly brown mustache, had once come to the hospital to get a course of antibiotics for some bad food he'd eaten. Otherwise Leila knew their names, Randolph, Shucman, and Cox, but did not know who was who. It was not much of a stretch to plead ignorance to her father.

Her duty to the mujahideen done, Leila settled in for a long weekend. That evening Umm Naji put her to work scrubbing out the cupboards; it seemed an age ago that the al-Ghanis had had servants to do that kind of work. At least the cleaning gave Leila something to do. Weekends were stultifying and slow. When she wasn't helping her mother with the housework, Leila tried to catch up on the medical journals that Dr. Whitaker sent home with her, finding some much-needed mental stimulation. Her English improved every time she plugged her way through one of the journals. She started to dream about seeing her own byline, l. Al-Ghani, in some prestigious academic tome.

"Here's one for you, Leila," said Umm Naji, when the mail arrived on Friday.

"Oh?" Leila said. She stretched out her hand to take the yellowish envelope. When she saw the handwriting on it, her nose wrinkled as though it were a bad smell. It was from cousin Abdul.

She thought she'd taken care of Abdul's unrequited love. After reading his initial letter of proposal, Leila had composed a careful response that said she was flattered by Abdul's attention, but that she could not consider marriage to him or anyone else until she finished her medical degree. It was not personal, Leila wrote. It was her decision, and in the meantime she would be happy to be Abdul's friend and honored to be his cousin. The letter was polite but a definite no. So, Leila wondered, what could Abdul have to say to her now?

Avoiding her mother's keen look of interest, Leila ripped open the envelope from the side and pulled out a single piece of paper. She scanned Abdul's words with growing astonishment.

It was another proposal of marriage, but this time Abdul had made it to her father. He wanted to send along a quick word to Leila, just so that she was not in the dark about her own future. Abdul wrote that he'd sent a simultaneous letter to Tamir requesting Leila's hand, explaining the reasons why, and, he wrote, Leila would do well to remember that Mosul was not safe and Abdul's home village of Al-Hadr would offer her protection from the violence. He understood that she wanted to go to medical school, but doubted it was feasible these days for a young Iraqi woman to have such a career. He, Abdul, was family and as such had Leila's best interest in mind. He was willing to forgive and overlook her earlier rejection of him, for her own good of course.

"Well?" Umm Naji said. "What does it say?"

Leila bit her tongue to keep from crying out in frustration. She could not believe the nerve of Abdul. After she had rejected him, he persisted to this point of extreme annoyance, like a typical male with a typical huge ego. A shadow of revulsion passed over her as she remembered everything about Abdul that bothered her. His short little hands. His greasy, receding hairline. His darting eyes. His obnoxious son, Mohammed.

"It says nothing good," Leila answered Umm Naji. "It's from Abdul."

"Abdul, yes. A good match for you, Leila."

"Mama!" Leila said. "How can you say that? He's awful!"

"He is your cousin! Do not speak ill of family, Leila."

"I think Abdul is unattractive and arrogant and he thinks so highly of himself. He must believe himself to be a good catch for any woman." Leila gave a bitter laugh. "He's wrong, you know. Mama, if you are so blind as to think Abdul's a match for me, then you need to get your eyes checked. Really."

"He is a doctor, you are interested in doctors. . . ." Umm Naji shrugged.

"I want to *be* a doctor!" Leila grew louder and more upset with each word that flew from her lips. "I refuse to marry Abdul. Do you hear? I refuse."

A wily look came over Umm Naji's broad face. She pursed her generous lips together and crossed her arms, looking satisfied at something Leila could not know. "Your marriage will be something for your father to decide."

"Excuse me?" Leila could not believe her ears. No one in the modern world arranged marriages. Though Fatima and Khaled became engaged after some finagling by their families, in the end they both had regard for each other, even love. Nowhere in the Quran did it say that the parents should arrange marriages for their children, because even Allah was aware that such things could turn into disasters. Arranged marriages were the stuff that suicides, murders, and runaways were made of.

"Your father will want to speak with you when he returns from mosque," said Umm Naji.

"He's always at mosque," Leila muttered. "I'm going to the cybercafe. You can weep for joy over Abdul's letter for all I care." She tossed the offending piece of paper at her mother's lap and fled the room.

The wind felt good on Leila's face after the stuffy prison that was her house. She bicycled as fast as she could toward Jedd Cyber on the corner. As a small mercy, the cybercafe was not crowded at four o'clock on a Friday, since many of the men were at prayers. Leila sat down in front of a computer console and tried to get lost in the machine, tried to forget about Abdul's letter that lay in wait for her at home.

She started by checking Sammurabi's Web log again. There were no new posts; in fact, the server notified her that there had been no new activity on the site for months. To Leila this seemed ominous. Any day now the blog would be taken down, and instead of information she would get the dreaded Page Could Not Be Displayed message. Sammurabi's account of strangeness might be dangerous to someone. Leila wondered if he was still alive and well in Egypt, or if something had happened to him, if he had disappeared the way that people under Saddam's regime used to disappear.

There was nothing new under the sun, Leila thought. Just different perpetrators of the same old crimes.

For a moment Leila thought about keeping her own Web log and posting for the world to read everything that was happening in Mosul. Then she decided that she did not need one more thing to get her killed, by the Americans or by the mujahideen. No, it was better to spend her spare time teaching belly dancing classes to a bunch of harmless American nurses.

She ended her Internet session with another quick, guilty search for James Cartwright's name, just to know what she was up against; as though some mundane information about his life before the army might give her a clue as to why he'd proposed treachery to her. She was left disappointed. There was little else about him besides his scholarship win when he was fourteen.

When Leila walked out of the Internet café, she saw a big white van lumbering down the main thoroughfare outside Jedd Cyber. Its sun visors were down and she could not see the faces of the two men inside, and that made her suspicious. Everything on the street seemed to go still in the wake of the vehicle. A sigh, a pause, a glance. Even two goats that wandered along the side of the road stopped chewing on their garbage for a moment.

She was not the only one to look; other pedestrians and shopkeepers peered at the van as it passed. No one was about to let it park or idle, for the big white vans often turned out to be bombs. Leila decided it was a bad idea to linger and turned down the little alleyway where her bicycle was chained. She pedaled down the alley where, after several twists and turns, she knew it would link up with another road.

Behind her, there might have been the dull crump of a car bomb. Or it might have been a car backfiring, or thunder off in the mountains. Leila did not stop to wonder. She had her own disaster waiting for her at home.

Her two-story house, once considered grand and elegant, looked hunched-over and miserable. There were things she'd never noticed before: broken tiles on the roof, rust on the gate, pockmarks and peeling paint on the front walls. It was downright shabby, the sense of orderly maintenance run away. Leila thought it fitting of her family situation and just for spite, she scratched at a peeling section of paint on her way in, making it a little bit worse.

Just as the heavy front door closed behind her, she heard her father's voice.

"Leila! There is something important we must discuss." Tamir's feet appeared first as he came down the stairwell, then the rest of his tall frame. His eyes burned and his head bobbed up and down like a bird's.

"Hello, *Baba*," said Leila, dipping her head at him.

"Into the sitting room." Tamir raced ahead of her and whirled, his clean white djellaba whipping around him like a woman's dress.

Leila got a sudden image of her father belly dancing and had to suppress a snorted laugh. She felt a bit hysterical and would rather laugh than weep.

"Sit, sit!" Tamir said, motioning with his hand. "Sit."

"Father, if this is about Abdul—"

"It most certainly is about Abdul! You're a lucky girl, do you know that? You have the chance to leave Mosul. And with so many people dying in this city every day . . ."

And whose fault is that? Leila wanted to say.

"These Americans," continued Tamir, "they shoot at everything that moves. Did you know that elderly Abu Mohammed, from next door, was shot and killed yesterday? He was just walking down the road! He never lifted a finger against the Crusaders! And the day before that, your cousin Mahfuz lost three goats when the Americans shot at his herd. These things are happening every day, which I think you do not appreciate, so safe at the American field hospital." Tamir glowered at her for a moment, but bounced back into his speech. "Abdul sent me a letter. He's asked for your hand in marriage. I must tell you, Leila, I was expecting this. Ever since Abdul's visit . . . I am not blind, you know. I hoped he might decide to ask me for you.

"He's offered you a home and family. You will move to his village. Abdul has a large house there, a fine house, and it is already suited for a woman. His late wife made the house most suitable, yes. You will even gain a son without the pain of childbirth! I know how you adore little Mohammed."

"Adore, yes, indeed," said Leila. The sarcasm was lost on Tamir.

"He is willing to marry you within three months. He can afford to keep a wife. And with your sister, Fatima, away, it is appropriate that you, too, should marry." Tamir smiled at Leila in encouragement, but it made her angrier.

"I can't believe you, Father," she said. "What in the world makes you think I want to marry Abdul? He's a foul little man with a brat of a son."

His eyes flashed. "Watch your mouth, girl." He inhaled deeply as though calming himself and then continued. "You will accept Abdul's proposal. You will continue your work at the American military base for now, and when it comes time to marry, you will quit the job. In a few months' time"—Tamir let out a little huff of laughter—"there will be no need to have a spy in the Americans' camp."

"What do you mean?" Leila asked, ignoring the rest of his orders. "In a few months' time?"

"It does not concern you." Tamir waved his hand in dismissal. "Your job remains to tell me about the Americans. In the meantime, I will write to Abdul on your behalf."

She opened her mouth to protest, but Tamir shushed her, making a gentle motion with his hand. "Don't press me on this, Leila. You do not know what is best for you. I do. To lose you would be—this way you will be made safe and happy. You remember what happened to Mr. al-Juburi. His girl Alia was killed for working at the Red Crescent center. She was engaged to be married but delayed the wedding . . . now he will never see her happy. I couldn't bear for my last daughter, my prettiest daughter, to be hurt. If you marry Abdul, I will not be like al-Juburi. I will not have to see you buried so young." Tamir's voice had become thick as though he were speaking around an emotion held in check. There was a shine in his eyes. "The most holy Quran instructs us to care for our women and their welfare, and that is what I am doing for you, my child."

Leila's thoughts whirred to a halt. For a moment she felt horribly guilty for having taken the job with the Americans, and she realized that she was part to blame for pushing her father into worrying about her so, but . . . Tamir was really going to try it. He was going to arrange her marriage to her disagreeable cousin, and Leila had no one to turn to for help. Umm Naji would be thrilled; Leila knew she would find no support there. Fatima had no influence over their parents, and Naji was too old to know or care much about his youngest sister. In ignorance about the situation, Naji would encourage the marriage to Abdul, too.

The electric lights flickered off and then back on as though in a silent cough. Leila glanced up at the ceiling lamp dangling from the center of the room. She stared into it for a moment, at the lightbulb surrounded by fine metalwork, the hanging bauble at the bottom. Caged light. That was how she felt. "All right, Father. I will marry Abdul," she said.

Leila retreated to her bedroom. She could not forever be pulled in two different directions. She stood at the crossroads between her parents' wishes and the way of her life up until now ... and on the other road, the Americans, and James, and a gleaming, frightening future. There was but one correct way to go from here.

Tomorrow, at work, she would seek out James, and tell him she'd changed her mind.

Later the next day, an unfortunate incident with two Military Police in the city threw the hospital, and the American soldiers, into a rage. An armor-piercing RPG blew apart the back section of a Humvee, part of an MP patrol, killing the gunner and forcing the others out of the vehicle. Once on the street they were vulnerable; they came under heavy fire from a nest of jihadis and had to shelter in another house while the insurgents surrounded them. One of the MPs was shot through the left eye, killing him instantly, and another bled out from an arterial wound while waiting for the reinforcements.

James was on the rescue patrol, and he carried one of the wounded men out of the combat zone. He came to the hospital to visit the injured MPs: to get a straight story on what they'd experienced, once they felt up to talking about it. The Ninewa Road incident, as it was being called, was an example of how the jihadis' tactics were improving, rehearsed, disciplined.

He was in the ward, chatting to one of the wounded, and when he emerged Leila intercepted him, looking directly into his eyes. It made her feel bold, confident. She wore tight Western-style jeans beneath her white lab coat, there was a stain of iodine on her left sleeve and what was probably blood flecked on the hem of the jacket; it was a busy day in the field hospital. "James," she said.

"Hi, Leila," he said. There was caution in his eyes, in his low voice. He was well trained to judge intention.

"I need to talk to you," she said. "Come." She grabbed his hand and tugged him along the hall toward the glass front doors, taking off her lab coat along the way. Like a panicked bird her mind flashed and fluttered, trying to hang on to her plan, her thoughts, her loyalties.

"I need to talk to you, too," James said, but Leila could scarcely hear him over the *thwack-thwack* of a Black Hawk flying overhead like a great black bug in the sky.

"Can we go to the MWR? I need coffee," Leila shouted. It would be a good place to have a quiet conversation.

"Sure," said James. "Do you need to tell one of the doctors where you've gone?"

"I'm on break," said Leila. "Hurry, James, before I change my mind."

Heedless, Leila scurried across the gravel a half step ahead of him with her dark ponytail dancing behind her. She breathed in deep, cool air tinged with exhaust and a whiff of sulfuric gunpowder and the faint pop-pop sound of rifles being fired from the shooting range nearby. *Killing practice*, she thought with a shudder.

They pushed through the swinging glass and wooden doors of the recreation hall, now bare of Christmas decorations and reflecting the harsh sky of February. There were a few officers hanging around inside, two of them shooting a customary game of pool, and Leila noticed a twenty-dollar bill pass between them. There was a vacant table in the far corner.

"We can sit over here," James said to Leila as they made a beeline for the table.

They sat, James flagged down someone to bring them coffee, and a heavy silence settled between them.

Leila did not wait for him to speak, for fear of losing her nerve. "James. I have thought about things. I will tell you everything my father does. Whatever information you need, I will get it. I know a place to eavesdrop on the sitting room. Whenever he has people over I sit there and I can hear things through the hole in the wall. Numbers, weapons, everything I will tell you." She caught her breath at the end and it sounded ragged in her head.

"Are you serious?" James asked. He tilted his head at her. "Leila, are you sure?"

"I am positive," she said. "He has become a bad man! Before the war he was fine and now he has gone crazy. It is your fault, you Americans—it is, don't deny it—and everything is upside down now." She bit her lip and lowered her gaze. The tiny childhood part of Leila that was her father's daughter had become a thing of the past. Neither of them said anything as their coffee arrived, and neither one touched their cups.

"I didn't know you felt that way about your father," said James, puzzled. "What has he done, Leila? A week ago you were furious at the suggestion of—of turning away from him. What changed?"

"It is nothing," said Leila. She turned her head away from him, her nose and jaw tilted upward, her gaze directed off toward the windows. "It is everything."

"He hasn't hurt you, has he?"

"Oh, James," Leila said, and tiny tears sprang up in the corners of her eyes. "He has arranged my marriage to my cousin Abdul. He is making me leave Mosul, leave my job, give up everything I've ever wanted. He does not care that I want to be a doctor. And Abdul is disgusting, annoying, I do not like him at all." She hung her head so that the loose strands of her ponytail fell around her face. Tears dripped into her lap. She sniffled with subtle grace, taking the napkin from the table and dabbing her eyes without fuss so that the other soldiers in the room would not notice.

"An arranged marriage," James repeated. "Your father's decided this, and you can't say no?"

"I cannot refuse," said Leila. "He has already written to Abdul to accept the proposal, and if I backed out, it would cause tremendous shame."

"You can't marry a guy you don't even like!" James burst out.

"Please, keep your voice down," Leila said.

"Sorry," said James, glancing around. No one else in the room paid them any attention. "This Abdul guy. Where does he live?"

"A village called Al-Hadr. It is an hour's drive away, when

anyone even bothers to drive there." She frowned and narrowed her eyes. "I've never been there. But it sounds like a—what do you call a place? A nowhere place?"

"A backwater?" James suggested.

"Yes. A backwater."

"So your dad has arranged for you to be married to your cousin." James thought it was weird, Leila could tell; based on the films she'd seen, Americans made fun of people who married their cousins. James continued. "So that's why you want to pass information to us. To get back at him."

"That describes it," said Leila. "I cannot go along with him anymore. It's his way, or your way. I cannot play in the middle. And the way he . . . he just . . . disregarded me, like my feelings and my future mean nothing to him! Why would I be loyal to that?" She finally took a sip of her coffee. It was not hot anymore.

"It's dangerous, Leila," said James. "I stand by what I said before. I don't want to see you involved in any kind of espionage. Bad things happen to people who get into this stuff, you know that, right?"

She was silent for a weighted moment. Images flashed through Leila's head, some of the bodies she'd seen, Iraqis killed by their own countrymen and tortured first. Tongues swollen and black from floating in the Tigris River; lacerations and bruises on lifeless skin. There would be no going back and no changing minds. Torn between the family of her past and the dream of her future, Leila comprehended why her fellow Iraqis made the sacrifice, why they risked everything to help a foreign power.

"You can just talk to me, if you want," said James. "You don't have to deal with Travis Pratt or, God forbid, the contractors. Just talking, you and me. I know it'll be hard—"

"That's not all," Leila interrupted. He deserved to know the entire truth, and that included her career in spying up to that point. She took a deep breath, holding James's eyes with her dark liquid gaze, twisting her fingers around the handle of her

half-empty coffee cup. "I am very good at passing information," she said. "Right after the time you dropped me off, in
December, my father discovered that I work here at the field
hospital. He gave me a choice. Quit, or give him information
about the Americans. I would not quit."

James's jaw dropped. "What? You've been giving your father, the terrorist, tactical information?"

"No," Leila said quickly. "No. I've been careful not to give
important details. I tell him things like how many wounded
mujahideen are in the hospital, what their injuries are, this
kind of thing. He wanted me to mistranslate, too, but most of
the insurgents do not know much, anyway. James, I have *never*
told him things about the schedule kept here, the troop movements, nothing I see. I had to keep my job, you see? There was
no other way."

"Why didn't you come to me?" James asked. "This is a big
deal. A really big deal." And it was; it meant the insurgency
had a source inside the American base. It was not the first time
it had happened, of course, and counterintelligence was wary
of the Iraqis working on-base for that very reason. Mistrust
would be forever associated with Leila now and that could not
be undone.

"I was afraid the hospital would fire me! Or that they
would use me to pass disinformation to my own father, and
oh, he can see straight through me when I try to lie to him. He
was a judge. He has seen every excuse and every lie there is. He
cannot be fooled." She smiled wryly, remembering that she'd
tricked him for some weeks into believing she was working at
the Al-Razi pharmacy. "Well, he cannot be fooled often."

"But now you're willing to try," said James. His blue eyes
looked skeptical, but he wanted to believe her. That much was
obvious.

"Yes. I am willing," she said.

"Right. This will be between us, then. We'll work together. I
don't trust anyone else to handle it."

"I do not trust anyone else, either," said Leila. She smiled at him, feeling a little lighter, as though the wheel of fate had spun and landed and the air had clarity.

"Right," James said again.

"Oh, but one thing," she said, recollecting her last "debriefing" session with Tamir.

"Yeah?"

"One night my father wanted a name. He wants Americans to put on the lists, you know, the ones with the bounty attached. On the Internet."

James nodded.

"Anyway, I gave him a name." She leaned forward, lowering her voice. "I told him Travis Pratt."

A deep-throated laugh floated on the air between them and Leila was shocked to realize that James found it amusing. He was laughing. With a flash of a grin he said, "The only way the mujahideen will ever see Pratt is if the whole of Camp Marez is overrun and defeated. Did you say the spook because he never leaves base?"

"Yes."

"Quick thinker."

"Thank you." Leila sat back. James's reaction made her feel devilish and she liked it; it also solidified the decision in her mind. She'd done the right thing even when pressed into a bad situation. "I have made up my mind now, James. These Iraqis are doing wrong. They kill women, children, innocents, heedless of anything but their stupid cause. It has to stop, and I want my father to stop. And I'm going to do it."

"Take it easy, sweetheart, don't get too far ahead of yourself," said James. "I'll be handling your case, I'll request it with my superior officer. We'll write up weekly reports and send them along to military intel. It won't be too much different from your current duties, just meetings like this one, with me."

"Sounds like a real hardship," said Leila with a little smile, still glowing from his use of the word *sweetheart*. It was too good to be true; didn't Americans in the films call their girls "sweetheart"?

"I'll do my best to make it easy on you," said James.

"I am sure you will," she replied.

Something passed between them in that moment; they were bonded now. They shared a secret. They gazed for a few minutes above the coffee cups while mortars thumped in the distance, gunfire crackled from the practice range, shouts erupted from the pool table in the corner as one of the officers won his round.

"So," said Leila, "if I spy for you, will I get a visa? To go to America?"

James laughed. "I knew you had other motives!"

"It's a valid question." Leila shrugged, but the corner of her mouth turned up in a dimple of amusement. "But really, James. Does the United States help the people who help them? Would there be a possibility? Because . . . see, if I go down this road, I am making a decision for my future."

James gave her a wry smile. "I can't speak for the U.S. government. It's a beast all its own. But if anything could give you an opening, it would be your work for us here."

"I suppose that will have to do," said Leila. Glancing at the worn face of her watch, she saw it was 1420. They had been talking for over an hour. "I must go back to work. It gets late."

"I'll tell the doctors you had other business, so you're not in trouble," James said.

"If you like," Leila said, standing up.

He stood, too, took a step closer to her. "Thank you for doing this, Leila. Whatever your reasons are, you'll be doing good."

"I hope so." She looked away from him and her old uncertainty threatened to gain on her, but she pushed it aside, as was her habit. "Walk me back to the hospital."

"Yep."

Chapter 19

It was no small matter to be an informant for the Americans. Affiliation with the occupying army was enough to get an entire generation wiped out. Several years ago, Naji al-Ghani had known a friendly man named Mohammed who ran a shop and restaurant with his seven brothers. Naji had sold him the tables and chairs for the establishment. The family were upstanding citizens and did not even pass word about the activities of the mujahideen; they simply got a little too friendly with the Americans, socializing, inviting them to try the specialties of Iraqi food. Later, Leila remembered, Naji sat in the al-Ghani sitting room and gave them the news that Mohammed and his seven brothers were shot and killed, all of them. Their bodies were dumped in the Tigris. The wife was raped and her arms cut off, her tongue torn out. Leila, home for a break from the Cairo University, had been horrified. That had been the first time it dawned on her that her country would not be improving any time soon.

Leila struggled to come to terms with the inalienable fact that she was now among the ranks of those most likely to be disposed of in violent fashion. Tightrope-walking was not her cup of *shai* and it stretched her nerves to their limits.

Leila gave her first official "informant" report on the last Monday of February. Spring loomed like a black thunderhead brewing with fresh green rain and the weather was already starting to turn. Little birds hopped around the base, eating the first of the insects, heedless of the human violence around them. The birds were industrious but quiet, as though not wanting to draw attention to themselves. James had decided to hold their intelligence meetings in the MWR Center, a safe and innocuous place, to make it look like a normal chat over coffee.

It took her a minute to get going, as though her tongue did not want to speak, but she made an effort and soon the information flowed from her mouth. James had a pen and paper to take notes with one hand; with the other hand he sipped his coffee.

The imam, Abdul-Hakam, was now a daily fixture at the al-Ghani house, Leila told James. He and Tamir talked endlessly and she listened in when she could. She thought they were planning something big; Tamir kept speaking as though Judgment Day were coming to Mosul. Leila counted the dishes coming from the courtyard that her mother washed and dried in silence and estimated there were now five mujahideen hiding in the well. There were weapons, too, Soviet-made RPGs and rifles and ammunition stored along with the terrorists—Leila saw them when she peeked through her bedroom curtains late at night.

James wrote it all down with a concerned frown. The month of March was going to be messy and they both knew it.

"I still don't know how to get out of my marriage to Abdul," said Leila. "My father sent positive word. Abdul wrote back with a list of linens I should bring as my dowry."

"Linens?" James asked, confused.

"It is the man's duty to provide the house, the facilities, the car and water and windows. It is the bride's duty to bring the linens, bedcovers, cushions, curtains, these things to the home at the time of marriage."

"Oh, I see," said James, not seeing. Leila wondered how they did dowrys and linens in America.

"As long as Father plans for me to marry Abdul, he and Mother stay in a good mood," said Leila. "But I will not marry that man." She waited for James to finish writing. Was he noting her personal problems? Would the U.S. Army be aware of her disdain for her first cousin? It felt like a weight off her chest to speak of it to James but she hoped he would stick with the relevant intelligence in his report.

"We have fifteen minutes left," James said, glancing up at the wall clock. They had designated one hour for the meetings. "Is there anything you have questions about?"

"Yes," said Leila, smiling and crossing her arms as she sat back in her chair. "I want to know more about you. Your family. You know everything about me, it is only fair."

"I doubt I know everything about you," said James. "It would take a lifetime to unravel the mystery."

Leila laughed. "I'm a mystery to you, James?"

"Frankly, yes. You are so damn determined about everything. I can't figure out what made you this way."

"It is just my Kurdish blood," said Leila. She waved a hand. "Warriors, you know. But enough about that. You."

"Me." James, too, leaned back in his chair. "What do you want to know? My life's an open book."

"How many siblings do you have?"

"I have a sister named Marybelle. I call her Belle. She's about your age, just graduated from college. She's engaged to a guy named Adam."

"Everyone is engaged," sighed Leila. "And your parents?"

"My father is Sam, who was a pilot in the air force, then for a commercial airline, and he's retired now. My mom, Jenny, does a lot of volunteer work."

"They live in Virginia still?" Leila asked.

"Yeah. It's a nice place. A lot different from here, though."

"Will you be in the army forever?" Leila watched him with narrowed eyes.

James lowered his voice, leaned forward. "No," he said. "Absolutely not. After this tour, I'm done. But, Leila—don't mention it to anyone. I haven't."

"But you have reached the rank of captain," said Leila. "They might give you more promotions." She opened her mouth again to ask if he was ambitious but waited instead, assessing James with a test of her own device. If she was supposed to be his friend, his interest, she wanted to be sure her trust was well placed . . . in a man who had his priorities straight. A man who would do the right thing.

"I don't care about promotions," said James with sincerity. "It's not worth it. Advancement means headaches and paperwork and politics. I wish I'd stayed low on the totem pole . . . I miss the simplicity. And I don't like what my job has become here." He sighed and ran a hand through his hair. "God, I was so gung ho at first. Couldn't wait to get in on some action. Now I don't know where it's gone. Every day is like . . . like a trip to the dentist. Miserable. There's just one thing that brightens it up."

"And what is that?" Leila whispered.

"You," he whispered back.

Across the scratched table, they could barely hear each other, but it was enough. Leila's eyes went wide and she averted them, down to the floor. *Oh, this is far gone*, she thought, and knitted her fingers together.

"Sorry," said James. "That was a little out of line. But I was being honest."

"I know you were," said Leila.

That was the end of their meeting.

On a day in early March, a dreaded but expected situation arose at the detainment center: two of the contractors from Asset Protection International, in the process of "working" on an insurgent named Yousef, had taken it too far and he had become unresponsive. Dr. Whitaker was called from the field hospital, along with Leila, who was meant to translate for Yousef if he regained consciousness. It was the first time she'd been inside the white-walled concrete building where terrorists were held (though it would not be the last time). The grim compound was enclosed in barbed wire fence and high towers with powerful spotlights. A bland facade hiding quiet violations of the human spirit, where detainees and their interrogators came out as different people.

Inside, the corridors smelled like a combination of disinfectant, fresh-cut wood, human urine, human fear. Leila was warned that the premises were classified and she was not allowed to talk about what she saw or heard there. The implication was that if she did, she would find herself a prisoner, and the cold squeeze of fear worked at her heart. Behind the solid doors Iraqis, guilty or innocent, awaited judgment. She trailed in the wake of Dr. Whitaker as a soldier led them to a large, square interrogation room where the wounded man, Yousef, was laid out on a table. A sizzled, singed odor hung in the air, like acrid smoke.

Two surprises awaited Leila. One was the presence of James Cartwright, who stood off to the side, mouth frozen in a troubled expression. He met her eyes briefly and then looked away.

The second surprise was the large tub of water in the corner. It was overfull, sloshing at the sharp metal lip, and the surface of the water glimmered dark and shiny beneath the fluorescent lights. Leila noticed two snaking power cords discarded on the floor next to the tub. She knew what they had done to Yousef. The greatest shock was that Westerners would do this, whereas it was more common for rogue Iraqi police and Shia justice squads to engage in torture . . . her mind cycled back to one of the first detainees she'd treated at the 67th, known as "number 1256." Turning away, Leila also noted the presence of a portable CD player resting on the dusty floor. She wondered what music they played when they interrogated prisoners.

"Good Christ," said Dr. Whitaker, stepping up to the table where Yousef lay. "What happened here?" Then he shook his large head as if not wanting to hear the answer.

"Sir," said James. "This detainee has been in the company of two of our API contractors."

Leila understood. James wanted it on the record that he was not present for the incident.

One of the contractors, a large bear of a man with a graying handlebar mustache, stepped up. "This man brought it on himself," he said. He had no name tag and no accountability. "We tried our best to make things easy, but . . ." He shrugged as if such methods could not be helped.

"Can you fix him up?" asked the other contractor. Leila recognized him as Reaper, the Australian who'd once come to the hospital for antibiotics.

"Frankly, no," said Dr. Whitaker. "Leila, write this down. Contusions across the chest and arms. Head injury, possible concussion, with consequent flesh wound; skull is visible. Reddish cast to skin indicates severe electrical shock."

Leila scribbled it down on the clipboard, nauseated. She tried to focus on the words in English rather than on the pitiful thing they described.

After they categorized his injuries, Dr. Whitaker said, "He either goes to the hospital now or he dies. Even now I doubt we can save him. For chrissakes, Captain," and he was addressing James, "how could you allow this to happen?"

"I didn't," said James through gritted teeth. "Randolph and Reaper were—"

"It's not a question of blame," said the big mustached man, Randolph, putting his hands up in supplication. "We have reason to believe this detainee is a major player in the insurgency. We're saving lives by questioning him."

Leila repressed a snort.

"All we're saying is that we don't want him to die, we want him to talk," said Reaper, backing up. When he stepped aside, his foot knocked against the CD player, and it kicked into life.

"I'm going all the way to the Emerald City to get the Wizard of Oz to help me . . ." Judy Garland's voice sang through the room, her childlike voice an eerie contrast against the electric wires and the prone Iraqi man on the table.

A tremble ran down Leila's neck and spine; it was just like she'd read in that Sammurabi's blog. It was too strange for words and so she let the music wash over her, hearing what Yousef must have been hearing until he lost consciousness.

A groan came from the table.

"Hey, he's awake!" said Randolph.

Yousef's eyelids fluttered and his lips moved. He appeared to be saying, "*No, no.*"

"Translate," Reaper ordered Leila.

James nodded at her in encouragement.

She leaned her head down and tilted her ear toward Yousef's cracked lips.

"*Kulkhara,* American pig," Yousef said.

"You don't need to translate that," said James, who understood some Arabic but was not fluent.

"I don't think I need to be here at all," said Leila in a whisper.

Yousef spoke again. "I know nothing."

"The hell you don't," said Randolph. Out of nowhere appeared a baton in his hands and he clapped it against his palm; Yousef winced.

"The music," Yousef said. "No more, please."

"What is this music?" Leila asked in English.

"He needs the hospital," Dr. Whitaker said.

But then Yousef began to speak, the contractors shushed the doctor, and they all leaned in. Leila listened to the Arabic and spoke in hasty English. "My cousin, he is the one you want. His name is Mohammed. He lives near the children's hospital, I will tell you the street, it is Ibn Atther Street, you will find him there, everyone knows him . . . please no more hurt . . . I tell you . . . he is mortar, my cousin, he has mortared you . . ."

And so it went on, with Randolph looming, James pacing and tense, Dr. Whitaker standing with his arms crossed, and Leila scribbling down the conversation on the clipboard as she spoke. Everything sounded like nonsense, and *The Wizard of Oz* CD clicked over to the next track, and the moment was so surreal that she pinched herself inside the wrist to make sure she wasn't dreaming. To her disappointment, she was not.

Yousef licked his lips and croaked out a few more words for Leila to translate. "There were four of us," he said, sounding on the brink of tears. "Always four."

"Always?" James asked. "The same four?"

"No, no," Yousef said. "I was forced. My cousin made me do it."

"Is your cousin the devil?" James said. The contractors grinned at each other.

"Devil, no, no," said Yousef, missing the reference in English. "The same four. We do not know commander, only that he is very important man. We have contact with one who gives us orders, over the phone. I can know the voice, but I do not know who."

"Where did you stay in Mosul, you little pig?" Randolph threatened Yousef with the iron baton again, but it was unnecessary.

"A house, a house, I do not know who," Yousef stammered. Leila knew, she *knew*, it was her own house.

"We believe you," James said. "I really don't think he knows," he said in an undertone to the contractors, who still glowered at the Iraqi on the table.

"Let's teach him how to talk," said Reaper. He pushed his sleeves up and stepped toward Yousef. Alarmed, Leila glanced at Dr. Whitaker.

The doctor and James intervened at the same time. Dr. Whitaker said, "Enough! He's going to the hospital. I don't care what your corporate bosses say. It stops here."

"But we need him to *talk*—"

James hit the switch on the CD player and the music stopped. "What the fuck is the matter with you guys? I'm the ranking combat officer here and I *order* you to stop. . . ." He trailed off. Yousef had fallen silent again. Had they killed him? "The hospital. *Now*."

For once, Randolph and Reaper did what James said.

They threw Yousef into the back of a white pickup truck, the lone vehicle immediately available. His eyes rolled up into his head and his arms and legs flailed in spasms, held in check by the plastic handcuffs and bindings. Dr. Whitaker and Leila knelt next to him, gripping the metal edges, and they sped off toward the hospital. The dusty wind had to be making the pain worse and Leila noticed that James took off his jacket and draped it over Yousef's shaking body.

The blood soon soaked through the fabric, rendering the jacket ruined, and it looked like Yousef would die before they even got there. They all let out a breath of relief when the truck squealed to a stop in front of the service entrance to the 67th CSH. Dr. Peabody poked his head outside with widened eyes.

"What the hell happened?" he said.

"Detainment center," came the curt response from Dr. Whitaker. Leila scurried through the door, eager to be back in a more comfortable zone with the nurses and her own lab coat and supplies.

James gave the doctor a long, solid look in the eye. "We got him here as soon as we could," he said.

Peabody called for a stretcher, some orderlies rushed out, and the business began. Fifteen minutes later, Leila's hands were still shaking from the ordeal as she prepared for surgery on Dr. Peabody's orders along with Baby Doll Quinn and Nurse Pavlopolous. A voice interrupted her work.

"Psst! Leila!" It was James.

Nurse Quinn heard and waggled her eyebrows but Leila ignored her.

With a word under her breath she left the group and came over to James. "What is it?" she whispered.

"I tried to stop them," he said, pulling her by the elbow out into the corridor. "The whole thing was so weird."

"Leila!" Dr. Peabody said, rushing by them. "Stand by for a while. The patient is under anesthesia now, but he might come out of it in a few hours after we get him stabilized. Until then, just hang tight." She knew why: the doctor did not want her to work with the massive damage done to Yousef's Iraqi body, he did not want her to feel torn loyalty or distraction from her work. Leila appreciated it, for it meant she could have a chance to talk to James and discover the precise chain of events.

She glanced up at the sound of approaching footsteps. It was Pratt, his brown hair combed in a neat side part, and it made Leila think of Yousef's torn hair and exposed scalp. Pratt raised his eyebrows and stopped in front of James as though expecting a full report.

"This is on you," said James. "It's yours, Pratt. It was your damn precious contractors. Take it and run. I wash my hands." He turned and strode away down the hall.

Pratt rolled his eyes and walked in the other direction, muttering something under his breath.

"What the hell is happening?" Leila said, trotting after James, frustrated and upset. She was caught up in something she didn't understand; who was responsible? On whose side could she judge? James looked down in surprise at her language.

"The contractors got out of control," said James. "I don't think the intelligence was valuable enough to be worth it." He swallowed thickly, and sweat beaded on his forehead, but he said nothing more. The wall was up. He was in his realm of "dealing with it," of his training and coping mechanisms, and Leila wanted to get through it. To reach him. Torture was cowardice and she had the feeling that James preferred things to be clean-cut within the realm of a battle, a firefight, a war.

"James!" she said. "Come on. Come outside. You need air. Follow me, now."

He let her lead him out a side door and he sat on some metal steps, bowing his head between his knees. "There, now," she whispered. Her hands moved in circles over his sweat-damp T-shirt. "Take it slow. *Shweh, shweh.* You are lucky to have a woman here, hmm?"

This made James chuckle. "Yeah," he said.

"Not many of the soldiers get this kind of treatment," Leila continued. She kept her voice low and sweet. Comforting. "A massage, a helper, a listening ear . . . you know, I think you have it best in Mosul, James."

"How do you do it?" James said. He sat up straight and the color had returned to his face.

Leila patted his back a few times and then knelt in front of him. "How do I do what?" she asked.

"Make me feel so much better," he said. "You're the antidote to this whole goddamn thing."

"For the sake of heaven," she said, "I am not. But I think you need some teasing right now. It was not your fault."

"I can't believe what they did. It was just so *weird*. I—I probably shouldn't be saying this to you. Anyway, weird." It was an understatement; the last thing James needed was a criminal charge of breaching national security. Pouring his heart out to Leila was not an option. To say a word about the methods and madness of the API contractors could get him in trouble, and Leila did not want the burden of hiding James's words from her father.

"The music from *The Wizard of Oz* was weird, yes. I have heard of it before."

Silence, except for the dull crackle of rifle fire from the range, a distant thump of helicopter blades, the whisper of wind across gravel.

"You have? Where?" James asked, his voice low, cautious.

"I have heard stories, too." She motioned for him to scoot over on the narrow metal step so she could sit. Their legs touched, hip to knee. "I have been meaning to ask, but I know about your rules of, um, what is the word? Secrecy?"

"Yeah . . ."

"Some weeks ago I found an account of an Iraqi man taken from Baghdad. He wrote about it in a blog, you know what that is?"

"A blog, yeah, of course."

"He is called Sammurabi. His name on the Internet, you know. Screen name. He wrote about what happened when the Americans took him, that he went somewhere north, a cold country. They talked about *The Wizard of Oz*. I can show you the link, if you want."

"He was a detainee?" James asked.

"A *prisoner*," corrected Leila. "They are not detainees and you know it. No one can be a detainee for two years."

"Fair point. So this guy's writing about his experiences? How do you know he's for real?"

"I wondered about that," said Leila. "But then he admitted that he'd been forced to drink pig's blood. No Muslim would claim it, unless it were true and they wanted to tell about how bad it was."

"Unless he's not a Muslim," said James.

"He is," said Leila. "The blog is on an Egyptian server. But he has not updated it in a long time."

"Huh."

The similarity was there. *The Wizard of Oz.* Shadowy contractors, shadowy government players, nameless prisons in deep-forested countries in the north. And it was all real. Leila knew it; she'd seen the white unmarked planes take off from Diamondback and they bore detainees to God knows where. Sometimes the detainees were released, like the Sammurabi blogger, and other times they disappeared. She wanted to find out more, but could not do it on the military Internet; it was monitored, the log-on and log-off sessions were recorded, and any page that Leila hit would be sent to military intelligence. No, if she wanted to show James, they would need to use an Internet café in Mosul itself.

"You remember the Web address?" he asked Leila.

Beside him, she nodded three times. "Yes. I can show you."

"I'll have to do it at a civilian cybercafe," he said, dovetailing with Leila's thoughts. "They monitor us here."

"So, they did use . . . what do you call it? Psychological warfare? What is it about, James? Why?"

"I haven't the foggiest idea," he said.

"Maybe I should go back inside," she said. "I need to be there in case he wakes up." She made a move to stand up, using James's shoulder to lift herself off the cold steps.

"Leila, wait." He grabbed her hand. Electricity seemed to

buzz in the center of her palm. She tried to keep steady like the best doctor's bedside manner. "Can you do me a favor? When you write your translator's medical report on Yousef, make two copies. Don't show anyone this other copy, but bring it to me. It's important."

"You are collecting evidence!"

"I hope I won't need it. But just in case—" James released his grasp on her and spread his hands. "If this thing blows up in my face, I don't want my men to take the fall for it."

From the few bits she'd heard, from the small influences she'd seen, the contractors from Asset Protection International operated by their own rules. In spite of those terrible photographs from the Abu Ghraib prison, from her own experience Leila knew better: torture was not systemic behavior of American soldiers. It was an aberration, a result of weak commanders, a rare and unfortunate by-product of their war. She liked the Americans. She wanted to believe the best of them, and of James, who looked out for her. She did not want him blamed for what the mercenaries did.

"You think like a mystery writer," she said. "I will do as you ask."

"I'll be back tonight," said James. "I'm coming with you back into the city this evening. I want to find out more about API and I can't do that from the Internet here."

"Okay," she said.

If the scope of this prisoner torture racket was as big as she was beginning to suspect, then it could not go unnoticed. Perhaps the major news networks wouldn't touch it, but these were real incidents happening to real people who, on occasion, got released. They could write down what happened to them and share it with the world. The truth would remain with her: truth against her father, the mujahideen, the private contractors, the occupiers, the bullies of the world.

At six, James was back at the field hospital, waiting for Leila in the thin shadow of a flagpole. When she emerged on time, carrying her black handbag and wearing the simple black blazer over her black trousers and white shirt, she noticed him in the darkness.

"Leila," he said, stepping out.

"Hi," she replied. Up close, he looked even more weary than he had earlier in the day.

"Don't take the bus today," he said. "I'll drive in one of the pickups. I don't want to draw any attention. Can you come with me?"

She twisted her heel into the gravel. "I do not know if this is a good idea," she said. "I should not be seen with a Western man. Mosul is a big city, but word gets around."

"We'll go into a neighborhood away from your house," he said. "And I have this." From his satchel he produced a red-and-white-checkered kaffiyeh, the traditional male head scarf. With sunglasses on, he could pass for a local. He even knew enough pleasantries in Arabic to enhance the illusion.

Leila looked off toward the city. It glittered on its rolling hills, so pretty from a distance, like a Monet that got messier on the approach. The air was quiet of the sounds of war at the moment; perhaps that was why she felt she could agree with him. "We will find a cybercafe, they are everywhere. Then you will go to the Al-Razi Hospital so I can get my bicycle. Then drop me off close to my own neighborhood, but not too close. Okay?"

"Sounds good."

He put on the kaffiyeh with an expert hand. They were like a Thermos for the head: kept cool in summer and warm in winter. Leila gave him an appreciative glance when she saw how well he tied the Bedouin headdress and told him he looked like a local.

Just as they started the ignition on a beat-up old white pickup that the Special Forces used when going "native," one of the military orderlies ran out of the hospital into the twilight and flagged James down. Heedless of Leila's presence, he gasped out the news: Pratt wanted James to know that Yousef the terrorist had died.

Chapter 20

Leila kept her hands clasped in her lap as the pickup bounced along the airport road into the dark dusty streets of Mosul. She felt strange to be riding in a car with a man, unaccompanied by a relative, until she reminded herself that she was not a *Saudi*, for heaven's sake, and she could do what she wanted. This was the modern way. And she trusted James with her life by this point.

They found a parking place in a stinking alley in a neighborhood safe from the prying eyes of Leila's neighbors and family. Leila wore her *hijab* tight about her head and kept her gaze low. She did not want to take chances that someone might recognize al-Ghani's daughter. James, too, kept a low profile in his headdress, old clothes, and sunglasses, even though the sky was dark and hours bereft of sunlight.

"The Unique Cybercafe," Leila read aloud in English. The sign was painted in battered red and white, with a mobile phone ad plastered next to it. She pointed at the shop below, a hole-in-the-wall place that did not look crowded. An older man sat at the first computer, plodding away at the keys, so Leila decided it was perfect. "Come on," she said.

They sat in adjacent chairs at a machine that looked at least fifteen years old. It was a slow connection but Leila was a fast typist; she entered Sammurabi's blog address from memory. It took a few seconds to load, agonizingly slow to Leila's hurried mind; she could not help glancing around like a child with its hand in the jar of sweets.

"Stop looking so suspicious," James whispered in her ear. He sounded amused.

"Sorry," she whispered back. "Oh, here it is."

She let James take over the mouse and scroll through the blog at his own pace. He made the occasional noise of surprise or confirmation. Then he got out a pen and notepad and jotted down quick-hand notes in messy penmanship.

He asked if she'd found any more stories like this; Leila said no. It was hard to sort through the fluff and lies on the Internet. To do a full search would take hours, or a special program that knew what key words to look for.

"The computers at intel could do it," said James. "But they probably already know what goes on in these prisons."

"Do they?" asked Leila. "It is not—what is the word—information kept apart, um—"

"Compartmentalized," said James. "Actually, you're right. I doubt anyone knows the whole story here. There are only bits and pieces. Tiles on a mosaic. But what pattern is emerging?"

"Torture," said Leila. She shifted in the plastic chair. "Pop culture. Brainwashing. Isolation."

"Weirdness," James agreed. "I can't help but feel like someone, somewhere, is benefiting from this whole thing. Like they're manufacturing trouble."

"The contractors?" suggested Leila. "The corporations?"

"Yeah," said James. "Just a sec." He leaned over and hit the link for a popular search engine. He typed in "Asset Protection International."

An immediate list of hits popped up. The corporate Web site, a spare page with no specific information, just a snazzy logo and some contact details. API's Virginia address, the name of the company president and CEO. Back button. Nothing to learn there. They clicked on a few more links to vacuous news stories and a dull description of the ribbon-cutting ceremony of the company headquarters building.

Leila pointed her pinky finger at a hit at the bottom of the search page, with the address of something called Corporation Black Watch. They hit gold.

"Yes," James muttered.

Corporation Black Watch was a nonprofit organization based in Spain that monitored the nefarious activities of multinational corporations. They focused on arms dealers, pharmaceutical companies, and the now-ubiquitous security contractors that popped up like weeds on an unkempt lawn after the invasions of Afghanistan and Iraq. They had an entire page devoted to API.

According to the Web site, Asset Protection International had several operations ongoing in the world. They hired South Africans, Americans, and Britons, and preferred former Special Forces. "Like Cox," said James. "He was a Navy SEAL." They hired out to the highest bidder and worked equally well with all governments. No one knew their annual profit margin; it was a privately held company and not listed on the stock exchanges. They were connected to several nasty incidents in other countries: a cover-up of a massacre in Serbia, collusion with rebel forces in Sierra Leone. The murder of a detainee at Bagram Air Force Base, Afghanistan, which was later blamed on a couple of military officers. Dodgy dealings all over the globe.

Leila scanned down the page: API was owned by another corporation. The bigger whale, a very recognizable name, was involved in construction, energy, and, strangely, a popular children's cable television channel. They had the contract to supply building materials to the American military. They built the stalls at Guantánamo Bay, Cuba. They built a large detainment center in Egypt. They contributed millions of dollars to both political parties in the United States, and were rumored to have several high-ranking politicians and bureaucrats in their pocket. Like James, she wrote down everything they found; it would be stored with the rest of the information in the silver puzzle box in the back of her closet.

"They are profiting from this war," said Leila.

"I'll say," said James. "Even the salaries of these guys are an incentive to go to war." He let out a laugh, humorless and gray. "You know what they're doing? They're drumming up business. Holy shit."

Leila nodded.

James said that ever since the API contractors arrived in Mosul, they'd been getting odd sets of orders that did not alleviate the violence, but exacerbated it. He got a look on his face that had become all too familiar to Leila these days: guilt. "I suspected as much," he said into his hands.

"What do you mean?" Leila asked, unfamiliar with his slang.

"I've just played right into it," said James. "Like an idiot. A naïve idiot. They get the army to do the dirty work, and they stay on-base, driving these *muj* detainees bonkers and coming away with a nice fat paycheck." He glanced around the little Internet café; no one was listening to them, but when he spoke again, his voice was nearly a whisper. "This isn't war. This is a scam. No wonder it keeps deteriorating. They *want* civil war. It means more business for them. Jesus."

Leila sat in silence, letting the implications sink in. The Iraqi constitution, the American occupation, the bombings and offensives and rebuilding efforts . . . all a smoke screen so that some very rich people could make even more money.

Asset Protection International could not be behind the invasion. The scope was too great for that. Even a powerful multinational corporation could not pull those kinds of strings, she reasoned. But the terrible violence that pulsed through her native Iraq was being encouraged, condoned, left to simmer. She let out a small huff of dismayed laughter. *And we aren't even taking into account the oil companies.* The energy corporations were salivating over Iraq's plentiful oil fields and Leila had always suspected that if Iraq had been a resource-poor country with an evil dictator, the world would have averted their gaze, just like those poor people in Africa, places the world had forgotten, where men like Saddam reigned but there was no money to be made from stopping them.

Leila saw the bitterness and disillusionment on James's face. Much of what he was fighting for was a farce, a commercial enterprise.

"We should go," she said gently. "It gets late."

"Yeah," James said. "Yeah. Come on, we'll pick up your bicycle."

Leila threw a few dinars down on the plywood counter for the cybercafe owner, who was on the phone and did not even glance at them as they left. It was good, thought Leila; because James wore his kaffiyeh and his vivid blue eyes were hidden behind his sunglasses, people assumed they were husband and wife, or brother and sister, nothing unusual at all. The disguise worked.

As they drove through the narrow back streets toward the Al-Razi Hospital, Leila's head swam with images and thoughts, struggling to keep track of it all. She thought about the sick joke that was the interrogation system the Americans used: *The Wizard of Oz.* Psychological persuasion. A subtle system of brainwashing that made the guilty out of the innocent, and left the true culprits to fade back into the shadows, living to fight another day.

Her own people, too, took the bait. Her father, though vastly different in his ideals, was more like James than he ever would have imagined: playing into the hand of those in power. Tamir al-Ghani was just what the doctor ordered for this new war. He rose in anger, responding to violence with violence, creating the perfect conditions for endless security contracts and rebuilding contracts and defense contracts. Leila wondered what he would say if he ever knew. But she could not tell him about API and the torture racket; it would reveal too much about her working relationship with James, the true goings-on at LSA Diamondback, and her own independence of thought that led her to research the whole thing in the first place. Tamir did not value independent thinking in his daughters anymore.

The darkness of the night made Leila feel claustrophic, and she turned her head to look at James as he drove. His profile was strong and taut. He was thinking, planning, mulling over the same revelations that tormented Leila. She pulled her head scarf closer about her face. They reached the hospital and Leila darted out of the pickup to unlatch her bicycle from the cold metal bars; James helped her put it into the bed of the truck. They hurried, for Leila did not want to be recognized. Given Tamir's penchant for knowing all the facts, it would not surprise her if the insurgency had its own complex system of espionage, made easier by the gossiping nature of Arab culture in general.

"Back home now," said James.

"Yes," said Leila.

They drove in silence for several minutes. Then Leila could not resist interrupting James's thoughts. "What now?" she asked. "What do we do with this information?"

"Well," he said, rubbing his chin with his hand, "I've written it all down, for one thing. Every time, ever since that first incident of torture with that guy back in November—remember him? Electrodes, just like this last?—and the API guys. I've kept records. I don't know what I'll do with it. If they try to court-martial me, then I can turn around and throw this stuff in their face."

"Court-martial? Why would they?"

"Yousef is dead, Leila. It's just like that case at Bagram, in Afghanistan—they'll blame it on the military. And I was the ranking officer present."

Leila sent up a prayer that James did not get exposed as a torturer and murderer; the man sitting next to her was anything but. She would vouch for his goodness and strength, she decided, if she were ever called in for evidence.

"I hope they leave you out of it," she said.

"Where do you want me to drop you?"

"There's an old park that I sometimes cycle past. It has low-hanging trees; we can stop beneath them and I will continue on. Take a left on this street up here."

The Al-Rumi Park was named after a Sufi mystic and sage, but little of its grand heritage remained. Now the park was littered with trash and bullets, scarred after the violence and never taken care of. The people of Mosul had more important things to worry about than the state of their green spaces. The park was not safe at night, either; it was the haven of criminals on the run, the homeless and dispossessed, beggars and thieves. Leila asked James to wait until she was clear of the park before driving off back to Diamondback.

He stopped the pickup and left the engine running. He lifted his hands off the steering wheel and reached out to brace his arm around her seat. Leaning in, he said, "Thank you for helping me." Did she imagine a trace of hoarseness in his voice?

"You are welcome," she said. She could not think of anything else to say. Outside the pickup's dusty windows, the Al-Rumi Park was all evil shadows, the branches of trees reaching out to snag her. She saw the flicker of firelight past the tree trunks, in the gloom, and the hunched-over figures of men clustered around for warmth or tea or scheming. Leila wanted to stay suspended in this moment forever, safe in James's company, sitting quiet and still inside the metal cocoon of the truck. Then her father's face floated in her mind's eye, wrathful and suspicious. "I should go," she said.

"Yeah. I'll get your bicycle out of the back." James hesitated for a split second as though he, too, wanted to stay, but then with the quick and efficient motions of a soldier he opened the door, checked their vicinity for threats, opened the door of the pickup bed, and pulled Leila's bicycle out, setting it upright for her. "Time to fly," he said to her. "Be safe, Leila."

"Thank you," she said. "This is not the first time I owe you for a safe trip home."

He glanced down at her. Their faces were not very far apart, perhaps four inches, and that air seemed hot, magnetized. Leila felt something warm in her solar plexus, a lump in her throat; her lips tingled. They were unprotected from the eyes of whoever was in the park and the dark square windows of the houses on the other side of the street, but Leila made a split-second decision. Lifting up on her toes, she whispered in James's ear, "I think I will dream of you."

In the heavy night Leila saw the twitch of a smile on his lips.

She whirled away and pedaled fast on her bicycle, giving no time for anything else, for she did not trust herself and she did not trust Mosul to leave them be.

That night, Leila kept her promise—she dreamed of James, her sighs quiet against a backdrop of the clatter in the courtyard. The noise eventually woke her and she watched from her post behind the curtain as Tamir moved three mujahideen into the modified room at the bottom of the well in the courtyard, three more guests of the Insurgency Hotel al-Ghani, putting the count at eight.

The next morning, Leila's head was a muddle of James, of API, of terrorism and the latest news that a bomb had exploded the day before in a neighborhood in Baghdad in which they had family. It was a market, at noon, the peak of traffic, and over thirty innocents had been killed. The worst part was that Leila was not upset. These incidents had become such an everyday occurrence that they rolled off her back. She had no time to think about it; she had to get ready; she had to go to work.

The field hospital was in an uproar when Leila arrived. Whitaker and Peabody were arguing, a rare sight, and the rest of the staff cowered from it as though no one wanted to get hit with the backlash. Nurse Pavlopolous bustled past Leila without saying good morning, a rarity for the outspoken nurse, and Leila was puzzled. She found Jessica Quinn.

"What's going on?" Leila asked.

"Shhh," said Quinn, trying to stay by the door to Dr. Whitaker's office so she could eavesdrop on the argument.

Leila, an expert in the art of eavesdropping, followed Quinn's example and cocked an ear toward the doctor's office. From what she could hear, the two men were at odds over the proper procedure for dealing with a "death in detainment" and what cause of death to put on the certificate. Dr. Peabody quoted Pratt, which Leila took as a bad sign, and advocated the vague phrase "accidental death" on the certificate. Dr. Whitaker (who as a colonel was higher ranking than Peabody) disagreed, saying the detainee was beaten to death, and had to be ruled a homicide.

They were talking about Yousef, no doubt. Leila had a flash of an idea, based on James's plan to gather evidence. She had access to the hospital morgue, and she could take pictures of Yousef's body. If the army tried to cover up the fact that he'd died because of torture, then it would be vital to have photographs that proved it. Everyone knew the power of photographs. They could be printed, distributed, flashed across screens the world over, just like those terrible images from the Abu Ghraib prison.

"Jeez," said Quinn. "This could go on for hours. Come on, let's have a cigarette break."

Leila agreed to join her in the hope of getting the hospital gossip. It turned out not to be much; Quinn said that Bonnie, the buxom blond nurse, was now engaged to a master sergeant in the Stryker Brigade. The doctor at the pharmaceutical dispensary was addicted to painkillers. There was a dispute about funding, which did not surprise Leila; money was something that everyone argued over. Leila tried to get Quinn on track by asking about the death of Yousef.

Quinn made a soft noise. "Oh, boy. That one is gonna be a mess. Did you see him? I'm kind of amazed they would let it go like that. Probably he was in the hands of the Iraqi police first, right? Then we took him?"

"No," said Leila. "This man has always been in Coalition custody. He was in fine health until yesterday, so I understand."

"Oh," said Quinn. She said nothing to what that implied

about her countrymen. Instead she tossed the end of her cigarette and grabbed Leila's hand. "Let's go back inside. So, have you decided to make our belly-dancing lessons a permanent fixture?"

Leila was dismayed with the way Quinn could turn her head away from torture and change the subject and pretend not to understand. "Yes," she said, "the dancing lessons are a good thing. If you can book the exercise room, I will give another one. The charge is—umm—Diet Coke for me."

Quinn laughed, sounding relieved not to talk about anything so serious as Yousef's cause of death. "Excellent!" she said in her sweet little voice. "See you later, Leila."

The rest of the day passed in heavy chores and silence; for even though all the hospital staff pretended that everything was normal, everyone knew that something bad was happening in the low-slung gated grounds of the detainment center.

On her way home, Leila was caught in an early spring thunderstorm and her bare face was pelted by an angry rain. She arrived, dripping wet, just as Khaled and Fatima arrived for a visit. Khaled chatted with their parents, and Leila and Fatima embraced with the force of long-parted sisters. Leila changed into dry clothes and they settled alone in Leila's room. Khaled's shop was doing well, Fatima reported, although a small car-bombing across the street had broken the main window. It had yet to be fixed. Their home was still most agreeable; Leila had visited a total of three times since January and though it was small, Fatima kept it clean and inviting. The house was no more than two small rooms and a water closet, without a courtyard or outdoor space at all, and no fruit trees. Leila suggested they move to the country.

"I've suggested it, also," said Fatima. "But Khaled is reluctant to leave his business. He has a cousin who could run the shop, I suppose, but my husband likes to be in control. Besides, then I would be so far from my dear sister and family!"

Leila hugged her sister again, and the shape of her sister's figure had changed, something she'd not noticed at their first greeting. A suspicion dawned in Leila's medical mind. "Fatima!" she said. "You're pregnant!"

A blush confirmed the fact. "Since just after the wedding, I think."

"Wow," said Leila in English. She gazed into her sister's reddened, solid face. Fatima had the look of a woman pregnant, a suffusion of new life in her cells, the care and nurturing that would bring a person into the world in some months' time. It was Fatima's dream, but to Leila it looked like prison. Leila imagined herself pregnant with cousin Abdul's child. Abhorrent. But it brought her to another point with Fatima.

"So," Leila said with a sly smile, "you have never given details, Fatima. What is your husband like in bed?"

Fatima giggled and covered her face with her hands. "Leila, you have become so bold!"

"Jessica's influence."

"Who?"

"Never mind. Really, though, what is Khaled like?"

"It's—um—not what I expected. I can't explain. Not unpleasant, Khaled is very gentle, and I think those magazines have helped."

"I'm glad of that," said Leila. "I had to grovel to get them."

For all the prying, Leila could not get specific details about sex out of her sister. The sole concession Fatima would make was that it was "all right," and she said that there were worse things about getting married. It wasn't much to induce Leila toward matrimony. They discussed the imminent April wedding of their friend Hala Rasul and Hala's sister Souad; it was to be a double ceremony. It was a smart idea to get both girls married at once because it cut the opportunity for violence in half.

"And what of you?" Fatima asked in the hour before she and Khaled were supposed to depart for their own home. "What about"—she lowered her voice to a just-audible tremor—"the American? James?"

Leila sighed. "I think about him all the time. He's not mar-ried, by the way! And perhaps I imagine it, but he likes me. But there's nothing to be done about it, Fatima, nothing. We're in the middle of the war, on opposite sides, each doing things we are not proud of. How can there be love or even friendship in such a bad situation?" She sighed. "Besides, you know that Mama and *Baba* keep trying to convince me to marry Abdul. I keep pushing it away. In the end, they can't be too serious about it. They can't force me. But I also can't be with the one I . . . I want, either. *They* would never agree to an American."

Fatima smiled. "You might surprise yourself yet, Leila. I refuse to believe that you'll let a bit of civil war get in your way."

With a laugh, Leila agreed with her sister in theory, thinking how nice it was to have a relative with her best interests in mind. Her mother was unsuitable for anything except giving orders and hinting at the social status of various cousins, asso-ciates, and neighbors. Umm Naji would never think to ask after the American men stationed in Mosul. Yet Fatima's praise worked on Leila's mind: could she be so headstrong? Was there a chance that she might end up with an American soldier through sheer force of will? The combination of daily peril to and from work, the stress of the hospital, and the un-palatable reality of the misdeeds at the detainment center pre-vented Leila from having a clear heart. Her feelings swung back and forth between dismay at James's involvement, pity for him, total trust, and suspicion that she was being manipu-lated. It was not the recipe for heartfelt affection. She ignored the fluttery feelings that rose from deep inside when she thought about his presence, his eyes upon her, the nearness of him when they had bade each other good-bye outside the Al-Rumi Park that night.

Fatima and Khaled left in a whirl of kisses and good-byes. For those few moments, everything was normal, and the fam-ily was whole and strong. Leila hung back, and Fatima gave her a tiny, knowing smile on her way out the door.

* * *

Leila's preoccupations went unnoticed in the al-Ghani house, for Umm Naji bustled about concocting special teas to aid pregnancy, smiling and joking and almost her old self again. Tamir seemed pleased though distracted at Fatima's news, spending most of his time at mosque or hosting the rounds of mujahideen. Leila knew it was a matter of time before her father was arrested; pragmatic as it may have been, Leila wished it might happen before cousin Abdul got his hopes too high for marriage. Without Tamir to orchestrate it, the arrangement would fall apart. She also hoped the arrest would happen without anyone getting hurt. Would James warn her if the Americans planned to come to her home? After all she was doing for them, she felt she deserved a forewarning for her safety if nothing else . . . or maybe she could even request her father's arrest, should he try to force her hand with Abdul. She smiled, thinking it would pay to have her American connections.

The next Monday she had another meeting with James. Neither one spoke of the Yousef incident, or the information they'd learned about API, or even the care they held for each other's welfare; the MWR Center was too crowded and they were fearful of being overheard. She gave him the information that eight insurgents now occupied the hole in the courtyard; he gave her thanks.

"But, James," she said when they were safe outside the building and in fresh air, "I have an idea. I think we should take independent photographs of that man's body. Yousef. That way we can prove he died because of torture. It's being kept in the cold locker." Leila had been troubled to learn this, for custom dictated that Muslims were buried within a day of their death.

James hesitated at her suggestion; Leila thought she knew why. He was there when it happened. Of course the military would have taken their own photos of the body, but there was no accessing them aside from a leak.

"We do not have to do anything with the pictures," Leila insisted. "Just have them. In case."

"Okay," James said, appearing to have made a split-second decision. He reached into one of his many cargo pockets and pulled out a small silver digital camera. "Use this. I'll pick it up from you before you leave tonight. Don't let anyone see you. But if they do, say that you were instructed by me to take photos; my name's on the camera, see? But it would be easier if no one saw you at all."

"Right," said Leila. "See you tonight, then."

"Tonight," he repeated. They parted ways.

The hospital was quiet that afternoon; Leila helped set a sprained ankle and bandaged a grazed cheek. Another Stryker came in with a twisted wrist from playing basketball. Later in her shift, Leila was able to take time away from her medical duties and she walked down the hall toward the cold room where bodies were temporarily stored. The shining steel door was unlocked.

Her heartbeat pounded with adrenaline as she looked this way and that, making sure no one saw her enter the room. Yousef was the only body in there, zipped up in thick black plastic with a name tag dangling off. Swiftly, expertly, Leila unzipped the body bag and made a face at the sight and the smell of it. She pulled the plastic away to get a clear shot with James's camera.

Click. Puffed-up eyes seeping dried blood.

Click. Burn marks from electrodes.

Click. Massive bruising across the chest and torso.

The job was done. Leila turned off the camera and pocketed it. Then she zipped up the body bag; the rubbery quality of it and the chill of the room combined to create a sense of unreality, as though it were the set of a film. She glanced behind her to make sure nothing with Yousef looked amiss and saw that it was fine. Pushing her ear against the door, she listened for footsteps in the outside hallway and heard nothing; she used the sleeve of her jacket to open the door so there would be no fingerprints. Without hesitation she stepped into the hallway, closed the door behind her with a satisfying thunk, and walked away.

No one was the wiser. James picked up the camera that night in a fast little handoff and a smile. Leila remembered to breathe again on the bus ride back into the city.

Chapter 21

Spring was Leila's favorite season. So full of promise, the weather cool and fresh, the birds pairing off and the bees humming on their rounds. This year, however, spring was slow to get started in Mosul, bound and chained by bloodshed. The birds were around but hushed. The season's first bees looked sluggish and morose as they buzzed indolently about the al-Ghanis' private courtyard, taking sniffs of the first flowers but not tempted to dive in with their normal vigor. Leila read her book, a large medical text, while sitting cross-legged on the worn stone bench in the courtyard. She wore her hair uncovered. The light was harsh and unforgiving, and did nothing to warm her. In the corner of the courtyard, the pomegranate tree leaned wearily toward the sun with scrawny branches. It could not bear fruit any longer.

Leila shivered, drawing her light woolen shawl closer about her shoulders. She leafed through the book, her eyes glancing across diagrams of molecules, complex biostructures that she could not picture right now as floating in her own body. Leila's body was numb and sluggish like the bees, not wanting to work on these terms.

Through the dirty window into the kitchen she could see Umm Naji, rolling dough for flatbread, her face a blank expression of habit rather than decision. Ever since Fatima's wedding, Leila's mother had done nothing but follow Tamir's directions. Umm Naji had even stopped hinting about marriageable men. This was due to the tacit arrangement with cousin Abdul, but Umm Naji did not act as though she anticipated the grand marriage of her youngest daughter. She'd said nothing about celebrations, about the traditional string of meetings and parties. It was as though the whole thing was a secret from the world, but Leila just took it to mean it wasn't serious. Abdul was an option, one that her parents wanted, but she felt sure they wouldn't begin planning until they secured Leila's permission.

It was Thursday but Leila had the day off. The previous day, the surgeons had told her she didn't need to come in on her normal schedule; a four-day weekend, they said. Just relax and stay at home. It seemed odd, the sudden holiday, but Leila did not question it.

So she caught up on her reading and even prepared some printouts of medical school applications. Later in the day she might work on her admissions essay. However, this was done half-heartedly, for a piece of her felt she would never live long enough to go to medical school. The psychology of danger was a quicksand trap of pessimism; why make plans for the future when she would be lucky to live through tomorrow? Leila contemplated this phenomenon with a different part of her mind, the serene analytical part that tended to think in English as a way of showing off to itself.

From across the wall, she heard the squishy sound of wet cloth being wrung out; it would be the widow Umm Mohammed, doing her wash. Her children had all left her; Leila knew the son, Mohammed, had been killed in a bombing several years ago, and the six girls of that family were long married with children of their own. Leila wondered why one of the daughters did not take the old lady in, but the answer was logical enough. Poverty afflicted much of Mosul, even these graceful old neighborhoods, now crumbling and dusty by the war. With poverty came the fraying of family ties, just not enough room, too many mouths to feed, and the widows were left to fend for themselves. Society had more important things to worry about.

Umm Mohammed was a tragic figure; Leila had seen her walking last week, hunched over, draped in black like a crow, making her way back from the market with a tiny bag of flour and some withered onions. Just after the invasion, when the cease-fire was a cease-fire and Mosul brimmed with hope, Umm Naji used to take fresh flatbreads to Umm Mohammed's house to save the old woman the trouble of baking, but those days were past. Now they had a well full of mujahideen to feed and no bread to waste on nonterrorists. Leila made a mental note to check on Umm Mohammed this weekend, perhaps take tea with her for the sake of neighborliness and some normality.

The days were supposed to be getting longer. To Leila it felt the opposite. Her days passed in shadow-stretching rapidity, a blur of medical terms read on the page, interspersed with wild thoughts and images. The patients on the ward at the field hospital. James Cartwright's face. Burned, charred fingernails resting on the end of an Iraqi hand. Cousin Abdul, leering at her, and his face morphed into that of Sayyid, the boy-man who worked at the Al-Razi Hospital pharmacy. Those initial days of promise, of getting a job, seemed like a glowing age ago. If only her life were so simple.

Then her wandering mind told her it was hungry, a reminder that she was still alive, welcome and yet not. Leila put her textbook away in her room and wandered into the kitchen, opening the refrigerator. No electricity. She shut it so as to keep the cold air in. Outside, the sun hit the tiled roof and painted wall on the other side of the courtyard, reflecting back into the kitchen window as a mockery of gold. Leila did not need the overhead lights to see her way into making a *shwarma* sandwich, so the loss of power was not so bad.

Cooling in the oven was the flatbread from earlier in the day. Leila grabbed a piece of it, put it on a plate. Opened the refrigerator again and chose some cold chicken and yogurt.

That would do. She chopped a few slices of cucumber, rinsing it first in the tap water, hoping she would not become ill from the polluted water but not caring too much if she did. That was what a medical degree did, after all: made a person more aware of all the things that could cause sickness and, eventually, death.

She brought her food back up to her room, unwilling to run into her mother or, worse, her father. She'd been eating there a lot, snatched meals on the sly, avoiding the family. If Fatima could just be around, things would be easier. An ally was a fine thing. But Fatima's loyalties had shifted just like the rest of Iraq. Leila tasted bitterness mixed in with the yogurt, the cucumber, the meat. She swallowed her food with difficulty.

The fall of darkness brought the imam to the house. Leila, compelled to listen, crept down the stairs in bare feet and a housedress. Her head was covered just in case a strange man should happen upon her. With Tamir's mood being what it was, the simple sight of Leila without a head scarf in the presence of a strange man would provoke him.

"—way is prepared," her father was saying.

Muffled sounds.

"Next week it will begin," said the imam.

The clinking of glasses. Leila's muscles tensed as she heard Umm Naji's footsteps in the main hall, thinking her mother might be heading for the water closet in the back and would discover her eavesdropping; the footsteps kept going into the sitting room. Leila relaxed. She heard her mother murmur some respectful thing and heard a clunk; she would have set down a fresh teapot.

"Discipline is the key," said Tamir. "No matter what the Americans do in the meantime, we must wait until next Friday. Only then will we have enough martyrs. Let them wait for us. We're on the offensive now."

To Leila it sounded like a lot of babble. Like boys gathered in a clubhouse, hatching grandiose plots against the neighbors, like those American cartoons she'd read about the little blond boy and his stuffed tiger. Just as she was about to leave, the conversation took a more serious turn.

They were planning a key offensive against the Americans and against all American "sympathizers." They had a list of Iraqi families who were to be murdered because of their close ties with the Americans: those who sold goods to the Americans from their shops, those who had them at their restaurants, those who had children working as translators or cleaners at the base. At this last, Leila swallowed a gulp of horror. As she was spying for the Ansar al-Sunna mujahideen (or they thought she was), she was safe from it. But her Iraqi coworkers, those that rode the bus with her every day, were now named targets. They would be hunted down at their homes, their families punished. *Oh, dear God.*

Then it got worse: her father spoke in hard, logical tones about the damage that would be inflicted on the Americans. They would engage the Stryker patrols using a stash of new RPG-7, shoulder-fired rockets that would home in on the hot vehicle engines like bees to a honeypot. Where they had gotten such weapons, Leila did not know. She pressed her ear hard up against the wall to hear the rest.

The jihadis in the sitting room gloated and congratulated each other over the incident several weeks ago, when the MP patrol was set afire and two of the soldiers killed. Then they moved on to the worst yet: they wanted to take as many alive as they could. After they had hostages, the Ansar al-Sunna would offer to make trades for Iraqi prisoners: twenty Iraqis for every one American soldier.

Her father, in a voice filled with cold joy, said, "No, the Americans will never negotiate. We should offer, of course . . . but these trades will not happen. Instead, we can behead the soldiers, and release the videos to Al-Jazeera. Then they will see how serious we are." To hear him say it made Leila want to cry.

She bit her bottom lip to give herself something to focus on. She closed her eyes and fought the urge to run away. Instead, she kept listening.

Murder, torture, and public beheadings were not the only items on the mujahideen's agenda. They rehashed the successful dining hall bombing at Camp Marez of several years ago, speaking with glee about the body count, the carnage, the Americans' impotence in finding the culprits. Then the imam gave a blessing for the greater bloodshed that was to come. Leila felt her heart drop.

Two bombs. One would target the Combat Support Hospital after the commencement of the offensive, when it would be full of soldiers recovering from the attacks on their patrols. The other bomb would target the downtown precinct police station when it was full of Iraqi police.

This was not some half-baked operation anymore. The plans were laid, the traps set, the supplies gathered. Somewhere in Mosul City, or perhaps on a farm just outside the limits, there were stores of weapons and explosives and the tools for making jihad. From the sounds of it, the big bombs were to be in trucks driven by suicide bombers, that classic technique of martyr making that drew enthusiasts from as far away as Saudi Arabia, Africa, Indonesia. She wondered who would drive the bomb into the field hospital.

James. She had to warn James. Her whole body was shaking, and she made herself wait a few more minutes crouched at the wall, making sure there was not more to hear, until she could pull herself together. The imam descended into quoting the Holy Quran; the others made interjections of piety and their faith in violence. Leila stood up, dizzy after being down on the floor so long, and put her hand on the wall to steady herself. She tiptoed on her bare feet back through the front hall and locked eyes with her mother.

"What are you doing?" Umm Naji asked, narrowing her eyes.

Lie. Think of a lie, quickly for the sake of Allah! "I'm not feeling well," she said, clutching her stomach. "I could only make it to the downstairs bathroom. Goodness, Mama, I haven't been this ill in ages! Really, I was sick, and then I threw up—" Leila stopped, seeing that her mother did not want details. "Perhaps there's a flu going around," she said.

"Hmph," said Umm Naji. "You'd better rest. Your cousin Abdul is arriving here tomorrow."

"What? Why?"

"For a visit."

"He was just here for a visit."

"He is family, Leila, you will welcome him. He'll be more than family to you soon."

Leila rolled her eyes. "Whatever, Mama." She knew what this was. Abdul was going to try to convince her in person to marry him. This prospect was enough to make Leila feel genuinely ill. *Ugh*, she thought. When she went up to her bedroom and closed the door, she banished Abdul from her mind and instead wrote down all she had heard downstairs. She made extra care to write down the specifics, the names and dates and places. James would be very happy with her and the thought made Leila happy, too. But how would she get him the information? She did not go back to work until Monday, which gave four days' warning of the mujahideen offensive, but Leila wanted to get rid of the burden as soon as possible.

She folded up her notebook paper. It was packed margin to margin with vital intelligence, ready to go into the puzzle box. Perhaps she should strike a firmer bargain with the Americans? Citizenship for information? Her shoulders drooped as she thought about it. The U.S. Army would never do it, though she had a feeling James would speak in her favor. But the rest of them would use her and lose her. It was a well-known story in Iraq now. Even at Camp Marez and Diamondback, the Iraqi translators who worked so hard and risked life and limb were not allowed access to medical treatment at the field hospital. The insurgents were treated there, but not the translators. If

Leila ever broke her ankle at work, they would haul her off the base and to one of the Mosul civilian hospitals. Gratitude was in the form of a handshake and maybe a pack of cigarettes, not anything useful.

Despite all that she'd heard that night, Leila's sleep was deep and dreamless until three in the morning. Then she woke up with a start. She was unable to put her finger on what was wrong; all was silent. She pulled back her curtains and the city was in blackout, which was not a great surprise. The power was off more often than it was on. She stared out the window for a few minutes and, seeing nothing, crawled back into bed. She punched her pillow to get it into shape and laid her head down on a cool spot.

The noise rolled over her skin before it reached her ears. An explosion, loud, long, and very close by. Leila sat up straight, clutching the sheet in her hands, fearing for a terrible moment that it was her house up in smoke by a mortar or bomb. An angry orange glow blossomed outside and filtered through her curtains. Leila was up again in a flash, yanking back the fabric, eyes widening as she saw a mushroom of flame in the direction of the Al-lah Al-Hasib Mosque.

And the mosque it was; there was the minaret tower, collapsing into itself. Flames licked the sky as the primary explosion dimmed down. She knew there were classrooms in there full of wooden furniture that would feed the fire for a while. But who would bomb a mosque at three in the morning? Someone who wanted to minimize casualties, so not the local homegrown terrorists. A suspicion dawned in Leila's mind like the false sunrise out her window, but it was too terrible to acknowledge. *No, they wouldn't do that. They couldn't.* No company, not even API, was powerful enough to go around setting huge explosions . . . unless they had the complicity of the U.S. military . . . and Leila stopped herself right there.

She watched, fascinated, as the smoke roiled and churned into the night sky, smoke lit by the fire beneath it, smoke carrying with it the remains of dreams and religions. Despite the horrible violence happening just outside her window, Leila had time for one crazy thought: because of the bombing, there was no way she would have to see Abdul tomorrow. She could tell her parents she was needed at the base first thing in the morning. She would be able to see James and present the evidence she'd overheard from her father. Leila feared the mosque bombing would anger Tamir and his nest of insurgents; they might bump up their timetable. Even more reason to get to the army base as soon as possible.

It was impossible to sleep anymore. She watched the flames out her bedroom window. The phone rang downstairs. Tamir answered and spoke in clipped, terse tones. Leila crept to the top of the stairs, hoping to hear details, but her father had ended the conversation by the time she got to the top of the stairs. Oh well. Back to watch the city burning.

The flames faded after a while and Leila snatched a few hours of sleep. When she opened her eyes again, the sun had risen. A column of black greasy smoke rose against the sky, bent by the wind.

She would find out later that she'd witnessed the beginning of an American offensive called Operation Clean Sweep, but by then it was too late to make any difference to Leila's decisions that day.

It took a few moments to get dressed and gather her papers. Leila disguised the notes from her father's most recent conversation in a sheaf of medical reports and journal printouts, then put it all in her handbag and closed the metal clasp around it. Perfect; it looked as it always did. Her shoes went on her feet and the head scarf around her hair.

Downstairs she met with disaster at every turn.

First, it was cousin Abdul, standing in the doorway to the sitting room in fine white djellaba and formal headdress. His face lit up as he saw her, making his skin look shinier than ever, and he bowed to her. Leila said nothing to him but kept walking past him into the kitchen so she could grab a pastry on her way out the door.

Then it was Umm Naji's chattering, coming through from the sitting room, followed by Tamir's voice.

"Leila!"

"What?" she said with a sigh. When she emerged from the kitchen into the front hallway with a small raisin-filled pastry in her hand, Umm Naji was standing next to Abdul. "Where do you think you're going?" she asked, her eyes catching on Leila's shoes and handbag.

"I have to get to work," Leila said. She took a bite of the pastry and headed for the front door. "Don't you know there's been a bombing?"

"For goodness' sake, don't talk with your mouth full of pastry. You're spraying crumbs all over the place," Umm Naji said, glancing toward Abdul with embarrassment.

Leila rolled her eyes. "I'll be home tonight, unless I have to work through."

"Stop."

Her father's quiet command stopped her in her tracks.

"There's a citywide curfew. No one is allowed on the streets," said Tamir, stepping past Abdul and toward her. "You cannot leave the house today."

"What?" Leila asked. "But I need to go to work!" She registered once again that Abdul was wearing his best clothes; her mother was in a fine embroidered dress. This gave Leila cause for concern and she wanted out of the house, away, toward the modern escape of the American base. Where once it was the camp of the enemy, now it was her sanctuary. "What's happening?" she asked when no one said anything.

Umm Naji stepped forward and took Leila's arm. "Upstairs," she said.

"Let go, Mama," Leila said. "I'll call work. I'm sure they've given me special permission to go to work, I—"

"We'll be down in a little while," said Umm Naji over her shoulder to Tamir and Abdul. Leila thought she heard another voice from the sitting room but could not be sure. Her head was buzzing with some kind of confused internal noise.

"What the hell?" Leila asked her mother when they were back in her bedroom.

"Do not swear at me, child," Umm Naji said.

With wide eyes, Leila sank down into her chair and watched as Umm Naji opened the painted wooden wardrobe and began riffling through the clothes there, muttering. Then she turned back around with Leila's best dress in her hands, confirming Leila's worst suspicions: Abdul had come to the house to marry her.

Leila noticed her mother, properly noticed her for the first time in weeks. Umm Naji was thinner and yet flabbier. Her skin hung from the bones as though it were melting. Her face was bloated, the skin pale, and she had dark circles under her eyes. In contrast to the nice dress she wore, her unwashed hair peeked out, stringy, from beneath her head scarf, revealing the many strands of gray in her once-lustrous raven hair, more salt than pepper. Umm Naji must have aged ten years in the past month. Leila knew why, too; it was the worry. Anxiety about Tamir, feeding the extra mouths down in the old well, knowing that one of these days the Americans would catch on and haul her husband away and leave her alone in the world. The worst part of it was that Leila could not muster up feelings of sympathy for her mother. Umm Naji had made her bed and she must lie in it.

Her parents had sprung the marriage on her, hoping to surprise her, thinking that in her daze she might wed her cousin without complaint and be taken away from Mosul forever. The timing was too good for it to be otherwise: on a holy Friday, the week before the mujahideen launched their violent plans and things really hit the fan, and her father wanted her out of the city. Only now, Leila thought with a manic burst of humor, there was a bombing at the mosque and it was all falling apart, anyway.

Tamir must be going insane in his thirst for revenge, impatient to throw his mujahideen into action; no wonder Umm

Naji held the fine dark dress out to Leila with an expression of urgency on her sagging face.

"Put it on."

"No." Leila took a breath. "I know what you're doing. You want me to marry Abdul right here, right now, don't you?"

Her mother's silence confirmed it all.

"I refuse," Leila said. "Absolutely no way in hell. Get that thing away from me." She ripped the dress from her mother's hands and flung it to the floor.

"Leila, you must!" Umm Naji said, tears of desperation cleaving down her face in wet streams. "There is no choice. Mosul is too dangerous. Your father—you know about your father. Please. Once you are married, you will be safe. Safe from the bad things here. It's what I've wanted all along, only the best for you! You don't know what you want. You are too young. Your father knows, so obey him, as is your duty as a daughter. This is not a choice. Oh, Leila, say something!"

Leila listened to her mother ramble on, the anger swirling in her chest, but this time the anger was pure and clear; Leila knew exactly what she must do. She reached down and retrieved the dress. "Can you leave me for a moment?" she asked. She gazed at Umm Naji, memorizing her face.

"Please tell me you'll do this thing, Leila," said Umm Naji.

"Yes," said Leila. "Yes, I see now. Tell Abdul I will marry him in just a few moments' time. I will put on the dress and fix my hair and makeup. A bride must look pretty, yes?"

Umm Naji's taut shoulders collapsed with relief. "Oh, dear daughter," she cried, clutching Leila's hands. "You will be safe now, taken care of! I will not worry anymore." A hint of the old Umm Naji came back for the flash of a moment in her enthusiasm. Then it disappeared again as she said, "I'll serve tea to the men now. We had to call the imam Rashdi, because Abdul-Hakam has—disappeared—this morning. But you don't need to worry about all of that because you'll be in Abdul's village by nightfall."

As her mother left the room, Leila gazed down at her finest

article of clothing. The dress was indigo blue, made of finest silk, with intricate gold-woven threads of flowers along the collar, cuffs, down the center, the hemline. It was an old-fashioned garment to be sure, made as a gift for Leila's graduation from the secondary school. She fingered the fabric and thought back to that quiet year before the world went crazy.

The September terrorist attacks in America had not yet happened when Leila graduated from secondary school. Her life had stretched ahead of her like a rainbow promise. She was accepted into the Cairo University program. Her father, still a judge, still a pillar of Mosul society, had the kind of money and connections to provide his daughters with nice things. Her parents had been so proud of her, not the least concerned about her getting married, and Tamir was the most steady, stable, caring father that a girl could ask for. He said she was beautiful, clever, he praised her grades. He called her nicknames and they had deep discussions about the state of the world; Tamir had been far more politically moderate in those days. He was even open to the idea of trade and cultural relations with the West. Leila agreed with him wholeheartedly.

Umm Naji was fit and large, Fatima was happy with her new job at the nursery, Naji was just married with his first child on the way. And Leila, the darling little one of the family, was given this fine dress to wear at her graduation from Mosul's best private girls' school.

Leila held the dress in her hands, recalling those warm memories as though in a matching haze of gold and blue. Then she looked out her window at a thread of smoke still sputtering from where the mosque had been. She thought of Abdul, waiting downstairs to snatch her from her dreams, her parents eager to get rid of her.

The carefully constructed life of the al-Ghani family was shattered and torn, never to be whole again. Leila understood it in that moment, just as she understood what her own role must be. How could they ever hope to bring back the familial warmth in conditions such as these? It was the war that turned her father into a violent terrorist, her mother into an impotent sack of bones. Iraq's descent into madness left no family untouched.

Untouched. That was what Leila would be where it concerned Abdul. She would be damned forever if she let that man marry her and make her his property.

Leila threw open her wardrobe and reached into the back of it, pulling out a small student backpack. She stuffed her fine folded dress into the bottom. Next came a few items of jewelry from a mother-of-pearl case on her shelf: solid gold bracelets, diamond earrings, an heirloom gold ring. She would sell them if she had to.

The most important thing to go into the backpack was the folder with her written minutes of her father's mujahideen meeting. The planned jihad would not occur without Leila warning the Americans.

She ripped open the frame that contained her diploma from Cairo, the first honors degree of which she was so proud. It, too, went in the folder. She added a stack of six or seven photographs of her family, all taken in the good old days, but she did not glance through them or allow herself another minute of nostalgia. That would come later.

Leila's hand hovered above her well-thumbed copy of the Holy Quran, resting on her bedside table. She was so mixed up about her own religion right now. It gave her hope, assurance that Allah saw everything and knew everything, and that there were angels hovering above her in love and light. But she felt that Islam was also the root of her predicament. If she could just go back in time and tell the Prophet, *peace be upon him*, to be clearer about loving mankind and not engaging in violence. Too late for that, though, and useless to dwell on it. She threw the Quran into the bag.

Last, there came the puzzle box, tarnished and heavy. It sat on Leila's bed like a lead weight. She knew every paper, every record, by heart. Within the box was the evidence of crimes from both sides, journal entries and records of the things her father had said and done . . . other copies of her reports from the field hospital. Some of it implicated her friend James in unsavory activities, but that could not be helped; most of the papers pointed to the U.S. military's helplessness over the nasty behavior of contractors and Iraqis. She stared at the box for a few seconds, then took out the sheaf of loose papers inside. Wrapping them in a rubber band, she replaced them in the box so that it closed; then she locked it. The silver square went into the backpack and she patted it once for safety. Things were ready.

It would not do to shimmy down the wall wearing her *abaya* and work shoes. So Leila stripped down in ten seconds flat, leaving her clothes pooled on the floor, and she pulled on some Western-style jeans, a loose T-shirt, and a light woolen sweater over top. Her hair she left in its strict bun beneath the head scarf. The less attention she attracted, the better.

Leila's plan was to sneak across the hall to Fatima's old room and somehow get into the front courtyard from the second floor. Her own bedroom overlooked the mujahideen-infested private courtyard and was not an option for escape. She took one last look around her room; she regretted leaving her treasured collection of books. If she could take one with her, one of the medical texts, perhaps . . . No. No room, no time.

Leila left her bedroom neat as a pin, filled with her essence, her intellect, her possessions. The one concession to her panic was her work dress bunched up on the floor. She turned the knob of her door before closing it so that it did not make a click. Then it was across the quiet hall to Fatima's old room. Leila heard no noise from downstairs and assumed that the men were all in the sitting room, waiting for the bride to show up, and her mother might have been in the kitchen or sitting with Abdul, the man who would never be a son-in-law.

Once Fatima's door was closed and the window open to the street side of the house, Leila's plan gnashed to a halt. The cement courtyard was at least five meters down from the window, an impossible height to jump without risk of serious injury. The last thing she needed was a broken ankle. But she had no rope, nor a ladder, nor any way of getting down to the ground.

As if to reinforce her predicament, a wind kicked up, howling down the fine asphalt street and whipping across Leila's face as she peered out the window. It was like being at the top of a cliff, with all the implications of jumping. Was she crazy?

Umm Naji's voice floated up the stairwell. "Leila! Hurry up. I'm sure you look beautiful."

It galvanized Leila into action. She looked around Fatima's room for something to climb with, something to hang on to—Leila looked at the small bed. She measured the width of the mattress with her hands and compared it to the window jamb. If she bent the mattress, she might be able to shove it through so it would provide her with a soft landing.

It took thirty seconds to strip the bed of its sheets. Leila lifted the mattress, which was heavier than she thought, and she made a muffled noise from the effort. *Mustn't drop it*, she thought, lest her family hear the thump. When the long mattress was leaned up and ready to lift, Leila opened the window as wide as it could go. It was the kind that opened like a door, with side hinges, and this was lamentable, for the hinges took up a precious inch of space and the mattress might snag.

Leila's heart pounded with fear and exertion. She made sure her backpack was secure on her shoulders and she gripped the dingy pink edge of the mattress and pushed it into a lengthwise fold. It popped back into shape as soon as she let the pressure down for an instant. "Damn it," she swore in English.

Through the open window the breeze came, a hard spring breeze, whispering to Leila about freedom. She gathered her strength and bent the mattress into a fold again, gritting her teeth, willing it to go through. She lifted it, keeping it together, and roughly pushed the end out the window. The cloth cover snagged for a heart-stopping moment, but Leila shoved with all her might and with a ripping sound the mattress was free. It

flew out the window and she heard it land in the front courtyard with a soft thud.

"Now," she said to herself, her throat dry. She swung her
leg up over the windowsill without looking down, then her
other leg, and saw her target. The mattress looked very small
indeed from such a height. It had landed at a diagonal, which
was unfortunate, but at least it was flat on the ground. She
would have to propel herself off the windowsill in order to hit
it just right.

Leila suddenly remembered a conversation she'd had with
James some weeks ago. He was telling her about his training in
the army and how he'd gone to jump school at a place called
Fort Benning in Georgia. James had many fabulous stories to
tell about jumping out of airplanes and he made it sound like
fun, an opinion Leila had shared until confronted with her
own jump from her two-story house. But as she hovered between leaping off the ledge and putting her feet back inside
like a sensible person, Leila recalled something James said
about the technique of the paratrooper.

"It's all in the landing," he'd told her. "You have to land
right. Even though a parachute is slowing your descent, it's
still going fast and the ground rises awful hard to meet your
feet. It's no good to try to land feet first, stiff and strong; that's
the best way to snap an ankle or a leg. You have to roll with
the landing, hit the ground with the softer, muscle-bound spots
on the body: first the calf muscles, then the thighs, the fleshy
part of the hip, the back and shoulder. Roll and bounce and
stay pliant and come up shooting."

Leila played the motion in her mind to let her muscles get
used to the idea. Roll. Bounce. Hit that mattress like a hopping
little ball.

On the rusted metal gate that led out to the street, a small
bird of a rich brown color settled and hopped from foot to
foot. It regarded Leila with sharp eyes. Then, pausing for a
moment as if to make sure she was watching, the bird flew off

again, up and up into the sky until it swooped behind another house and out of sight.

She jumped.

On instinct her arms and legs flailed, wild, uncontrolled. She remembered to tuck her elbows in and coil into a flexible ball just milliseconds before hitting the mattress. It was not a direct strike; Leila's shoulder rolled off the mattress and ground into the cement, but almost all of her momentum was broken by that point. She doubted she would even have a bruise.

For a breathless second she lay there, unable to believe she'd done it, and then she was on her feet and looking back at the house, up at the window from which she'd leapt. Through the open window she heard Umm Naji knocking on her bedroom door across the hall, nervous voice pleading with her to come out and get married.

Leila pulled open the gate and ran.

Chapter 22

Mosul was dead. Any person who saw it as Leila did that Friday morning would have thought so; there was not a soul on the streets, no movement, no vehicles. Even the curtains in the windows seemed afraid to sway with the wind.

Leila scurried along the walls and back alleys away from her house, hunched over, moving fast. She did not want her father to pursue her, though it would take her parents several minutes to realize that she'd run away. But more than that, she did not want an American patrol to spot her.

The people of Mosul had learned the hard way that there was no negotiating with the twenty-four-hour curfew. It was in the Arab soul to negotiate, but curfews were a brick wall of American will that could not be argued away. Any person out on the streets during curfew was picked up and taken to a police station or detainment center; many curfew breakers were liable to be shot dead, no questions asked. After all, the al-Ghanis' neighbor, Umm Mohammed, lost her husband of forty-five years in that very way, caught on the wrong end of an American armor-piercing bullet on his daily walk.

With such incidents the norm rather than the exception during curfews, Mosul hunkered down in the aftermath of the Allah Al-Hasib Mosque bombing to wait it out. Leila expected that most people knew of the bombing, though factual news was hard to come by. The electricity was off, too, so only those lucky few with petrol-powered generators could run their ArabSat televisions and get the latest from Al-Jazeera or the American-sponsored propaganda station, Al-Hurrah. So as Leila crept past house after house in her stately old neighborhood, her neighbors remained shuttered and closed off from the world, awaiting news, never letting their beloved family members go out to be cut down by a burst of gunfire.

After several blocks of breathless anxiety, Leila decided where to go. It would not be a good idea to try to get to Diamondback now; the buses would not be running and there were no taxis on the streets. She could not walk, for if some ignorant Stryker patrol saw her they would shoot her. Instead, she decided, she would go to Fatima's house.

Fatima and Khaled kept their home in a different neighborhood in Mosul, one that was poorer, older, and more crowded. It was all they could afford on Khaled's shopkeeper's income. In Leila's opinion, it was rather a step down for an al-Ghani daughter, but Fatima seemed happy enough just to be keeping her own hearth.

Her sister's house was about a half hour's walk from where Leila crouched. It was a hazardous business to be out on the streets for so long, but for once Leila's eccentricities paid off: her meandering routes through the city on her bicycle, to and from work, to and from the market, left her with a mapmaker's knowledge of Mosul. Leila knew the old city the way a spider knew its own web. The back alleys, the paths, the holes in ancient, crumbling walls. She planned the best way to get to Fatima and Khaled's house without being seen.

Leila ran down a side alley and she was on her way, winding, dodging, keeping her head down. Once she heard the menacing roar of American Stryker vehicles on the main street, but she was well concealed. These tiny warrens were unknown to most of the bumbling Americans and Leila allowed herself a smirk. Only the Special Forces went deep down into the city's guts the way Leila could.

Leila exhaled in relief when she rounded a corner and spotted

Fatima's door, sorely in need of a paint job. In this neighborhood, the houses were crushed against each other, sharing interior walls, a hive of humanity. Leila rushed forward and knocked softly three times.

Silence from within. Surely Fatima and Khaled had not gotten stranded somewhere for the curfew, leaving their house empty? But no, the exterior padlock was not attached; they must be inside. Leila thought perhaps her sister was engaging in newlywed activities with her husband, following the suggestions from *Cosmopolitan* magazine that said doing it in the morning could be "very spicy." Leila pushed the thought from her mind and knocked harder.

The door creaked and opened a fraction. "Who's there?" whispered Fatima's voice from the darkness.

"It's me, sister," Leila said. "Please."

"For goodness' sake, Leila," Fatima said, pulling the door wide. She was dressed in her house clothes.

"Thank you," Leila said. The inside of Fatima's house was like the cool shelter of a cave, dark and quiet, free of soldiers, terrorists, and nasty cousins who wanted to marry her.

Khaled greeted her from his lounging place on the thin dingy cushion on the floor in the front room. He held a cup of tea in his hand; Leila eyed it with enthusiasm. She needed some tea to calm her after that mad dash through the streets. "Good morning, Khaled," she said as though there were nothing out of the ordinary about her being there.

Behind them, Fatima closed the door and latched it double from the inside. "What are you *doing* here?" she whispered. "Don't you know there's a curfew?"

"Oh, Fatima," Leila said, and flung her arms around her sister. "You will not believe it. Mother and Father conspired to get me married! Cousin Abdul was at the house this morning, dressed in a best djellaba, and they even had Rashdi, you know, the imam from Nurridin Mosque."

"Abdul? The imam? You, married?" Fatima looked confused and overwhelmed by the information.

"And I saw the bombing," Leila rambled, heedless of her sister's growing alarm. Khaled sat up a little straighter to listen. "It was this morning, or middle of the night. The Al-lah Al-Hasib. A huge fireball out the window and it is still smoldering. I think that Abdul-Hakam, the imam, was killed."

"The mosque destroyed!" Khaled interjected, aghast. "Who would do it?" Such things might happen in the degenerate southern cities, in Baghdad and Najaf and Samarra, but not in Mosul. Not until now.

"I don't know who did it," said Leila. She kept quiet with her suspicions about the American mercenary contractors and their need for the business of violence. Those questions she would save for James, whenever she might see him next.

"Wait, so are you married to Abdul or not?" Fatima asked.

"God, no. I ran before they could make me."

Both Khaled and Fatima looked troubled. "Leila," Khaled said, "you have done something very serious."

"You're not my father!" Leila said. When would men cease trying to tell her what to do?

"Speaking of our father," Fatima added, "he will be so angry with you. I cannot imagine what he will do!"

The three of them were silent as they contemplated what, indeed, Tamir al-Ghani might do with a runaway daughter. Honor killings were for wayward girls who refused marriages or, worse, had boyfriends prior to being married. By her father's newly fundamentalist standards, Leila was almost guilty of both, though he was only aware of one transgression.

For a moment panic threatened to overwhelm her; she was uncertain of what to do next. She prayed that her father did not break the curfew to come after her, as the most logical place for Leila to run was to Fatima's. If she kept moving, she might outrun her father until she got to LSA Diamondback, where she would—do what? Ask for protection? Plead with Quinn to let her crash in the nurses' quarters?

Fatima made the tea, humming a soft song to herself, and Leila felt herself calm down at the sight of the kitchen ritual.

The cooking area was not more than an aging gas tank attached to a double-cooker hob by a rubber tube, and a wooden chopping block that stood on wobbly legs. Fatima did not seem put out by the spareness of it and had arranged the bags of rice, tea, flour, and the bottles of cooking oil on the wall shelf in a tidy fashion. A fresh white muslin cloth was draped over the chopping block.

Leila could not help but smile in spite of her inner turmoil. Her sister had always adored cooking, making tea, cleaning; when they were girls, they argued about playing doctor (Leila) or house (Fatima). Because Fatima was older, Leila had compromised with her and ended up playing the husband. Their play area had not been much bigger than Fatima's new abode. . . . Umm Naji had set up a playroom for them using the smallest upstairs room.

"I'm home, dear wife," said six-year-old Leila.

"Have some shai," replied Fatima, presenting her with a tray of child-sized, chipped teacups, empty.

Taking one, Leila made a show of pretending to sip the imaginary hot liquid inside. "Ouch! It's burned me. You make very boiling tea."

"I hope Allah has blessed your day," Fatima said, mimicking the words Umm Naji said to their father when he came home from work in the evenings.

"He has," said Leila. *"I cured three people."* When pretending to be a man, Leila was always a doctor as a profession. It was a way to interject her own fun on her sister's domestic domain.

"What illness did they have?" Fatima asked, also pretending to sip tea.

"One had a heart attack," said Leila. *"The other two had the flu. But I healed them all. The heart attack man was difficult, though, because he was so large."*

Fatima giggled. "Too much bouzat haleeb," *she said.*

Leila laughed, too, although she loved ice cream and could not imagine ever eating too much. Becoming fat might be worth it.

"We should have a party," said Fatima. "Especially with imaginary guests; then I won't have to speak with strangers."

"Can we have sweets? Let's ask Mama."

"She won't give us any," said Fatima. "You ask her too often. You're spoiled, Leila."

"I'm not spoiled, I'm a man!" Leila said, standing up and puffing out her chest as though she were indeed a prideful husband.

Fatima laughed at her. "We could have Naji ask for us. . . ."

"Naji has no time for us," Leila said, for their brother was at the boys' secondary school and thought himself above associating with his little sisters. "No, I'll just ask Baba. He'll tell her to give us some melfoof, at least."

"Mmm," said Fatima. "But wait! I'll bake some for us." She leaned over to a battered upside-down cardboard box that rested on the floor. It had been drawn to look like an oven using a black marker, with a pretend handle. Fatima tugged on a cutout section that opened like an oven door. "Here," she said. "It will be ready in five minutes."

"Just a few more minutes," said Fatima, peering into the teapot as she waited for the water to boil. "I have some *melfoof*, here, it will help you feel better."

Leila murmured her thanks as she chose a piece of pastry from the offered tin. It seemed impossible to think of a world without Fatima's quiet, humble, caring aid. No matter what happened to the rest of their family, at least Fatima would be keeping house, doing as she had always wanted. With the tea, made extra sweet with mint, Leila began to feel a little bit better.

Chapter 23

When Iraq was "liberated," satellite dishes had been among the first purchases in the new, free market. Even Khaled had a big satellite dish, aimed to the sky like a great ear, and when the power rolled back on later in the day, Leila could watch television. The signal was watched across the Arab-speaking world, by hundreds of thousands of people who had their own problems to deal with.

Leila thought about this as she sat in Fatima's closet-sized sitting room, gazing at the television, unable to rip her eyes away from it. For a moment she felt connected to the outside and that was why she was addicted to the signal. She felt part of something larger than herself, and somewhere, Beirut or Amman or Cairo, perhaps, there were other women watching this very same thing. Women without a terrorist for a father, a coward for a mother, or a smarmy cousin wishing to marry them. Once upon a time Leila would have fired up her ambition to be a modern woman, used it to fuel herself and stay afloat, but now she was not sure she would live long enough. It might behoove her to prepare herself for death, just in case. With a little flash of guilt she half turned in the direction of Mecca, sent up a prayer to Allah, and murmured that peace be upon the Prophet Mohammed.

The problem with having medical training, as Leila long ago learned, was that the whys and hows of death were de-

---

mystified to the point of inspiring agnosticism. A doctor could not afford to ponder deep metaphysical meanings; a doctor could do what she could with what she had and no more. Ease suffering, strap that bandage on, find a solution, give the right medicines, wield the scalpel wisely. For some reason the thought comforted. Maybe Leila could use a scalpel on her own city and cut out the cancer of terrorism that lived there. But when would someone arm her with a blade?

The male announcer on Al-Jazeera, a man with heavy orange makeup, brayed about the new spate of violence in Mosul. They showed the same footage over and over, a five-hours-old picture of the thin column of smoke rising from the mosque, the same that Leila had seen from her bedroom window. Then the TV showed some recycled footage of a woman crying over a body of a small boy and some men running around with blood on their clothes. Leila could see bare trees in the background and knew it was not new footage; in fact, she suspected it was from some random car bombing of many months ago. But it gave the effect that the news channels wanted: blood, violence, tears.

Khaled also watched the television with a tight expression on his face. "How am I supposed to work when the whole city is under curfew?" he said.

"Just stay safe, husband," said Fatima from the other room. She was wandering about with loose hands, tidying the place up, looking for something to occupy herself.

"We will have no money," said Khaled.

"Even if your store was open, brother, there would be no one to shop," Leila said.

Khaled made an inelegant grunting noise but did not complain anymore.

"Do you want to play checkers?" Leila suggested to Fatima. They played for three hours. They made rice afterward, along with a watery soup of lentils, for that was all the food in the house and the markets remained closed. Leila was not very hungry and told Fatima so, but her sister insisted on making dinner as though housekeeping were a joy, even in times like these.

Night fell. Neither of the parents showed up to retrieve Leila and she wondered what was happening at home. Abdul must still be there; travel was banned. From either side of Fatima's tiny flat, there were whispers in the walls, rumors spreading, little comments and worries voiced by neighbors. No one knocked on Fatima's door with news. The television remained on all day, to everyone's surprise, for the authorities tended to turn off the power when violence descended.

Leila, with her new knowledge of the way the Americans worked, thought with a trace of bitterness that they wanted anger on the Arab street this time. It meant more business for them. She wondered where James was. She wished she could get to the hospital and seek refuge there, make herself useful, and never leave. That little piece of land was America itself for all of Leila's intents and purposes. With a wistfulness that improved with distance, Leila thought of Nurse Quinn, Bonnie, the funny Dr. Peabody, the kind Dr. Whitaker. And there she was, Leila al-Ghani, split between two worlds and hovering in her sister's tiny apartment like a nervous bug.

The waiting was not so bad. With the power on, the television played through the night, distracting Leila from what she had done, delaying her decision about how to get to the field hospital. With music videos pounding out of Dubai stations, who cared about what came tomorrow? But the quivering pit of anxiety in Leila's stomach said otherwise. She bade good night to Fatima and Khaled at midnight; they retreated past the hanging curtain into the second room that could not quite be dignified with the word *bedroom*. Out of courtesy, Leila kept the volume on the television dim enough so that people could sleep but loud enough to disguise any noises that a virgin sister should not hear.

At around four a.m., in the middle of a restless sleep, Leila thought she heard shouts a few doors down, then the splintering of wood. But this was an unfamiliar neighborhood and she was not acquainted with its rhythms. It could have been a house raid by the Americans; it probably was. But Leila was not about to stick her head out and see.

The night was merciful and free of parents. In the dead hours between running away and what was to come next, Leila could almost imagine that everything was fine and she should not feel so uneasy and she was just visiting Fatima for a while, after all.

Yet as Leila stretched on her mat on the floor, the smallest things disturbed her sleep: the fly that buzzed past her head, the sensation of crawling on her calf muscle, an itch on her left hand. Maddening.

The morning came with the swift speed that characterizes spring in Mosul, as though the day itself couldn't wait to start blooming. She could not muster enthusiasm for spring and new beginnings while she huddled, scared, in her sister's apartment, unsure of what her fate would be.

Then over morning tea the word came from Al-Hurrah that the citywide curfew on Mosul had been lifted. A police spokesperson came on the TV and announced that conditions were "normalized," whatever that meant, and that people should go about their business. Even through the grainy pixels of the television screen, Leila could see the sweat beading on the man's upper lip, the dejected way he spoke, as if he knew that nothing good could come of it. She felt sorry for him.

"I will open the shop today," said Khaled. He wore yesterday's djellaba with faded brown dirt clinging to the cuffs. Washing the clothes meant going onto the roof, something Fatima was not willing to risk yesterday. "I will open the shop if just to get some more rice. We are almost out."

"Do you think people will do shopping today?" Fatima asked.

"The curfew has lasted over a day," said Khaled. "Milk, maybe rice, and meat. The people need these things. I am brave. Nothing ever happens when you are expecting it, anyway."

"See my brave husband?" Fatima said with a smile.

"Yes," said Leila, unable to quell the dread within her. No curfew meant that she needed to be on the move, for her parents would come. Tamir al-Ghani would be in a foul mood. Was she so important to her father as to warrant a time-out from his insurgent activities? Would he yank her back home and then go about his business of being a terrorist?

"I need to go to work, too," Fatima chattered on, oblivious to Leila's distress. "If students show up, there must be someone there to help them. And the orphans have nowhere else to go."

"I think you should stay home," said Khaled. "Too dangerous."

"You can work and I cannot?" Fatima protested.

"I am the man!" Khaled said. "It's different."

"It's not different. We need as much income as possible."

Leila kept quiet and tried to blend into the room.

"Besides," said Fatima, "it is like you said. Nothing ever happens when you are expecting it. And who would blow up a nursery?"

"I don't know," Khaled said. "Nothing makes sense anymore."

"Leila can watch the house while I'm gone," said Fatima. "I'll do a half shift. Just this morning; then I'll be home. If you can work, so can I." And for a moment, Leila was reminded of herself and her own stubbornness about being a working woman.

But Khaled still groused, saying he didn't need his wife to work, and he was man enough to provide for her all by himself. The man had a complaining streak that Leila had never noticed before and she was glad that she didn't have to live with it. He wrapped his head scarf without care so that it was askew and Fatima had to readjust it for him. The sun already blazed down on the street outside and it might be a warm day; Leila could see the sandy reflection coming through the crack beneath the door. When Khaled was out the door, grumbling still, Leila took off her woolen sweater and put it in her backpack.

"Fatima, I don't know if I'll be home when you return," Leila said.

Fatima gave her a long, searching look, eyes full of concern. "You think Father will come?"

"I don't know what to do, Fatima," Leila said. As she pronounced her doubts aloud, they flooded her and she felt tears spring up in response. "I can't marry that man, I can't! You know I can't. Not when I have so much to do with my life. Not when I'm in love with—well . . ."

Fatima stared. "You are in love with the American?"

"Oh . . ." Leila said. But she knew it was true. She did not know how she'd denied it for so long, so that now when hope faded by the minute she realized her own foolish feelings. So many disguises there were for love: care, regard, admiration, friendship, objective concern. All rubbish. And Leila knew that she'd loved James since she first struck gazes with him that night in Hala Rasul's house, for she'd thought of him ever since. Her rational mind did a stand-up job in trying to ignore it, but to say it aloud to Fatima released the tide. "Yes," she said, "I love him. God help me, I do."

Her sister had horror written on her face. "Father will kill you," she said. "You cannot love this James. Have some sense, Leila. I thought that you had—what do they call it?—a crush and that was all. You can't mean it. He's not a Muslim!"

"Not you, too," Leila said. "This idiotic religion business. I don't even believe in God anymore." Later, she would wonder if she'd brought retribution on herself with that statement. But in the heat of the moment, she enjoyed the thunderstruck expression on Fatima's face, enjoyed the shock of saying it. "That's right, I don't believe in God anymore and I love an American man and I've run away from the marriage my father arranged for me. Shoot me now!" She flung her arms wide, hitting the wall with a knuckle that sent a shooting star of pain up her arm. She did not notice it.

"You've gone crazy," Fatima said, standing up and putting on her *hijab*. "I want you to stay here, Leila, until I get back from work. I'm your older sister and I don't want arguments about it. Then we'll have a cup of *shai* and talk this over and see what can be done."

"I'm not staying here. Father will come."

"No," Fatima said, "he will not. Because I'm going to call him and say that you're safe here, that I'll fix you right up, and then take you home."

"You won't!" Leila said. "I won't!"

"Stop being stupid," Fatima said, and set her jaw. Her sullen obstinacy infuriated Leila.

"You think," Leila said, "that just because you're married, it gives you the right to tell me what to do? You are no better than our parents! I thought you understood me, Fatima! I thought you accepted me as your sister no matter who I loved or what I did. Isn't that the way it's supposed to be?"

Fatima opened her mouth to respond but there was no chance.

"No," Leila continued, "you get up on your high horse because you're married to some lousy shopkeeper with a grease-stained collar who complains every second of the day. It doesn't make you anything, Fatima. It doesn't make you anything."

It was as though she had struck Fatima across the face. Her sister's jaw dropped a little, mouth moving but words not forming. An angry flush rose on Fatima's face and she whirled away, bringing out a set of keys from the pocket of her dress. "I'm locking you in here," she finally said. "You've gone mad. You deserve to marry Abdul. Maybe it will get you away from this city and that job with the Americans that has given you crazy ideas."

The door creaked open, and the light invaded the house from the street. Fatima stood on the threshold and glanced back at her sister with remorse. Then, without knowing why,

Leila scrambled to her feet, wanting to soothe her sister's feelings into leaving the door unlocked, and not wanting to leave things unsaid between them. "Fatima, wait. I'm sorry. I did not mean those things. I'm just upset."

"I know," said Fatima, softly. "But I'm still keeping you here safe." Then she was out the door and it slammed in Leila's face and she heard the click of the tumblers on the external padlock that hooked through the bar of the door.

"Fatima!"

Then boredom, waiting, desolation. Leila searched the tiny house and found the old *Cosmopolitan* magazines that had been her secret wedding gift to her sister and was disturbed to find things circled with a pen in the love advice sections. She flipped through one of the issues to find the fashion pages, lost herself in imagining the clothes on her own body, and broke into tears about every half hour.

She heard a dull crump from across the neighborhood but tried to ignore it and the violence it most likely brought with it—she was too worried about how to get to the base, to James.

Then she remembered her cell phone, which she seldom used, buried in her backpack. She could call James—she had programmed his number into her phone some time ago, then forgotten about it.

"Stupid Leila," she muttered to herself as she scrolled through her phonebook and found what she was looking for, pressing the Send key without a second thought.

Interminable ringing. "Pick up, pick up," she urged.

Static. And then, "Hello?"

"James!" Leila shouted. "It's Leila, James, can you hear me?"

"Leila?" There was silence on the other end of the line, followed by a series of clicks and taps, and she could hear men's voices in the background.

"I'm here," she said, and because the connection was terrible, she launched into her tale about her father's plans, lest they be cut off. "My father says there will be two bombings," she said. "One at a police station, the central precinct, and the other at the field hospital itself. The 67th, James, do you hear me? And there is a new kind of missile—I don't know what it is called—it comes from Saddam's old stores. To explode, to destroy the vehicles. The mujahideen have new weapons. And he said the Iraqis who work on-base will be killed, their families hurt, there is a list of them! James, can you hear me?"

"I hear you," came his calm and professional voice. "Are you all right, Leila? Where are you?"

"I am at my sister Fatima's," she said. "I ran away." A burst of static interrupted her and she tapped at her phone, exasperated. "James?"

"I'm here," he said. "What neighborhood?"

She told him.

"Leila, tell your sister to stay home today. It's not safe out there."

To anyone else, James would have sounded cool and unaffected; Leila, however, heard a tone of warning in his voice and a shiver went down her spine. "She's already left for the nursery. Why? James?"

But he did not get a chance to tell her, to apologize, or even to thank her for the inside information that would, undoubtedly, save American lives. The connection had broken, gone dead, and Leila swore. She shook her phone as though it were a bottle with something stuck inside. Sitting back, heart pumping, she held the dead phone in her numbed hand and leaned her head against the solid white-painted wall. *I've done everything I can*, she thought. *Now I must wait.* Patience was not her strong point but she must learn.

The day wore on. Leila expected the door to open any moment bearing Fatima or her parents. She thought about what she would do.

For all Fatima's advice, Leila would not marry Abdul. She would threaten suicide before she would do it. However, she had brought great shame by running away like that and her father would be incandescent with rage; she knew him and his moods. He would blame it on the American influence. Amends had to be made.

"I'll just say I'm sorry," she said to herself. "I'll lie. I have no problem lying."

Noontime came and went. Leila began to wonder when her sister would return and decided that Fatima must have gone home to tell their parents where Leila was. The three of them would come together, outnumbering Leila, dragging her back to be married or worse.

Idly she flicked through the television channels, watched some Egyptian music videos, started watching an Italian movie dubbed over in English. Al-Jazeera said nothing new. In spite of the tinny blare of the TV, the room had an air of silence, a breathlessness, or it could have been Leila's lungs, not wanting to work.

When the clock hit three in the afternoon, Leila knew something was wrong.

Where in the name of Mohammed, *peace be upon him*, was Fatima? She had the key to the padlock on the door. She should have been home by noon. Leila pressed an ear to the door to attempt to hear what was going on outside. She heard voices and some shouts, the honking of horns, nothing out of the ordinary. But like the inside of the apartment, the street held an eerie stillness to Leila's eavesdropping ear. Had something happened?

Ten minutes later, Leila heard the fumbling of a key outside; then it slid into the metal padlock with a smooth click. She could have cried with relief. The door opened and sunlight poured in. "Fatima! Where have you been?"

Khaled stumbled across the threshold as though intoxicated. The silver door key dropped from his hands and clattered to the floor with an incongruous high note of cheer.

"Khaled!" Leila said, shocked. "What's the matter?"

Khaled's face was gray, his eyes were wild. He did not speak but looked back over his shoulder into the street. He pointed outside, where a white pickup truck idled.

It had splashes of dark red on it, dark red running off from the tailgate, dark human limbs dangling like rubber off the side. For a moment Leila's eyes saw, but her brain did not register. She ran out into the street.

There were three people in the back of the truck. The driver might have been trying to take them to a hospital but it was too late for them all. On the right was a small girl, too young to wear the *hijab*, her hair in braids and the lower part of her body blown off. Her eyes were closed. In the middle was a man, unidentifiable as such except that he wore the shredded remnants of trousers. And then there was Fatima.

For the ravaged wreck that was her body, her face was almost peaceful. The mouth was closed but the eyes were open, sightless, glazed over in death. Little flecks and smears of blood marred her olive skin. The neck was bent at an odd angle, and there were third-degree burns over most of the body. Her *abaya* was burned away. In places the flesh had melted, leaving pale glistening bone; Leila averted her eyes from a rib sticking out. This could not be her sister. This was a macabre doll, a false image, a joke.

She'd seen such things before, men in the field hospital, but it was far worse when it was a woman or a child. And when it was a sister, it was unthinkable.

Leila could not look anymore so she turned, not seeing the street in front of her. Some part of her rational mind still worked and went over the day's events. Fatima had gone to work. Who would bomb a nursery? Leila remembered hearing that dull thump in the distance earlier in the day. Could have been thunder, could have been a brick falling, could have been the unforgiving explosion that killed her sister.

As though pinching herself in a dream, Leila faced the truck again. With a shaking hand Leila reached out to close her sister's eyes and when she felt the lukewarm, stiff skin the knowledge crashed in: no more older sister to laugh at her and love her and support her.

It might have been thirty seconds, it might have been thirty minutes, but the grief could not keep track of time as Leila clutched the side of the truck for support and she fixated on a strand of Fatima's hair that had come unpinned and blew free from the head scarf.

Above Leila's head, the afternoon sun did not care about the human suffering beneath it. The rest of the street came back into focus. The buildings crowded together, two- and three-story apartments, bending toward the sky as though tired. Laundry hung from wires and strings, fluttering in the wake of pedestrians and goats. There was a woman in the door of a house, weeping. Other people stopped and stared into the truck of the dead, perhaps wondering if their relatives were among the casualties.

However, most went on as normal, walking, their feet moving, their mouths talking. Leila could not believe it. How could anything be normal after this? When she opened her mouth to talk to the driver of the pickup truck she tasted salt; she was crying.

"What happened?" she asked, and though the tears came down unstoppable, her voice sounded calm. Clinical. The voice of a doctor; the voice of a stranger.

"I don't know," the man said, and shrugged. He looked at her with sympathy. "You know one of them? Your daughter?" He gestured to the little girl.

Leila did not answer. "What are you doing with them?"

"To the hospital," he said. "I didn't know what else to do. There were several others, injured, killed, but what happened to them, I don't know."

Leila couldn't think, couldn't move. She gazed down at the dusty street, littered with the flattened remnants of animal dung and juice boxes. Khaled leaned against the door of the apartment with a vacant stare, stricken. The sight of her sister's broken husband forced her back into the moment and into action.

"Go with her," Leila said, grabbing Khaled by the arm and dragging him out into the street. "She needs you to go with her to the hospital." It seemed imperative that Fatima not be left alone or forced into the hands of strangers. "Ride in the front seat."

Khaled, in deep shock, climbed into the front seat without protest. The driver gave another look of distant sympathy and stepped on the accelerator of his idling engine. The rumbling made the bodies in the back shake around like jelly. They drove off and Leila was left alone, staring after the makeshift ambulance, eyes trained on the lump that had been Fatima, knowing this was the last time she would ever see her sister.

After she'd sent Khaled off, the horror came and made her move again, and she knew she had to return home. She had to tell her parents that their daughter was dead. Abdul, the forced marriage, the mujahideen . . . all else faded away; there would be no wedding on the day of a funeral. *Fatima, Fatima.* Leila felt like a little girl again, lost inside a cloud of disbelieving sorrow, and she needed her mother to hug her and her father to tell her that everything was going to be all right. There was no more curfew so she could run down the streets if she wished.

It was four o'clock.

Leila grabbed her backpack from inside Fatima's tiny house. She put away her empty cup of tea, washed it out in the little sink, in denial that Fatima would not come home to this modest kitchen ever again. *Don't think it*, she told herself, *don't think it, just get home, don't think it.*

With a presence that felt like an alien being had taken over her, Leila picked up the house key that Khaled had dropped, locked the door behind her, and gave it to their next door neighbor with instructions to watch out for Khaled to come home from the hospital. "Fatima is hurt," she told the woman, "so Khaled has gone to be with her." Then she was running through the streets, through the strange neighborhood and back into familiarity, past the corner shop, down the fine asphalt street, and into the front courtyard of her family home that she had fled only yesterday. It was like an age ago.

The mattress Leila had used to jump out the window was moved aside, under cover of the porch. She ran past it and into the house; the front door was unlocked. "Mama!" she called. "Mother!"

But it was Tamir she saw first. Tamir standing in the doorway of the sitting room, looking as he always had, tall and thin and stern, but there was something new in his eyes. A light, a fever, a sense of hope that was ridiculous on this day of carnage. Leila ignored it.

"*Baba!*" she said. "Something terrible has happened. An explosion. It's Fatima, she's hurt, I saw her, Khaled has gone to the hospital—" She wandered, unable to pronounce the truth, skirting around it and hoping that her father would catch on. But he didn't. His facial expression did not change; he showed no worry for his eldest daughter. Instead he gazed upon Leila with peculiar intensity, like a predator.

"Where's Mama?" Leila asked when he made no motion of understanding.

"Leila. My daughter." Tamir stepped forward to embrace her.

A sob escaped as her father's strong, wiry arms surrounded her. It felt so nice to lay it all back on him. He was the man of the house, the head of the family, the one with the answers. He would make it better. "*Baba,*" she said, and she was crying again. "My sister is dead. My sister is dead. She is blown up. What do I do? Why?"

"Shhh," he said, stroking the back of her head. "It is fine now. Everything is all right. Paradise awaits us. Allah will take care of us, it is in His hands now, shhh, don't cry, my little nightingale."

Leila pulled away, feeling better already, so happy that her father was back. He'd come to his senses and he would take care of her again. Then she looked into his eyes and was so terrified by what she saw that she wondered if she was in a nightmare. It was like talking to a puppet, a thing that looked and talked and walked like her father, but was some other creature. He looked more like a judge than ever, a white judge in a white robe, the primitive kind that pronounced death with the most careless manner. Blank eyes, hard and glowing like coals . . . his mouth smiling . . . his beard long and unkempt.

Leila could see that he hadn't listened to a word. He had no idea that Fatima was dead. It did not register at all. He looked over Leila's shoulder at some other point in the room and nodded.

She half turned and was aware of another person there, a man, not cousin Abdul but another; then before she had a chance to question, a dirty rag was shoved in her face. It smelled familiar as it covered her nose and mouth; Leila knew enough not to breathe it in. But the men held her fast. Tamir smiled at her as though he was proud, as though she were one of his soldiers or a servant who had done something right.

Through the haze of heartache and shock and surprise, she at last identified the choking smell on the rag: chloroform. It was Leila's last coherent thought, for her lungs burned for lack of oxygen, and she hissed as she inhaled the treacherous fumes in the rag. The world went black as she looked in her father's eyes.

The first thing Leila noticed when she awoke was that she was propped upright in a seated position. She could not feel or move her body, but her other senses returned like a checklist: sight, sound, smell. The world was blurry; she couldn't focus, and her lids drifted closed again. The pungency of the chloroform had given way to leather, motor oil, exhaust. She was in a vehicle, and for some reason this scared her. There was another smell underneath: a tinge of chemical, harsh, warning, almost like sulfur. It rang a bell of familiarity somewhere, but she couldn't quite place it.

Her eyes opened. Indeed, she was in a truck, and her hands were bound in front of her. She was strapped to the driver's seat with silver duct tape running across her lap and midriff. Something dug into her back, and she realized that she was still wearing her backpack. She could feel the hard edges of the puzzle box inside.

The steering wheel had a peeling leather cover on it and there was a layer of filth on the vinyl dashboard. With a glance over the gauges on the dashboard, Leila saw that the truck's fuel tank was full and it had a great many miles on the odometer. Beyond the dusty glass windows, the truck was parked in a dim place, a garage from the looks of the corrugated metal rolling door looming ahead. It was very quiet. Her eyes slid shut once more.

"Leila." A voice; soft, nice. "Wake up, little one."

She wanted to fall back into sleep. Sleep was safe. In the blackness of unconsciousness, nothing bad could happen to her, and if it did she would lie in blissful ignorance of it. She said something to this effect, but it came out all muddled.

"Wake up. Here's some tea. Drink the tea."

Someone was forcing the edge of a glass between her lips. A few drops of warm sweet liquid fell into her mouth. She sputtered a little, then drank reluctantly, coming back into herself. The tea tasted just like the kind her mother made with that bit of extra mint floating in it.

Leila turned her head to the side; her father sat in the passenger's seat next to her. She looked into his hazel eyes and for a moment it was as though the war had never happened. They were father and daughter, side by side, drinking tea. Then Tamir spoke.

"You have done something very serious, Leila," he said. "You've run away from home. You left your cousin Abdul humiliated in front of the imam. Do you understand this?"

She nodded, for she did understand.

"You were supposed to be married," he continued. "I tried my best to help you, Leila. I'm your father and I know best for you, but you are a stubborn girl. A disobedient girl. I see this now. If you knew why I arranged for your marriage to Abdul . . ." He paused, bringing his hand across his mouth as though it were a painful subject. "I wanted to make you safe.

You could have gone with your good cousin, your new husband, and made a life away from here. No danger to you. You see, Leila, I know better than anyone what must happen here in Mosul. It is *my* plan now that we are implementing against the Crusaders. I wanted to protect you."

Leila blinked, clearing away the chemical wool that clogged her head. Her father continued.

"But you refused to take my good blessing. I've been very lenient with you these past months. I've let you work with the Americans, doing a job that should not belong to a woman, interacting with strange men, foreigners. I've let you walk around in vile Western clothing. And this is how you repay my kindness? You turn your back on the man I choose as your husband?"

Leila shook her head in protest, unable to think of the right words, but her father shushed her, anyway.

"You have *shamed* the family," Tamir said. Little flecks of spittle flew from his mouth as his manner changed, as his fury rose and he lashed out like a wounded scorpion. "You have brought disgrace to the al-Ghani name. You deserve no better than to be removed from my family. You are a blight to us, a black mark, a girl who is out of control and who has forgotten who she is!" A note of high hysteria crept into Tamir's voice. "You have done it to yourself!"

"No!" Leila said. "I did nothing wrong, Father. Nothing. It is you who have changed."

"Don't speak, you impertinent girl! It is I who give the directions now. You will obey me. And you will be grateful to me, for I have worked out something that will give you a chance to redeem yourself."

At this, Leila eyed her father with one measure of hope, one of mistrust. In Tamir's current state of mind, redemption was open to interpretation.

He smiled. "Since you are so determined to make something of yourself, I have arrived at the perfect conclusion. You will save your own honor and make the name of al-Ghani remembered here forever. This thing you will do . . . it will be a noble, wonderful thing. And I will be proud of you, Leila."

"Father," Leila said, tears swelling in her eyes, fear growing in her heart. "What are you talking about?"

"You have joined our martyrs' brigade," said Tamir. "You are a strong and reasonable girl. And you can get revenge on the Americans now. They blew up your sister. Did you know that? It was their Hellfire missile that killed her . . . and now you both will find your place in Paradise. You must drive this truck into the American base and blow up the hospital there. And"—Tamir laughed for three short, high bursts—"you know your way around because you worked there!"

It had to be a joke, a cruel test of some sort; perhaps he wanted to know her loyalties. "Father, I can't drive a bomb," she said, attempting to bring some sense into their discussion. "You are being ridiculous. I am your spy in the enemy camp, not a bomber."

"Look behind you," said Tamir softly.

Leila strained against the tape that bound her to the driver's seat, but she was still able to peer around the headrest to look into the spacious back of the truck.

They looked like boxes stacked along either side of the truck, but they were not. She saw the silvery detonation cords sticking out at regular intervals, attached by long snakelike wires that met in a mass at the center of the truck's floor. Here there was a black box, improvised and held together by duct tape, simple and malevolent. It looked like a great mechanical brain sitting in the middle and plotting destruction. She squinted her eyes; the letters on the greenish stacked blocks were unreadable Cyrillic. It had to be military-grade explosives, perhaps taken from a storehouse from the old regime or imported from Iran. It was hooked up and ready to go.

Leila knew little about explosives, but she knew enough to determine that this was no trifling marketplace bomb. The weight of knowledge pressed on her from behind, and she could not help but feel that an evil black cloud loomed over her shoulders. She'd never been in such close proximity to so much destructive power. It was horrible and awesome all at once.

"I won't do it." She shook her head at her father, who waited with glistening eyes. "I won't. This is the wrong thing."

"It is the right thing," he corrected. He spoke as he had when Leila was a child, and she'd made some spelling error and he would point it out with gentleness, as if this current predicament, too, were a small error of her thinking and all it would take was the word of the father to change her mind.

Leila pictured the great stacks of plastic explosive behind her arriving at their destination and blasting open in a searing cloud of flame and chemical and black, dissolving heat. Her body would be disintegrated, the metal of the truck would melt and shatter and fly, the cloud of death would reach out and grab everyone within at least a hundred-meter radius. There would be bodies burned, scarred, and baked and left to peel apart, like Fatima was left in the back of that pickup truck. A wave of nausea roiled in Leila's stomach.

She looked back over her shoulder to remind herself that it was real, not a dream or a nightmare. Her father mistook it for her approval.

"See what you will do?" he said, gesturing into the boxy back of the truck. "It is glorious. I've planned this attack for many months now. The time has come to consummate our plans. The Americans tried to bait us, but we have the patience they lack. They wanted battle and they got it, and now they suffer, and soon more of them will die because of your sacrifice, daughter."

"A battle?" she echoed. "What battle?"

"You've been unconscious since yesterday," said Tamir. "Another martyr preceded you not an hour ago; he was a great success. He blew up the police station when a company of American soldiers was there. They say that at least ten of the Crusaders were killed and another twenty wounded. A great success."

"Which company?" Leila had to ask. A small dart of panic penetrated her consciousness that it might have been James's group of Special Forces soldiers.

"They're all the same, you silly girl. One American is like the other. All ignorant, all vicious dogs with designs on empire. But they will not last here in Mosul. No, we'll drive them out, and you will help us now."

The vitriolic propaganda was too much for Leila to take. She might die yet, but she would not take a hospital full of wounded men with her. She threw out a last desperate plea for her life. "Father," she said, breathless, head swimming. "I have a better idea. A more glorious plan. Let someone else drive your truck. I'll go back to the Americans and continue my work as a spy, your spy, and they'll never suspect. I can give you such good information! I'll be your eyes and ears."

"Women are cowards," Tamir said. "I give you a chance at glory and you try to squirm and bargain your way out of it! You are a little worm. No daughter of mine, unless you do this thing."

Tears sprang to Leila's eyes as she saw the hardness set into the deep lines of his judge's face. There were no alternatives anymore, not for men like him, not in a country where the bombs went off every day and the people teetered on the brink of self-destruction. "I'm sorry, Father, I'm not bargaining. I'm trying to find the best way to hurt—kill—destroy the Americans. That's all."

Tamir leaned into the passenger-side seat. "This is the best way. This is your chance, your *only* chance." From his robes he pulled a switchblade. With one quick stroke, he sliced the tape that bound her hands.

Leila's body went limp; he would not be persuaded otherwise. She was strapped in to her fate. The little demons of helplessness crowded in around her, laughing at her resignation, poking her until she felt she would go mad. Nothing to be done but follow her father's orders. A part of her understood why her fellow Muslims martyred themselves. They, like she, were left without choices, in situations where death was preferable to life, where only death would mean something. She, Leila al-Ghani, had but one method of escape.

Chapter 24

A herd of goats grazed along the shoulder of the Al-Muthanna road. The scrub grass was low and stubbly, but the goats' practiced teeth found the choicest blades and tugged and pulled at them, procuring for themselves a sparse breakfast. The animals were skinny; it was a rough life for city goats. There was never enough to eat in Mosul, not even for the people, and there had not been a year of bounty for so long that everyone, animals included, forgot what it was like to be well fed. Tending to the herd was a man that might have been very old or very young; his face was both.

Among the plaintive bleating of the animals, the daily traffic of Mosul City moved along. It was mostly foot traffic and bicycles; the occasional car was either beat-up and on the brink of collapse, or of an official capacity, bearing new foreign-appointed bureaucrats of the old city to their jobs. Every once in a while the road was disturbed by the dull, slow rumbling of a supply truck, the petroleum-fueled lifelines of the city. They brought vegetables, grains, bottled juices, imported goods.

But one large white truck that growled past the herd of goats carried precious cargo of the deadly variety.

Leila, in the driver's seat, fixed her gaze on one particular animal and watched its throat as it swallowed a mouthful of grass. A small detail in a day full of small details that added up to a terminus. She refocused on the road ahead. It was about a half-hour drive to Diamondback from where the abandoned garage had been. She had half an hour to come to terms with her fate, half an hour to say her prayers, half an hour until she did the unimaginable.

She had been driving for ten minutes. In that time she'd contemplated a few things, making general associations of herself with those suicide bombers that afflicted other countries, other cities, other families. It could not be real and yet the smell of gasoline was strong in her nostrils, the truck rumbled and groaned through the pedals beneath her feet, the steering wheel vibrated with automotive life. Progress was an exertion with the heavy weight of the explosives.

The duct tape bindings still held her body fast against the cloth seat. She'd already tried to get herself free, but there was too much of it, and it wrapped all the way around so many times that she would need a miracle, or a knife, to liberate herself. She damned the inventor of duct tape. Whoever they were, they'd done their job too well.

As she passed the last of the goats, she realized they would outlive her. She wondered if she was fortunate to know with specificity the hour of her death; most human beings were not graced with such foreknowledge. Fatima, for instance; she'd never expected to die yesterday morning, Leila was sure.

Paradise. The Quran was not very clear on what heaven was like for good Muslim women. Her father had told her she would go to Paradise if she became a martyr. But Leila thought otherwise; the deep parts of hell must be reserved for people who did such things as blow up a hospital. It was not just the patients, helpless and wounded; it was the nurses, Quinn and Bonnie and the women to whom Leila had just last week given dancing lessons. It was Dr. Whitaker and his new little grandson waiting at home, never to know his grandfather. It was Dr. Peabody and his jazz music. They were Leila's coworkers, her friends even, and here she was forced into the ultimate disloyalty against them. She had not even the benefit of dying an innocent.

The dread minutes ticked past. The base drew closer. Leila imagined she could hear the bomb behind her marking off time with anticipatory glee, tick-tock, tick-tock. When she turned onto the long road that would lead her past Camp Marez and into the base proper, her whimpers of panic grew louder and more insistent, and Leila could not quite tell if she made noises aloud with her throat or if they existed in her head alone.

The worst part of the scheme was that the bomb *would* go off at eleven o'clock in the morning. No matter where Leila and the truck were, it would explode. Her father had known better than to give her control over the fatal mechanism. The bomb was timed to precision, or so she hoped; it was on a timer that could not be turned off.

Tamir had counted on the suffusion of his idealism into Leila's foggy, drugged head; with nowhere else to go and no choice, she might as well take some Americans with her.

Well, that was where Tamir was wrong. Leila had made up her mind halfway to the American base. She would die, but she would not take anyone else with her aside from some insects and plants. She would drive the truck into a vacant section of rock and dirt near to the base and there she would wait. A morbid part of her wondered if there would be enough of her body left for the Americans to identify as being their former medical translator, Miss al-Ghani.

The truck lurched as she made her way down Diamondback Road. Spread out before her was the gloss of American occupation, all prefabricated and improvised and glinting in the sun. From here she could see military vehicles with their dull paint and shiny antennae. She could see the huge tent of a dining hall, once destroyed and now repaired, a big white sand dune sticking out of the flat uniform structures.

At Diamondback on her other side, the hangars, the runway, a C-5 Galaxy idling on the tarmac in wait of something. She had a brief fantasy of flying away on a jet plane. It lasted a fraction of a second. She could not fly, for she was driving, driving toward her death. Would it hurt? she wondered.

About two thousand meters ahead she saw her target. It was not the hospital but a high embankment with a ditch in front of it. There was nothing in its immediate vicinity except a barbed-wire fence. A bleak spot, unremarkable, perfect to detonate an unwanted suicide bomb. She would aim for that. It was in view of the Texas towers of Camp Marez and Diamondback but too far away for them to be able to shoot at her with any accuracy.

She fixed her thoughts on the embankment, her foot steady on the gas pedal, not deviating in course or velocity. All other considerations ceased. She thought she saw a Humvee patrol circling from far away, preparing to come down the road toward Mosul City, but she could not keep her attention on it for long.

She gave the engine a little extra juice; the truck jumped forward. It was traveling at just over thirty-five miles an hour when it passed the sandy lip of the road and plunged forward into the loose dirt, tilting forward, tires spinning in vain. There was a jolt as the nose of the truck hit the embankment, scattering rocks and pebbles across the windshield. Leila let go of the steering wheel out of instinct and slammed both feet on the brake pedal. She jerked forward, held in place by the duct tape bindings, her hands flying out to balance herself. The hood of the truck crumpled, and she held her breath and waited for the explosion.

None came. The vehicle sank nose first into the ditch. Leila was suspended by the bindings, leaning forward, and her head swung back and forth; she felt like a rag doll, boneless and wishing she was already dead, not wanting to wait any longer. *Just blow up and have it done*, she thought.

She heard a dull thud and turned to see a few blocks of explosive slide toward her into the driver's compartment, still attached by their wires to the master box in the center. They looked like creatures crawling along the floor to attack her, vicious and sentient beings still attached to their mother. It would be that much quicker, then, when they blew up in—Leila looked at the clock—eleven minutes, if the clock on the dashboard was accurate.

She slumped forward in defeat. This was how it would end: tied up, alone, her spirit crushed. Fatigue overwhelmed her and her eyelids closed against the tawny sunshine.

There was a rumble, a roar. At first she thought it was the bomb going off. Then she heard a shout—a voice, American, a male.

"Hey in there! What's going on?"

There was something so familiar about the voice. Leila decided the bomb had exploded and she was dead, already journeying into the world of spirits, and perhaps she'd ended up in the American version of the afterlife.

The barrel of a rifle poked inside the window. The man behind the rifle wore a helmet to match his desert camouflage. The black voice microphone of a digital radio stuck out from his collar. He was an Asian man, she saw with a bit of surprise. Not many of those around Mosul. And yet, like his voice, there was something familiar about the face and the name Nisson on the patch over his left breast. She might have treated him in the hospital or seen him around the base.

"I know you," Nisson said. "You're the translator, right?"

She could not move her mouth any more than she could move her body. It was all too terrible and unreal.

"Ike!" Nisson jerked his head back to shout behind him. "You might wanna take a look here."

Another man appeared. This one Leila did recognize. It was the warrant officer, Ike, that huge lumbering bear of a man with the broad face, the one who'd been at the raid on Hala Rasul's house. When she looked into his wide eyes, it was as though someone had pinched her back into the present time, and she realized that a Special Forces team must have found

285285285

her. She had not imagined the Humvees at a distance, after all. A sudden urgency crashed down on her and she spoke.

"Ike. It's Ike, right? You have to get out of here. It's a bomb. In the back of the truck. Any minute now"—and Leila's breath stopped as she saw the minute hand on the dashboard clock creeping at 10:58—"it's going to explode. Get out of here!"

Ike stared at her for a disoriented beat, a microsecond, and then he acted. He poked his head farther in the window and his eyes trailed down to the loose block of plastic explosive that had slid forward, wires attached. He followed the wire and could see the rest, just past the angle, and Leila heard the intake of breath through his nose.

"Shee-it," he muttered.

Nisson was already barking something into his collar microphone. Ike backed away from the truck and Leila was relieved. She heard the crackling static of a reply over the radio. Then Ike was back, his face floating in her vision.

"Open the door," he said. "Unlock it. Fast!"

She leaned over and unlocked the door; it swung open and Ike saw that she was strapped in, taped up, unable to get out of her own accord.

"It will explode at eleven!" she said. The clock was at 10:59. She did not know what the clock said on the evil black box that directed the bomb.

Ike clicked open a blade. He spoke to Nisson over his shoulder. "Sergeant, get the company away, move the vehicles. Do it, get the hell outta here!"

Then there was no time to speak as Ike worked at the duct tape. It was stubborn; at least an entire roll had been used to bind her. Piece by piece his sharp army-issue knife worked through the metallic stuff until Leila could lean forward. Her torso was free. Her legs remained bound to the bottom of the seat. "Give me the knife!" she said. "I'll get the rest!"

"No way in hell," said Ike. He started on freeing her legs, implacable. It was as though there was no bomb at all in his mind.

Leila could but stare at the clock in horror. The minute hand clicked over to 11:00. She wrenched her eyes shut, expecting to be torn asunder. The bomb did not go off, but she knew it would; they had no time. Ike cursed. Seconds elapsed; they seemed like hours. She threw a glance back into the truck to look at the bomb, certain that she would see the red bloom of an explosion as soon as she did.

Then freedom as the duct tape was cut away and her right leg went slack, but the left one was still attached to the tape. Ike grabbed her by the arms and pulled her from the truck. "Let's go!" he shouted.

She ripped her leg free and Ike grabbed her hand. Together, they scrambled up the embankment toward the road. Dirt and loose pebbles slipped through her fingers as she stumbled and righted herself. No time, there was no time. Any second now. She felt the soles of her shoes hit the asphalt and she ground her heels in and ran.

Ike let go of her hand but held his own pace to make sure she did not fall. A gentlemanly act, she thought, and then she ran as fast as she had ever done in her life. Her *hijab* came loose and fluttered free, the wind gusted into her face, blowing her hair out behind her. *Go, go, go*, she urged her drug-clouded muscles.

The explosion was loud, strong. The searing wind hit her back, lifting her up and then knocking her flat on the road. There was an odd ringing noise in her ears. She coughed as the deadly heat shimmered through the air above her, followed by a black, dense cloud. She was aware that things were clattering to the ground around her, metal things, pieces of the truck and pieces of rock. They might have been pieces of her.

Her eyes streamed involuntary tears. She lay shaking there on the road like a fallen leaf for what might have been seconds or minutes or hours; time had no meaning anymore.

Then she was aware of someone crouching next to her, a large bulking figure; Ike. He touched her shoulder. "You okay, Leila? Are you okay?"

She could not move but managed a little mewing noise of assent. Strong arms lifted her from beneath her shoulders, propping her up. There was another man there, someone she didn't know. They helped her walk, half-carrying her away, and they leaned her up against the reassuring solid metal side of one of the Humvees. An uncontrollable urge to retch rose in her throat and she doubled over, heaving, but nothing came out. She felt vague embarrassment at such a display in front of strange men, but they did not seem to think it unusual, for one of them patted her on the back to help her as though she were an infant.

It was then that she was strong enough to turn and face the sunlit sky and the firelit ground behind her. It was a shock, even for one who was used to car bombings and violence.

The truck was gone. Once a large hunk of solid machine, it now assumed the shape of a dead flower, splayed apart and melting. It burned with a mix of rubber and petroleum, choking out black clouds that were so thick they might have been solid. All around the truck, the asphalt was blistered and cracked, and bits of shrapnel were embedded into the road and the dirt like scattered demon's toys. Some of the shrapnel burned and twisted and fluttered in the light breeze.

Another wave of nausea hit her, and she had to look at the horizon until it passed. She could not believe how close she had come to being part of that ghastly display. Without a doubt, the bomb would have destroyed the field hospital. She felt sick to her soul.

There was the distant sound of a siren approaching. So reassuring, the wailing sound of postdisaster. It meant that she was still alive.

"Leila?" Ike looked into her face with concern.

"Thank you," she said. "I—thank you."

"All in a day's work," he said. "C'mon, let's get you cleaned up."

Ike had saved her life. With chagrin, she recalled her first impression of Warrant Officer Ike Champlain as a burly, scary man who could not be trusted. She allowed herself to be helped into the Humvee. When the soldier in the driver's seat started the engine, she jumped as from an electrical shock. She felt hypersensitive and at the same time numb. In shock. The doctor's part of her brain diagnosed it, separate and floating in rational calm above her real self. *Interesting.*

The Humvee idled on the road. Leila waited, unconscious of time, aware that it was just the driver and herself in the vehicle while the other soldiers loitered outside, smoking, watching the smoldering wreckage that might have hurt their own.

The soldier at the wheel turned his head to say to her, "Sorry, ma'am, I have orders not to go anywhere yet."

"Huh," was what Leila could muster in response.

Soon another car came, this one official-looking and black. It stopped by the patrol and James Cartwright got out. He wore clean digital-patterned fatigues and a beret. Even from some meters away, Leila could see the tautness of his features, panic kept under control. She was only half aware of opening the door and leaping from the Humvee. She ran a couple of steps and halted, breathing hard, wanting nothing more than to feel his solid arms around her.

James saw her. He jogged forward and then he did what she wanted. He swept her up into a tight embrace, strength wrapped about her; she could practically feel his heart through the cloth of his shirt. He was careful of her face, which bled from a laceration, but she buried her face in his neck like a child coming home.

"Shhh," James whispered in her ear. "Shhh. It's okay. It's gonna be okay." Sweet nothings that comforted.

Her tears came then, tears from inside, not as a reaction to smoke and dust and fire. James let her wipe her eyes on his sleeve. "I'm so sorry," she said. "It's my fault. I've been so stupid."

"It's okay," he said again. "Don't worry about it now. You're alive. Hear me, Leila? You're alive. You're fine." It sounded as though he were convincing himself of the fact as well as her. "God," he said, his eyes bright with emotion, "I was so worried about you."

She had nothing to reply with, so she dropped her wet eyes to the ground, although her hands held tighter to his collar and she leaned into him. James said something about taking her to the hospital and she let him help her back into the Humvee. He took the front passenger seat and Leila stared in unwilling fascination at the ruined carcass of the truck as they passed. She could not tell front from back, end from end, so warped and sharp was the metal. As they drove away an army firetruck came racing to the scene, though why they bothered Leila did not know.

In the clear again, Leila rolled down the window a bit and breathed deeply. The rushing air felt nice on her face.

Everyone at the field hospital must have heard the explosion and anticipated casualties. The hospital was on alert with paramedics standing by at the service entrance. Dr. Peabody was there, too, in operating room scrubs, ready to do his work. Leila wished that it were Dr. Whitaker with his spry, grandfatherly manner, but Peabody would do. She gave a feeble wave as she was helped down from the Humvee.

"She's injured," said James, holding her arm. "And in shock, I think."

"What happened?" Peabody asked.

"A bomb," said James. He didn't elaborate further.

"We'll fix her up," said Peabody. "Come here, then."

It did not take long, but James stayed by her side. They cleaned off the little scrapes, put on some gauze bandages, applied a salve for the bruises. There were some minor burns on Leila's exposed hands and neck; these stung but she knew they were first-degree, nothing to worry about. Like a bad sunburn.

When Peabody offered her sleeping pills on a little paper tray, she refused them. Whatever her mental state, she needed to deal with it on her own, not sink into a soft, drippy haze to forget it all. Besides, she whispered to Peabody, she'd been under total anesthesia from chloroform. No more consciousness-altering substances if she could help it.

When she mentioned the chloroform, James sat up straight. "Chloroform?" he asked her.

"Not here," Leila said. She was well aware that Nurse Quinn, buzzing around and helping Peabody, would gossip with Bonnie and Michelle. Quinn kept making noises of sympathy and patting Leila on the shoulder; it must have been exciting to see her coworker and dance instructor so close to the violence.

Her body thus patched and aided, Leila allowed James to lead her to the officers' quarters; Leila had never been there and would normally have looked around in great interest at the rows of accommodation trailers. But they were a white blur to her and she had to focus on the gravel beneath her feet so as not to fall down. She stepped onto a small makeshift wooden porch made from a leftover pallet, a door opened, and they were inside the hooch with its thin metal walls and sharp-edged furniture.

"Do you want some tea?" James asked.

"No," Leila said, thinking of her father forcing the home-made perfect tea through her chemical-dried lips, telling her that she must blow herself up. She did not think she could ever drink tea again. "No tea."

"Okay . . . um . . . coffee? Oh, wait. Here." He rummaged through a drawer to procure a packet with the words Swiss Miss on it. "Hot chocolate," he said. "This is the kind my mom always used to make for us as kids. She sent it from home. Trust me, it'll make you feel better." He stood up and turned on the little electric hot pad and set out a small pot. Beneath the hot pad was a mini refrigerator from whence came a little jug of milk. He measured out a cup to be heated. The milk in the pot issued forth little hissing noises; James stirred with a metal spoon. His back was to her as he spoke, his voice gentle.

"Whenever you want to talk, I'll listen."

"Yes, I know," said Leila. The silence that followed was not awkward but rather the opposite: domestic, comfortable, understood. She took the opportunity to glance around his quarters with more interested eyes. It was neat as a pin, of course, for he was a military man and it would be his habit. On his desk was a framed photograph of an American family: a gray-mustached man with his arm around a plumpish, nice-looking woman; a pretty young woman about Leila's age with blond hair; James himself, kneeling down, with his hand resting on the head of a big Labrador dog. They all looked so happy in their forever-preserved sunshine.

"Is this your family?" she asked.

"Yeah," he said, turning to look at her. The milk was steaming and he poured it into a tin mug and stirred in the packet of chocolate mix. "That was taken right after I graduated from college."

"They all look nice."

"You'll meet them someday," said James as though it were a given.

"Hmm," said Leila. "How will you introduce me?"

James smiled as he handed her the mug. "Careful, it's hot. How would you want me to introduce you?"

"Oh, I do not know," said Leila. She took a sip of the hot chocolate; it was good. It tasted like someone's home. "As a friend."

"A friend you are," said James. He took a seat, not next to her on the bed but in the green plastic chair opposite. "How are you?"

"Fine," said Leila.

"No, I'm really asking. How are you? What happened, Leila?"

"I—" She wanted to tell him everything but it was too much all at once. She took another sip of cocoa to brace herself. "Oh, James," she began. "Such terrible things have happened these days."

"I know," he said. A shadow passed over his face and she

realized that she was not the only person to have confronted war, to have looked upon death. They were in this together. She was not alone and it made her strong enough to talk.

"It started the night the Al-lah Al-Hasib Mosque was bombed," she said. "That was your people, was it?"

James said nothing but the admission was in his face.

"I thought so. I woke up that morning and Father was in such a state. He was waiting, I guess, to give the orders to attack. In the meantime he and Mother did something else. They wanted me out of Mosul. He knew what was coming. So they tricked me, deceived me, and my cousin Abdul was at the house. So was the imam." She sighed. The rest of the story flowed after that: the arranged marriage, her flight, taking refuge at Fatima's house from where she'd called James with information. The argument with Fatima and how her sister left to go to work and came back as a corpse.

At this, a tightness grew across his features that Leila took at first to be sorrow or sympathy. When he glanced away from her, however, she realized he must know something.

"Who was it?" she asked. "The bomb that killed Fatima?"

Silence.

"James?"

"I told them not to," he finally said. "I told them the risk was too great, that civilians would be killed. They didn't listen."

"Who is 'they'?" Leila was becoming agitated. The insanity in which they were embroiled had no depths.

"There's something you've gotta understand. The army is not the only power operating here . . . the corporations have a lot of say over what happens. Their bosses are civilians, just like ours. And sometimes, like with API, they put pressure. They want violence. We already know that. So when an incident like those Hellfire missiles in the city . . ." James paused, reluctant. "I'm not going to say anything else, Leila, but you can draw your own conclusions."

Leila understood. It was as they'd discussed. The contractors from API wanted a basis for their contracts; they wanted an insurgency. That was why the curt command to kill was given, making Fatima another innocent casualty in their war.

"They cannot do this," Leila said. "I did not think the mighty United States Army was under the orders of a corporation!"

"Times have changed," said James. "We do what we have to do. God, it's fucked up. Sorry. But it is." Standing, he opened the gray metal locker beside his bunk and pulled out an old mangy boot. In confusion Leila watched as he reached inside the boot and pulled out a small diary-sized book, bound in thin green leather. "I've written this stuff down. Journals are admissible as evidence in court, you know." He used his thumb to flick through the pages of the leather-bound journal, absentminded, distant.

"What's in there?" Leila asked, gesturing at the book. "What other evidence? What are you planning, James?"

He stared at her. It was a struggle to circumvent his built-in barrier against trust, she knew it, and then, in a gesture she would never forget, he reached out and placed his hand on her cheek. His thumb brushed her skin. She could but stare back at him, overcome with an alien happiness. For a tiny moment in the midst of it all, they were two people and nothing else, looking into each other's eyes with perfect understanding.

A knock on the door interrupted the moment. James stepped across the tight space and pushed the door open, revealing Travis Pratt, flanked by four military policemen.

"May I help you?" James asked. There was ice in his voice.

"She's under arrest," said Pratt, pointing past him at Leila sitting pretty on the bed with the half-finished hot chocolate in her hand. "On charges of terrorism."

"Don't be crazy," said James. "She's not a terrorist."

"Sorry, man," said Pratt. "Whether she is or isn't, orders are orders."

"Who do you take your orders from, Pratt? Huh? Who the hell gives you the right?" James was angry. Leila felt gratified that it was on her behalf, but she could hardly deny the charges of terrorism; a few hours ago she was driving a truck bomb toward their base. She set her cup down.

The rest happened without delay. She was ripped from the safe shelter of James's company and placed into custody. She would have gone without a fuss, yet the MPs insisted on shackling her and marching her with four strong arms holding her tight, bruising her skin. James protested with vehemence, but the sound of his voice died away as she was put into a large white SUV and driven away. It was obvious where they were headed: the Camp Marez internment center for "security detainees." Finally Leila felt like she was a real Iraqi.

Chapter 25

In the detainment center for the second time and under far different circumstances, Leila noticed details that had escaped her before. There was a peculiar smell in the air, below the obvious, and it was harsh like rubber or electricity. The concrete floor was stained in places. The long bars of fluorescent lighting flickered on and off like a strobe light. The effect was shabby, not what Leila might expect from a U.S. government–funded building. Trying not to see the place or let it taint her spirit, she squared her jaw and kept her eyes looking forward.

She was placed in a small interrogation room. The requisite bare lightbulb hung from the ceiling. She was shackled with plastic strips to the chair upon which she sat. There was a single table in front of her and another chair, empty, in the corner. She stared at the cement floor, pockmarked with dents from God only knew what.

There she waited for about an hour; she was just starting to get bored when there was a scuffle of boots outside, the sound of a key in the lock, and three men entered the room. One was James; the others were the CIA agent, Travis Pratt, and one of the contractors—Leila was pretty sure his name was Cox, the ex–Navy SEAL that James had mentioned before.

"What the hell?" James said when he saw her. "What are you guys doing? She's in *cuffs*? She's *innocent*."

It felt good to be stood up for.

"That has yet to be determined," said Pratt in his silky voice. A wave of severe dislike came over Leila and she saw her own emotion echoed on James's face.

"Chill out, James," said Cox. "We're just taking precautions."

James focused on Leila instead. "How are you?" he asked her. "They haven't hurt you, have they?"

"No," she said. She shook her head to reinforce her statement and her black hair tumbled about her face. "No, I am most fine."

"Good." James turned back to his colleagues, who regarded him with blank stares. "Let's step outside for a minute, gentlemen. There are things to discuss." As they filed out of the room, James was the last out and he turned to Leila to mouth the words "I'll be right back." She nodded in acknowledgment. Once they were out of the room, Leila scooted forward on her chair to try to hear what was being said in the corridor; bits and pieces floated past her ears and she tried to reconstruct their casual sentences.

First she heard her father's name; then Pratt said, "On the way." Leila caught the words *muj*, *sweep*, and *operation*.

"Within the next hour . . . I'd bet," said Cox.

"Cool," said James, and his voice was clear and loud, making Leila wonder if he knew she was listening. "Why don't you guys handle him? I'll take over here."

Pratt again. ". . . some kind of attachment . . . interrogate . . . conflict of interest."

"Oh, come off it," said James. "Pratt, our job is to question these terrorists. I have seniority here as the ranking military officer, and I would remind you that you are in a *military* facility. You will question Mr. al-Ghani, and I will take charge of the daughter. That's how it's gonna be." He was almost shouting.

Leila felt a squirm of delight. That would show the CIA, so famous in these parts. And James must really like her and trust her to take that tone. She did not hear Pratt's comeback, but he must have acquiesced, because when James reentered the room he looked calm.

"Leila," he said, just beneath his breath.

She jerked at the sound of his voice. Tugging at her plastic bindings, she longed to be free, to explain herself, to go back in time and redo every decision she'd made beginning the winter past. She was unjustly detained, she was in shock, she had just survived a horrific explosion with naught but a few cuts and bruises and shattered innocence.

"What will happen to me, James?" she asked.

"Hey," he said. He closed the door behind him but did not lock it. "Hey," he repeated, kneeling down before Leila, his gentle manner that of working with a cornered, wounded creature.

"Why am I held here?" she asked.

"It's just a precaution they took," said James. It was an unconscious echo of Cox's words. "They want to know what happened. Why you were driving a truck bomb onto the base."

"I did not!" Leila said. "I ran it into the embankment so no one would be hurt! I tried to save you, the hospital, everyone!"

"I know. Shhh, honey, calm down." James put his hands on Leila's thin, quivering shoulders. "You did well. You did the right thing. I know that."

"Then why am I here?" Tears threatened to spill out of her eyes and she saw it made James nervous; men did not like crying women. She tried to stem the tears. *Honey, he called me honey.*

"It's that little jerk. Pratt. They want a scapegoat; they want a victory. But you'll be in the clear. Listen to me, Leila. I *will not* let anything happen to you. Do you trust me?"

She nodded, flinging tears. James brought out a handkerchief, a red patterned one that belonged around a cowboy's neck. He dabbed her eyes and nose for her. "Okay," he said, "I'm going to take off these plasticuffs. I don't know what's

wrong with these guys to chain up a woman. They have no respect." He kept talking along those lines as he cut off the re-
straints with a quick, slicing motion. Leila let out a breath of
relief and she flexed her wrists around in their freedom.

"Thank you," she said.

What she did next, even she could not fathom. Leila threw
her arms around James's neck and fell forward to hug him. Because he knelt on the floor, it meant that she ended up with
knees on the cold hard floor, too, but she didn't notice it.

James brought his arms around Leila's waist and what
started out as an embrace of simple gratitude turned into
something else. She buried her face in the crook of his neck
and he brought one hand up to stroke her hair in comfort.
"Thank you," she whispered again, but at that point her
words did not matter.

Their faces pulled back to look at each other, but not for
long. Leila's hand ran through his hair, nails scraping along the
nape of his neck. Then there was no more space between them
as James leaned forward and kissed her on the mouth. It was
not a long kiss; Leila tasted its honeyed sweetness and she
pressed herself up against him in response.

They were both breathing hard when they pulled away.

Oh God, thought Leila. She'd broken all the rules that day;
one more wouldn't matter. A hot flush warmed her cheeks and
a tiny smile worked at her lips. She made no move to extricate
herself from his hold. "James," she said.

"Leila," he said. Then he shook his head as though clearing
it of cobwebs. "We don't have a lot of time." And his tone was
all business again. "I've got to explain some things. Do you
have any personal effects with you?"

"Just that," she said, pointing to her backpack in the corner.
"I do not know how it is still with me. I had it when I ran
away from home, and then I suppose my father never took it
off my back when I was drugged and tied up. It has my
diploma in it, and some clothes. Jewelry. Little things that are

important to me. And . . . the things I've kept, records and papers. Our researches."

James was already up and carrying the pack to her. "This is good," he said. "You're going to need to carry some things. Here." He helped her to sit back in the chair. He dragged the other plastic chair across the room to be close to her. He took her small hand between his large ones and held it fast. "First things first. They've arrested your father."

Leila closed her eyes against the news, but when she opened them again the room was steady, not spinning, and she felt clear and composed and not at all surprised. "What about my mother?" she asked.

"I don't know," said James. "I'll try to find out for you. I have a plan now, so listen up."

She sat up straighter like an attentive schoolgirl.

James had given the plan some thought. Leila was in a tenuous position and they both knew it.

With a father who was Mosul's number-one terrorist, her job as a medical translator was over. Added to the black mark on her name was the fact that she had been driving the suicide bomb intended for the hospital. It would not matter that Leila had driven the truck into an embankment instead of the target given her by the mujahideen; she was still an attempted bomber, and she would be fired. It had happened before: translators were thrown back out without recourse or protection. They were marked by their own countrymen as traitors, because they had aided and abetted the Americans. There was nowhere to turn.

Then, on the other side of the issue was Mosul. Since Leila had not completed the task assigned to her by her father, it was obvious to whom her sympathies belonged. If she were released from the detention center and back into the city, she would be lucky to have a few days to live before the *muj* found her and "dealt with her." She was a turncoat, a failed martyr, a girl who had brought shame on her father the terrorist. Leila held no illusions about what would happen to her. She would be another body mutilated, shot or beheaded or worse. They might film it and put it on the Internet to set an example. They would hurt her in the worst way a woman could be hurt.

"It's no longer safe for you here," James said. "We both know that. You can't stay in Mosul."

"I have nothing to stay for," she said. "My father arrested, my sister dead in a bombing. I want to leave this place, but where do I go?"

"That's where I come in," said James. "I'm going to take you out of here. We're going north, into Kurdistan."

"I have family there!" Leila interjected, but James held up a hand.

"No," he said. "You have to get out of Iraq. The jihadis will find you, Leila. Even if you go north to your mother's family, they will track you down. You've been an embarrassment for them, you see: their own leader's daughter was working for the Americans all along. They're going to want to punish you for it. If we can't get anything solid on your dad, we might even have to release him, and then *he* will definitely find you."

Leila scoffed. "You will find my father guilty. How could you not? He is the main leader of the Ansar al-Sunna. The top jihadi."

"Well. In any case, there's no way you can stay in this country. Do you have your passport in your bag?"

She nodded.

"Great. But, Leila, here's the thing: the army doesn't care about you. If they decide you're innocent, which they will, and then release you, you're on your own. They don't care that the insurgency will kill you. But"—and here he sighed—"I told you I would protect you, and I will. I'm going on a reconnaissance mission to the north, me and a few other soldiers. That's the cover. We're going to take you along with us, drive you north through Kurdistan, to the border with Turkey, and then from there you're going to Istanbul. You'll catch a flight to Europe. You'll claim political asylum when you get there. And you'll be safe, Leila, because they can't send you back. They can't."

She had no idea he would go out on such a limb for her benefit; from the sounds of it, James had arranged her escape. On one hand she was upset that the U.S. Army could use her as a translator and drop her so fast, but there was hope there, too, hope at the thought of fleeing to Europe. The seriousness of Leila's situation was not lost on her: if James did not take an active role in smuggling her out of the country, then she would never make it on her own.

"How will you do it?" Leila asked. "I am a prisoner here. Will they release me?"

"Yes," said James. "When we get your father here, it'll clear up. He's already been arrested. We're leaving in a few days, you and I and six other soldiers. Warrant Officer Ike Champlain is one of them—you know him, the big guy—and we're taking Ali Mugnih along as a translator. They're totally trustworthy. Ali's going to help you cross the border, he has a cousin—"

Leila laughed. "This is Iraq, of course there is a cousin!"

"Yeah," James said, smiling with her. Then he sobered. "I want to get you out before Pratt or someone can protest. They would never let me off on a reconnaissance mission if they knew it was to take you to the border."

"You are breaking the rules for me," Leila said, and smiled.

"Yeah, you have that effect," James admitted. He smiled back.

To bring an Iraqi civilian along on a mission, Leila knew, was to invite the harshest consequence. It was not worth contemplating what would happen to James's career if he was caught at it . . . a disciplinary action, perhaps even a demotion . . . it said a great deal that he would risk so much for her.

"When?" she asked.

"Three days from now. I know that's a long time to sit in the detainment center, but at least you'll be safe here. Is there anything you need to take with you from on-base? Anything I can get for you?"

Leila contemplated for a moment but shook her hand. "I think I have what I need," she said. "Oh! But can you give me paper and a pen? I want to write letters to the doctors and nurses. To say thank you."

"Sure," said James. He withdrew from his pocket a standard-issue leather-covered notepad and a push pen with the words *10th Spec. Forces, Fort Collins* stamped in white on it. "You can use this."

"Thank you." The plastic chair made a harsh scraping noise as she pulled it toward the table. Bending her head down, she felt James's hand brush her hair, and she smiled without looking up when he left the room.

Chapter 26

Leila waited. She did not like what seeped into her nostrils: stale urine; the sharp tinge of gunpowder or ammonia, she couldn't tell which; the scent of human fear. Prisons around the world held the same kind of odor. She was sure that all of API's contracted "detainment" operations in nameless Eastern European countries, in Afghanistan and North Africa and the forgotten places of the world, had this aura of quiet suffering. Those faraway places did not matter, though, not when it was she who was the prisoner.

Every ten or twenty minutes, Leila started shaking. It was a symptom of her shock, she knew, and yet it did not make the spasms of delayed panic any easier. One part of her rational mind analyzed all of this and told her that she'd suffered too much all at once. The voice of reason was tinny and powerless, however, when the waves hit her. She was in a dark swamp of sorrow for Fatima's death; an oppressive guilt over everything her father had done and made her do; plus the baffling, warm survival instinct that told her she was still alive after running for her life. Leila had to pinch herself to be sure she was real and not in the afterlife. Then the shakes would subside into general calm for another few minutes. She wished that James would return to put his arms around her.

James. The solid, unchanging presence who had not judged her or assumed the worst of her. The one who was going to save her very life. When they kissed, Leila had felt like she was returning home to something safe and happy and light. She knew she was in love with him, but this fact had to be set aside for the time being, for there were things to do in the meantime—things that would determine the course of the rest of her life.

She'd settled into her chair and finished her letters of thanks to the people of the field hospital, for she did not know if she would ever see them again. Just as she was signing her name on the note intended for Jessica Quinn, there was a knock on the door.

It was an MP, one of the prison detail. He looked surprised that Leila was not shackled and told her that she was to be moved to a cell. "Temporary," he said, "until the interrogation can be continued."

"Super," she said in a very American voice. It was a term she'd picked up from Bonnie and Quinn, who said it a lot. The MP blinked at the word.

She told the MP she was capable of going with him without a fuss and would not try to escape. "After all," she said, "I am just a woman." It would have worked better on an Arab man, but the soldier nodded after thinking about it and did not attempt to bind her hands. He took her elbow but did not grip hard. They went down another corridor and Leila found herself in a harsh empty cell with a too-small window, set high and facing the west.

The setting sun made an orange rectangle of feeble light on the other side of the wall, punctuated with shadows of steel bars. Leila watched the patch of light as it moved, weak, without vigor, as though the sun were a woman succumbing to the overwhelming strength of darkness from the east and unable to put up much of a fight. Or maybe Leila was just projecting her own thoughts onto Nature.

James had said they were leaving in three days. A flood of potential worries occupied Leila for a moment until she reminded herself that she was not doing her job. Her job was to be calm, to abide until James retrieved her, and to get herself prepared for what was to come. She settled for breath exercises, which she did until the patch of sunlight was dead and gone and the cell left in darkness.

For three days she waited. For three days no one came for her, not to question her or free her, and her twice-daily contact with a human being was when her meals were pushed through a metal sliding drawer to the side of the door. The food was plain but not meager; that, at least, was a benefit of being a prisoner of the Americans. Despite the dismal surroundings, it occurred to her that she was in the safest place in Mosul. Logic told her that her father was close by, that he, too, had been arrested, and it must be why they hadn't given her a brutal interrogation. Perhaps Tamir had spilled her innocence already. James would back it up; he would have detailed in his report how Leila had been double-informing all along, how she'd given them forewarning about the bombings and the special rockets, how she'd driven the bomb away from the hospital.

On the evening of the third day, as Leila stood on her tiptoes, watching through the barred window as the sun melted into another puddle of depressed orange on the horizon, James returned to the detainment center.

She knew it was him from the knock on the door—soft and respectful. The door swung open a few seconds later with the jingling rattle of a key and the man himself stepped inside.

"Hey," he said.

Leila wanted to hug him again, to kiss him again, but she forced herself to keep a distance and settled for a simple "Hello."

"Is there no light in here?" James said.

Leila shrugged. With the shaft of light from the well-lit hallway, she could see an empty light socket inside a metal cage in the middle of the ceiling. She pointed up at it.

"Typical government operation," he said, glancing upward.

"Anyway. I have your backpack. You've been cleared and you're free to go."

"Oh," said Leila. She could not muster up anything more profound. She extended her hand to take her familiar old student pack from James. He put a hand of support on the small of her back and she straightened in pleasure at the touch.

"I'm going to take you to the MP guard station," he said. "They'll check you out." Absurd words, as though the detainment center were a hotel. "Normally, with released detainees, they take them back into the city; you'll insist on walking. You'll say there's nowhere in the city for you to go and you will walk. Can you do that?"

"Yes."

"When you go out the gates—they'll escort you—thank them and wait there. Walk until you hit a dark patch on the road, beyond the perimeter lights, and I'll find you there."

"How will you find me if it's dark?" she asked, afraid of being left on the shadowed road.

James paused his stride and glanced down at her with amusement. "You're forgetting who you're talking to," he said with a quirk of a smile. "We have ways around stuff like darkness."

"Oh yes," said Leila, remembering the Americans' miraculous technology. Indeed, a black night was nothing to a soldier with night vision or infrared. She would hide in shadows and be plucked from them, whisked away, forever gone from Mosul. For a moment her heart was a leaping tiger, ahead of itself, snarling and yearning for freedom from the cage that had held her since the war began. Steps, mere steps, until that freedom.

James led her out of the cell and passed through a long wide corridor painted pale buttery yellow. There were shouts and the sounds of a scuffle coming from one of the doors left ajar. Leila could not help but glance inside. Her eyes widened.

She wanted to cry his name, "*Baba!*" but her tongue had turned to lead. Tamir's eyes locked on to hers over the shoulders of the men restraining him. They flashed with some emotion—love or hate? Leila could not tell. Beside her, James gripped her hand, trying to pull her away from the sight.

Leila's father saw this, too, and his lips pulled back into a grimace, his hazel eyes gleaming as he struggled. There was a great deal of shouting; the American soldiers pulled his arms behind his back. Leila saw a rip in his robe at the shoulder and the angry bloom of a contusion there.

"*Baba*," she said. She took a tiny step toward the doorway. James relented his pressure on her hand.

"*Eib*!" Tamir shouted at her, the Arabic word for shame. "You are not my daughter!"

Leila flushed. "I am sorry for you," she said. "I forgive you." She did not forgive Tamir, not yet, but she knew that someday she would. She knew, in the deep place of her soul, that this was the last time she would ever see her father, so she had to say the right thing even if it wasn't true at that moment.

Then Pratt's unwelcome visage hovered in front of her, blocking the view of her father's struggle inside the cement-block room. "This is classified business," he said. "You were never here." Pratt closed the door in her face.

"Come on," said James.

So it was that Leila last saw her father, the great judge, the loyalist, the Iraqi patriot Tamir al-Ghani. He was a prisoner, with the loveless duration of his life stretched, long or short, in front of him. The evidence against Tamir was too overwhelming, she knew, and he would never be released. He might be shuffled from prison to prison, tortured in faraway places, left to rot, his cause forgotten.

Leila lingered outside the door for a moment longer. "Will they hurt him?"

James was silent. That was her answer, one she'd expected, but it was no easier to receive for all her anticipation of it. She wondered where her father would go and what would become of him; she wondered where her mother was. The al-Ghani family was blown to the winds now. Would she ever recover?

318 Morgana Gallaway

There was no time to think about it; Leila was operating in survival mode, hanging on to the essentials that would keep her alive.

She walked with James farther along the hallway, past a row of closed doors, and he pointed around a corner toward a desk manned by men in uniform. "Go to the guard station," James said, low in her ear. "I'll be out of here as soon as I can." He squeezed her hand and then turned, walking back the direction they'd come.

She acted out James's instructions on autopilot. There stood a couple of stern-faced MPs in front of her, each with clipboards, each with too many lines on their young faces. They had seen much. She gave her name, they confirmed her release. They asked her to sign something. Leila glanced over the page: it was a nondisclosure agreement, acknowledging that once she was out of American custody she would not reveal details of the facility or its staff. She signed it without a choice in the matter.

She turned over her backpack so that the MPs could riffle through it one more time. What on earth Leila would smuggle out of the detainment center, she had no idea, but the search was conducted like a bad habit of power. They returned it to her with gruff nods.

"Thank you," she said.

"Where are you going now, Miss al-Ghani? There's a car that can take you back into the city," one of the men said. His name tag read ROSARIO.

"This is all I have left." She hefted up her backpack. "I will walk for a while. Please, I insist on it." She held up a hand as the soldiers looked ready to protest. "It is not yet curfew. I want to walk."

One of them might have said "stubborn women" under his breath, or perhaps it was "stupid woman," but she was not concerned either way. Two MPs flanked her walk out the door and into the severe lights beneath T-towers and barbed wire. The sigh of relief did not escape her lips until she was outside the gates of the detainment center and the MPs had left her there, disappearing back into their station.

She was alone on a gravelly road with the dead silence of night closing in around her. A tiny shard of fear stabbed into her heart and she pushed it away, just as she'd been pushing everything away. She made for the darkest patch of road she could see; a cover of clouds had rolled in after sunset, obscuring the stars and reflecting the eerie orange city lights. It was half as bright as it should have been, for the main power grid was off in Mosul again and the lights belonged to the few fortunate enough to have generators.

In her jeans, dark sweater, and black hair, Leila disappeared well enough into the unlit shadows of the road. She stood, unsure of what to do, not knowing if she'd gone far enough. The thought that James and his soldiers would have night-vision goggles reassured her. They could pierce through the darkness to sweep her off and away.

For about half an hour she waited on the shoulder of the road, shifting the weight of her backpack from shoulder to shoulder and glancing this way and that. Nothing sounded, no crickets or night swallows or bugs. The space around Leila was sheathed in oppressive silence. She wished for some familiar noise to distract her from her thoughts.

Then she got it: the engine of a vehicle coming toward her. She crouched down in case it was not James in his white jeep, but as it drew closer the vague ghostly shape of it resolved. The headlights were off so Leila was not blinded. It was James, as promised; she could see the pale shape of his face hovering in the window. She drew in a deep breath, unaware that she had forgotten to breathe. The jeep slowed down and the back door opened for James to hop out.

"In you go," he said, grasping her hand and helping her up into the vehicle. In the driver's seat was Warrant Officer Ike, who turned to smile at her.

"Hey," Ike said.

"Hello," said Leila, smiling at the man who'd saved her life.

"Drive on, good soldier," said James. As the jeep gained speed on the road, James introduced her to the man in the front passenger seat. "This is Ali, our translator," James said. "He's very trustworthy."

"*A-salaama*," said Ali, nodding at her. In the shadows Leila could not tell much about him, except that he was a young man with a serious yet friendly face. She hoped he was indeed trustworthy.

They did not head out of the city, as Leila had expected. Instead Ike turned the vehicle back toward the main operational part of Camp Marez and the hangars.

"Here," James said, reaching into the back of the jeep to procure a dark wool blanket. "Climb into the back," he told her, "and cover yourself with this. There's another vehicle of soldiers coming north with us, but they don't know about you. I'm splitting up the company when we're out of Mosul, so there is actual reconnaissance done on the mission. Allay suspicion. They'll fork up to the northwest and we'll continue up to Turkey without them knowing about it."

"Killing one bird with two stones?" Leila asked, modifying a phrase she'd picked up from Dr. Whitaker.

James and Ike both laughed. "Yeah," said James. "Something like that."

She climbed over the backseat and scooted herself into a little corner. There were supplies in the back, bottled water and petrol and long boxes of what must have been weapons or ammunition or something. James leaned over and helped her hide beneath the blanket.

"Not a word," he instructed. "Not until I tell you it's safe. And keep your head down, too; they can't know there's a fourth person in the jeep."

"Okay," she said. Her voice was muffled by the blanket.

After that it was just noises, some of them baffling, and Leila longed to poke her head out and to look, but did not dare. Voices, boisterous and confident, so very American. Vehicle doors opening, doors closing. "Yes, sir." A discussion of the route to take out of Mosul. Someone asked the time and another person replied that it was 2230. There was the distinctive metallic clicking and rattle of weaponry being handled.

Her internal panic kicked up when she heard someone open the back door of the jeep into the very compartment where she was hiding. She willed her muscles to not move and held her breath, hoping either that it was James or that the person would not notice the shape in the corner. She heard a harsh, hollow *clack* as something was stacked, very near to her feet. Then the door closed again. She breathed.

It seemed ages that she huddled there unmoving. She stopped trying to deduce what was happening around her. The ways of the Special Forces were unknown to her, anyway, even if she'd had the faculty of her eyes, so she had no point of reference to understand the noises she heard. Finally the jeep rumbled to life, vibrating beneath her as the engine started, and she heard Ike's voice say, "Let's roll, boys. And girl."

Her skin jumped a little when a hand fell upon her shoulder, patting her, but it was just James. "You can come out from under the blanket now," he said. "You'll have to keep your head down for a while longer, though."

Grateful, she pulled the blanket off her face to see more darkness, though with the outside headlights on, a whitish light was cast on the interior of the jeep. She sighed in the cool air and pushed her hair out of her eyes. "Thank you," she said.

"Ah, so nice to have a woman around," Ike intoned from the front. "You know, Leila, we're not used to having sweet feminine voices to make our patrols so pleasant."

They drove. Leila never got her last look at Mosul because she had to keep her head down. She did, however, stretch her legs out flat across the boxes of bottled water and bundle the blanket up to make a nice little pillow beneath her head. She lay there, low and quiet, until James poked his head back over the seat.

"We're almost past the city," he said. "In about an hour the other vehicle will take off in the other direction." As if to confirm this, he fished out a little microphone from his jacket and it made a whining noise as he turned it on. "Tango Four, come in. Over."

A scratchy noise. Then came a disembodied voice speaking into James's ear, which Leila could hear faint whispers of. James nodded to himself. "One hour until split-off, confirm." He spoke in a series of words that Leila did not understand, code names for things, shorthand and slang that was its own warrior dialect. He flicked some little switch and the inside of the jeep was back to straight human voices. "You okay back there?" James asked Leila. "Need anything?"

"No," she said.

"Can we have some music?" Ike called from the front.

"I have a new CD from Egypt," Ali volunteered, the first time he'd spoken on his own. His English was good, as good as Leila's.

"Naw, none of that Arabic shit," Ike said. "Captain, sir? You have your David Bowie on you?"

"I just might," said James. Leila heard rummaging. "Yeah!" he said. "Put it on. And please spare us your singing."

Ike did not, and for the next hour they had to endure his warbling voice, including an enthusiastic rendition of "Major Tom." "Too bad you're not a major. And your name's not Tom," Ike said during an instrumental moment.

"Yeah, yeah, too bad," said James.

Leila thought they were a little crazy.

Soon the vehicle slowed down, the radio crackled, and James told Leila that she could sit up now, but she was drowsy and not inclined to move from her position. She drifted in and out of sleep until just past midnight, when the jeep slowed down again and pulled off onto the rocky shoulder of the road. "Here good, boss?" Ike's voice, still loud, floated through the haze.

"Yep," said James. Then his head appeared over the back of the seat again, peering down at Leila. "We're going to rest here, sleep until sunrise. I'll set up a blanket outside."

Leila nodded, bleary-eyed. They'd stopped near a rocky out-cropping, sheltered from the sight of the road by several large bushes. The sky was still overcast, but no longer was there the glow of city lights; they were in Kurdish territory now, Leila was sure. A sweet night breeze waved through the sparse stalks of grass that grew in bunches around them. She could not see far in the dark, but the space around them had the soft feel of wilderness, an emptiness that would shelter and protect them.

And, of course, there was the fact that this jeep was ar-mored beneath its innocuous chipped paint, and its occupants armed to the teeth. Leila slept well on the thin bedroll swept out onto a flattish rock. Two men rested a few yards away, not too close, and they changed identities throughout the night: first it was James and Ali, then Ike and Ali, then James and Ike. They were rotating shifts of playing night watchman. Leila's sleep was dreamless, punctuated by startled fits. Aftermath of shock, her doctor's brain told her, and when dawn rose swift and furious on the eastern horizon she awoke, amazed that she'd lived to see a new day.

Everything from now on would be bonus time in a bor-rowed life.

She wanted to make herself useful, so when James built a small fire of twigs, Leila found a teapot and boiled some water. Being Americans, they had powdered coffee instead of tea, but that was fine with Leila. The taste of tea would still bring back the taste of betrayal from her father. Forever she would associ-ate her mother's *shai* with awakening as a suicide bomber. She set out four tin mugs, standard military issue, and when the water boiled she measured out the coffee powder.

The silence as they all drank was not uncomfortable. Leila reverted into her customary cultural behavior of being seen and not heard. She did not know Ali, the translator, or what his impressions of her would be, but old habits of demureness died hard. She did notice that when she helped to clean up their breakfast and put the dishes back into the jeep, James placed his hand between her shoulder blades in a light caress, making her wish hard that they were alone. They had to settle for a quick look of longing between them.

As they drove through tiny hamlets and villages, nothing approaching the size of a town, Leila saw that they were very much in Kurdistan. The slopes rising around them were rough, rocky, but still verdant with spring's growth. The road wound back and forth, serpentine about the hills, avoiding the clusters of conifer trees that clung to the edge of the mountainside. Ike had perfect control of the vehicle on its winding path and Leila relaxed for a moment, secure.

"Did we pass Dohuk?" she asked, referring to the main city of the far northern region.

"Last night," said James, sitting in the backseat beside her. "I think you were asleep."

"It was my sweet lullaby voice," Ike called from the front. They ignored him.

"I have family in Dohuk," she said.

"That reminds me!" James said. "I forgot to tell you. Your father told the interrogators that your mother's gone north to her Kurdish relatives. Your house in Mosul is closed up, something about your brother doing it."

"Naji," she said. "My brother. He's stayed out of it all, I think. And so Mother's gone. That is good." Leila felt weird to say it. Her family was truly splintered. Her grief over Fatima bloomed afresh, though she was leaving it behind, along with Iraq itself. She swallowed and banished her sorrow for another day. Yet she was glad her mother was with her other relations, far away from the violence of Mosul. More, Leila was glad not to be with Umm Naji, for a life in Kurdistan would be stultifying and dull. She would have had to put her dream of being a doctor aside forever and therefore her current journey with these American soldiers took on a new meaning.

She was *going* somewhere. Wherever she ended up, she knew it would not be Iraq. She would be an exile from her own country and there was something exciting about it. Leila allowed a tinge of hope to color her thoughts. Outside the window of the jeep the countryside rolled by, dry hills and dry vegetation, getting hillier by the mile. She let her head rest on the glass and her imagination reeled forward in time to take her to places unknown. Cities. Further education. New people and new experiences, a plunge into a foggy future that sent a little thrill down her spine. Escape by flight, not martyrdom. Who knew what she might find?

The morning turned to noon. The terrain was rough and the road rougher. They bounced and jostled down the road with its potholes and gravel; there were bizarre stretches that were paved.

"It's chaos," said James, gesturing out the window.

"Mmm," Leila agreed.

It was dusty, too, from their slow pace on the primitive road. The windows stayed rolled up, encasing the occupants in stale but clean air. For a while Leila had a conversation in Arabic with Ali, learning more about him and where he was from. He came from Baghdad originally, she learned, and started working for the Americans two years ago at the age of eighteen. He'd requested a transfer to Mosul when his Baghdad neighborhood got too dangerous. Leila understood this; the capital of Iraq was even worse than Mosul these days.

Ali, she discovered, was a Shia Muslim and therefore at risk of retribution from angry Sunnis. He was also at risk by virtue of his working for the "occupying Crusaders," just as Leila had been. Ali seemed a cheerful and optimistic young man, clever as a whip, full of hope for someday going to America and making a life there. She was encouraging to him. They talked shop for a while, lamenting the difficulties of translating some things from Arabic into English. Arabic was a language full of nuance, often with several different words for something, each with a minute difference of meaning.

"English is a blunt language," said Ali.

"Descriptive in some things, though," said Leila. "Emotionally blunt. Arabic, I think, is more . . . courtly."

"Yes, courtly!" Ali said with fondness. "Yet I would give it up forever."

"I hope you get to go to America," Leila said, and meant it.

"*Shikram!*" Ali thanked her.

"Hey," Ike interrupted, "what are you guys talking about? We can't understand you."

"We are talking about you," Leila joked. "Saying all mean and nasty things." She laughed.

"See how she gets?" James said. "She's out of control." He winked at her, a flash of blue brilliance, and Leila smiled at him. Then James reached out in the privacy of the backseat and took her hand, squeezed it for a moment. A few small threads of pleasure ran through her nerves, all focused on her left hand.

Then the jeep swayed as it went over a rocky patch of the road and the bump forced their hands apart again. *Just as well*, thought Leila. She understood why the Holy Quran forbade that unmarried men and women be left alone together. It was far too dangerous.

Chapter 27

They stopped ten miles from the border with Turkey. The road on which they traveled was loose gravel, fading away at the edges into the landscape. It was not a well-traversed route, that much was obvious, and Leila was sure that James had planned it that way. The border between Turkey and Iraq was porous, not worthy of being called an international boundary at all, given that the entire region was restless for autonomy under the name of Kurdistan. The instability worked to the advantage of Leila, James, Ike, and Ali, however.

"You'll be taken as far as Kayseri by Ali and his cousin," James said as the jeep ground to a halt at the side of the road.

"Break time," said Ike, jumping out of the driver's seat and lighting a cigarette.

Leila took the opportunity for some fresh air. It was chilly outside the jeep and she slipped her woolen sweater on over her clothes. They had stopped at the crest of a mountain that overlooked the wrinkled, magnificent ranges that defined Kurdistan. Scrub brush, small trees, and high-altitude wildflowers grew along the slopes, although it was too dry to be called anything but harsh. The roads up here were curvaceous and sometimes dizzyingly close to the precipitous edges.

The feet of the four travelers crunched in the rock of the jeep track as they each stretched their legs. They had been driving a total of seven hours out of Mosul, but it felt like longer to

Leila. Part of the road had been washed out, so a detour had been necessary; another time, James ordered them to take the off-road option to get past a checkpoint of Kurdish militia. That had been an adventure in large rocks bumping against the axel, and the danger of flattened tires, but they'd come through all right.

In the jeep, the radio crackled. "Come in, this is Tango Four, over," said a faraway-sounding voice.

Ike picked up the mouthpiece. "Charlie Two. Go ahead."

"Wanted to report a discovery just north of Dohuk . . . we're runnin' around up here and we've found a supply of old howitzer shells, some rifles, other stuff."

"Righto, mark the location, we'll radio back to base."

The disembodied voice gave a rapid series of coordinates, degrees and minutes and seconds.

"Taken a note," said Ike, scribbling it down on a piece of paper. "That all?"

"That's all. Tango Four, out."

The radio fell silent as Leila watched the exchange. She blushed when Ike looked at her, afraid he might accuse her of eavesdropping, but instead he grinned and gave her the paper. "Give that to the captain, would you?"

"Sure," she said, ducking her head as she took it. She walked up to James, who was standing a good twenty feet away, holding a cigarette and gazing over the terrain below their feet. "Ike said to give you this." She held out the coordinates.

"Thanks," he said, pocketing it. "I have to radio back to Marez in a couple of minutes. Give them something to work with. They don't know we're this far up."

"And they do not know Ali and cousin and I are sneaking into Turkey," added Leila.

He laughed. "Uh, no. Illegal incursions are not on their agenda."

"You don't have to do this. I can take a bus or—"

"No, you can't," he interrupted. "No way. It's too dangerous. Besides, I . . ." He paused, looked around. "I'll give you more details when we're alone for a minute, but there's something important I want you to take. Some papers."

Leila gasped. "Records? To go with mine? Your journal?"

"Shhh," he urged, grasping her arm. "Yeah. There's no other way to get it out of the country in any reasonable time."

Leila narrowed her eyes at him. "Are you using me?"

James shrugged sheepishly. The wind kicked up, blowing his dark hair up from behind, making him look haphazard. "You caught me," he said. "Do you object?" As he said it, his hand trailed down her arm to find her bare fingers.

"Not really," said Leila, smiling. "I suppose it is the least I can do, since you are saving my life."

"Excellent point," James said. "Come on. We've got to talk about how you're getting past the border."

Together they walked back to the jeep. Ali was just finishing his cigarette and preparing to take over the driving duties. Ike was rummaging around in the back for something, making a great deal of noise, until he brandished a package of Oreo cookies.

"Where the hell did you get those?" James asked, astounded.

"Found 'em in the city," said Ike. "At a shop. During Clean Sweep. You know, things got pretty boring while we were waiting for the *muj*, so I did a little shopping."

For a moment James looked about to admonish him, but instead shrugged. "Cool. Good thinking," he said. "Right. Now before we get under way again, we need to talk about our story here. Leila, I have an entry visa stamp for your passport, so that when you try to exit Turkey later on, you won't have problems. We're trying to avoid an official border crossing at all; these stations are so remote they won't know the difference. All you need is a stamp saying you crossed. We're driving as close to the border as we can and meeting Ali's cousin—what's his name?"

"Yezdi."

"Right, Yezdi, just shy of the line. They'll take Leila across."

"Wait a moment," Leila said. "We're leaving the jeep?"

"Have to," said James. "For one thing, the Turkish government won't let our vehicle in without a record of our passage. And if we leave Iraq . . . well, that could get us court-martialed. Ali and his cousin are more free to come and go. But they won't be gone more than a couple days. Ike and I will run around, do some recon, make the daily reports to Marez, and hold the jeep here until Ali returns. Right, guys?"

"Yes, sir," said Ike.

"How are we getting across the border?" Leila asked.

"Donkeys," said James.

"Oh my God," Ike laughed.

"It is true," Ali said. "My cousin is waiting for us ahead with three donkeys. There is a goat track that crosses behind the mountains and meets the main road again."

"You'll walk the main road until you can find a taxi," James continued. "Get yourself to Diyarbakir; from there you'll drive up to Kayseri. Leila, you'll take the train to Istanbul. I've written down the information for you and the fares."

Head spinning from the prospect of jeeps, donkeys, taxis, and trains, Leila stared at a rock near her foot so that she could ground her thoughts. "What happens in Istanbul?" she asked.

"This," said James. He reached into his pocket and took out an envelope, handing it to her. Leila opened the sheaf and found a printout for an e-ticket: a flight, British Airways, Istanbul to London Heathrow, in her name. It departed in three days. Also in the envelope was cash, in the incredible amount of one thousand U.S. dollars.

"James, what is this?" She waved the envelope at him.

"I'll explain in a minute," he said in an undertone. The meaning was clear; James did not want to give details to Ike and Ali. "I want us to focus on getting across into Turkey now; we have to drive us up close, but not too close, or the border guards will see us. Oh, and I'll need your passport for the Turkish entry visa stamp I . . . uh . . . *acquired*."

Ike chortled. "The ways of the Special Forces are mysterious," he intoned to Leila. "Don't ask, don't tell."

"Sure," she said weakly.

The four of them piled back into the jeep. Leila readjusted the straps on her backpack to prepare for an overland journey and filled the pack with extra bottles of mineral water and some army-issue energy bars. With a lurch the jeep started rolling forward with Ali at the steering wheel. Next to her, James brandished a dried-out wooden stamp and an ink pad.

"The entry visas are in blue at this border station," he said. "Here, give me your passport."

She handed it over and he flipped through it. "Nice picture!" he said, laughing.

"Lemme see," Ike said, turning in the front seat.

"No! It doesn't even look like me," Leila said. The jeep jolted over a bump in the curvy road and she yelped.

After twenty minutes of careful driving, they came to a stop again, this time before a bend in the road. There was nothing distinguishing about the place in the road, not a sign or a tree, but Ali seemed to know what he was doing. For a moment Leila wondered if he was trustworthy or if he was leading them into a trap with the mujahideen. In Iraq, one never knew. It was fortunate that James and Ike were there.

"We are arrived," said Ali.

"Where's your cousin?" Ike asked.

"There," said Ali, pointing. Sure enough, the slight figure of a teenage boy came around the bend, three scrawny donkeys in tow. Leila wrinkled her nose; she did not trust the stamina of these donkeys. Ali laughed. "He is a very prompt boy, my cousin," he said.

"I guess so," said James, sounding amazed. "Thanks, Ali."

"It is no problem, good sir," said Ali. "As long as I get paid, eh?" It was a jest, and Ike laughed.

"Same for all of us, my friend," Ike said, clapping Ali on the shoulder.

"We've got to move," James reminded them. "Leila, all you need to worry about is your backpack. I've got the supplies ready in bags. Stretch your legs for a minute, there's a long ride ahead."

Leila did; she watched as Yezdi, the teenage boy, was given a small box with soda and a few CDs from Ali, for his trouble. James approached the donkeys and strapped on the bags of water, extra ammunition (for everyone in these parts traveled armed), and clothes. He moved expertly with the animals and Leila wondered if he had a history with horses. It was easier to respect a man who worked well with animals; it spoke of stern gentleness. A man who was good with animals tended to be a man who was good with children.

With cautious footsteps Leila stepped toward the donkeys, reaching out a hand to pet the nose of one of them. It stared at her with baleful eyes but did not object to the touch. "Nice donkey," she said in Arabic. "Good donkey." She switched to English and asked James, "How far is the border?"

"The crossing is about three miles away as the bird flies. By road, a bit longer. It's good for us that the terrain is so rough; they won't be able to see the dust kicked up by the jeep or the donkeys." James paused to retie the kaffiyeh he wore around his head. Then he regarded Leila's attire. "Do you have a more traditional dress with you?" he asked. "Something to blend in?"

Leila sighed. "My graduation dress. It is very fine, though, with gold threads and embroidery. It would attract more attention than this." She motioned at her jeans and shirt. "I did not think."

"Mmm," said James. "Oh well. Maybe you can buy something to help you blend in."

"Yes, I could do that," she said.

Ike wandered over to them. "Are they about ready, Captain?"

"Yep," said James. "Can you guys give us a minute?"

Ike smirked. "Yes, sir," he said, then turned away as James beckoned to Leila.

James glanced up at the rocky ledge hovering over the road; there looked to be a way up. The sun sizzled above their heads, a hint of the baking summer to come. The air was cool at this high altitude, but still Leila was grateful for the spare head scarf she'd remembered to pack. It might be the last time she ever wore it if she were to live in the West. For the moment it seemed incredible that she was living at all. Inside her shoes, she wiggled her toes, just to reinforce the fact. The difference between safety and danger was an invisible line on the ground, and that seemed fitting; Leila hoped she could cross the line and consider it done.

"Come," James said, extending his hand.

She slipped her small hand into his and allowed him to lead her away from the white jeep, away from the three others who stood backs turned to them; the scramble up the rocky slope was not difficult and then Leila and James were fifteen feet above the road, with an outcropping of bare pink rock between them and their fellow travelers. The wind was blowing up the mountain, which was good since it stole their sensitive words away from curious ears below.

"I don't want to say good-bye to you, James," Leila began, knowing that he would be the thing she missed most about her life in Iraq.

"I know," James said, and his hands were on her waist, his face bowed toward hers. "But you'll be safe. I promise you that. Now, listen carefully."

She nodded.

"When you arrive at Heathrow Airport, you're going to declare political asylum. Tell them that your life was under threat in Iraq. They can't send you back if your status is declared as a refugee." James pulled one more trick from his jacket, one more essential document, a seal for Leila's fate. It was in a pale yellow envelope. "I've written a letter, see, with the signature of one of my superior officers. It says that you worked for us as a translator, and that your life is under threat from political elements here. I'm afraid it's all I can do for you. Not allowed to take direct action. But if you can get to the West on your own, then there's nothing stopping me from supporting you in words." He pressed the envelope into her hands.

James's military self seemed more prominent than ever. He had to stay detached from her. His words might be her salvation, but the irrational part of Leila wanted him to throw his orders to the west-blowing wind and come with her. Self-reliance was frightening at the moment.

"And there's this," James said, taking his hands away from her for a moment to reach into his worn-out backpack. He pulled from it the leather journal he kept; it had been filled with notes and she could see the edges of extra papers folded inside, threatening to burst out. "It has everything I've written down from these past months. It frees the involvement of my men, my team, and of you, and that's why it's so important. The memory chip from my camera is also inside, in the envelope, so keep it out of danger."

Leila's eyes widened; she remembered the pictures of Yousef. She nodded again, vigorously, and clutched the book close to her. "I will keep it very safe."

"It's best if you don't look through it," said James. "It's safer for you if you don't know everything."

It would be a challenge to suppress her natural curiosity, but Leila nodded. She owed everything to James and that included following his instructions to the letter. "What should I do with it until you . . . until . . ."

"I'll join you as soon as I can," said James, staring into her eyes in the manner of a vow given. "That's a promise. Take the journal, your puzzle box, and open a safe-deposit vault in a bank. Something random, not where you have an account. Put the papers there, keep the key on you at all times, and then banish it from your mind. Don't dwell on it, Leila. Just . . . go ahead in your life. When I see you again, you'll be a top med student and everything will be clear. Don't worry."

Leila gave him a wavering smile. "When you see me again? For sure?"

"Of course," said James. "Something good has to come from all of this, right?"

"Of course," she said.

Then, as the wind picked up, making Leila sway on her feet, James held her close with the hard edges of the book between them. He lowered his head and kissed her, with urgency; it was very much good-bye. Leila had never been kissed that way in her life. She felt herself weak and wishing they had more time, another night, hours alone in which to express that which had no words. But on that mountain's edge in the deepest disarray of Kurdistan, time was a luxury unafforded. Leila had to leave, for she had a train to catch, a new life awaiting her.

James held her hand with a firm grip as he helped her down the slope to where Ali and Yezdi waited, each smoking a leisurely cigarette. The journal went inside Leila's old school bag next to the Persian puzzle box and she hoisted it onto her back.

"Take care, Leila," said Ike, with a crooked smile and a cheery wave.

"I cannot thank you enough times," Leila told him.

James helped her up onto the braying, scrawny donkey. He laughed and so did she. The sun was steady above them. He did not let go of her hand, even as Ali and Yezdi clicked their tongues and they got the donkeys moving off the road and down the narrow goat track. Leila's own donkey took a few tentative steps and she found there was a tearful lump in her throat.

James, leaning in, kissed her on the cheek and brought his hand to cup her face for one last, stolen moment. "Be good."

"I will. Be safe."

"I will. I would say something else . . . but I can't, you see. I have to save it. It will give me a reason . . ." He trailed off.

Leila knew he meant it would give him a reason to stay alive. And she could understand that. She knew what he felt for her, anyway, for her feelings were the same. As the donkey started on its way, she looked back at Captain James Cartwright; she saw not only James but Fatima next to him, Umm Naji, her friend Hala, the kind doctors and nurses at the field hospital. For a split second she even thought she saw her father. The donkey was slow and she wished it could hurry up. Instead she turned her face ahead toward the unfriendly mountains and ordered herself to be brave and strong and good.

Chapter 28

Eighteen months later

The rain came down hard and straight in London. There was no wind to send it astray from its downward path onto streets and roofs and the occasional patch of lush green grass of the public parks. The air was damp and dark, as it had been all season. Though it was just past four o'clock in the afternoon, twilight hovered beyond the clouds, and some of the city's lights flickered on, warm patches of orange encased in cast iron.

Leila al-Ghani walked beneath a black umbrella, dressed in her long knee-length coat. She wore leather boots, heeled against the occasional back splash of a passing car. A hat covered her head. She looked like any other Londoner, one of Eastern descent, obviously, but a modern woman. She was often pegged as Pakistani or Indian by those who could not tell the difference. The warm brown tones of her skin suited this climate, for the cool damp air created the bloom of roses on her cheeks and her face was a hint, a promise, that warmer climes existed but London was first choice.

In one hand Leila carried a stylish black leather satchel that looked like a physician's bag. It was heavy with textbooks and papers. On this gray day she was on her way home from a lecture. She'd just come off the London Underground, not too crowded in this hour before the rush, and walked toward her four-person student flat in Ladbroke Grove. The flat was run-down and not so expensive: perfect for four medical students to share.

Leila felt comfortable in this neighborhood. There were families here, and it had the feeling of a suburb with its low-slung town houses in orderly rows. The sidewalks had weeds growing between the cracks. The nights found some drunken hoodlums on the streets, but they were always the same locals, not anyone to worry about. Leila could stay anonymous.

When she first settled in London she'd thought about living in one of the Muslim-dominated neighborhoods in the north of the city, or perhaps trying to blend in to the Bangladeshi population in the East End. But then she figured that was the first place they would look for her—jihadis who knew her name; intelligence services who had her on a list of former de-tainees. She didn't want encounters with either group.

She was registered at Imperial College under her own full name, Leila al-Ghani, but it was not too rare of a name. She'd looked in the London directory first and found listings for many other al-Ghanis; one more would not be noticed. Her given name, too, was common among Muslims. However, she did not give the school her home address on their registry; she listed a post box in the far-flung neighborhood of Elephant and Castle. She had to make her way across the city every week to pick up her mail. The safety margin was worth the in-convenience.

There was no tangible reason for her paranoia. She'd never been threatened, never been confronted; she had never even had an incident with the fixed presence of crazies in London, the ones who must inhabit every city. Every day was a study in normality. Yet there was something beneath it all, a feeling of being watched, a sensation that perhaps someone was taking her photograph with a long-lens camera. She noticed the work vans idling on the streets with men inside, smoking and chat-ting; they could have been what they appeared, just blue-collar workers going about their jobs as plumbers or electricians. Or the men in the vans could be watching her. The little hairs on the back of her neck pricked up sometimes. Her pulse quickened. And she never knew why.

There were other things, too. She had a mobile phone, a snazzy little silver thing like everyone had, but sometimes she swore it malfunctioned. Once in a while she would hear a faint clicking on the line. It could have been a crossed signal. Or it could have been a tap.

As James had instructed so long ago, she had put the puzzle box, stuffed with its sheaf of incriminating papers, in a random safe-deposit vault at a bank where she had no account. The papers burned a hole in her consciousness sometimes, the photos and the accusations and the *implications* of what those papers held, but she had not received instructions from James on what to do with them. She thought he must be figuring it out for himself. It was a vast game of chess they were in, and they could not move until they were sure of checkmate. It was difficult to hear the news out of Iraq and not go public, but she held firm. James was the one person in the whole business that she trusted. She would wait for him. The key to the safe-deposit box was kept on her person at all times, within the hollow space on the large locket she always wore. She never opened it and none of her friends knew what was inside it. When pressed she acted as though it were an emotional issue, with the image of someone loved and lost. This was the case; accompanying the safe-deposit box key was a tiny photograph of Fatima's face.

She knew James's tour was almost up, or perhaps it already was. He sent her an e-mail once a month, full of friendly pleasantries for the censors. She had learned some patience by now, and so she responded in kind, letting him know that she was all right. The e-mails were the only anchor to her previous life. Since coming to London, she'd put her feelings for James on a cool hiatus. If he couldn't be with her, Leila needed to stay in control of herself, no matter how much her heart sang when she saw his name in her e-mail in-box.

In London, Leila always went home via a different route, just as she had in Mosul. Under the pitter-patter of rain on her umbrella, she glanced behind her and around her before ducking through the low iron gate and up the stairs to her flat. The keys were already out and in her hand and she turned the lock with quick expertise. Then the door was closed and she was safe.

It was a typical student flat, messy with papers and books, but the four girls kept it clean of dishes and wine bottles. Leila's flatmate, a buxom girl named Rose, was lounged on the sofa, flipping through a stack of notes.

"Hey, Leila," Rose said.

"Hi," Leila said. She put her umbrella on the stand by the door so it could dry. "Raining hard outside."

"Yeah! Good day to stay in my trackie bums and get some work done."

Rose was, indeed, in what she called her "trackie bums": exercise pants, exceedingly comfortable. Leila had three pairs herself.

"Yes, I must study, too. I have an exam next week for neurophysiology," Leila reported.

"My stuff's bad enough," said Rose, who was studying to be a pediatrician. "You're crazy to be doing pharmacology."

"I like it," said Leila. "Do you want some coffee? I'll make some."

"When are we going to get you drinking tea like a proper British girl?" Rose teased, flashing a smile out of well-formed lips. "I thought you drank tea in the Middle East."

"I prefer coffee," said Leila. The English way of drinking tea, with milk, was removed from her bad memories, but still too close for comfort. "And I always will," she added.

Rose harrumphed from her spot on the sofa but said nothing more.

The flat fell quiet for a few hours as Leila retreated into her bedroom to study. Her computer was on and running, connected to the Internet and set to her favorite medical reference search page. She fell into her Zen-like zone of learning, a happy place for her. Her mind was quiet and aware, expanding to accommodate new information, in its natural state. Leila had decided to specialize in pharmacology for her medical degree. Despite her early distaste at distributing pills from the Al-Razi pharmacy, here she was after a doctorate in the subject. But, after her work with the Americans, she'd done enough hands-on medicine to last a lifetime. Besides, there was room in this field for Leila to do great things and her marks were already tops.

She'd been in London for a year and a half. Her days of working in Mosul at the army hospital had congealed into memories; the idea that she'd almost been a suicide bomber was ludicrous now. It only returned in vivid, gruesome detail in her dreams. In her nighttime episodes, Leila sometimes ran too slowly (or Ike did not cut the tape fast enough) and the bomb exploded and killed her. Other times she drove the truck into the field hospital itself, killing everyone there, yet somehow she survived to walk around and witness with oppressive guilt what she'd done. But when Leila awoke in the mornings to see her neat-as-a-pin London bedroom, decorated with clean wood furniture, and the big elm tree waving its affable branches at her through the window, it all faded back into the dim clouds of memory.

"I'm making a run to the shop," Rose called at her from the sitting room. "Need anything?"

"No, thank you," Leila called back. She heard the door slam, leaving her alone in the flat. It was now dark outside and the raindrops on the windowpane magnified the lights outside into a million little constellations on flat glass. Leila kept working. For a moment she distracted herself with wondering whether Rose had locked the door. She hadn't heard the click of the lock. It drove her a bit mad sometimes that her flatmates were not security-minded, but then they'd never had reason to be. All were upper-middle-class British girls with nothing but private schools and idyllic summers behind them.

Leila heaved herself up from her desk, unable to study with an unlocked door at her back. She was just reaching for the latch when the doorbell buzzed, loud and grating in her ears. She almost jumped out of her skin and bit down on her tongue to keep from screaming. Her heart knocked in her chest.

"For heaven's sake," she muttered in Arabic, and she put her eye up to the shutter hole to see who it was.

A man. He wore an old-fashioned hat with a brim, which shielded his eyes but revealed the line of his strong lower jaw and a stern, well-formed mouth. It was enough. Leila flung the door open to find James Cartwright in the hallway, dripping from the rain. He removed the hat; his intense blue eyes were a familiar comfort.

Without knowing what she was doing, she flung her arms around him and he staggered backward with the force of it. It had been so long that his face and build had faded into generality, just like the rest of her memories of Iraq. To have him before her in the flesh was a miracle.

"Ah, Leila," he whispered in her ear. His voice was husky, perhaps with cold or something else.

"James, James, James," she murmured. "You've come to see me!"

"Can I come in?" he asked.

Leila released him and stood back. Her shirt was soaked through in places with the raindrops he'd borne from outside. "Oh," she said. "Yes! Sorry." She opened the door wide and he stepped in. He seemed to fill up the entire sitting room with his presence. She had an uncontrollable urge to stare at him and she indulged it, regarding him frankly and without pretence. The longing must be in her eyes but she did not care.

James took off his coat, hung it on the rack. "Do you want me to take off my shoes?" he asked. His hat, too, was hung to reveal fashionably short black hair, thick and wavy.

"No, it's fine. I need to Hoover the floor, anyway," she replied, feeling very anglicized all of a sudden, self-conscious of it. What would he think of her now? Had she changed?

"You're lovely as ever, Leila," he said, relieving her of her fears. But there was something impersonal in the statement, an awkwardness that did not used to exist.

Leila decided to cut to the chase. "I've been waiting for you," she said. The air was silent in the flat and for a split second she sent up great thanks to Allah that they were alone. From the outside she could hear the hissing, water-on-pavement sound of cars driving by; music was playing from another apartment. And in the space of that moment she knew what else to say; the one thing that was, up to that point, desperately unsaid between them. "I love you, James."

His mouth opened a fraction. His eyes widened. It took a good five seconds for him to compose himself and then he smiled, genuine, wry, familiar. "And I love you, Leila." It was out of the way, out in the open, and they kissed for several long, sweet moments.

When they finally broke apart, each unable to quit the smiles on their faces, Leila tried to get serious. "The papers," she said, and that did it.

"The papers," James said. "They're safe?"

"Yes."

He looked around as though afraid they might be overheard. "Does anyone else live here?"

"I have three flatmates. But they are all out. Rose might be back any time, though, she just went to the shop."

"Where's the bathroom? The toilet, I mean?"

She pointed, thinking he needed to use it. But instead James took her hand and led her into the small bathroom and closed the door. "James, what are you—?"

"In case of bugs," he whispered. He turned on the tap in the bathtub and then the one in the sink. "Running water will mask our voices, to some extent. And whisper."

"Really, James, do you not think it is paranoid?" But as she asked the question she knew it was not. After all, did not she herself think she was being surveilled, and take random routes home every day? She put an accepting look on her face in spite of her question.

"Shhh," he said.

She did not mind talking in the bathroom so much after all, because it forced them into close proximity with each other. Bold in her home territory, Leila wrapped her hands around James's waist and smiled when she heard his breath catch in his throat. "Now," she purred into his ear, "what you were saying?"

"Umm." He cleared his throat and continued. What he said made Leila's blood run a degree or two colder than usual. "It's time. I want to release some of those documents."

She stiffened in his arms. It did not take effort to whisper because her voice did not seem to be in proper working order, anyway. "Are you sure?"

"Yes," said James. "I can't stand it anymore. Knowing what happened. And my tour is over; I left the Special Forces. My commitment was up and I'm a mere reservist now. Now's the time."

"I will do whatever you tell me," said Leila. She smiled up at James because whatever happened next, she would help him, and he was her friend. The future was murky and frightening, and she knew they might need lawyers, Allah forbid, but that was all right. Leila stood on her toes and took James's face in her hands, then whispered into the shell of his ear, "Can you stay awhile?"

James, as it turned out, could stay a long while.